Brush of
Angel's Wings

**Center Point
Large Print**

Also by Ruth Reid and available from
Center Point Large Print:

The Promise of an Angel

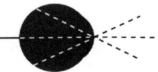

**This Large Print Book carries the
Seal of Approval of N.A.V.H.**

Brush of Angel's Wings

A Heaven on Earth Novel

RUTH REID

CENTER POINT LARGE PRINT
THORNDIKE, MAINE

The text of this Large Print edition is unabridged. In other aspects, this book may vary from the original edition. Printed in the United States of America on permanent paper. Set in 16-point Times New Roman type.

ISBN: 978-1-61173-381-5

Library of Congress Cataloging-in-Publication Data

Reid, Ruth, 1963–
Brush of angel's wings / Ruth Reid.
pages ; cm
ISBN 978-1-61173-381-5 (library binding : alk. paper)
1. Amish—Fiction. 2. Michigan—Fiction. 3. Large type books.
I. Title.
PS3618.E5475B78 2012b
813'.6—dc23
                                                2012003138

To my husband, Dan,
and our three children,
Lexie, Danny, and Sarah.
I'm blessed to be surrounded
by your love and support.

Pennsylvania Dutch Glossary

ach: oh
aemen: amen
aenti: aunt
againish: stubborn, strong-willed
Ausbund: Amish hymnal used in worship services
babrag boi: rhubarb crisp
bauch shmartzlich: stomach pain
blabbermauls: blabbermouths
boppli: baby
bruder: brother
bu: boy
Budget: Amish newspaper
daed: dad
denki: thank you
dokta: doctor
doplich: awkward
Englisch or *Englisher*: a non-Amish person
fraa: wife
geh: go
grossdaadi haus: grandfather's house
gut mariye: good morning
guder nacht: good night
gut: good
haus: house
hinkle: chicken

hohchmoot: pride
jah: yes
kaffi: coffee
kapp: a prayer covering worn by the women
kumm: come/came
leddich: unmarried
lieb: love
Loblied: praise song
mamm: mom
mammi: grandmother
mariye: morning
maydel: girl
mei: my
meiya: tomorrow
nacht: night
narrisch: crazy
nau: now
nay: no
nett: not
onkel: uncle
Ordnung: the written and unwritten rules of the Amish
Pennsylvania Deitsch: the language most commonly used by the Amish
redd-up: clean up
rumschpringe: running-around period that begins when an Amish youth turns seventeen years old and ends when the young person is baptized into the Amish faith
schnitzboi: split moon apple pie

schul: school
sohn: son
vass iss gut: what is good
wundebaar: wonderful
yummasetti: traditional Amish dish using hamburger, egg noodles, and cheese as the main ingredients

Chapter One

Rachel Hartzler wove through the wedding crowd, then dashed toward the line of parked buggies. Now that her sister Iva's wedding ceremony had ended, Rachel needed to rush home and help with the meal preparations. It wouldn't be long before the throng of wedding guests migrated from her *aenti's* house to her parents' home to continue celebrating.

She hitched her horse in haste, hoping to avoid the guests and their comments. Several had already mentioned that she would be the next Hartzler married. The *last* Hartzler, she'd inwardly corrected. She wasn't holding her breath. Marriage wasn't around the corner for her. At age twenty, well past the prime time to court, she had yet to be offered a ride home after one of the youth singings. Lately she'd been praying about becoming a teacher. A good job for a *maydel*.

Rachel climbed into the buggy and fastened the canvas leg covering over her lap. Despite the clear sky and sun overhead, Michigan's early spring wind produced a teeth-chattering chill.

"*Geh* on, Ginger." She tapped the reins. The horse obeyed and the buggy lurched forward. Once on the main road, she gave the horse a free head.

The mare, feeling her morning oats, picked up the pace. A retired harness racer, Ginger ran faster than any of the other horses in her father's stock.

As a steady clopping of hooves from behind them grew louder, Ginger must have sensed competition approaching and her pace automatically increased. Rachel dismissed the fleeting notion to rein in the mare. After all, the icy winter had kept them both off the roads. With only a thin layer of slush on the pavement, it wouldn't hurt to let the horse burn her energy.

She glanced out the window opening at an approaching buggy. Shaded inside, the male driver's identity wasn't visible. His sorrel gelding came alongside her, nostrils flaring from the quick pace. The horse didn't have the zest to pass, despite his driver's calls to go faster.

It had been a long time since her last race. A flash of pride spurted through her veins. Ginger could win without an ounce more energy. But strategy was important.

Rachel caught a glimpse of how close the other buggy's wheel was to hers. Too close. Any connection would tangle them both into a heap. A good excuse to move faster. She clucked her tongue and Ginger happily obeyed. Her heart rate increased to match the faster clopping of Ginger's hooves. The brisk air burned Rachel's cheeks and a chill traveled down the back of her neck. She'd never gone so fast.

The stiff breeze caught her winter bonnet and slipped it off her head, saved from blowing away only by the loosely tied strings around her neck. Her flimsy prayer *kapp* flapped as a few of the pins holding the head covering in place loosened. She shifted the reins to one hand and used her free hand to grasp the strings of her *kapp*.

A few of her *aentis* had skipped the ceremony to prepare the meal, so she certainly didn't want to arrive home with her hair askew and her covering in disarray. Buggy racing was only something that happened between the boys, and even then the elders did not always overlook their boyish pranks.

The last buggy race she'd won caused some undesirable attention. She shouldn't want to risk spoiling her sister's wedding festivities just to prove she could handle a fast horse. Still, the excitement surging inside spurred her on. She would pull back on Ginger and drop her speed when they reached the bend on Northland Drive where the dirt road leading to the farm came into view. Continuing the race around the corner wouldn't be wise.

"Get over, there's a—" The man's muffled yell was swallowed by a blaring horn.

Rachel stuck her head out the side opening. A semitruck driver laid on the horn again as he sped past. The truck's draft pushed Ginger off the road and onto the dirt shoulder. The shuddering buggy wheel dipped into a large hole. Rachel slid across the seat and slammed hard against the door. Another jolt lifted her off the bench and hurled her toward the window. Something solid thudded against the side of her buggy and kept her from catapulting out.

She clambered to get back into position and held the reins tightly in her hands. She leaned back and pulled steadily on Ginger's reins. "Come on, girl, whoa!" she shouted, her voice shrill with fear. Finally, the horse stopped. She held her hand over her ribs and inhaled a few quick breaths. Her muscles quivered, but she didn't dare release her grasp on the reins, not with Ginger pawing at the ground.

Squeezing her eyes closed, she whispered, "*Denki*, God. You spared *mei* life."

"You got that right."

She jumped, startled by the appearance of the man and the harshness in his tone. She opened her eyes to come face-to-face with Jordan Engles.

"You nearly killed both of us." He cocked his head to gain full view of the inside of her buggy, narrowing his mossy-green eyes.

"I did? You were certainly intent on racing." She bit her tongue to keep from adding, *And you lost*.

He rubbed his neck while cranking it side to side. His expression relaxed and he cleared his throat. "Are you okay?" The edginess was gone from his voice.

Reality of the near accident sank in and rendered

her speechless. She couldn't offer more than a mere nod. She rubbed her sweaty hands against the folds of her dress. Her palms, raw from the leather reins rubbing them, burned.

He squatted in front of the wheel, poked around a bit, then rose. "You've damaged the wheelbase."

Ach, her father wouldn't be pleased with the news. "I heard a loud thud. What did I hit?"

"Other than a hole? Nothing."

Before she had a chance to respond, he opened the door and made a short jerk of his head. "Get out. I'll drive you."

She flipped off the leg covering and lowered herself to the ground. Ginger lunged forward and the buggy shifted. Rachel jumped back inside, scrambled over the seat, and set the brake. Something she should've remembered the moment the buggy stopped.

"Take it easy," Jordan said.

Not knowing if he meant her or the horse, she moved with caution. With the buggy on the edge of the ditch, and his unwillingness to stand aside, there wasn't much space to step out. When she did, her arm brushed against his chest. She followed the hooks and eyes on his dark vest to his thick neck and snug-fitting collarless shirt. Then she lifted her eyes and focused on the dimple indenting the center of his chin.

He grinned. "You think you can move aside now?"

"I . . . uh . . ." If she could find a deeper hole,

she'd bury herself. The entire incident left her stunned. But so did staring into his eyes.

Looking more closely at him, she realized his teeth were clenched and he'd pinned his shoulder against the wheel. When she glanced at the soft ground, reality of the situation soaked in like a stale slice of bread sponging up milk. Her movement threatened the buggy's stability.

"Move away from the buggy." He tossed his head, knocking the straw hat sideways on his head, revealing a thick mass of auburn waves.

She inched passed him. Instead of waiting for him at his buggy, she went around to the other side to calm Ginger, who hadn't stopped stomping the ground.

"Easy, girl." She glided her hand down the horse's neck and along her back to the harness buckle. After releasing the straps, she freed the mare. Unbalanced, the buggy shifted.

Jordan's strained groan sounded like a growl.

"*Ach*, I'm sorry."

She rushed back to the other side of the buggy as his boot slid over the mixture of gravel and slushy mud.

His jaw squared, causing the veins in his thick neck to swell with pressure. "Stand back!"

"You are not alone, child." The ten-foot spread of Nathaniel's unfurled wings engulfed Jordan under its protective canopy. Braced against the wheel, Jordan hadn't realized his burden had been lifted. He still pressed, still struggled, laboring against what had already been done.

Nathaniel covered Jordan's hands and pushed the limp wheel onto stable ground.

Standing mute, Jordan rubbed his hands together as though he recognized the source of the penetrating heat.

"Acknowledge God in your heart," Nathaniel whispered, spreading a warm breeze over Jordan's face. Even Nathaniel's gentle touch to his shoulder didn't awaken Jordan's spirit.

The young man glanced up at the sky. His mouth clamped tight.

Nathaniel's wings retracted. His radiance dimmed as he moved away. He could do no more at present. He would return to the perimeter of the ethereal realm, where he watched over his charge. Until called again by God.

Jordan bent his knee and touched the wooden rim. His heart hammered against his chest. He hadn't enough strength to push the buggy onto safer ground, yet he saw the movement. He'd read how adrenaline can surge during a crisis. The idea seemed logical. He stood and rubbed the back of his neck.

Rachel's sharp breath broke his concentration. As he turned to look at her, his arm accidentally brushed against her shoulder.

"*Denki*," she said softly.

If he hadn't witnessed her racing the buggy, he never would have believed that this small-framed girl standing beside him could control a horse that strong and that fast. He'd barely held on to his gelding after the semi spooked him.

Jordan opened his mouth to say something about her foolish driving on a major highway, but stopped when he saw her trembling lips.

A gust of wind lifted her *kapp*, exposing long wisps of untamed hair. In the sunlight, her wheat-colored hair took on a reddish tinge. He froze, captivated by the shine.

She spun away and attempted to straighten her head covering. An impossible task while she held the horse's reins.

Jordan came up beside her and took hold of the mare. "I'll tie her to the back of my rig."

"*Denki*." She kept her back to him and in a flash had the pins out and the *kapp* refastened.

The mare held her head high, looking about her, while he lapped the leather strap through a metal ring and pulled it tight.

Instead of climbing into the buggy, Rachel was frowning, staring off in the distance.

"You do want a ride, don't you?" he asked as he came up behind her.

Rachel glanced at his extended hand and climbed into the buggy unassisted. Seated ramrod straight on the bench, she tucked her chin against her chest and closed her eyes, while her fingers fumbled to shove more stray strands of hair under her head covering.

Her hair looked fine spilling out from the *kapp*. He would have told her so, but he didn't dare add more tension to the situation. Apparently, riding in his buggy had put her on edge. Her dress wasn't wrinkled, yet she repeatedly hand-ironed the folds on it.

He realized he was staring at her while parked on the shoulder of a busy road. Not wise—for more than just safety reasons. He picked up the reins and released the brake.

When the buggy jerked forward, she grasped the edge of the seat and peered straight ahead, offering a perfect profile of high cheekbones.

"Where's the bucket brigade?" he asked.

She looked confused. "For what? A fire?"

"You were running that horse hard. I figured there could only be one reason: a fire." Her blue eyes sparkled like the reflective surface of his favorite fishing hole and appeared just as cold. "Where are you going?"

She shifted on the seat. "I live up the road. We're hosting a wedding for my sister."

"Are you Micah Hartzler's daughter?"

"*Jah*," she acknowledged curtly, then faced forward.

"I've been helping the Troyers close up their farm. They're moving to Wiscon—you already

19

know that, since Iva will be moving too."

"*Jah*, Iva and Fanny," she mumbled.

Rachel finger-pleated the same fold in her dress over and over.

"I'm Jordan Engles."

"*Jah*. I know about you."

Since his mother died and he'd recently moved in with his Amish uncle, it seemed everyone in the community knew something about him, or more accurately, about his shunned mother.

"Here it is." Rachel pointed to an average-sized farmhouse. The wide wooden porch wrapped around two sides and lanterns hung from the overhead roof beams. He pulled into the gravel drive and stopped Blaze near the smaller of the two barns.

"*Denki*." Rachel jumped out of the buggy.

"Hey, where are you going?"

She spoke over her shoulder, "I have chores."

He motioned to her horse. "You ran that mare. You cool her down and wipe off the lather."

Without offering a rebuttal, she returned, reached for the leather strap, untied it, and led the mare toward the barn. Jordan watched her go, admiring her spunk. His adrenaline had relaxed, and now he could enjoy the humor of this slight girl having a road race on a busy highway.

A stream of buggies flowed down the driveway as the wedding guests began to arrive. Since coming to Mecosta County, Jordan had met only a handful of people. One buggy separated from the

20

stream and pulled up beside his. He recognized the driver as a young man about his age named Timothy King.

Timothy hopped down, walked around the buggy, and helped his pregnant wife from her seat, tucking her hand underneath his crooked elbow.

He brought her up to Jordan and patted her hand. "Jordan, this is *mei fraa*, Sadie."

Jordan touched the brim of his hat. "Hello."

Sadie smiled and returned the greeting. At that moment the bride and another woman swept her away from Timothy. The three put their heads together and spoke some sort of secretive woman chatter as they moved toward the house.

"Sadie's sisters?" Jordan asked.

Timothy grinned. "*Jah*. Those three are as thick as flies on a cow in summer."

Jordan didn't really know how to respond. He felt awkward in this group. He didn't belong. Didn't want to belong.

He didn't know what else to do with himself, so he stood next to Timothy, who greeted the bearded men and introduced each one to Jordan in turn. Jordan shook hands and returned greetings, but all the bearded men blended together. Matthew Troyer bounded up to them, clapping Timothy on the back. He smiled at Jordan. "You are staying for the meal and the frolic tonight, *jah*?"

"The meal but not the frolic." Jordan had done well to avoid the singings, frolics, and get-

21

togethers that involved the pairing of unmarried couples. He gave the honest excuse that he had no intention of staying in the community.

A buggy moving much faster than the rest came down the lane and halted in the midst of the growing crowd. Micah Hartzler climbed out and searched the crowd. When he didn't find what he was looking for, he breathlessly addressed the small group of men standing before him. "Anyone seen Rachel? Her buggy is disabled on the side of the road."

Jordan cleared his throat and raised his hand like he was in elementary school. "I gave her a ride. She's in the barn tending the horse." Heat crawled up his neck. Her father must not think much of him for letting a girl do the barn work while he socialized.

"She's okay?" Micah's heavy breathing slowed.

"The wheel's in bad shape, but Rachel and the horse are fine."

Micah visibly relaxed. *"Gut."* He paused as though gathering his thoughts, then looked at Jordan. "Would you ride with me and lend a hand with changing the wheel?"

He hesitated briefly before answering. "Sure." He didn't want to be in the position of having to explain what had happened to the buggy. On the other hand, if her father knew, maybe he would prevent her from running that horse on a busy highway.

Rachel came out of the barn, her hands black from dirt and horse sweat. *"Daed,* I . . ."" She paused, glanced at Jordan, then continued. "The buggy wheel's damaged."

"Jah, so I noticed. I'm going after it."

She stepped forward. "Let me help."

"No need." Micah clapped Jordan's shoulder. "I found me some strong hands, ain't so?"

If Rachel could slip off to the barn without others noticing, she would spend the remainder of the night with the livestock. Horses don't ask questions or hint about her approaching and passing the age for marriage and babies.

She finished drying the casserole dish and passed it to *Aenti* Leah on her right, then accepted the next rinsed one from *Aenti* Esther on her left. The rumble and laughter and rise and fall of voices in the other room continued.

Sadie reached for Fanny's hand. "I'm going to miss you and Iva moving so far away."

"You'll have to help Rachel find a *bu.* Then we can make the trip home for her wedding." Fanny handed Rachel a dry dish towel, relieving her of the soiled one. "Don't make Iva and me wait too long."

Rachel didn't even look at her sister. She focused on the pan that didn't have a drop of water left on it. "Don't hold your breath."

"If you'd prepare yourself to be a *fraa,* you

23

wouldn't have trouble finding a husband." *Mamm* touched Rachel's shoulder. "Preparations are a must."

A must. Her mother failed to add cooking, sewing, and cleaning. All the areas Rachel fell short in perfecting. At least to *Mamm's* specifications of what she deemed necessary to find a husband. So far, *Mamm's* coaching had helped her three sisters.

"Perhaps I should be a teacher," she said.

"Have you prayed about it?" Fanny asked, always the bossy older sister.

"Of course I have." She really did want to seek God's will in this. But she found it was hard to listen when she was still angry about James.

Katie Bender appeared with a stack of dirty plates and set them on the counter next to *Aenti* Esther. "I think this is the end of them."

If Rachel's brother, James, hadn't died, Katie would be another sister. Now she avoided her late brother's fiancée every chance she could. Although that was difficult. Except for intimate family gatherings, Rachel's sisters still invited Katie to all the family events.

"Iva's looking for you, Rachel," Katie said. "I think her singing is getting ready to start."

Rachel eyed Katie. Katie of all people knew why Rachel hadn't attended the singings since her brother's tragic death two years before. So why would she even ask, knowing it would bring up the painful past? "*Nay, denki.*" Her voice was curt and cutting.

Katie winced as the weighted words fell on her. "Okay," she said, her voice tentative. She wiped her hands on a towel and left the kitchen.

Rachel bit back what she wanted to say. She wanted to lash out, reminding Katie that if she hadn't insisted on looking for the angel at the river before the singing, James would still be alive. Instead, she sucked in a breath and did what she knew she had to do—apologize. Again.

Rachel followed Katie out of the room. "I'm sorry."

Katie's smile quivered. "I understand."

Rachel paused, still working at keeping back the words she really wanted to say. She took a deep breath. "I should get back in there and *redd-up.*"

Rachel hoped to get everything cleaned up before the singing began. If she did, perhaps she'd have a chance to sneak off to the barn and hide there during the youths' selection process. As she picked up a towel and stepped back to the spot she had left, the words of the other women washing, drying, and putting away moved around her without distracting Rachel's turbulent thoughts.

Rachel's hope for a fast and undetected disappearance vanished when Iva entered the kitchen. She could see the eagerness on her sister's happy face. Soon it would be time for the elders and other married folks to leave so the unmarried youth and the newly married couple could begin their own festivities that would continue well into the night.

"Can I steal Rachel away?" she said. "We want to start the selections."

"*Jah, geh* with them," Sadie said, nudging Rachel.

"Perhaps after the dishes."

Rachel slowed her drying until *Mamm* reached for her towel. "*Geh*, have fellowship."

Rachel leaned so her sister wouldn't hear. "*Nett* for me, *Mamm*."

"So you say. *Geh nau.* This is your sister's wedding. And this is a part of finding a husband."

Iva waited a moment and then moved through the door saying, "Hurry up."

Her hands weren't wet, but Rachel rubbed them on the front of her apron anyway. Perhaps the frolic would satisfy her family, and the remarks about her being unmarried would end. She hoped the guests would be gone before the embarrassing selections, and she could carry out her plan when she wasn't chosen—like she had done when Sadie and Timothy married.

After practically being pushed out of the kitchen, Rachel meandered down the hall. Inside the room where the girls would wait, the chatter was already under way. Soon the boys, sent one by one from the barn, would choose a girl. After the pairing, the singing would start in the kitchen.

Rachel moved toward the window and stood beside her friend Naomi.

"I keep looking for William," Naomi said, peering out the window.

Rachel watched the people leaving. Her *aentis* left together, her sisters not too far behind them. Timothy and Jordan stood next to the barn.

The barn door opened and the first boy headed to the house.

"That's William." Naomi tugged Rachel's arm. "*Ach*, do you think he'll pick me?"

Rachel smiled. "*Jah*, he's smitten with you."

Naomi squirmed in nervousness until William stood at the bedroom door, asking for her. Naomi clapped her hand over her mouth to stifle a squeal. Then she stood, gathered herself together, and walked out of the room almost composed.

Rachel turned her attention back to Jordan and Timothy outside the window. Whatever Timothy had to say, Jordan kept shaking his head. Their conversation seemed to get a little more animated as it continued.

"Please don't be sad," Iva said, breaking into her focus.

Unsure whom Iva was talking to, Rachel looked away from the window. Only she and her sister remained in the room. Closing herself off from the muffled commotion, she hadn't paid attention to the thinning number of girls in the room. Not that this was a surprise. Rachel expected this to happen. She wasn't ever chosen.

"I'll go upstairs. I'm tired anyway."

Iva reached for her. "*Nay*. I want you to—"

Heavy footsteps thudded down the hall and stopped in front of the room.

After a soft tap on the door, her sister opened it just enough to peek out at the caller.

"I . . . ah . . ."

The male voice on the other side of the door sounded indecisive. The back of Rachel's neck prickled with sweat. Why had she agreed to participate in pairing up for the singing? She imagined the night couldn't get much worse.

"Rachel is waiting." Iva flung the door wide open, revealing the young man who had requested her. "I'll meet you two in the kitchen," her sister said, bouncing out of the room.

"*Ach!*" Rachel said. She stiffened.

"Yeah. So you say." Jordan's eyes traveled over her like he was inspecting a horse at auction. "Timothy insisted I stay. He said there was one odd girl . . . I didn't know it was you."

Chapter Two

Rachel squared her shoulders after Jordan's statement stole the air from her lungs. "Timothy called me an *odd* girl?" How awful to learn that her brother-in-law referred to her in that manner. She'd grown up with Timothy and had always admired him even before he and Sadie married.

Jordan put his hand up. "No, no. I said it wrong. He meant there was an uneven number of girls." He shifted—with discomfort or annoyance, she couldn't tell. "Are you coming?"

She couldn't gather enough wits to move before he rubbed the back of his neck and shifted his weight. "Look, I don't usually attend your . . . frolics, but—"

"You don't have to tonight. *Nett* for me."

He didn't move, but a glint of mischief flickered in his eyes. "Don't get all ruffled. I gave Timothy my word." He held on to the door frame and stretched to look down the hallway. "I think they're waiting for us before they start."

She eyed him closely. The cotton material of his black vest strained at the seams. With his broad chest, he could use a larger size. With thick wavy hair, he certainly wasn't bad-looking.

She quickly reminded herself that he hadn't truly selected her. No one had. But standing vulnerable in front of him wasn't the time for self-pity.

"What did you tell *mei daed* about the buggy wheel?"

A grin split his face.

Unable to bear his mirth, she pulled at a loose thread on her dress sleeve.

"I told him the truth."

She closed her eyes. How would she explain racing Ginger? Her father had only recently given her the horse and she had come with strict rules. She couldn't drive at night. She couldn't go into town. Now she wouldn't be allowed to take the horse on the highway.

"I'm *nett* feeling *gut*." She headed for the staircase—the opposite direction from where the youth had gathered. "Tell Iva, will you?" Lowering her head, she started up the steps.

Jordan cleared his throat.

When she turned, he stood with one foot on the landing and the other on the first step, peering up at her.

"I told him a truck startled the horse . . . and you were a good handler."

His words warmed her like sweet rolls from the oven. Yet she contained her relief behind her masked expression. *"Denki."*

He took another step closer. "I should have told

him you were racing that horse over patches of black ice."

With him standing on the step below her, she only had to tilt her head slightly to be eye to eye with him. "There's Borium on Ginger's shoes for traction."

"Smart girl." He turned. "But *narrisch*," he mumbled under his breath.

Crazy? She followed him down the steps. "Do you know what you just called me?"

"My mother was Amish. Some words you never forget." He crossed his arms. "Yes. You acted crazy."

"The ice had melted."

"The road was still dangerous." He began to move toward the kitchen. "They're ready to start. Are you coming?"

"I don't want to join in. You already said you don't either."

He nodded, relief lightening his expression.

"*Gut nacht* then." Rachel continued her ascent, carrying the awful truth with her. Jordan had only made an agreement with her brother-in-law. He had not come of his own wishes.

When she reached her room, she crossed it to gaze out the window. Laughter filtered up from the kitchen. Then the singing started.

She didn't regret her decision not to join the youth activities. The evening wouldn't end until almost midnight, and tomorrow there would be plenty of cleaning chores.

Still, since the singing frolic was at her house, it made it impossible to avoid the activity without looking like she was sulking. She should've followed her original plan and hidden in the barn.

Nathaniel extended his wings and drew closer to Rachel. "Child, the Father loves you. Do not be dismayed. He has a plan, a good plan for you. Do not lose heart."

Rachel touched the strings of her prayer *kapp*. Earlier, when the buggy bounced off the road and she came off her seat, she was certain something stopped her from flying out. She closed her eyes. "*Denki*, God, for your protection."

"God cares a great deal about you. That's why He sent me to protect you," Nathaniel whispered.

Jordan fed the leather harness strap through the buckle. He'd stayed at the Hartzlers' longer than he wanted, but at least he got out of accompanying Rachel to the singing.

"What happened?" Timothy ambled toward Jordan's buggy. "I thought you said you would stay for the singing."

"Rachel refused." Jordan shrugged. "She might still be upset about the buggy accident."

Timothy rocked back on his heels. "Probably racing again."

Jordan laughed. "She won."

"You take losing better than most." Timothy wagged his head. "Micah should've never given her that horse."

Although Jordan agreed, he held his comment. The girl had been reckless. During the time he spent working with harness racehorses, he witnessed plenty of accidents. Today's incident should've shaken her to the core. He wasn't so sure it had. She certainly defended her driving and denied the hazardous road conditions. Rachel's only concern was that her father would find out, not that she gambled losing her life.

"Gambling will destroy everything you love," his mother had said over and over until he grew sick of hearing it. Now he wished he could say it as a warning to this girl. But he hadn't earned the right. What worried him was that with the competitive streak he saw in her, he knew she would race again.

"Here comes Micah," Jordan said in a low voice. "Don't say anything about Rachel racing."

Timothy chuckled. "Getting beaten by a girl is bothering you *nau*, ain't so?"

"Something like that." Jordan unhitched Blaze from the post and swung himself onto the buggy seat.

"I should find my *fraa* and head home," Timothy said.

Micah waved to Timothy but stopped at Jordan's

33

buggy. "*Denki* for helping me with *mei* daughter's buggy."

"Glad to help." Jordan gathered the reins, eager to get going.

"I'm planning to clear an additional field for planting. Your *onkel* Isaac mentioned you're looking for work."

"I will be." His uncle lived on the opposite side of the district, a two-hour drive by buggy, but Jordan needed the work. "I'll be done with my current job in a couple days. After that I would like to come."

Chapter Three

Rachel overslept. She crawled out of bed and slipped into a dress, her eyes still closed. Her internal clock never failed to wake her before the rooster's alarm, but this morning the rooster was crowing again as she fastened the straight pins on her dress. Yawning, she adjusted her prayer *kapp*, shoved her stocking feet into a pair of stiff work shoes, and then took her wool cape off its hook on the way out the door.

A horse, not of her father's stock, whinnied near the barn. Although it wasn't uncommon to find a new horse in the corral, this particular sorrel didn't pace the fence as did most young colts in need of training. He looked a bit familiar, but she couldn't place him.

She loved horses, and if it hadn't already been so late, she would have spent a few minutes checking out the new gelding. She glanced at the pink horizon and stepped up her pace. By now she and *Daed* should have the chores nearly finished. Once inside the barn she followed the dim lamp-light to the milking area.

Daed looked up from milking the cow. "*Gut mariye.*"

Rachel yawned. "*Mariye,*" she replied, picking up the feed bucket. Usually once she stepped out of bed she was wide awake, but not today. Today she couldn't keep her eyes open. Since Iva married and they no longer shared a bedroom, she'd spent restless nights listening to the wind brush the tree branches against the window.

Her shoulders slumped against the support beam and she yawned as she filled the bucket with grain. The wooden door leading to the pasture slid open, and Jordan Engles entered with a cow on a lead. His unexpected appearance stole her words away.

At least now she knew who owned the gelding in the corral and why the horse looked familiar.

"Good morning," he said as he tethered the cow to a post. He then reached to take the bucket from her hand. "No need. I fed the horses already."

Rachel grasped the handle tighter. "Then I'll feed the calves."

"Did that too." Jordan cleared his throat. "Besides, that isn't what calves eat."

Rachel glanced into the bucket. "*Jah.*" She instinctively bit her bottom lip as pride roared within her. She was tired. Certainly she knew the difference between what horses and calves ate. Jordan had merely distracted her a moment.

Daed stood from the milking stool and reached under the cow for the bucket. "Help your *mamm* get breakfast started." He glanced at Jordan. "Hungry?"

"Oh yes, sir."

Her father patted him on the back as though entertained by the appetite of the younger man. "*Gut.*" He turned to her. "Remind your *mamm* to set an extra plate."

"But . . ." A lump the size of her fist lodged in her throat. She swallowed. "I always help you in the barn." Ever since James died, she had tended the animals every morning with her father. They'd managed fine without hiring help before, so they certainly didn't need Jordan—half *Englisch*, half Amish—attempting to replace her brother. And wouldn't his presence just make that pain even stronger, a reminder every day that her brother was gone forever? *Daed* still wore a cloak of sadness even though he pretended to accept the Lord's will.

And pretended not to blame her for her brother's death.

Jordan reached for the feed bucket in her hand; this time he was successful. "The barn's damp. You should go inside so you don't catch a cold."

How dare he treat her like a small child or an imbecile. "I'm quite familiar with how drafty this old barn is. After all, I've spent plenty of hours working out here, ain't so?" She would have shown him her calloused hands to prove her labor had *Daed* not stepped forward.

Her father held the milk bucket out to her. "Rachel, take this one to the *haus*. We'll bring the other one when we *kumm*."

She glanced at Jordan but couldn't find it in her heart to return his smile. The longer she stared, the wider his smile grew.

Daed offered her no support. He shooed her toward the door. "We won't be long."

"*Jah*," she muttered.

Her brother's death was hard on her father in so many ways. Immediately after James was buried and the other farmers had to return to their work, she stepped in to help, enjoying working with her father, learning, becoming strong. She loved the livestock, the planting, the harvesting. It didn't matter that they rarely spoke of anything except the work at hand. It had been *gut*. Hadn't it? She had even felt lately that their strained relationship was on the mend. But now—how could he dismiss her so easily?

Rachel slipped through the kitchen door,

keeping the screen door from slamming behind her. She swung the milk bucket up and placed it on the counter with ease—something she could not have done two years ago.

Mamm glanced over her shoulder from the stove. "*Gut mariye.*"

"*Vass iss gut?*"

Mamm moved away from frying the peeled potatoes. A deep frown settled over her face as she swept Rachel's stray hair away from her eyes. "What are you upset about?"

"Why is Jordan Engles here?" The words escaped her mouth sounding harsher than she had intended.

Mamm's typical smile was slow and steady in coming. "Jordan is helping your *daed* ready the fields for planting."

Her father had talked of wanting to clear more acreage to farm, but she assumed the two of them would prepare the land.

"*Daed* needed help and asked Jordan. Since he's new to the community, he has more availability than the other young men."

Rachel hated the truth in *Mamm's* statement. She took a ladle along with some tall glasses and poured fresh milk into each one. No matter how careful she was, she could never seem to do it without slopping it down the sides and making puddles on the counter.

Her mother scraped the potatoes off the bottom

of the cast iron skillet and flipped the raw side into the grease.

"*Daed* knows I wanted to work with him." She took a cloth and swiped at the spilled milk.

Mamm added a heaping spoonful of lard to a second cast iron fry pan. "You're twenty and *nett* a child."

"*Jah*." And this year she was stronger. She could control the plow easier and not tire in the heat as quickly. If anyone was going to replace James, it should be her, not an outsider. Sure, Jordan might know a few *Deitsch* words from his mother, and he dressed like one of them, but he remained detached from the community.

"You need to spend less time in the barn," *Mamm* said stiffly, cutting off any further discussion. "It's time you put into practice your cooking and sewing skills." She handed her the basket of eggs from the counter. "When you finish with the milk, you can fry these eggs for your *daed* and Jordan."

Rachel groaned under her breath. Didn't she know enough about cooking? If the kitchen wasn't so stuffy and confining, maybe she'd like to cook. And maybe she didn't have the culinary skills to please the palate, but at least she could cook well enough to stay alive. She'd spent a good deal of every summer canning vegetables from the garden. And sewing too. What more did a girl need to know other than how to darn socks and patch pants? True, her stitches were not evenly spaced, but they served their purpose. Why did it matter when the boots covered one's socks and hid stitching imperfections? *Daed* hadn't once complained.

Mamm poured vinegar into a bowl. "*Kumm*, the eggs must be washed."

Rachel washed the eggs, then carried them to the stove. The first egg she cracked too hard and the runny yolk broke and splattered into the grease. The next one slipped into the pan with its yolk intact. It didn't break until she attempted to flip it. She left them for a moment to put the glasses of milk on the table. By the time she'd returned, the eggs had a small layer of burned crust on one side. But they were still edible, *jah*? She set those aside for Jordan. With the next two she took extra care as she cracked their shells and when she flipped them over. She peered at them while they sizzled in the pan. The yolks were probably cooked a little too long, but she supposed they would be runny enough. Those she reserved for her father.

"Here they *kumm*." *Mamm* stepped away from the kitchen window and wiped her hands against her apron, then eyed Rachel. "Straighten your apron." *Mamm* moved over to the stove and picked up the kettle. "I'll pour the *kaffi*. You can set the utensils in their places."

Rachel prepared the table as instructed. She

placed the plateful of hot biscuits and the butter dish in the center of the table as the men entered the kitchen.

Jordan handed her a milk bucket. She took it too roughly and the milk splashed against the side and over the brim, spilling down her dress front. "*Ach.*"

"Careful." Jordan grinned.

She looked inside the bucket. "This was all you could get?"

"Well, you spilled some," he said under his breath.

She placed the bucket on the counter next to the other, annoyed at herself, her *daed*, and especially at Jordan.

"You'll want to keep the cream separated," he told her, as if she didn't know.

Apparently he didn't know cream sometimes took twelve hours before it fully separated. Even she knew the method for gravitational extraction. "Most dairy farmers know it takes several hours to produce heavy cream."

Jordan leaned closer. "You must mean the farmer's *fraa*. I've never heard of a farmer with spare time enough to wait for the cream to be skimmed."

Something the opposite of Amish meekness rose up inside her. She glared at him. He responded with a grin that annoyed her even further. After a brief pause, she pasted on a smile and took the plates of food to the table while her mother poured the coffee.

Daed pulled a chair out and offered it to Jordan. "Have a seat."

Rachel set the plate of eggs on the table in front of her father. She swallowed hard, trying to remind herself that Jordan was their guest and she needed to treat him as such.

Mamm gave Rachel's shoulder a subtle nudge, and Rachel placed the other plate in front of him.

After a brief look at the platter, Jordan lifted his head, settling his green eyes on her. "Thank you. It smells good."

Was he lying? Or could he not tell that the kitchen smelled of burnt potatoes and eggs? If Jordan meant what he said, his senses were probably tainted from mucking out the horse stalls—which should have been her job.

Rachel crinkled her nose. "*Gut.*"

When her father cleared his throat, she forced a smile at her guest, trying not to ask him to change seats—she didn't like him sitting in James's chair any more than she liked him usurping her place beside her father in the fields.

Mamm leaned toward Rachel. "Sit. Your father is ready to pray *nau.*"

Rachel slid onto her chair and bowed her head, silently begging God for forgiveness of her jealousy. Had she lost her mind to be jealous over barn chores? Anyone would gladly welcome more helping hands. She chewed her bottom lip and forced herself to concentrate on her prayer.

God, with your blessing, every year our crops have provided a decent yield and our garden is larger than we need. Why has Daed *requested Jordan's help? Am I not enough?*

I thank you for this food, Aemen.

Jordan shifted in his seat, opening and closing his fist. Obviously he hadn't milked a cow before. No wonder he didn't get a full bucket. She grinned. He wouldn't last working for her father. Maybe God would answer her unspoken prayer and she would soon be back at *Daed's* side where she belonged.

Daed and *Mamm* opened their eyes at the same time.

Jordan bowed his head, then lifted it immediately. "*Aemen.*"

"*Aemen*?" Rachel raised her brows.

Jordan ignored her and jabbed his fork into his eggs. He paused to look at *Daed* soaking his biscuit in his runny yolks. Jordan made a slight shrug, then lifted his over-hard cooked egg on top of the biscuit.

"*Gut* meal," her father said, exchanging a glance with *Mamm*, seated at the end of the table.

"Yes, very good," Jordan echoed.

Miriam lowered her fork from her mouth. "Rachel cooked the eggs."

Her mother was always so careful not to sound

boastful. Why would she tell of Rachel's cooking, as though frying eggs was a great achievement? It wasn't like she'd mastered her grandmother's recipe for *schnitzboi*.

Jordan shifted his attention. "Micah, what do you intend to plant in the back field? Corn?"

"Soybeans," Rachel replied, eager to show her knowledge of their farming plans.

Her father looked at her. "We've planted soybeans in that field the past two years—"

"*Jah.*" Rachel made one sharp nod aimed at Jordan.

Daed cleared his throat. "We'll plant corn."

Corn? *Daed* actually agreed with Jordan.

"Why?" she blurted.

"Crop rotation." Jordan lifted his brows at her. "Helps control cloddy soil." He turned to her father. "Am I right?"

Her father smiled. "*Jah.*" He pivoted in his chair to give Jordan his full attention. "It also helps the nitrogen balance and groundwater runoff."

Jordan's eagerness to please and her father's elation with his new field hand gnawed away at her. How had Jordan weaseled his way into her family—and so quickly? She had enjoyed working in the barn with her father while her older sisters helped *Mamm* with the indoor chores. She preferred it. Now Jordan's presence threatened the thread of normalcy her family had found after James's death.

Rachel set the fork on her plate of half-eaten food. She'd lost her appetite. She stood, taking the plate with her.

"While you're up, maybe Jordan would like more *kaffi*," *Mamm* said.

Rachel and Jordan locked eyes. She forced herself to turn away from him and focused on picking up the coffeepot and refilling his cup without his asking for more.

"Thank you."

"*Kaffi, Daed*?"

"*Jah*. Warm it, please." He moved his cup closer to the edge of the table, then shifted his attention back to Jordan. "We can take a walk and I'll show you the property lines. If the ground is dry enough, I'll show you how to use the plow."

Rachel collected the dirty dishes from the table and loaded them into the sink. If she hurried, she could have the dishes washed before they finished their coffee. Then she would ask to go along. Maybe *Daed* would explain the importance of nitrogen balance to her.

Rachel emptied the kettle of hot water into the sink and added soap. She washed as *Mamm* brought more dishes from the table.

"Are you finished?" *Daed* asked Jordan.

"Yes, sir," he said and pushed back his chair. Jordan picked up his empty cup and took it to Rachel. "You want this in here?"

"*Jah, denki*."

As he leaned close to put his cup in the sink, his hand brushed against hers. The way he studied her bored into her, causing a whooshing sensation to speed through her, leaving her feeling off balance. He followed *Daed* out of the kitchen, but his woodsy scent lingered.

"They will work well together," *Mamm* said as she scraped the grease from the fry pan into an empty can. "You should have plenty of time to sharpen your household skills."

Rachel knew what she wanted to sharpen, and it had nothing to do with household skills.

The peas had sprouted despite last week's late frost. Thankfully, Rachel had listened to *Mamm* and waited before sowing the other seeds. The soft ground held a few wet patches, so instead of planting today and chancing seed rot, she would till the remainder of the garden. Although, this year, they wouldn't need a large garden. They'd planted extra last year anticipating Iva's wedding meal. Truly, there might not ever be a need for another large garden. Rachel had suppressed her hopes of marriage shortly after she became of courting age and no one paired up with her or offered to drive her home after the singings. The disappointment was easier to handle once she accepted that her life wouldn't necessarily follow the path of the other young women in the community.

Rachel worked until her bare hands became raw

from not wearing gloves and the cold April wind hindered her progress. She kicked off her dirty shoes at the door and padded into the kitchen, shaking her hands and then tucking them under her arms in an attempt to get them less numb.

Mamm set a water-filled jar on the counter, then proceeded to fill another one from the tap. She glanced at Rachel. "Is something wrong with your hands?" *Mamm* turned off the tap, dried her hands, then reached for Rachel's to examine them. "*Ach*, your hands are cold."

"I should've worn gloves."

"*Jah*, the wind is chilly."

Rachel put her hands into her armpits again and wiggled her fingers, hoping to get the blood flowing. "What are the water jars for?"

"I thought your *daed* and Jordan might be thirsty."

"They might want *kaffi* too." They were bound to be cold in the open field.

"*Gut* idea. And you might want to use some beeswax salve on your chapped hands. It's in the cabinet."

"I'll take the drinks out first," Rachel said.

Mamm pulled the thermos from the cupboard. The kettle already filled with heated water, she made the coffee as Rachel slipped back into her cape and shoes.

Rachel trekked across the field with the thermos clutched under her arm and a jar of water in each hand. Like the aroma of morning-brewed coffee, the scent of freshly turned ground jolted her senses. Her *daed* used to tease her that she liked dirt as much as the earthworms. She smiled. It was still true. She was not afraid of dirt and hard work. And considering her love for the animals, she wondered why she couldn't spend all her days outdoors.

She found Jordan and *Daed* squatting down in the center of the field studying the dirt. Probably analyzing the cloddy soil, maybe the nitrogen content, whatever that was. Rachel had never concerned herself with soil to that degree. She also had never shared long conversations with her father about water runoff. Jealousy pricked her conscience. She knew to rebuke sinful thoughts but couldn't just yet.

They both looked up as she approached. Jordan tossed the handful of dirt he held and returned to the plow, commanding Clyde forward. Her father stood, his dirt-smudged forehead wrinkled from squinting against the bright sun.

"I thought you might be thirsty." She held out one of the glass jars to her father. "And I brought you *kaffi* for later." She set the thermos on the ground next to other items they'd brought to the field with them.

While he took long gulps of the water, she stole another glance at Jordan. "*Daed*," she said, "why can't you teach me about cloddy soil and groundwater runoff? And I can handle Clyde as *gut* as anyone." She meant as good as Jordan. Better than Jordan. He didn't know the temperamental horse like she did.

Daed lowered the jar. "Take Jordan the water. He's thirsty."

She sighed. Why did he continually push her away?

Jordan lifted his head and pulled back on the reins as she approached, her dress flapping around her ankles in the breeze. She extended the jar toward him.

He pushed his hat down on his head and wiped his grubby hands across his thighs. "Thank you," he said, accepting the jar.

Jordan gulped down the water in one continuous drink, released a satisfied sigh, and handed the empty container to her. "How's the cream? Have you watched it separate yet?"

She ignored his wiggling brows and spun in her father's direction. Walking up to *Daed*, she said, "I'll work with you tomorrow."

"*Nay* need."

"But I've worked in the field ever since—"

"It's already been decided." The jagged lines around *Daed's* eyes softened. "I'm doing this for you."

"Me?"

"You won't learn how to become a *fraa* by working in the field."

What was he talking about? She had no marriage pledge.

He chuckled. "I saw those eggs you served Jordan."

A look of horror must have crossed her face because *Daed* laughed harder. Although it was wonderful to hear him laugh again—she hadn't heard him laugh much since James died—why did it have to be linked to Jordan's arrival?

She waited until Jordan and Clyde were far enough away that he wouldn't be within earshot. "Even if I could cook as *gut* as *Mamm*"—the ties of her head covering blew in her face, and she grabbed them and held them away—"it doesn't mean I'll find a husband."

Perhaps *Daed* sensed her embarrassment because he sobered. "In God's timing, I pray you will." He put his hands in his pockets and watched Jordan. With the reins draped over his shoulders, Jordan's hands held steady on the plow as it cut through the dirt.

"I might *nett* know much about cooking and sewing," she said, "but I do know Jordan isn't plowing a straight line." She waited for him to agree. Any farmer knew to keep his sight fixed in the distance and not on the ground. Jordan would have the corn growing in circles if he didn't guide Clyde properly.

Daed scratched the back of his neck. "*Jah*, he's got some learning to do, but it'll be *gut* to have a set of strong hands on the farm." He continued to keep his eyes on Jordan. "It's too far to make that two-hour drive back and forth from his *onkel's haus* every day, so he's moving into the *grossdaadi haus.*"

The *grossdaadi haus*? She tried to hide her disbelief. James had been given their grandparents' house when Katie Bender and he made plans to marry. Rachel couldn't bear the idea that Jordan was taking James's place living in the *grossdaadi haus*, or more importantly, in her father's heart.

"Walk properly, child, not in strife, for that is not pleasing to God." Nathaniel's words penetrated her heart, but they would only be empowered by her willingness to obey this truth.

Nathaniel smelled the stench surrounding Tangus before the fallen angel surfaced from a dense black fog. His scaly body flaked off shriveled layers of matter that once made up his radiance. His beauty, along with his towering size and strength, had shriveled when God cast him into darkness with the others. Guarding his several sets of eyes from Nathaniel's light, Tangus stealthily approached the girl, whispering syrupy words of deceit into her thoughts and heart.

"Your father lost the son he loved because of you. Your carelessness stole your father's heart forever. You know you can never take your brother's place. You are not as important to your father as your brother was. Turn around, Rachel. See how well your father and Jordan work together. Jordan will take the place in your father's heart that rightfully belongs to your brother—and to you."

Rachel kicked a clod of dirt as she walked away from her father. "*Ach*, why did Jordan have to *kumm* here?"

"Yes! He has no right to interfere!" Tangus said, crawling closer. He pivoted, gloating over his certainty. "She will open her heart to the spirit of envy, you'll see."

Rachel turned her face to the sky. "He has no right to interfere in our lives. He isn't even Amish."

"Seek God, child," Nathaniel urged.
Tangus inched closer. "God doesn't care about such silly things. Don't trouble Him with this frivolity."

"Why doesn't *Daed* see Jordan is worthless to him? He's *nett* going to be any help." She closed her hands into fists, frustration beginning to fill her. "He didn't milk the cow fully and he can't even plow a straight line."

"That's right. Your work is far superior to Jordan's." Tangus smirked. "You heard her,

Nathaniel. She's listening nicely to me, don't you think?"

Nathaniel's shudder kicked up wind, and he feathered the tip of his wings across Rachel's cheek.

The girl searched the sky, touched her face, and sighed.

Chapter Four

Jordan unfastened Clyde from the plow and led him off the field. As he rounded the corner of the barn, Rachel came into his peripheral vision—talking to a cow. He pulled back on Clyde's halter to have him stop.

He was far enough away that he couldn't make out everything she was saying. Had she really asked the cow how she was feeling? She probably expected the cow to answer too. He cocked his head when she squatted down and spread her hand over the cow's belly.

The cow swished its tail and caused Rachel to lose her balance and stumble backward. When she regained her balance, she lifted her foot, and judging her grimaced expression, she'd probably stepped in a cow pie.

Jordan subdued his mirth and coaxed Clyde forward. He didn't need to waste time watching

Rachel—especially since it was obvious she disliked him. He understood, but whether she liked him or not, the cows needed milking. He wanted to make a good impression by having the barn chores completed before Micah returned from his errands.

He led Clyde into his stall, unhooked the water bucket, and headed outside to the pump. As he pumped the handle, Rachel shuffled toward him.

"I'll just be a minute." He eyed her soiled shoe, then sniffed the air. "Do you smell something?"

Her nose scrunched as she breathed in, then she exhaled while shaking her head. "Nothing unusual."

"Hmm. I was sure I smelled a dung pile." He shrugged. "Must be the wind direction."

She leaned toward him with narrowed eyes. "You do know this is a farm."

Jordan grinned and made it obvious he was looking at her shoes. "Most farmers wear boots to do barn work." He filled the bucket, moved it aside, then continued pumping the handle. "Go ahead. Take your shoes off and wash them."

"I'm a big girl. I know what to do with dirty shoes." She put her hands on her hips. "And I can pump *mei* own water."

Jordan released the handle and stepped back, raising his hands in surrender. "I hope those aren't your Sunday shoes."

Nathaniel followed Jordan into the barn. "Do not strive against one another or cause one to stumble into anger. Rather, love one another as Jesus commanded."

Nathaniel entered the stall at the same time as Jordan. The horse nickered at Nathaniel's presence. "Be still," he ordered the beast. The horse pawed the straw floor, stretched its neck, and snorted.

"Easy, boy." Jordan lowered the full water bucket and picked up another to get feed.

Rachel entered and headed to Ginger's stall. Grabbing the feed bucket, she carried it to the grain bin.

"Apologize. Don't let the sun go down," Nathaniel prodded Jordan's conscience.

Jordan took a step toward Rachel, intending to say something, but sneezed instead.

"Bless you."

"Thank you." He sneezed again.

Jordan scanned the area for the fur-ball culprit. A litter of barn cats caused his last sneezing fit at the Troyers'. Earlier, when he helped with milking, he hadn't had this problem.

Rachel filled a tin can with grain. "You have a cold?"

He used a coffee can to scoop oats from the barrel, filling it to the brim. "Allergies." He inhaled slowly. His nasal passages weren't completely clogged—yet. The fluid inside his sinus cavity pulsated with increasing pressure.

"You look like you've been crying."

Jordan rubbed his eyes. "I'm like the TV commercial. Sneezing, itchy . . . watery . . . eyes."

Her nose scrunched.

He sighed. "I guess you've never seen the commercial."

"*Nay.*"

Of course she hadn't. No electricity. No television or radio.

She opened her big blue eyes wider. "You miss watching TV?"

"Sometimes." He missed a lot of things that were sold to pay his mother's medical bills or repossessed for lack of payment. He took Clyde's bucket and headed back to the stall, sneezing three times in quick succession.

"Every Amish family has a barn," she said, following him. "If you have hay allergies, why did you *kumm* to live with your *onkel*?"

He stared at her for a moment, wondering how much to tell her. He began to pour the oats into Clyde's feed bin, and the horse had his nose in the bin before the oats had emptied from the can. From the corner of his eye, he caught a glimpse of her bending down to pick up a gray, fluffy-haired cat. She stuck her nose in the cat's fur and nuzzled it. He could hear her talking to it in soft, muffled words, cradling it in her arms.

"I guess that's your cat."

She looked at him as though he were stupid.

"Does it have a name?"

"*His* name is Smokey." She craned her head toward the opened window. "*Daed's* back. He'll need *mei* help with the horse." She lowered Smokey to the ground and headed for the door. She stopped, the sunlight streaming into the barn, putting her in a silhouette outlined with gold. "Does my *daed* know you're allergic to the barn? Perhaps working here isn't such a *gut* idea."

"Who says it's the barn? Maybe I'm allergic to you."

Her eyes narrowed. "Another *gut* reason you should leave." She bolted out the door.

"Jordan, I want to help you find your way, but how can I if you don't listen?" Nathaniel peered upward. "Master, show me how to reach him."

Tangus hung out in a corner and chortled. "I think it's nice he's having fun."

Gravel crunched under the wheels of what sounded like a truck. Jordan peered out the window to see Micah waving his hands, giving directions for whoever was backing up the fancy horse trailer. Whoever owned this rig was serious about horses.

"Rachel, *geh* ask Jordan to help me, please."

57

Jordan trotted for the door, nearly colliding with Rachel at the entrance. "Sorry," he said, stepping around her.

"*Daed* said he needs help unloading a horse." She delivered her message as though it was painful for her to do so.

"Sure." He wiped his hands on the sides of his pants and followed her to the trailer.

Micah hand-signaled the driver to stop. He spoke to Jordan while still focused on the trailer. "This boy might give us problems unloading."

"New horse?"

"*Nett* mine. I only shoe, board, and train them." Micah waved to the man who was getting out of the driver's seat of the pickup truck, but Jordan locked eyes on the girl climbing out from the passenger side. She looked to be Rachel's age and was very beautiful. Her chestnut-colored hair fell over the shoulders of her jean jacket and bounced as she strolled confidently over to Jordan.

"Hi, I'm Kayla." She stuck out her hand, which he clasped. Her grip was firm, her hand very soft.

"Jordan," he said.

She dug her hands into the front pockets of her jeans and rocked back on the heels of her boots, considering him.

He didn't mind admiring her as well. A good Amish man would look away and not tempt himself. But he wasn't Amish.

Delight spread over her face and she couldn't

stand still. "I'm excited. This is my first horse."

"Is that so?" Why was it that girls squirmed when they were excited? It was like every muscle was bursting with energy.

"I suppose since you're Amish a new horse wouldn't be a big deal to you."

He wasn't sure how to answer, deciding it was less complicated to let her believe as she wished.

The trailer ramp hitting the ground with a heavy thud riled the horse. "I need to help Micah," he told her and stepped closer to the trailer.

"Easy *nau*," Micah said calmly to the horse. "Jordan, if you could stand on the other side of the trailer . . ." He took in the area around him, mentally measuring what he needed to do for safety. "Rachel, go in the *haus* and help your *mamm* with supper."

She gave Kayla a long look but did as her father instructed.

Nathaniel shadowed Rachel across the gravel drive. He wanted to assure her of God's love and steer her away from jealousy. But hearing Tangus provoke the horse, Nathaniel turned back to protect his other charge.

Micah opened the access window to the trailer and attached the lead to the horse's halter. The horse snorted and moved about, causing the trailer to rock. "Easy, boy," Micah said, calming him a bit. He stepped inside the trailer and unlatched the barrier that had supported him during the ride. He took hold of the lead and began to back the horse out, speaking in soft tones.

The moment the appaloosa cleared the trailer, he reared, pawing his front hooves in the air above Micah.

Tangus pounced on the animal's back and clung like a bur at his withers.

Micah pulled the rope taut, seemingly unruffled at the horse's dangerous behavior. "He's got some vinegar in him." The horse tossed his head, his eyes wide, his feet in constant motion.

Nathaniel drew his sword. "Leave the animal alone!"

Tangus slithered off the horse. "You're no fun."

Once Tangus was gone, Nathaniel lowered his sword and tethered it to his armor. Then, gently touching the horse's neck, he spoke soothingly. "Peace, be still."

The horse stopped his fight, and Micah looped a rope around his neck and passed it to Jordan.

The horse snorted and sidestepped in Jordan's direction.

"Easy, boy." Jordan gripped the rope with both hands as Micah eased closer. The horse, although somewhat calmer, still kept his ears back against his head while nervously raising his head high, breathing heavily and pawing at the ground.

Micah spoke to the *Englischer*. "George, will you open the barn door the rest of the way? Gently, so the noise doesn't spook him."

Once the door was open, Jordan and Micah guided the horse into an empty stall.

"I'll get some feed. Maybe that will calm him." Jordan headed to the grain barrel. The girl followed.

"What do you think of him?" Excitement bubbled out of her.

He paused from filling the can. "Not that my opinion matters . . . but he seems too high-strung for a beginner to handle."

Obviously deflated and defensive, she said, "He comes from good stock."

Jordan finished scooping the oats. "For what?"

"Barrel racing."

"I drive horses and ride but not around barrels." He left her standing by the feed and sneezed on his way back to the stall.

"God bless you," Micah said. He gestured to the other man. "This is George Davy, and George, this is Jordan Engles. He's helping me on the farm."

The men shook hands, exchanging words of greeting.

"Well, I guess I'd better get going. There's always something to do on a farm, isn't there?" George stepped toward the door. "Are you ready to go, Kayla?"

"I want to say good-bye to Pepper." She climbed

the first rung of the stall gate and leaned to stroke the horse's neck. "I'll be back to visit soon."

Jordan tossed a flake of hay into the stall, then grabbed the empty water bucket. The horse's name seemed reasonable. Not only did he have black spots, but he had fire running through him.

He took the bucket outside to the well, and as he pumped the handle, the Davys climbed into their truck. He returned Kayla's wave, then picked up the full bucket.

Jordan sneezed as he was returning to the stall with the water. He tipped his head back to search the rafters but didn't see the cat.

Micah walked up to Jordan. "Barn dust?"

Feeling his eyes beginning to water, Jordan wiped his shirtsleeve across his face. Rachel's words returned to him, asking if her father knew of his allergy. "I'll be fine." Even as he spoke the words, another sneeze triggered. Perhaps he was allergic to barn dust as well as cats.

"April is early for pollen."

"I still want the work." His words were rushed.

Micah cocked his head. "*Gut*. Have you ever shoed a horse?"

"No." He guarded his breathing, taking in only shallow inhalations.

Micah clapped his shoulder. "I'll teach you how but *nett* today." He patted his stomach. "I'm hungry. You too?"

"Yes, sir."

• • •

Rachel set the dishes on the table so hard they rattled. Her mother stood at the stove, oblivious to any attempts Rachel made to temper her anger. It wasn't that she despised women's work. She disliked her father's cold dismissal. Several times in the past she'd helped unload horses that arrived for buggy training or shoeing.

Rachel set the utensils next to the plates and wandered over to the window ledge. The last time she looked out, the *narrisch* animal reared and both *Daed* and Jordan were trying to control him when he came down. Once the horse settled, she wasn't sure who stood prouder, the spotted horse or the owner's daughter.

The truck no longer in the driveway, she moved away from the window. Her mind reeled with thoughts of how Jordan had shown no shame eyeing the beautiful Kayla Davy. Rachel understood how the girl's figure, made more obvious in those tight-fitting jeans, would attract his attention—but why should that bother her?

Mamm poured the gravy from the beef roast into a serving dish. "Put the bread and butter on the table. Everything should be ready when they *kumm* in to eat." She placed the pot in the sink and ran some water into the empty pan to soak.

The back door opened. The men doffed their hats and placed them on wall hooks.

"I use bar steel and always leave a very small

bit of expansion room." *Daed* held up his fingers, indicating the minuscule space. "I'll show you when we shoe next week."

"Great," Jordan said and pulled out the chair where he'd sat during breakfast.

Daed took his place, continuing the topic of shoeing.

Her father had bonded quickly with the hired hand. Too quickly. Rachel set the bowl of potatoes in the center of the table and pulled out the chair across from Jordan.

When she opened her eyes after offering an abbreviated quiet grace, she noticed Jordan's eyes roaming from the food to her parents, then stopping on her, smiling.

Daed opened his eyes and picked up the knife to slice the roast.

"I tilled another row before putting Clyde up," Jordan said, then added, "I'll work on it tomorrow too."

"*Nett meiya*. Timothy needs help with his addition." He glanced at Rachel. "Maybe you and *Mamm* will bake a pie to bring?" Without waiting for Rachel's reply, *Daed* spoke to Jordan. "You like pie, *jah*?"

Jordan looked at Rachel. "I like anything sweet."

Like Kayla Davy. Rachel shot him a quick saccharine smile. "I think there're some crab apples left over from last fall."

Chapter Five

"I wasn't planning to make anything." Rachel sawed the knife through the stalk of rhubarb and handed it to Naomi. "Everyone knows I'm *nett* a *gut* cook." She cut off another section. "That's why *Daed* hired Jordan—so that I could prepare for being a *fraa*."

"Does he want you to marry Jordan?" She leaned closer and, without giving Rachel a chance to answer, added, "Wouldn't it be *wundebaar* for us both to have fall weddings?"

"*Nay!*"

Naomi pouted. "I thought you wanted to get married."

"You and I both know that without being asked to be taken home after a singing, it's *nett* likely that someone will marry me." Rachel pushed aside the rhubarb's leafy cluster to expose the stalks.

"Maybe Jordan is the right *bu*. He seems different than the rest." Her friend's brows lifted.

"He's different because he's *nett* Amish."

"His *mamm* was Amish."

"His *daed* wasn't."

Naomi wiped her hands on her apron. "Why else would he *kumm* to live here?"

"He doesn't seem interested in our ways."

"What you see on the outside isn't always the same as the inside."

"Did someone tell you why he's here?"

"*Nay.* I have heard nothing." Naomi tilted her head in thought. "I guess he's here to marry you." She chuckled, putting her hand over her mouth.

"That's *nett* funny." Her friend had meddled in trying to match Rachel with a *bu* more times than any of Rachel's sisters. But teasing her about Jordan wasn't something to laugh about.

"You'll see. He'll ask you home from the singing."

Rachel had learned shortly after they both became of courting age not to encourage Naomi. Once Jordan made it clear he wasn't interested, as all the others had, Rachel hoped Naomi would back off.

"This should be enough for a pie." Rachel handed Naomi another stalk to add to the bundle. She swept the dirt from her dress. Rhubarb season usually started in another week or two. She hoped cutting some early meant it would be more tart.

"I'll help you prepare it. I love cooking." Naomi let out a long dreamy sigh. "I hope William likes what I made. It's *Mammi's* recipe for *schnitzboi.*"

Rachel smiled. "Of course he will." William was outspoken about liking everything Naomi cooked. Rachel wondered how Jordan would react to her rhubarb pie if she accidentally forgot to add sugar.

●●●

"Rachel, if your pie is ready, we can start loading the buggies with the food." Sadie plucked a pickle out of a jar and took a bite. "I can't wait to see the *boppli's* room."

Rachel opened the oven and pulled out a golden-brown crusted pie.

"That one will win a certain someone's attention," Naomi whispered.

Rachel smirked, then quickly hid her expression with a dish towel. "I think it will," she said after composing herself.

She picked up the pie using a set of pot holders and carried it to the buggy. Once all the food was loaded, they headed for her sister's house.

Pulling into Sadie's yard, Rachel's heartbeat quickened when she caught a glimpse of Jordan on the ladder, hammering a nail into a two-by-six. She looked away before he caught her gawking like a *schul* girl.

Katie Bender's buggy pulled in and parked a little ways away from them. Rachel couldn't help the bitter feeling rising up within her. She had no right to be there. She spoke to Sadie. "Who—" Rachel bit her tongue.

"I invited her. She was practically family." Sadie waved at Katie.

Until James died. Rachel took the hot pie and stepped gingerly down from the buggy. Naomi lifted the bowl of potato salad out of the back of the

67

buggy, and both waited for Sadie to load her arms.

"I wonder if Katie brought her pen and paper," Naomi whispered. "I heard the bishop has given Katie permission to write for the *Budget News* again."

"*Jah*, I heard that too." She didn't understand why the bishop would allow it, especially after all the trouble her writing had caused. "I'm trying to keep *mei* mouth shut." Admittedly, she hadn't tried too hard in the past. But lately, an inward voice of conviction pushed her to attempt to reconcile. She wanted to continue ignoring it, but it was pressing down on her.

Rachel let her focus travel up the ladder and stop at Jordan.

He looked down and grinned.

Heat crawled up Rachel's neck. Sure that her face looked as if she'd spent the day in the direct sun, Rachel dropped her head so he wouldn't see. She picked up her pace, looking at her feet as she went. She began to think about Katie. Maybe she could use her endless curiosity to her advantage. Katie could drill Jordan about why he came and how long he planned to stay. She'd presumed it was for the summer only. But what if *Daed* wanted him to stay through harvest? And worse, what if he wanted him to stay through winter?

Rachel maneuvered the pot holders underneath the hot pie before setting it on the table, then turned to go back for more food. She wondered if she should suggest the interview or not.

Timothy climbed out of the new addition's window opening, stood back, and admired the structure. "What do you think?" he asked as Rachel was passing.

"It looks *wundebaar*. That's an awfully big room. Is Sadie expecting more than one *boppli*?"

"She's starting to look that way." A sheepish grin filled his face. "I'll take multiple boys."

Rachel pretended to scowl. "And what if she has *maydels*?"

He pointed to the opposite end of the house. "Then I'll build another room on that side for the boys we'll have the next time."

"And if she has another *maydel*?" Rachel enjoyed teasing her brother-in-law.

He laughed. "Then we go up. Multiple levels if we must."

Timothy's animated facial expressions always had a way of making her laugh. Sadie had certainly found a wonderful husband. Rachel wished there were more men like Timothy. She would have been jealous if it hadn't been her sister who married him.

She stepped back a few paces to further admire the addition.

Timothy nudged her arm. "There's probably a singing this Sunday." He nodded toward Jordan.

Rachel put her hand to her chest, horrified. Timothy had looked out for her welfare more as a brother than a brother-in-law even before James died, but he had never been so bold.

"I thought you were *mei* friend," she said.

"Jordan's new. I think he would like the sing-ings."

"I don't know why he would."

"He could become Amish. It's not impossible."

"Please don't encourage him to stay." She wanted to sound firm, not begging. She didn't know if she succeeded or not.

"Your *daed* needs help, and I'm swamped with work myself."

Daed didn't need help—he had her. Besides, Jordan wasn't a farmer. He proved that when he stopped milking because his hands were too weak to finish filling a bucket. And he plowed a row so crooked it looked like a snake had slithered through the field.

Timothy stepped toward the table of food. "Looks like the food is ready."

"*Jah*, I need to get a salad from the buggy," she said. "Excuse me."

The men lined up around the tables, except for Jordan, who sat under a tree an unsociable dis-tance away. His auburn hair rippled down the back of his neck and rested on his thick shoulders. If he were wise, he would get a haircut before tomorrow. Since this week's Sunday service was on their side of the district, the bishop would have something to say about the length.

She reached into the buggy and pulled out the salad. With Jordan under a tree, she could walk with her head up, her strides confident.

Sadie tapped her on the shoulder as she set her salad down. "Jordan might be shy. Why don't you make a plate of food and take it to him?"

Rachel didn't care if he was shy. She didn't care if he starved to death.

"He would probably like to sample your pie."

Rachel grinned as she reached for a plate, her mood suddenly lightened.

"I'm sure he would."

Jordan turned when someone cleared her throat behind him.

"Hungry?" In one hand Rachel held a plate, and in her other, a glass of tea that she thrust toward him.

Ravenous was more like it. The sandwich, mound of potato salad, and generous slice of pie made his mouth water. "Thank you."

"You're welcome." Rachel began to move away, her back toward the table laden with food.

"You didn't say what you made."

She turned around and walked backward, not slowing her pace. "The rhubarb pie."

"Then I'll eat that first so I know I'll have enough room for it."

"*Gut*, you do that." And then said under her breath, "And choke."

And choke. The girl had spirit. He filled his fork with pie. The moment he closed his mouth around it, his lips puckered and he found it difficult to swallow. He washed down the sourness with great gulps of tea. At least she hadn't withheld the sugar from the drink.

Rachel looked over her shoulder at him and he touched the brim of his hat. Although he admired someone with her spunk, he wasn't about to give her any satisfaction of besting him. He took another bite.

Rachel sat at the kitchen table and peeled potatoes while *Mamm* made a batch of biscuits.

"Sadie's place has a lot more room *nau*," Rachel said.

Mamm sprinkled the table with flour. "I told her we would go over next week and help her make curtains. That will give you some sewing practice."

Rachel forced a smile. "Oh. Sure." The thought of sewing frolics had never interested her. And she didn't want to talk any more about this one. So she changed the subject. "Has Jordan mentioned his *mamm* to you? He doesn't seem to say anything about her."

An odd expression crossed *Mamm's* face. It was so quick, Rachel didn't know how to read it. *Mamm* split the dough in two sections. "It must be painful to talk about."

The peels fell steadily from the potato. "Was she shunned like people have said? Did she marry an *Englisch* man?"

"Rachel." *Mamm* wagged the rolling pin and spoke firmly. "I won't participate in gossip." She lowered the pin on one section of dough and rolled out a thick layer.

Rachel sensed that her mother wasn't telling her everything. Her mother knew more than she let on.

Jordan and her *daed* entered the kitchen talking nonstop about farming as though she and her *mamm* weren't even there. They washed up and sat at the table for supper. When all heads had lifted from prayer, Rachel reached for the bowl of potatoes directly in front of her. "Jolly looks like she might deliver soon."

"Is that so?" *Daed* tapped the table, his eyes on Jordan. "Have you birthed a calf?"

Jordan swallowed, a spoon of potatoes hovering over his plate. "No." He let the potatoes fall from the spoon and dug some more from the bowl before passing it on. As he shifted, his wavy hair covered his eyes.

Ach, why did she bring up the pregnant cow? She hoped they wouldn't leave her out of that too. Rachel reached for the vegetables. "Tomorrow's service is at the Yoders' *haus*."

Mamm exchanged the creamed corn for the

73

potatoes. "Will Naomi be hosting a singing?"

"I suppose." Rachel didn't really want to go to that topic either. She'd only wanted to change the conversation from farming, so *Daed* didn't have a chance to exclude her from helping to birth the calves.

She tilted her head as though noticing Jordan's unkempt hair for the first time. "You could use a haircut before service."

"I'll shape it up after supper," *Mamm* said.

Jordan shifted in his seat. He opened his mouth to say something, then lifted a spoonful of creamed corn to it instead.

"She cuts *mei daed's*." *Not always even on the sides*, she almost added.

Daed chuckled. "Don't worry. She's *gut nau* about not clipping the ear."

Jordan cut a glance from one to the other.

Rachel stifled a snicker and stabbed a piece of meatloaf. When they finished supper, she cleared the table and washed the dishes while *Mamm* cut Jordan's hair on the porch. When Rachel had finished her tasks, she stepped outside.

Mamm lowered the scissors. "What do you think? His hair is much thicker than your father's. It doesn't lay the same."

Rachel cocked her head. "It isn't even." She pointed to the left side. *Mamm* trimmed it more, and Rachel reevaluated. "Too much. *Nau* the right side needs shortening."

She held her expression even, although her stomach wanted to twist with suppressed laughter.

"*Ach*, his hair is too thick." *Mamm* extended the shears toward her. "Maybe you can do better. I'll go fetch him some clean towels for the *grossdaadi haus*."

"Have you learned not to clip ears yet?" Jordan asked, sounding a bit worried.

"I haven't clipped any yet." She didn't tell him she hadn't cut anyone's hair, so she hadn't had the chance to clip an ear.

He closed his eyes when she lifted the scissors.

The softness of his bangs took her by surprise. A tingle spread from her fingertips through her arms and deep into her core. For a moment she froze.

He peeked through the locks, his green eyes taking on a puppy dog appearance. She drew a deep breath and readied the scissors. "I've only sheared sheep," she said, snipping off a hunk of hair.

"Then I don't know if I want you to cut—"

Chunks of hair fluttered to the ground. He lifted his hand and, guiding it over what remained of his bangs, let out a growl under his breath.

Rachel cringed. "Maybe I took off too much."

"So you say." He reached for her wrist and gingerly removed the scissors from her hand. "I'll finish."

Rachel swiped the hair clippings off one of his shoulders. His muscles tensed, causing a ripple of heat to surface over her face. She jerked her hand away. "I'll fetch the broom and sweep up these shavings and put them in the garden because they'll keep the deer away." Her words ran together like a little girl's. Embarrassed again, she put her hand on the door to go inside just as *Mamm* appeared on the other side holding a handful of towels.

Mamm looked at Jordan and her eyes widened. She handed Rachel the towels. "You better carry these for him. Jordan's covered in hair clippings."

Jordan set the scissors on the stool and grabbed his hat from the railing. He raked at his head with his fingers as though searching for his missing hair, then slammed his hat over his ears, grumbling something about looking like a Dutch boy.

They walked silently to the little house. He opened the door and stepped aside to let her in. "There's an oil lamp on the table if you need it," he said.

"*Jah*," she said softly, "this was my grandparents' place until they passed away." Although it wasn't her missing grandparents that gave her an aching heart. Stepping into the small house reminded her of James and all the hope that had been a part of the house when he was to take it over. He and Katie talked about adding on another bedroom when they started their family.

Rachel set the towels down on the table next to the lamp. The pack of matches lying there felt damp. After the third match failed to light, Jordan came up beside her, produced a pack from his pocket, and lit the wick.

"I'll find you a bar of soap." She scooted into the kitchen, grabbed the soap next to the sink, and returned. "You'll want to wash up so you're—" For a split second all words fled from her. Jordan had unfastened the top eye hook of his shirt. "—not itching. I mean scratching all *nacht*."

"Thanks for your concern." His fingers moved down to unhook the next one.

Rachel lifted her hand to shield her eyes and hurried to the door. "*Nacht*." She grasped the knob, but her sweaty hands couldn't get a firm grip. As she stopped to wipe her hands on her apron, the sound of his boot steps came up behind her. She caught a glimpse of the small patch of chest hair centered over his breastbone, and her heart rate increased. She rubbed her hands against the folds of her apron once more.

Leaning close, he reached in front of her for the door handle. "Having problems?" With an effortless twist, the door sprang open.

A welcoming gust of night air immediately cooled her hot face. Unable to form a simple thank-you, she rushed outside. He should've known how improper it was to bare any skin in front of an unmarried woman. Was he trying to mar her reputation?

Chapter Six

Jordan closed the door, still puzzled by Rachel's panic. He was only taking off his shirt. Surely with a father and a brother in her family she would've seen a guy without a shirt before.

He looked around at the lamplight flickering against the bare walls, the handmade wooden furniture, and the tattered braided rug in front of the stone fireplace. The Amish were more primitive than he originally thought. Judging by the way his nose clogged and his eyes itched, the musty-smelling house had been closed up for years. Still, there was something special about the rustic home.

Nathaniel circled the room alongside Jordan. "Don't focus on their lack of material possessions or overlook the family's closeness with God. The value of love far exceeds gold."

Jordan plopped down on the chair next to the fireplace. He opened the lid of the wicker basket next to the chair and found it full of newspapers. Jordan enjoyed reading, and since his arrival, he hadn't had the time to find a library in town. He pulled out a newspaper and read the masthead.

Budget News. Although he'd grown up with an Amish mother, he'd never heard of the publication. He flipped the pages and skimmed the columns. Amish news from Holmes County . . . Lancaster . . . Mecosta . . . Hope Falls. It amused him that instead of communicating by phones, it seemed they kept in touch through this newspaper. He set the paper back into the basket and closed the lid. He would wait until he was more desperate for something to read. Even then, he couldn't imagine that plowing stories or canning news would be of any interest.

Although his mother never mentioned an Amish newspaper, she had talked about the tight bonds within Amish families. They passed furniture and quilts, farming land and houses, down to their children. From one generation to the next, the Amish faith and Plain ways continued.

"Your mother ran away. You stay much longer and you'll experience the same suffocating bonds that force these families together and forced your mother to leave. Once they get you, there's no way out." Tangus strutted the length of the room. "Jordan, you know this. First they give you hand-me-down clothes to dress like them. Your own buggy. A horse. Now it's the haircut. You look silly.

"The noose around your neck comes next. Every move you make will be watched and reported—and probably scorned."

Jordan rubbed his neck, then jumped to his feet as tiny hair shavings prickled his back. He pulled off his shirt without bothering to unfasten any more of the hooks. Holding it carefully by the collar, he opened the door and snapped it a few times.

Jordan combed his fingers through what was left of his hair. He dreaded looking in a mirror, knowing his Dutch-boy cut probably resembled an untreated case of mange. Thankfully, the Amish didn't have large mirrors. "Maybe this is why Amish men wear hats," he grumbled. "The women can't cut their hair right." He gave his shirt one final snap and looked toward the lit main house. "I'll find a way to get even with your antics," he said under his breath.

Rachel rubbed the knot in her lower back during church service until she caught Jordan watching her from the men's side of the barn. His mouth curled into a smirk and she dropped her hand and straightened her shoulders. With guarded breath and a tightened abdomen to deflect the soreness, she maintained her proper position.

He turned his eyes away.

She sighed. Her shoulders slumped and the muscle tightness returned. She'd never hurt like this after gardening. It was Jordan. After she left, she saw him shirtless at the woodpile. The vision had messed with her sleep. Apparently she tossed more than she thought during the night. She continued to squirm until the service ended with Bishop Lapp's dismissal. Thankful for the release, Rachel eased off the wooden bench.

Jordan strolled toward her, his hat in hand. "You think you're stiff *nau*, walk behind a plow."

"I can *nett* only handle Clyde better than you, *mei* rows are straight too." A shard of pain shot through her squared shoulders, but she was determined to hold the rigid stance until he walked away.

"You're cringing." He glanced quickly around the room, then leaned close so only she could hear. "You should take a breath. You hold it too long and you'll pass out."

She exhaled loudly. "I'm sure you'd let me fall to the floor."

And understandably so after eating her bad cooking for several days. She liked his wide-eyed expression yesterday the most when she had served him eggs she'd poached in milk. The slightly undercooked eggs jiggled on the plate and his face had contorted into a dreadful shape. But after a brief hesitation, he ate them without complaint and even complimented her in his dry humorous way, telling her she would get them right someday.

"I ought to catch you," he said, "and put you in a soiled wheelbarrow for the bad haircut you gave me." He tugged on his exposed earlobe before placing the hat on his head.

Rachel imagined him dumping her on top of the compost pile.

Naomi practically skipped over to them, taking Rachel's hands in hers. "Please tell me you plan to attend the singing tonight." Naomi's mouth turned down lower the longer she waited for Rachel's response. "*Ach.* You forgot?"

Rachel hadn't forgotten about her friend's get-together, she simply relished the idea of going to bed early. Besides, Naomi knew she didn't attend any singings.

Her friend's lips puckered into a pout.

"If my parents permit me to use the buggy, then *jah*, I'll *kumm*. For a little while." Rachel immediately regretted the promise, but at least if she drove herself she wouldn't have to depend on a *bu* to drive her home.

Naomi smiled and glanced at Jordan. "You're invited too."

"*Denki.*" Jordan tapped the brim of his hat at Naomi and exchanged a brief glance with Rachel before he walked off.

"He probably won't *kumm*," Rachel said.

Naomi sighed. "I know. I hear he hasn't attended anyone's singing." Naomi weaved her arm around Rachel's elbow. "I don't care if he is *Englisch*. He's over twenty so he should be thinking of marriage."

"Not all men should be married," Rachel said.

• • •

Jordan walked away, the image of Rachel's blushing cheeks still on his mind. Maybe the suggestion that he would catch her in a wheelbarrow was a little harsh. The timid girl had made a mad dash out of the house last night. Perhaps she pulled a muscle in her back as she tugged on the door.

Yet she still showed up to help milk the cows before church. She grimaced when Micah sent her back inside.

Micah was right.

She needed to learn how to cook, or the man she married would go hungry. Although he was certain she'd spitefully left out the sugar in the rhubarb pie. He figured that out when he returned his plate and saw her wry grin. And had she lopped his hair off on purpose? He wasn't sure.

Perhaps Micah had hired him merely to force Rachel into performing more womanly chores—he wouldn't be surprised. Without certain skills, an Amish woman had a difficult future.

Attending the evening singing would be a step in the right direction for her. She'd be around other women, exchanging recipes, or whatever they did when they were together. And that couldn't hurt. He observed her from a quiet corner. Even as she favored her lower back with the support of her hand, she was beautiful.

He blinked a few times to get the vision of her out of his mind. He'd kept his distance from everyone since coming to live with his Amish kin. He didn't need a woman confusing him when it came time to leave.

He moved outside to the yard. The unmarried men had gathered in the meadow to play stickball, while the married men milled near the wheat thrasher. Timothy stood next to his father-in-law, Micah.

Onkel Isaac waved Jordan over to the group; his uncle wanted him to feel welcomed into the Amish community. He even made a point to invite him to church service on this side of the district to introduce him to more members.

Shoving his hands into his pockets, Jordan strolled toward the wheat thrasher.

Onkel Isaac clapped his shoulder. "Brother Micah tells me you're a hard worker."

Jordan leaned forward to acknowledge his appreciation of the good words of Micah, who stood on the other side of his uncle. "Thank you."

"Brother Micah said he's going to show you how to shoe horses. That's a fine trade."

"I'm sure it is," he said, then turned to scan the yard.

The men's conversation shifted and diminished into the background of Jordan's drifting thoughts. The menfolk's interest in taking him under their wings surprised him, since his own father—a truck driver—never found him important enough to come see in all the years Jordan lived at home.

It had been very difficult growing up without a father. School friends invited him to their church activities and family outings, sharing their fathers for a few hours or a day. But the stand-in fathers never replaced the longing in his heart to know his real dad. Sure, his mother made excuses for him, but even at a young age, he knew truck drivers could still come home.

Jordan studied the fine, dusty film on his shoes. It didn't matter who his father was, he hadn't been there for his mother when she lay dying and he wasn't there for him after she passed on. What remained for him was an uncertain future, vast and open, void of the direction usually offered by parents.

He'd promised his mother he would learn about the Amish life before moving on. After her death, when *Onkel* Isaac invited Jordan to come live with him for a little while until he could get on his feet, he accepted. He'd never intended on staying, but the people brought him into their lives as though he was. Yet no matter how kind they were to him, after experiencing living the simple life, he knew it wasn't a path he wanted to choose.

If his mother were alive, she would consider him *againish*, too self-willed to study the *Ordnung* and learn the truth about the faith. Before she died, she repeatedly told him he must approach faith with his heart, not with his head. It had to be through his heart. But he had opened his heart when he needed God the most—and God didn't respond. As a result, Jordan didn't know if he'd lost what little faith he had or if he just walked away. How could a good God ignore his continuous prayers that his mother get well? If God wasn't going to care enough about him to spare the only person he had in the world, why should he care about God anymore? It was time to walk away. Time to live the best he could, the best he knew how. If it wasn't for his promise to his mother that he would give faith a chance by returning to her birthplace, he wouldn't be here in the Amish community. He was thankful, though, that being here also offered him the opportunity to work and try to sort out what he wanted in life. Unless sending him to live with his uncle was God's will, which Jordan doubted.

Jordan glanced up at the clouds. *I'm fulfilling my promise to my mother, but, God, I still don't understand so many of their ways. Did she think I would feel a kinship and want to become Amish? Is becoming Amish what she wanted? After all that happened to her?*

"What do you think, Jordan?"

Hearing his name spoken broke Jordan's thoughts. Lingering in the past had choked his voice. He cleared his throat. "I'm sorry. I wasn't following the conversation."

"I asked what you thought of planting oats near the barn," Micah said.

"I think it's a good idea. The angle of the sun and the positioning would give them optimum growth opportunity."

Micah looked over his shoulder. Jordan followed his gaze and saw Rachel and Naomi, locked arm in arm, strolling across the yard toward them. They must've come to announce it was time to eat. Not at all too soon, given that his stomach had started growling over an hour ago. They stopped in front of the group of men.

A few strands of Rachel's golden hair came out from under her bonnet, and the sunshine cast a perfect glow on her face, making her freckles look even more pronounced.

Naomi jabbed Rachel's side and nudged her forward.

Rachel cleared her throat. "*Daed*, there's a singing at Naomi's *haus* tonight. I would like to drive myself."

Before Micah answered, the cast iron bell clanged to announce the meal was ready. Jordan blew out a breath as the group headed toward the house. If Jordan had any smarts, he would've kept walking. Instead, he looked from Rachel's down-turned head to Micah. A dullness had cast a shadow over his employer's eyes.

Micah made an apologetic sigh and admonished his daughter. "I don't want you driving the buggy after dark. Unless . . ." Micah turned to Jordan. "Are you going?"

"No! I mean . . . I didn't plan to attend." It wouldn't be right. Those evenings were intended to provide the youth with time to socialize in hopes that they would find a suitable mate within the faith. He wouldn't be suitable for any Amish woman. Nor did he want to be.

Rachel looked straight at him with narrowed eyes while slowly shaking her head as though giving him some kind of message. Obviously she didn't want him to go. But there was something more. A veiled threat? The thought of aggravating her a little was tempting, especially after the haircut she'd given him. Jordan turned to her father. "I'll see that she gets home."

He tugged his earlobe at Rachel when she trained her angry eyes on him.

Micah patted his back. *"Denki, sohn."*

Instantly Jordan changed from mischievous to serious. He swallowed an emotion he couldn't grasp.

"Kumm on *nav,"* Micah said, looking at the people standing at the tables. "I think they're waiting for us to say grace."

Jordan walked behind them, his head bowed. He'd never been called son except by his mother. He'd quickly developed respect for Micah as he worked with him, but Micah referring to him as son left an unpleasant knot in Jordan's stomach.

Chapter Seven

After Micah and Jordan had taken care of the evening chores, they were leaving the barn when Micah's forehead creased with concern. "She's *mei boppli.* I trust you'll bring her back early, *jah?*"

"And I'll keep her safe."

"*Gut.*" The tension lines on Micah's forehead relaxed. A wide smile crossed his face. He clapped Jordan on the back and began to take long strides toward his porch.

Jordan went the other way, to the small house, wondering what he had gotten himself into. He didn't want anyone getting the wrong impression about his taking Rachel to the singing. He had done well to avoid joining the youthful buddy group thus far. They ran in packs, dated in packs, and joined the church in packs.

His Sunday shirt and vest lay sprawled over the bed where he'd tossed them earlier. His pants hung draped over the back of a chair. It seemed pointless to spend so much time changing clothes. From barn clothes before church to his Sunday clothes, then back to barn clothes, and now, once again, he must change into the handed-down, too-small vest. For what? Couldn't he dutifully monitor Rachel without having to wear church clothes?

He heated water for washing up, missing the ability to just turn on the tap and have the hot water flow. He propped a small, chipped oval mirror against the shelf ledge. As he shaved the stubble off his face, he considered all he had left behind—friends, job, technology. Not that any of those were all that satisfying. He'd been ready to move on from the friends who were choosing lives he didn't care for. His job was one he'd considered quitting anyway. And the technology? Well, taking a small break wouldn't hurt, although he had to admit it was tough the first few weeks. He hadn't realized how much he'd come to rely on it.

Before leaving the cabin, he added a few more logs to the fireplace, hoping that would make for a nice bed of hot embers waiting when he returned.

He stepped outside, tugged the edges of his vest, and headed for the corral. Blaze trotted to the fence to greet him. "Hi, boy," Jordan said as he gave the horse's forehead a little rub. He took the halter and slipped it easily over Blaze's nose and buckled it behind his ears. He talked to him under his breath as he harnessed him and tethered him to the hitching post. After another quick rub on Blaze's forehead, he walked the short distance to the Hartzlers' home and climbed the porch steps. After drawing a deep breath, he knocked.

Miriam opened the door. A warm smile filled her face. "You don't have to knock. You're part of the family *nau*."

"Thank you, Mrs. Hartzler. That's very kind." He wished his heart felt what his words said. But he didn't, and he couldn't, create them out of nothing. He just didn't belong. Not here. Not anywhere. His feet dragged over the braided rug in the hall as he followed Miriam into the sitting room.

"Have a seat. I'll see if Rachel is ready."

Jordan eased onto the wooden rocker. The Bible on the stand next to the chair had a tattered leather binding that clearly indicated someone's priority for reading it. His mother's dog-eared Bible pages had frayed over the years as a result of her own extended time in the Scriptures. The Bible she'd given him remained stiff and unused.

He leaned back in the rocker and looked up at the ceiling. "What am I doing here?" he asked under his breath. "I'm not Amish."

"Knock, child, and the door will be opened. Seek and you will find." Nathaniel drew closer. He longed to administer compassion and dry Jordan's watery eyes, but some tears will cleanse the soul for those who recognize their spirit's cry. When Jordan closed his eyes, Nathaniel pumped his wings, creating a gentle wind that lifted the pages of the book lying next to him.

Tangus crept along the room's crown molding. A filmy brume dispersed from his mouth. "Nathaniel, you keep revealing your perceived truth to someone who refuses to heed your call." Tangus edged closer and flitted above Jordan. "He listens to me. Don't you, Jordan?"

Jordan shot off the chair and twisted around, sure someone had spoken. No one was there, but the room didn't feel empty. The planked floor creaked as he walked over to the wooden-sash window. Sprigs of green buds on the maple tree filled the branches with life. A strange heaviness caused him to turn. Yet no one had entered the room. His gaze locked on the lamp's flickering orange flame and how its shadows licked the wall.

Jordan returned to the side table and picked up the Bible. Scanning the open page, his eyes caught on the verse, *"Cast all your cares . . ."* He stopped reading when he heard footsteps tapping down the wooden stairs. He had just set the Bible back on the table when Rachel appeared. His breath unexpectedly caught in his chest, causing him to cough. With her prayer *kapp* set back from her forehead, her wheat-colored hair looked vibrant against her plum-colored dress, and she looked even more beautiful. His hands moistened and he wiped them down his pants to dry them.

Rachel darted into the kitchen. A moment later she reappeared holding a covered dish, her mother at her side.

"Let me carry that for you," he said and reached for the food container. Something inside the warm dish smelled good. He hoped it would be tasty too.

The door opened and Micah stepped inside and wiped his feet on the rug. "I asked Jordan to bring you home early."

"Yes, sir." Jordan reinforced his promise with a stiff nod.

"*Gut*," Rachel said sharply.

Miriam placed her arm around her daughter's slender waist. "Be gracious to your host."

"*Jah*, I'll be sure to." Rachel removed her cape from the wall peg and put on her bonnet, tying the strings in a bow under her chin.

Miriam escorted them out to the porch. "Enjoy the fellowship."

"Yes, *Mamm*." Rachel glanced at Jordan, her eyes mirroring his reservations.

He waited until Rachel climbed into the buggy, then handed her the dish. This night might prove more challenging than he expected.

If it wasn't the first time Naomi was hosting, Rachel would have continued her avoidance of all singings. But how could she disappoint her closest friend? So with a mixture of excitement for Naomi and dread for herself, she settled into Jordan's buggy.

Rachel touched her neck. She hoped her dry throat, partly from the dread, and somewhat raw from the cool breeze, wouldn't affect her singing. With Jordan attending, she didn't want to sound froggy.

Jordan climbed on the bench beside her and released the buggy brake. Once they were on the road, he tapped the container she held. "What's in the dish?"

"*Babrag boi.*"

His brows crinkled.

"Rhubarb crisp."

"With sugar?"

She almost smiled but managed to hold it in check. "I didn't make it. *Mei mamm* did."

"Then it's safe to eat, I suppose." He looked at her, his eyes full of laughter.

For some reason this time she didn't mind his teasing. "I don't know. Maybe I've learned my cooking secrets from *Mamm*."

Jordan burst out laughing. Rachel liked the sound of it. It made her insides swell with a different kind of joy than she was used to.

After that, they grew silent. Rachel had so many things to ask him, most of which would be prying. It was unlike her to be so curious about someone's life. Perhaps because he came from a world she hadn't much experience in.

Thankfully, Naomi's house was a short distance from hers and the rest of the awkward silence wasn't too insufferable.

Jordan pulled the buggy in front of the house to let her out before taking Blaze and the buggy by the others near the barn.

Instead of taking her hand to assist her, he offered to hold the dish as she stepped down. At the door, he handed it to an eager Naomi, then excused himself.

Naomi looped her arm around Rachel's and giggled. "How was the ride here with Jordan?"

Rachel rolled her eyes. "We both know it was arranged." Naomi had heard it as clearly as she when Jordan hesitated to agree.

"The others don't need to know that. Besides, maybe—"

"Don't say it. Jordan and I don't get along." Rachel removed her cape and bonnet and hung them with the others on the hook.

"Have you prayed about it?"

If the truth were told, she hadn't prayed about much since her brother's death. She hadn't moved away from her faith, but she struggled to speak with a God who didn't always make sense. "Not yet," she said. "I don't know that I need to."

"You need to pray about everything, Rachel Hartzler."

Rachel pointed at her dish. "Where shall we put that?"

Naomi sighed. "You do that a lot. You change the subject."

Rachel shrugged and followed Naomi into the kitchen.

Naomi's kitchen was small compared to the one in their farmhouse. The cookstove and firebox took up one portion of the room, while shelves of canned goods lined another wall. Since cabinets wrapped around the other walls, there wasn't much space around the long wooden table, which seated ten.

Rachel eased over to the window to see if she could find Jordan. He stood in the midst of the fellows but didn't appear engaged in their conversation. He seemed intent to remain an outsider. It made no sense to her. Even if he was leaving, why would he not at least enjoy the time he had? The Amish treasured their close friendships. They bonded their tight community and fostered their strong belief not to be of the world. She had to remind herself that he wasn't Amish.

It wasn't long before the men shuffled into the kitchen. They sat opposite the women at the table. All except Jordan, who stood near the entry, as though ready to make a quick escape. Rachel couldn't get the image of him out of her mind. There had to be more of a reason for his refusal to participate than just the fact that he didn't plan on staying in the community. He certainly wasn't shy. Yet, propped against the wall, he looked despondent.

Naomi paused at the entrance. "I'll fetch another chair."

"I'd rather stand," Jordan said.

Naomi's nose crinkled, then after a brief hesitation she said, "Let me know if you get tired."

The singing started with the familiar praise song "*Loblied*," taken from the *Ausbund*. Rachel looked over at Jordan. With his arms crossed, his eyes traveled up the wooden molding of the door frame as though inspecting it. He wasn't even humming along. He hadn't been with the community long, but he attended services so he had at least heard most of the songs. Instead, his mouth tightened, as if guarding himself from joining in.

Several songs later, the group took a break to enjoy refreshments. As they lined up in front of the food, Rachel ambled over to Jordan.

"Why won't you join everyone and sing? Don't you wish to honor God?"

His stare bored into her. "Who says you must sing to honor him?"

She stared back. "Why did you agree to *kumm* if it wasn't to participate?"

"To keep an eye on you as your father requested." Jordan pushed away from the wall and reached for her elbow. He moved her toward the dwindling food line. "Let's eat."

Rachel stepped in line, following the others, aware of Jordan close at her shoulder. She reached for the same spatula as Peter Wyse and pulled back her hand.

Peter gestured for her to go first. "Are you enjoying the singing, Rachel?"

"*Jah*, it's a *wundebaar* gathering." Her hand trembled as she scooped a serving of shoofly pie that was so large it teetered on the spatula. Peter brought his plate under her hand just as the slice slid out of control. "Perfect teamwork," he said when it landed on his plate. "Thanks."

"*Ach*." She handed Peter the server. "Please, you go first."

Peter selected a slice and reached for her plate to place it on.

"*Denki*."

Peter continued to offer help with her food selections as they made their way along the counter. At the end, she looked at the heaping plateful and gulped. In her eagerness to accept all that Peter served, she hadn't considered how foolish she looked with more food than she could possibly eat.

Jordan peered at her plate and grinned. "You have a hearty appetite tonight."

Rachel looked at him, everything in her pleading with him not to tease her in front of everyone or point out her folly. Whether he understood her silent plea or not, he pivoted to shield her from the others. "Slide what you won't eat onto my plate."

She eased a good-sized portion of her food to his dish, grateful for his willingness to rescue her from embarrassment. Perhaps he was thoughtful after all.

"I guess I was somewhat distracted," she admitted.

"So it seems."

Judging by his amused expression, the cherries in the cobbler were not colored as brightly red as her face.

He leaned closer. "Should we find a seat, Red?"

Naomi took the chair opposite William, while Rachel sat across from Peter. Anne, a small-framed girl, eyed the chair opposite Jordan. It seemed the pairing up had begun. At the other end of the table, Dorothy and her sister Tamara chatted with Noah and James, who had come over from the adjoining district. Clearly, by the ongoing prattle, plans of who would ride home together were already in the making.

Rachel's stomach knotted. Even though the last singing she'd attended was so long ago, she remembered feeling like she wore two left shoes. Timothy had kindly volunteered to drive her, but she didn't want to impose on Sadie and him. After that last time, even *Daed* didn't say much when she dallied in the barn feeding the animals on Sunday evenings.

"Do you have a favorite song?" Anne asked Jordan.

He looked up from eating long enough to answer. "No."

Rachel touched Anne's forearm. "He doesn't sing."

Jordan glanced at Rachel, then looked at Anne. "I sing. I just don't know any *Deitsch* songs."

"He's a distant sort," Naomi whispered to Rachel. "We'll have to work on that."

Distant wasn't necessarily the way Rachel would describe Jordan in a group. Impersonal, aloof, downright rude—she could name multiple descriptions of him. She could name more, and each one made her very aware that he was not one of them. Except for his attachment to her father, Jordan appeared content not interacting with anyone.

Several people excused themselves to talk on the porch. Rachel picked at her food. She didn't want to appear wasteful, but this was still too much. Without looking up, she could feel Jordan's eyes piercing her.

He slid his empty plate across the table. "You can trade with me."

Rachel considered him. "You sure?"

"Yes, just pass it over."

She quickly glanced around the room to see if anyone was watching, then traded his empty dish for her barely touched food.

Jordan ate in silence while she watched in gratitude. His kindness to her tonight was undeserved and unexpected. Had jealousy of his relationship with her father skewed her view of him?

She took the empty dish to the sink and tapped Naomi on the shoulder. "If you get some water warming on the stove, I'll wash the dishes."

"*Ach, nay.* I'll do them after everyone is gone."

Peter brought his dish and came up beside them. "Rachel, would you like to get some fresh air out on the porch?"

Rachel wiped her hands on the sides of her dress, but they weren't wet. No one had ever requested to talk to her alone on the porch.

Jordan squared his shoulders, glanced sideways at them, then continued eating.

"*Jah*, Peter, I'd like that." Rachel walked with him to the door, took her cape and bonnet from the hook, and strolled with him into the cool night air. Several couples hushed their conversations as Peter led the way to a vacant section on the wraparound porch. They stood next to the railing, both silent.

Peter's lanky frame shifted. "The sky is thick with stars tonight."

"*Jah*, the moon is full too." She fiddled with the side seam of her cape and discovered a loose thread to twist around her finger.

The fresh scent of apple blossoms filled the air. She loved it when the trees bloomed in April.

Several minutes passed before Peter turned

sideways and faced her. "I haven't seen you at a singing before." He stepped closer. "Would your parents object if I escorted you home?"

"*Jah.*" Jordan's abrupt reply startled Rachel, and Peter flinched at his appearance.

Jordan folded his arms across his broad chest.

Rachel bristled at his possessive stance. Jordan was out of bounds. She wasn't under his authority. "I think Peter was asking *me* the question."

He cast a brief glance at Peter but steadied his eyes on Rachel. "It doesn't matter." He turned to Peter. "I brought her, and I intend to see that she gets home."

Peter raised his hands. "I didn't mean to—"

"You didn't." Jordan reached for Rachel's elbow. "I promised your *daed* I'd have you home early."

"Perhaps I'll meet you after you get the buggy," Rachel said.

"I'll wait." Jordan took two steps backward and waited next to the house. Even after her steely glare, he merely shifted his stance and displayed a lopsided grin.

"Maybe another time, Peter?" She felt she should apologize but couldn't with Jordan standing right there.

Peter glanced sideways at Jordan, then turned back to her. "Sure."

"I'd like that."

Jordan moved closer to them. "Okay, now that you've made your plans, we should be going." He stepped between her and Peter and reached for her elbow. "I don't want your *daed* upset with me for not returning you early."

She twirled around to get away from him and shot off the porch in the direction of the buggy.

With a few long strides, Jordan reached her. "If you had a *bruder*, you would understand."

She gasped. If James were alive, he wouldn't have interfered. "You're not my keeper."

"I am for the evening." He opened the buggy door and reached for her elbow. "Do you need help getting in?"

Rachel jerked her arm free. "I forgot. I have to get my dish and say good-bye to Naomi." When she flitted to the house, he kept her pace.

"Both Esther's and Anne's *bruders* were there and neither one hovered over their sister," she said.

"*Jah*, and both Jacob and Enos had interests other than their sisters. I'm only interested in you—keeping you safe."

"*Nett* necessary."

Once inside the house, she found her dish on the counter.

"I wish you could stay longer." Naomi squeezed Rachel's hand. She leaned in, gave her brows a suggestive wiggle, and whispered, "I understand."

No, she didn't understand. Still, Naomi's statement caused Rachel to bite the inside of her cheek.

"Thank you for inviting us." Jordan turned

to Rachel. "Are you ready to go, Red?"

Rachel growled under her breath and turned to Naomi. "I'll see you soon."

Naomi winked. "*Jah, Red,* soon."

Once they reached the buggy, she drew a deep breath. "Because of you, everyone will tease me for my face turning red."

His eyes searched hers. "I happen to like the color red."

Rachel climbed into the buggy and plopped on the bench.

He lit the lantern, looked at her, and grinned. "It's a nice shade. Besides, your face isn't as red now as when you were talking with Peter."

"Which you rudely interrupted."

He shrugged. "I was ready to leave."

"Peter offered to drive me home. That's the purpose for the singing."

He raised his brow in amusement. "Didn't you accuse me of not honoring God because I wasn't singing? I'm sure you said *that* was the purpose for the singing."

Rachel turned to face the window opening.

They drove back in silence. Once in the drive, Jordan pulled back on the reins and Blaze stopped. He set the brake and jumped off the seat. He followed her up the steps to her house.

She reached for the door handle and paused. "Is this where I'm supposed to tell you I had a nice time?"

"That's not necessary." He cocked his head and smirked. "It wasn't a date." He tapped the brim of his hat. "Good night."

"*Ach*!" She pushed the door open and stepped inside muttering, "It certainly wasn't."

Lamplight glowed from the sitting room. Her father had waited up. When she reached him, he was closing the Bible. "How was the singing?"

"Fine."

"You don't sound like you had a fine time." He placed the Bible on the table next to the rocker. "Everything go *gut* with Jordan?"

"He thinks he's my overseer."

Daed gave a slow, understanding nod, then cracked a smile.

"I won't allow him to take James's place," she blurted.

Daed's smile faded.

She should've guarded her tongue. His eyes dulled.

"He's a *gut* man," *Daed* finally said. "He offered to drive you home."

She nodded slowly, then turned to head up the stairs. Maybe her father didn't know. It wasn't a date.

Once inside the cabin, Jordan dug his hand into his pants pocket and pulled out the treasured photograph of his mother.

"I don't understand this way of life, Mom. Why

105

do you want it for me when you couldn't live it yourself?" He sat in the chair next to the fireplace, taking her photo with him. "Maybe I'd fit in better as a truck driver. Travel the country like my father."

The empty eyes that stared back from the photograph uttered words only his heart understood.

Forsaken.

"Jordan, you are not forsaken. God loves you," Nathaniel said. He stirred the embers in the fireplace to gain Jordan's attention. "Read the Living Word, child. It is a lamp to bring you out from darkness and to light your path."

Jordan sucked in a breath when flames shot up in the fireplace. The wood had been consumed. He moved closer. Ashes don't flare up. The room filled with an orange and red glow. He turned a complete circle. The open Bible on the lamp table caught his attention. His mother's Bible.

Chapter Eight

"Northern Wisconsin is colder than Michigan." *Mamm* read to Sadie. "Fanny says April there feels like March here."

"The way I feel, I'd rather it be cold than hot,"

Sadie said, patting her belly. Five months pregnant and Sadie looked debilitated sitting with her legs propped up on the kitchen chair beside her. Because of her size, nearly everyone believed she would have twins.

Mamm continued reading highlights from the letter. "Their garden is small. They planted late so they aren't anticipating much yield."

Rachel went to the kitchen window where she could watch Jordan and *Daed* talking near the barn. She'd read Fanny's and Iva's letters when they arrived yesterday. Then she heard them at dinner as *Mamm* read them aloud to her father.

Mamm's reading droned on. The part in the letter where Fanny asked about her came next.

"'So Rachel cut Jordan's hair? Should we be saving our money to *kumm* home for a wedding?'"

Rachel rolled her eyes. "Please tell me you're *nett* going to read that letter at the sewing frolic later." The thought of entertaining similar comments was dreadful.

Mamm folded the letter and slipped it back into the envelope. "I'll skip the stuff about you and Jordan when I share the news."

Gut. Since last week, Jordan had been colder than a fish stored in the ice *haus.* Even if she wanted, she wouldn't be able to figure out Jordan Engles. Wearing the clothing, suspenders, hat, even the haircut, didn't make him Amish. Her sisters should know, not many outsiders became Amish as adults.

"Timothy says Jordan is a hard worker." Sadie sipped her tea.

"*Jah*. Your *daed* is very pleased."

"According to Timothy, Jordan could become a building framer if he wanted."

The entire family sang Jordan's praises. Rachel frowned. Why couldn't they see he was nothing like Timothy, who was a role model of a *gut* husband for her? If she married, she would want the man to love her the same way Timothy loved Sadie. Rachel wanted someone grounded in faith, who read the Word daily . . . like her *daed*. She closed her eyes. *Grounded in faith*. Why would she require of him the thing she could not do herself? Her own faith was a constant struggle. Not that she had fallen away. She loved God, she just doubted whether she had a purpose. A God-given purpose. From an early age, Sadie knew she wanted to marry and have children. So did Fanny and Iva. Most Amish women shared the same desire. Rachel used to but now had lost hope for marriage and children.

God, please forgive me if I've messed up your purpose for me . . .

"Sadie? Are you feeling okay? Your face is awfully red," *Mamm* said.

"It's this heat." Sadie fanned her face.

"Why don't you go lie down? There's still

plenty of time before the women arrive."

Sadie lowered her feet to the floor. "I think that's a *gut* idea."

Rachel waited for Sadie to leave before whispering, "Is something wrong?"

"She's retaining a lot of fluid," *Mamm* said. "But so did Ellen Fischer when she was pregnant with twins."

Rachel nodded, but one thought led to another and soon she was thinking about her cows near their delivery dates. Since she wasn't working in the barn, she hadn't kept a close eye on them.

Mamm opened the cookie jar and peered inside. "We can make a batch of peanut butter cookies for the frolic." She closed the lid. "But first we'll get a load of laundry washed so it can dry on the line while we're quilting."

"I'll fill the washtub." Rachel headed to the door. The wash *haus* was near the barn. She could check on the cows while she was out there.

"Be sure to gather Jordan's clothes for washing. He's part of the family," *Mamm* called out from the kitchen.

"Sure." She pulled the door open.

Tangus smiled. Rachel's inner rebellion would play nicely into his hands. "Soon your mamm will call him son," Tangus jeered. "He's part of the family . . . James is no more. Nearly forgotten." He swooped closer to his prey. "But you can get rid of Jordan. The power is in your tongue. He doesn't want to be here anyway. You would do everyone a favor to convince him to go."

Rachel kicked a rock, then winced when it didn't budge. Her thoughts were wrong—twisted with sin—but Lord help her, she didn't want to rebuke them.

She opened the door to the wash *haus* and got a bucket to fill with water. It took seven buckets to fill the tub depending on the size of the wash load. She usually sloshed more water on her dress than what made it into the tub.

Opening the door to the *grossdaadi haus*, she paused. The wooden floors shined as if Jordan had applied a fresh coat of mineral oil. As much as she polished the floors in the sitting room, she'd never had them shine like this. She wiped her finger along the fireplace mantel, then inspected it for dust but found no trace. There was no doubt Jordan was tidy. In the bedroom, his clothes were folded neatly too. Rachel plucked the garments he'd worn from the bed. She stopped midway across the wooden floor. Her wet footprints had created a trail from the door to the fireplace to the bedroom. Since the floor would likely dry before Jordan returned, she continued on her way.

A nest made of twigs and straw on the window ledge caught her eye. She rose to her tiptoes and leaned over the porch railing. She counted three bright blue eggs, another wonderful sign from God that it was spring. There were always many nests in the trees about their farm. But it was unusual to find one low enough for her to see into.

Inside the washhouse she dumped the pile of laundry into the water.

The door opened and *Mamm* stepped inside with a basket of dirty clothes. "Room enough for these in the tub?"

"*Jah.*" Rachel added the clothes and pushed them under the water. On days like today, she wished they owned a gasoline-powered wringer washer like Naomi's family. But *Mamm* never wanted to ask *Daed* for a gasoline washer, not with a household of women who were able to hand wash. Perhaps now that her sisters were all married, her mother would change her mind about what she termed an expensive convenience.

Mamm rolled her sleeves to her elbows and dipped the piece of clothing up and down. "Too much soap again." *Mamm* glanced at Rachel's wet dress. "I see you overfilled the tub too," she said playfully. She chucked her daughter under the chin. "A husband will expect his *fraa* to be neat and keep a clean *haus.*"

Rachel knew her mother was making light of the situation, but how many times would she hear what a husband expects? She wasn't like her sisters. She tried, failed, and accepted her shortcomings.

She only wished her mother and father would.

Rachel cranked the handle as *Mamm* fed the clothes between the rollers. The flattened pants came out the other side and fell into the basket. In between each piece, Rachel changed arms to turn the crank. Some of the heavier work pants of her father's took both hands and all her strength to send through the wringer.

After the last article of clothing fell into the basket, Rachel paused to wipe the back of her neck. She was glad they had a washhouse. She and *Mamm* generated their own heat in the closed area so they didn't require a potbellied stove in the winter. It was tough in the warmer months.

Rachel took hold of the basket. "I'll hang them." She took the clothes to the line and set the basket on the ground. Rachel reached for a pair of pants and gave them a stiff shake before she clipped them to the line. In the distance, Jordan and *Daed* worked the field. From where she stood, she couldn't see if Jordan's rows were straight. From the way his head was bowed, she decided they were not. He certainly wasn't much of a farmer— he still hadn't brought in a full milk bucket.

Rachel positioned her chair next to the quilting frame. Because of the overcast sky, the diffused light entering the sitting room made watching her mother's hands difficult.

"Make your stitches fine." *Mamm* drew the

needle up from the fabric. "Like so."

Rachel followed her mother's lead. This wasn't her first sewing lesson—she'd had many—but she still hadn't been able to master stitching. She watched *Mamm* demonstrate how to feed the needle through the fabric and pull the thread taut.

"*Nau* load your sharpie with as many stitches as possible."

Rachel's already tender fingers fumbled with the needle.

"*Gut*," *Mamm* said. "*Nau* keep your stitches evenly spaced and on a straight line."

This wasn't an easy task. Rachel would rather keep Clyde plodding straight across the field than aim her needle along an imaginary line.

Judith Lapp rested her hoop over her pregnant belly. "It *kumms* natural after practice, Rachel."

"*Jah*, for sure and for certain," Sadie added. Her belly wasn't much smaller than Judith's, yet she had several more months before term and Judith was due any day.

Katie lurched forward to check Rachel's work. "Are you getting the feel for it?"

Rachel forced a smile. "I'm trying."

"Judith, have you names picked out for the *boppli*?" *Mamm* asked.

Judith shared a smile with her mother-in-law, Mary, Bishop Lapp's *fraa*, before answering, "Andrew Zechariah if a boy, and Mary Elizabeth if a girl."

"After you, Mary. How lovely." *Mamm* winked at Sadie. "You'll have to think of names." *Mamm* beamed. "Maybe twins, ain't so?"

Aenti Leah turned to *Aenti* Esther. "Twins," she said loudly.

"I'm *nett* deaf," *Aenti* Esther replied.

"How is your *bruder* Samuel?" Sadie asked Judith.

Judith's face lit up. "Growing stronger every day. He helps Andrew after *schul nau.*"

Katie looked up from her sewing. "I heard there are plans to build another *schul.*"

"*Jah*, this fall," Mary Lapp replied.

Rachel waited for someone to mention her as the possible teacher. Not that she hadn't considered asking the bishop for the position. If God intended for her to remain unmarried, teaching would provide an income.

A shadow spilled over Rachel's hoop, making the stitching difficult to see. She glanced out the window at the clouds. "It looks like we're going to get rain."

"I hope *nett*," *Mamm* said.

"Ouch." Rachel pulled her hand out from under the hoop and examined the needle stick. It wasn't bleeding, but it was enough to make her put her work aside until there was more light. She stuck her needle in the fabric to mark her spot. "I'll make *kaffi.*"

"Give me a minute and I'll help." Naomi

114

quickly finished her block. She was working on a much larger log cabin block. Having mastered her technique years before, Naomi could stitch quickly while alternately lifting her head to carry on a conversation. Naomi had added incentive to finish the quilt for her hope chest now that William had shown interest in courting.

Naomi tied off her thread and pushed her work aside while the others continued looping their stitches. With all the years the womenfolk spent sewing, they could keep a straight line in any amount of light.

Once in the kitchen, Rachel opened the side of the woodstove and fed a few sticks of oak onto the bed of embers. Then she filled the kettle at the sink.

Naomi came up beside her. "I thought it was cute when Jordan called you Red."

Rachel glanced at the kitchen entry, making sure they were still alone. "He did his best to embarrass me all *nacht*. In front of Peter too."

"I caught Jordan gazing at you. He pretended not to be part of the group, but he was watching you closely."

Rachel set the kettle on the stove, then leaned against the counter and crossed her arms. "He thinks he's in charge of me. Like he's *mei bruder*."

"Your eyes are foggy if you can't see that he wants charge over you, but certainly *nett* like a *bruder*."

Steam rose from the whistling kettle, expelling a blast that drifted toward the ceiling. Rachel lifted the kettle and placed it on the wire rack away from the direct heat. "Tell me about the size of the garden you put in." They shared a knowing smile. When a girl started planning a wedding, the family automatically increased the size of the garden. Most information was kept between the couple, but Naomi and Rachel were too close to keep such secrets from each other.

Naomi clasped her hands behind her back and swayed. "He hasn't gained courage to ask for my hand if that's what you mean. He's only started *kumming* to sit with me on the porch."

"I'm sure you've given him plenty of hints," Rachel teased.

"Of course. He's shy. I'd still be waiting for him to sit with me in the evenings if I hadn't told him about the new wooden bench *mei daed* made."

"New bench?"

"I told him I'd never sat with a *bu* on it." Naomi tilted her head, considering Rachel. "You need to be forward too."

"I've only been asked once to be driven home from a singing and Jordan interfered with that. He could have let me ride with Peter. What harm was there in that?" She balanced the plate of peanut butter cookies over the cups.

Naomi grabbed the other cups. "Forget Peter. He drove Anne home after you left. Jordan is the one.

116

I'm telling you, you're blind if you can't see he's interested."

Rachel's mind reeled. *He took Anne home?*

Naomi nudged her. "You have a porch swing." She cast her eyes toward the window. "And the evening *wedder* is pleasant."

Rachel wanted to tell her friend to leave it alone, but she held her response and headed for the sitting room.

After serving the women, Rachel sat next to the window. The women's chatter merged into the background as she sipped her coffee and gazed outside, lost in her thoughts. A pickup entered the driveway and stopped in front of the barn. Rachel scooted closer to the window for a better view.

Kayla Davy climbed out from the driver's seat.

"Is that someone in the driveway?" *Mamm* craned her neck, as did most of the women.

"An *Englisher*," Katie said, taking in the outside activity.

Rachel set her cup on the side table and stood. "George Davy's girl. She's probably *kumm* to check on her horse." Rachel rose to her toes to see where Kayla had gone. The lilac bushes in full bloom obstructed her view. "I'll tell her that *Daed's* working in the field," she said, walking to the door.

Once Rachel rounded the bushes, she stopped. Wearing a blue-and-white checkered shirt tucked into a pair of skintight jeans, Kayla rocked on the heels of her boots while talking to Jordan at the edge of the field.

Jordan leaned close to Kayla, his attention never leaving her lovely face.

Chapter Nine

Jordan eyed Kayla Davy's stance. With her thumbs laced through her belt loops and her fingers tapping the pocket rivets on her Wranglers, he couldn't help but notice the shiny buckle that was centered over her petite waistline. The adornment boasted of a champion barrel racer, and Kayla seemed mighty proud to wear it as she rocked on the heels of her boots. The sun's reflection off the silver buckle sparkled.

Jordan cleared his throat. "What can I do for you?"

She smiled. "I thought I would go for a ride."

Jordan scanned the area. "It's too muddy for trail riding, and I wouldn't trust that horse on the road if I were you."

"Maybe you should be my guide and keep me safe." She raised an eyebrow.

Jordan steadied his focus on Micah as he approached them. Maybe in the absence of her father, Micah's caution would influence her not to ride today.

"Good afternoon, Kayla. I hope you don't mind if I shoe your horse on Monday."

"That's fine. I was actually hoping to ride today."

Micah glanced at the clouded sky.

"I asked Jordan if he wants to ride along with me"—she bowed her head slightly while directing her eyes up at Jordan— "but he hasn't answered."

"Not today," Jordan said. This wasn't the time for trail riding. It was time for hard work. He needed to prove he was worthy of his pay. He spoke to Micah. "We've got that last patch of ground that needs turning."

She cleared her throat. "Okay, I'll go alone." She spun around and walked away.

Tangus chased after the girl, filling her head with flirtatious ideas and movements, while Nathaniel held his position next to his charge.

Dancing around the girl, Tangus caused the sunlight to shift and shadow about her. "She's a beauty, isn't she, Jordan? Probably the prettiest girl you've ever seen. And she wants to spend time with you! She'd be clay in your hands—moldable to fit your desires." Tangus curled his lecherous tongue over his lips. "You find her beauty enticing; don't deny yourself. She's yours. Don't let her walk off alone."

Nathaniel created a gust of wind that shook the branches of the poplar trees. A balsam scent filled the breeze and drew Jordan's attention upward.

"That's right, Jordan, look away. Flee temptation." Nathaniel pressed his hand on Jordan's shoulder. "Turn from temptation."

Tangus spoke louder. "Your heart desires her. It's okay. God wants to give you the desire of your heart. Embrace it and run after her—after fate." Tangus purred with satisfaction when Jordan's focus shifted from the sky.

Jordan watched Kayla head to the barn. She was so different from Rachel. She was open and eager to spend time with him.

No! He closed his eyes to ward off being distracted. To mentally shake off Kayla's image, he spoke to Micah. "You think we can finish before the sun goes down?"

Micah evaluated the unbroken ground. "If *nett* today, then next week we will." He looked at Jordan, considering him. "Grace would be pleased with you."

"Thank you, sir. But I still have a lot to learn. I don't know much about plowing." He fisted his hand. "I'm not good at milking yet either."

Micah smiled. "I meant not yielding to temptation."

Jordan shifted awkwardly.

"May I ask a personal question?"

Jordan coughed into his hand. "Sure."

"Where's your father?"

All kinds of emotions let loose inside him. "I don't know. I guess he's a truck driver. I haven't seen him since I was . . . a kid."

"He hasn't tried to reach you since Gracie became ill?"

Gracie?

"I'm sorry. Is this too hard to talk about?"

Jordan shrugged. Micah was easy to talk to, but he'd never talked much about his father, even with his mother.

Micah cleared his throat. "I'm sorry. Sometimes I miss the long talks my *sohn* and I had." He peered at Clyde standing in the field. "What do you say we finish the plowing another day? I'll fetch Clyde. You start the evening chores."

"I heard about your son. I'm sorry. It must be difficult without him. No one told me what happened." Jordan wished he hadn't said anything after seeing the pained look in Micah's eyes.

"It happened two years ago. He tried to save a stray sheep from the river and the current swept him under."

Jordan swallowed. He hadn't thought about it before. No wonder Rachel was adamant about not being brothered.

"I'm sorry."

When Micah's eyes watered, Jordan had enough sense to give the man space. "I'll start the chores." He walked to the barn.

Kayla looked up from tightening the saddle cinch. "Change your mind about riding?"

He leaned against the support beam and crossed his arms. "No."

She flipped the stirrup down and gave it a quick tug, then took the reins in her hands. "Would you get the door?"

He pushed off the wall and unlatched the door.

The sudden light spooked Pepper, who side-stepped the entrance.

"It's okay, boy," Kayla coaxed softly. The horse took a few steps back until he backed into the wall between the hay and the milking area, then he burst forward. The reins slid through Kayla's hold.

Jordan reached out and grabbed them as Pepper was about to speed by. "Whoa." He pulled the horse's head around so he could do nothing but move in a circle. "Ride another day. He isn't settled."

She crossed her arms and planted her feet. "I'm not frightened by a horse."

She was foolish not to be. Dripping wet, she probably didn't weigh much more than the saddle. She'd be tossed off him like a fly if Pepper decided he didn't want her there anymore.

"Are you sure?" This horse was clearly too much for the girl to handle.

"Absolutely sure." She let Jordan lead Pepper out of the barn and into the sunlight. Rachel was not far away, standing at the clothesline. He sensed her pretending not to notice him as she unfastened the clothing from the line. His stomach pitted with an odd sensation.

Kayla came around the horse's left side. "Will you give me a leg up?" She stood on one foot, her other leg bent at the knee, and looked at him, not giving him much choice.

He hesitated. The horse rippled with energy, unable to stand completely still. Kayla hopped about to stay with him.

"Jordan, please?"

He put his hands underneath her bent leg, supporting it. She began to bounce gently. "One, two, three," they counted together. On three, Jordan lifted and Kayla expertly swung her free leg over Pepper's back and set herself in the saddle. As she secured her feet in the stirrups, he said, "Stay out of the field. It's too muddy. I'd take the trail through the woods, but watch for downed limbs—"

"Maybe you should ride along with me." She smiled, looking coy and enticing.

"I'm not crazy."

"And you think I am?" She held the reins tight as the horse sidestepped. "You wouldn't be riding Pepper, you'd be riding a much, much tamer horse." Her brown eyes flickered with an untamed spirit similar to that of her horse. They both seemed to have vinegar running through their veins.

He grinned. "Should I call you a fool instead?"

"If that's what you think of me." She reined her horse in a tight turn. "But a good Amish *bu* would repent over saying that." She loosened the rein at the same time she nudged Pepper with her calves. The horse bolted forward and mud soon shot up behind his pounding hooves.

He wanted to yell that a real horsewoman warmed up her horse before asking for speed. She wouldn't hear and she wouldn't care anyway.

A moment later Rachel walked up beside him. "What did you say that Kayla said you should repent?"

"She was teasing." He shifted his weight when Rachel didn't drop the scowl. "I called her a fool. That isn't a big deal."

The women near the house were bidding each other good-bye.

"They heard what she said too." Rachel nodded toward the women who had just finished their sewing time. "A *gut* Amish *bu* would—"

"I don't have anything to repent over. I'm not Amish," he said with a sparkle in his eye and a grin on his lips.

The long-haired cat meowed, and Rachel stooped down to scoop him into her arms. "Smokey!" she cooed. "Where have you been?" As she rubbed him, he began to purr.

Jordan backed away before the cat's dander blocked his breathing. He collected the water buckets from each stall, then held his breath as he moved past her. So far his chest hadn't tightened, and he wasn't wheezing in the close proximity to the cat. But he could sense a sneezing fit about to take over.

Jordan set the buckets under the well spigot and cranked the handle to prime the pump. Hooves pounded the ground. Jordan spun. Galloping to the barn, Pepper was riderless.

Jordan bolted toward the barn to catch the horse. He grabbed the dangling reins, and as he quickly mounted the prancing horse, Rachel stepped out of the barn. He wasn't thrilled about getting on this tightly wound bundle of energy, but he had no choice. It would take too long to saddle up another horse. He only hoped Pepper had a lot of his fire.

"Tell Micah I went to find Kayla. She might be hurt." He guided the horse to head in the same direction he'd watched Kayla go. *God, I know I don't pray often enough, but let her be okay.*

On the wooded trail, the budding birch trees offered an open view, but the fading light would become an issue if she wasn't found soon. He spotted fresh hoofprints and began to follow them.

"Kayla?" His voice echoed. He swept his eyes across the path. The rushing river grew louder. She had to be somewhere close. His eyes locked several feet ahead on her checkered shirt. Jordan prodded the horse to move faster and dismounted before the horse stopped a few feet from her.

He looked her over from head to toe as he knelt beside her. She was caked with mud, but he didn't see any blood. He tapped her shoulder. "It's Jordan. Can you hear me?"

She groaned.

He reached for her hand. "Where do you hurt?" Just because there weren't visual signs of injury didn't mean she hadn't suffered internal injuries.

She managed to pull herself up to a wobbly sitting position, then winced and laid back down on the ground. "I'm fine. I'm just dizzy."

"Are you sure? I don't want to move you if you're injured."

"Jordan, stop. I fell off a horse, I didn't . . ." Her voice trailed off as she closed her eyes. "I'm okay," she mumbled, clearly not okay. "Really."

Jordan took a few moments to assess her. Nothing looked broken, and he presumed she would feel worse if she had more serious injuries. He slipped one arm under her shoulders and the other under her knees and lifted her into his arms. "Just relax."

She leaned her head against his chest. "Is Pepper all right?"

"He's fine." He hoisted her up into the saddle. She held on to the horn, swaying and barely staying upright. He slid his foot in the stirrup and swung his leg over. Once situated behind her, Jordan held the reins in one hand while steadying Kayla by the waist with his other.

126

He clicked his tongue and Pepper headed home.

Her silence bothered him. He'd read once how a concussion caused a deep sleep. She hadn't slumped over, but he hadn't heard anything more than a faint moan.

"You still with me?" He nudged her gently.

After a short delay, she replied, "Yeah."

"Don't go to sleep."

"On a horse?"

He smiled. Perhaps her silence had been more a case of humility.

Jordan held a tight rein on Pepper to keep his pace slow. In the background of the horse's steps, bluebirds chirped and a squirrel scurried over the pine-needle-covered ground.

"You were right about it being too muddy for riding." Her voice slurred a little as though she were sleepy. "And that Pepper was a bit too crazy to be out on the trail."

He smiled.

"Why is he so calm now?" She tilted her head back to look up at him.

"Maybe because he's done a lot of galloping this morning." He shifted, very aware of her closeness. "You have to take control and show him who's the boss."

"Maybe you can teach me how to do that."

"Maybe."

At the back side of the Hartzlers' barn, he reined in the horse near the entrance. Pepper, glad to be home, was willing to stand still.

Rachel rushed out of the house, Micah out of the barn.

Keeping his hand on Kayla's waist, and with Micah positioned on the other side to make sure she didn't fall, Jordan slid off the horse. He slowly eased her down from the saddle.

"Are you all right?" Micah's forehead creased with lines.

Still in Jordan's arms, Kayla raised her head off his shoulder. "Yeah."

The deep lines on Micah's forehead receded. He blew out a breath, putting a hand over his chest.

"If you can take care of Pepper, I'll take her home."

Micah nodded.

Jordan carried Kayla across the lawn to her parked truck.

Rachel ran ahead and opened the driver's side of the truck.

"The passenger side, please," Jordan said.

Rachel rushed to the other side and opened the door.

New automobile scent penetrated the air. He glanced at the gunmetal-gray leather seat and hesitated to lower a mud-covered Kayla onto it.

"It's okay. Mud won't hurt the leather. I'm such a fool."

"I wasn't going to remind you of that."

"Because you're a good Amish *bu*." She started

to giggle, then grabbed her side and took a sharp breath.

He pulled the seat belt around her and clicked it into place. "By the way, I'm not Amish." He closed the truck door and, turning, almost plowed Rachel over. "Sorry," he said, reaching out to steady her.

Rachel looked surprised. "You're driving her?"

"I have a license."

Jordan trotted around to the other side and climbed into the cab. He cranked the engine and marveled over the brand-new, high-tech system blaring music through spectacular speakers. This was one nice truck.

After paying for his mother's medicine, he had nothing left to make his truck payments and his vehicle was repossessed. Still, his stripped-down S-10 had cloth seats and a factory-standard radio. It wasn't anything like Kayla's top-of-the-line dual-wheel king cab.

"Listen to how all this power purrs under your control. The same way she did in your arms. She's not hurt." Tangus chortled. "But you knew that when she pretended to be dizzy. She wanted your arms around her. And she felt good there, didn't she? This doesn't have to be the only time. It can be the first time."

Micah tapped on the window. Jordan pressed the down button, thankful to be distracted once again from thoughts that seemed to pull on him incessantly when Kayla was around.

Micah looked over at Kayla. "I hope you feel better soon." He turned his attention to Jordan. "I'll fetch you in the buggy."

"Thank you. *Denki.*"

He waited for Micah to move away before putting the truck in gear. At the end of the driveway, he glanced at Kayla slumped against the window. "Which way do I turn?"

She pointed to the right. "Go about two miles, then turn left on Davy Lane."

He waited for a car to pass, then eased onto the road. Once he made the left turn, the name of the road dawned on him.

"You have a road named after you?"

"After my grandfather." She weakly waved her hand. "At one time he owned all of this."

Jordan read the sign on a brick building as they passed.

"The school's named after him too," she said.

Because he was watching Kayla instead of the road, the tire dipped into a pothole, jostling them both.

Kayla groaned. "I wish this road was paved."

"Sorry." He concentrated on the road and was able to avoid the other washed-out areas.

"I live just over the hill."

They reached the crest of the hill and his breath caught. A long, tree-lined drive led to a sprawling two-story house with multiple wings and a covered porch. As he drove down the hill, he couldn't help but admire the place.

"You could have a place like this one day, Jordan. Comfortable. Everything you want. All the horses you want." Tangus wanted to touch Jordan's shoulder but was restrained from doing so.

Jordan parked the truck and jogged over to Kayla's side of the vehicle, trying to push envy aside. It was hard. This was so close to all he'd dreamed of. "You have a nice place," he said, trying to sound casual. Although she seemed she might be okay, she still looked shaken up. He offered his hand to help her out. Kayla moved it to her waist and reached for his other hand. "I'm too wobbly. I need you to steady me." Jordan again felt trapped into being close to her. And felt uncomfortable at how much he enjoyed it.

As he set her on the ground, she put a hand against the truck and it seemed her knees buckled slightly. He wasn't sure if it was part of a show or if she was still very weak. He put his elbow out so she could take it.

"Thanks." She tugged his elbow. "Look, the builders finished the stable yesterday."

Jordan took in a full view of the impressive stone-sided structure. An iron staircase curled above the horse stable to what looked like a second-story living area. A rooster weather vane capped the roof. Floodlights surrounded the elongated riding arena in the front of the building. The place looked straight out of a magazine.

"Daddy's talking about putting in an enclosed arena as well. Then I can ride year-round."

Tangus trotted up to Jordan. "You remember the thrill of working with the harness racehorses. All that speed, strength, high-strung temperaments. You can have that and more. You don't want to walk behind a plow all your life. You're not Amish. Instead of smoldering in this heat and coughing up field dust from your lungs, you could work with horses again. Air-conditioned stalls . . ."

"I worked on a horse farm. They bred harness racers."

"Where was that?"

"Farmington Hills. It's about four hours south of here."

"I know where that is . . ." Kayla waved her hand dismissively. "This is small compared to those farms. We only have eight stalls."

"Air-conditioned and heated, too, probably."

"I'd take you on a tour if I didn't feel so rough." She pushed her tousled chestnut hair behind her ears, exposing her dirt-smeared cheeks. Her knees buckled a little.

"Can you walk?"

"I think I'll be fine. As long as I can hold on to something . . . someone. Working on a racehorse farm must've been exciting. Did you go to the races too?"

"Most of them." His mother had never liked that going to the races was part of his job. She'd repeatedly warned him not to become entangled in the excitement of gambling. She said it so often he heard her words at every race. *"A gambler eventually sells his life—and then his soul."*

Kayla pointed to the back door. "You can take me in there and then wait inside for Micah."

He rubbed his free hand along his thigh, leaving a trail of dirt down the seam, and walked beside her to the door.

"If you're not Amish, then why—"

"Am I wearing the funny clothes?" He snapped his suspenders, then pulled off his hat. "Or are you wondering about the Dutch-boy haircut?"

"Hey, I wasn't going to mention the haircut."

He laughed. "Rachel did this. Apparently, until she got hold of me, she'd only sheared sheep."

Kayla laughed but stopped to grab her side.

Concern took over. "Are you hurting?"

"Only when I laugh. So don't make me laugh."

She paused at the door. "If you aren't Amish, then why are you at the Hartzlers'?"

"My mother was Amish. Before she . . . died." His voice quivered and he swallowed. "She made me promise to spend time with her relatives. My uncle arranged for me to work for Micah, so I'm here until I figure out what's next."

He glanced at her truck. "Do you think when you're feeling better you could drive me into town? The library should have computers. I'd like to go online and get information on truck-driving schools."

She smiled. "Sure, but you don't need the library." She dug her hand into her pocket, pulled out a rhinestone-studded phone, and held it out. "You can search the Internet on this."

His phone, before the contract expired, had only the basics—and they could barely afford that. It didn't even have texting options like most of his high school friends had.

She touched it and the screen lit, then handed it to him. "Just type in what you want to search." She nudged the door open. "Come inside."

Jordan looked at his grubby clothes and mud-covered shoes. "I better not." He extended his hand to give back the phone.

"I'll get it from you later. I have unlimited texting, calls, and Internet. Call your friends if you want."

Jordan smiled. "I lost track of them after high school. They left for college, and I started working at the stables. I would like to do some searches, if you're sure you can do without it."

"That's the least I can do for someone who

rescued me." She leaned closer. "Besides, I have a laptop and a phone in my room. I won't miss it—much." She laughed. "It's so weird how our parents never had these things, and we can't live without them."

"Thanks." He looked down at the phone in his hand, then back up at her, taking in her beautiful eyes. "I'm glad you weren't hurt badly."

"You mean other than my pride?"

"That will mend." He waved and continued down the driveway, glad it seemed she was getting stronger by the minute. With each step he took, a battle raged within him. He attempted to push away all that enticed, trying to settle his mind on what his mother would say was truly important.

Chapter Ten

Rachel held Ginger at a steady trot until she caught up with Jordan walking along the edge of the dirt road. When he saw her, he jammed something sparkly into his pocket. She stopped the buggy and waited for him to board.

"I figured you'd be enjoying Kayla's hospitality." *Ach*, why couldn't she keep the sarcasm out of her tone? She glanced behind her out the window and, spotting another buggy, she signaled Ginger to trot.

Jordan inched closer to her on the bench. "Careful, jealousy is a sin."

"I'm *nett*—"

His grin widened.

"What did you shove into your pocket? Are you trying to hide something?"

He reached into his pocket. "You're awfully nosy for someone who isn't jealous." He showed her the shiny item and said, "It's a phone."

"I wouldn't have guessed your style to be so fancy." She had a good idea Kayla gave it to him so they could stay in contact.

Rachel snapped the reins and Ginger picked up her speed. Maybe they would reach the house before Jordan pried open a deeper gash in her heart. Kayla was beautiful. She certainly had plenty of worldly stuff to entice him. Jealousy was a sin, and the last thing Rachel wanted was to admit her jealousy.

She heard the clip-clop of a fast horse coming up from behind them. She gave the reins another light snap and Ginger picked up her pace.

He glanced behind them, then glared at her. "Are you racing that buggy?"

She ignored his question.

He reached out and firmly covered her hand with his.

A discharge of current zipped through her body and curled her toes. Distracted by the effects of his touch, she released control of Ginger to him.

"Whoa." His shoulder brushed against hers as he pulled back the reins.

Ginger obeyed, slowed her pace, and stopped when Jordan called, "Whoa," again.

Before he started lecturing about buggy racing, she blurted, "We don't believe in worldly—"

The phone suddenly blared with a song Rachel had never heard. Jordan fumbled and nearly dropped it before answering the call.

"Okay . . . Yeah . . . Yeah . . . Okay, thanks for letting me know." He jammed the phone back into his pocket. "That was Kayla. She wanted to tell me how to find the songs and games on this thing."

Rachel's hands trembled as she straightened the folds on her dress. "You're bringing sin into *mei* father's *haus*."

Jordan's eyes broke from her gaze. He straightened his position on the seat, took up the reins, and used the words the horse understood. "*Geh* on, Ginger."

ಬಬ

"Jordan, the Master is calling," Nathaniel said, standing over the charge's bed.

Jordan forced his eyes open. Had someone tapped his shoulder? He peered around in the darkness. Of course, there was nothing and no one. *Just a dream,* he thought, and closed his eyes.

"Jordan," Nathaniel repeated.

Now fully awake, Jordan sat up in bed. From under the door, yellow light seeped into the otherwise dark room. It crawled along the floor in a dense fog. Suspended in a dream state, he saw himself throwing back the bedcovers and rising. Given freedom to move about the room, he stepped into the warmth of the fog and, as it coursed its way, he was drawn to the source of heat.

An icy breeze alerted Jordan's senses. He opened his eyes fully. Familiar with his surroundings, Jordan understood he was seated in the sitting room's rocking chair with the Bible lying on his lap. He touched the vellum texture and heat radiated off the pages.

"For I know the thoughts that I think toward you, says the LORD, thoughts of peace and not of evil, to give you a future and a hope."

Jordan let the words of Jeremiah sink in. *"Future and a hope . . ."* Did any of this have to do with the information he'd been able to gather about truck-driving school?

Timothy motioned for Jordan to follow him out of earshot of the Sunday crowd. "So Rachel was racing again?"

"Who said Rachel was racing? When?"

"Yesterday. On Davy's Road."

Jordan tapped his chest. "I had control of Ginger when the buggy passed."

Timothy nodded pensively. "I was driving the other buggy, and seeing Rachel on the driver's side, I assumed she was racing."

Jordan smiled. "She didn't willingly give me the reins, but I don't want her in trouble with Micah. She already thinks I've come between them."

"She needs to understand her place."

Jordan crossed his arms and shifted his stance, feeling unreasonably defensive for this girl.

Timothy slapped him on the back. "Don't get worked up. I've always been fond of Rachel, but I'm afraid she'll stay *leddich*."

"*Leddich*?"

"Unmarried." Timothy rocked back on his heels. "She's too competitive. She isn't a *gut* cook." He chuckled. "Would a man want to say he lost a buggy race, and then lost his heart to the winner?" Apparently, he didn't expect Jordan to answer. Timothy continued, "Sadie won *mei* heart with her cooking."

Rachel needed practice. Sure, her eggs were inconsistent, sometimes hard and sometimes runny, but he ate them.

"Let's eat." Timothy's expression changed suddenly, his forehead creasing.

"What is it?" Jordan followed Timothy's gaze to his wife holding her belly.

"Sadie, she isn't feeling *gut*." He picked up his

pace across the yard. "I need to take her home so she can rest."

Jordan continued into the house. He bowed his head, as though in a silent prayer of thanks with the rest of the folks, until he heard others moving about. He filled a plate and grabbed a cup of coffee. He moved toward the door, hoping to pass through the crowd unnoticed. Watching his feet instead of his surroundings, he bumped into Rachel, spilling the coffee all over himself. He buried a yelp. The hot liquid soaked through his vest and thin shirt and dripped down his pant leg. His skin felt scorched. Thankfully, the coffee had spilled over him and not on her Sunday dress.

"*Ach*, I'm so sorry," she said. "I'll find you a towel." She rushed over to the sink.

With his plate in one hand and his half-empty coffee cup in the other, he couldn't stand in a room full of people and remain silent in his pain any longer. He fled the house, stopping under the maple tree. Placing his plate and cup on the ground, he lifted the corner of his saturated shirt to inspect the burn. He hadn't thought of himself as a spectacle until he heard Rachel's gasp.

He looked up at her wide eyes and dropped the corner of his shirt.

"I brought you a towel." She extended her hand. "Are you . . ." Her eyes darted up and down the soiled area.

"Burned?" He reached for the towel in her hand.

"It isn't bad." He dabbed the cloth over the soiled area of his shirt.

"Your *gut* clothes too. I'm sorry."

"It wasn't your fault." When he glanced up, an unexpected jolt struck his core as he caught the concern in her eyes. Why didn't the unmarried men see this side of her?

"Are you sure you're *nett* burned?"

"Do I need to remove my shirt to prove I'm fine?" He placed his hands on the top hook and eye of his vest.

She spun. "I don't find you funny, Jordan Engles."

"I was joking."

She marched off without looking back.

Jordan sat under the tree to eat. Even though the green bean casserole didn't look appealing, he selected it knowing Rachel had made it. One bite of the mushy mixture, and he couldn't deny her cooking skills still needed lots of work. He considered dumping the plate of food somewhere near the barn and going through a fast food restaurant in town. His mouth began to water as he considered a greasy hamburger and fries versus mushy green bean casserole. When he spied the host family's dog, he clicked his tongue and the dog ran to greet him.

"You like Rachel's cooking, don't you, boy?" Jordan waited in anticipation as the dog licked the plate clean. He left the empty dish on the table and headed to his buggy. Once he pulled onto the road, he thought over his decision and wondered if it would be wise. He didn't want to be disrespectful of Micah or the others in the community by eating in town on the Lord's day. He sighed, turning the buggy onto a different road than he'd planned. Too bad making the right decision didn't stop his mouth from watering.

As Blaze trotted along the dirt road through the farmlands, many of the *Englisch* farmers were plowing their fields with tractors while the Amish homes were void of activity.

He admired the Amish way in many things— but at the moment he'd give anything to have that burger and fries followed by the luxury of a hot shower.

After arriving at the Hartzlers' house, he unhitched Blaze from the buggy and turned him out to the pasture, then headed to the little house to change into his work clothes.

He tossed his Sunday clothes over the chair and picked up the pants he'd worn earlier to milk the cows before church. As he fastened the suspenders, he noticed the picture of his mother had fallen out of his nicer pants and was lying on the floor. His breath caught. It looked wet—had the coffee splashed on it? He picked it up and inspected it. Seeing that the photo was not destroyed, he breathed easier and tucked it back into his pocket before heading outside to do the chores.

Jordan fed the calves and horses, but it was still too early to milk the cows. He scooped chicken feed into an empty coffee can and trekked over to the henhouse. The chickens flocked around him, clucking as he scattered corn over the ground.

Kayla's truck pulled into the drive and stopped. She climbed out and waved. He tossed the remaining grain to the chickens. She probably wanted her cell phone.

"Hello, Jordan," she said as she walked in his direction.

"I'll get your phone." He set the coffee can on a stump and headed for the little house.

Kayla followed. "Were you able to find the information you wanted?"

"Yeah, thanks." He opened the door and stepped inside.

She followed him. "Whoa." She looked around the room. "Does Rachel clean for you?"

"No," he said as he continued to the bedroom. "I'm self-sufficient."

"You make your bed too." She smiled as she stood in the doorway.

He took the phone from the dresser and handed it to her. "Sorry. I ran your battery down."

She laughed. "I forgot to give you the charger. Not that it would matter since you don't have electricity here." She slid the phone inside her pocket.

"Let's go," he said and led her back toward the front door.

Kayla stepped outside and put her hand up to shade her eyes. "It's probably still too muddy for riding. What do you think?"

"I hope you're not serious."

She smiled. "I guess it would be foolish to ride today."

"Yup." He stopped near the woodpile and took hold of the ax. "Thanks again for letting me use your phone."

"Anytime." She started to walk backward to the barn. "I'm going to check on Pepper."

He started to follow her with his eyes, then purposefully focused on the wood to be split. His ax strike hit dead center. As he picked up the split pieces, he noticed Rachel and Micah stepping out of their buggy, each carrying a small bundle. Rachel looked in Kayla's direction, then at Jordan.

His heart thumped hard. Had Rachel seen him watching Kayla walk away? He placed a chunk of wood on the block and wielded the ax.

He didn't owe Rachel any explanations.

He tossed the chopped oak into a kindling pile and readied another log to split. With his constant pace he had cut enough wood to service the cookstove for a week. But with his thoughts still fixed on Rachel, he needed the hard work of the ax to process them. When he paused to wipe the sweat from his neck, Micah was heading toward him. "I see you've been busy," he said.

"Yes, sir." Then, noticing Micah's sober expression, he asked, "Did I do something wrong? I thought you'd be pleased."

"I understand . . . more than you think. Come with me."

Jordan sank the ax into a stump and continued on with Micah. Nothing was said until they both entered the barn. "She's distracting, I know, but Sunday is a day of rest."

He wasn't sure if Micah was referring to Kayla or Rachel, and he wasn't about to ask.

Micah motioned to the back door. "Slide it open, please."

Jordan did as instructed. He sheepishly waited for the cows to enter.

Micah chuckled. "Don't look so grim, *sohn*."

"I view wood as a necessity, like milking the cows," Jordan said. He slid the door closed after the last cow entered. "I didn't mean to offend God . . . or your faith. I'll be more mindful."

"You didn't offend me. And God understands your heart." He tied the cow to the milking post and arranged his stool. "Hard work tends to keep a man out of trouble." Micah sat and dipped a washrag in a sudsy bucket. "David certainly had too much time on his hands when he watched Bathsheba bathe."

"God forgave him. He didn't remove him from kingship."

Micah looked up from washing the cow's udder. "God forgave him because he repented of his sin. It is a lesson to us all. We all fall short." Tossing the rag into the bucket, he stood and placed his hand on Jordan's shoulder. "Since you've arrived, I see your heart is heavy. Is there something you wish to talk about? I could drive you to the bishop's *haus* for a visit."

Jordan shook his head slowly at first, then with firm refusal. Jordan didn't know where he'd find what he needed. But he knew the bishop couldn't offer him relief from his heavy heart. His mother had claimed he would find that relief as a gift of peace that could only come from God.

"I appreciate your kindness, but I'd rather not discuss it."

Micah sat on the stool and positioned his hands. Milk sprayed against the metal bucket.

Jordan watched a few moments, his hand resting on Florri's flank. "I gave the cell phone back," he blurted.

Micah looked over his shoulder. His forehead wrinkled.

"Kayla Davy's phone. I borrowed it."

Micah's expression stiffened.

"I'm sorry. I didn't mean to disrespect your ways."

Micah stood. "A cell phone isn't sinful."

Jordan blew out a breath.

"The reason we choose not to have phones is

146

to maintain separation from the world. Some settlements allow them for business purposes, but *nett* us. We rely on God's provision." Micah patted Jordan's shoulder. "Did the phone help with what you were looking for?"

Jordan cleared his throat. "I think so."

Chapter Eleven

Micah added coal to the forge. "Would you fill a bucket with water for cooling the tools?"

"Sure." Jordan grabbed the bucket beside the anvil and headed to the pump. He looked forward to learning how to shoe the Davys' horse even though he wouldn't need the skill in his future plans. Not that his plans were firm yet. Truck driving beckoned to him. Not because it was the dream career he'd always wanted, but partly because of the freedom it offered. Like his father, he could find his purpose "out there" somewhere. And maybe it would help him understand why his father couldn't stay with his wife and son.

Black smoke curled from the pipe extended above the roof of the lean-to attached to the barn. When Jordan stepped back inside bearing a full water bucket, Micah was pumping the piston bellows to get the coal hot.

Jordan remembered a school field trip to the

Pioneer Days exhibit. The man wore a bib-style, oil-tanned apron while hammering the molten metal. How different this was. Micah wasn't putting on a demonstration to show how blacksmiths once worked; he was a real tradesman.

Micah looked over his shoulder. "Once the tools are heated, I'll have you get the horse." He swept his shirtsleeve over his brow before turning the tools over in the forge. "You can arrange the nippers and hammers according to size."

Jordan did as instructed. "Why the different hammers?"

"This one is a straight hammer." He pointed to a long-handled tool with a blunt, snub-nose end on one side and a wedge on the other. "I use it to shape the bar stock into a horseshoe." He pointed to the next hammer. "The driving hammer is to set the nails in the hooves, and this one is a rounding hammer for refining."

Jordan mentally rehearsed the name and uses of each hammer. The driving one had a claw end similar to a carpenter hammer. He should be able to remember that one.

"Okay, I'm ready for the horse," Micah said.

Jordan brought the horse into the shoeing area.

Micah fastened a second lead on the halter and clipped each lead to an iron ring on opposite sides of the wall. "First we crosstie the horse—for the same reasons you did in your previous job."

Jordan watched intently.

Micah's hand traveled smoothly from the horse's neck to the withers and down Pepper's front leg. He picked up the hoof and rested it on his slightly bent leg, then after a careful inspection, Micah lowered the horse's hoof to the ground.

"If this was the heart of winter, I'd braze a few Borium rivets on the shoes to give him traction over the icy roads." He smiled. "*Kumm* fall, you'll be able to apply them with your eyes closed."

Jordan's stomach knotted. Come fall, he planned to be gone. He wondered how long it would take to complete the course he needed to take to get his Class A Driver's License.

Micah gave explicit details of each step, but Jordan's thoughts drifted from trying to remember what Micah said to being in a truck, driving from state to state. First, he reminded himself, he had to earn enough money to take the truck-driving course and pay for the special license. He'd better pay close attention. Even if he didn't learn all the ins and outs of blacksmithing, farrier skills could be used anywhere.

Jordan jammed his hands into his front pockets and marveled at Micah's skill. He worked with confidence and a steady hand.

"Now for the hind legs." He slid his hand cautiously down the leg and asked for the horse to pick up its foot. "Sometimes the horses are touchy about having their back hooves handled." He used a sharp metal hoof pick to clear the packed soil and trampled dung from the bottom of the hoof. "On a new horse I do them last and work fast."

Micah explained his process while he sized the shoe. "I leave expansion room. Their feet grow faster in the spring than the winter."

Sweat dripped down the back of Jordan's neck and down his chest. Standing this close to the forge, he would have thought it was closer to August than the end of May.

Pepper neighed and his ears flickered.

Micah seemed to sense the horse growing impatient and worked quickly without taking additional time to explain his activity. When he finished, he studied the horse. "I like to let the horse stand on them a minute or two before walking."

The tools sizzled and steam rose when he dipped them into water.

"*Mei* father made this hammer and passed it down to me." He picked up the one used to drive the nails and turned it over in his hand. Instead of seeming nostalgic, he seemed sad. His eyes held a dull cast. "I taught *mei sohn* all I knew and planned to pass this down to him." His voice quivered. "You won't be an apprentice long. If you decide to become a blacksmith, you'll need a *gut* set of tools." Micah's eyes glazed and he stroked his beard. After a moment of silence, he cleared his throat. "Will you walk the horse so I can monitor his stride?"

"Sure." Jordan unfastened the horse from his cross ties and led him in a large circle around the pump, then back to Micah.

"*Gut.* Now at a trot, please."

Jordan trotted the horse in both directions in a circle before Micah gave his approval.

"You can put him back in the stall while I *redd-up* the forge."

Jordan led Pepper toward the barn, figuring this was Micah's way of asking for time alone. As Jordan latched the gate, Rachel appeared.

She narrowed her eyes. "You've taken everything from me."

He cocked his head to get a look into her eyes. "What are you talking about?" He tried softening his tone, but nothing altered her hardened expression.

She dragged her sleeve over her face. "Lunch will be ready shortly."

Jordan wasn't sure who to look at during the meal, Micah's long face or Rachel's glaring eyes. Miriam must have sensed the coldness at the table because she stared at her plate and ate in silence too.

Rachel's accusations puzzled him. What had he taken? He merely wanted to work hard, earn some money, and move on.

A boom of thunder broke the silence at the table. Rain pattered against the kitchen window.

"The clothes." Rachel bounced to her feet and ran to the door.

Jordan lowered his fork. "I'll help her," he said, seeing Miriam start to stand.

Miriam smiled. "*Denki*, that's very kind."

He grabbed his hat from the hook and bolted outside.

The bedding flapped in the stiff wind. He jogged to the line and unclipped the shirt in front of him. "I'm sorry, Rachel."

She stopped in front of him. "How long are you planning to stay?"

Jordan unclipped a towel, unsure how to answer.

She reached for the towel next to his. "Why won't you talk about your mother? Or why you're here? Do you have some big secret you don't want anyone to know?"

His jaw tensed.

"That's it, isn't it?"

He spun to face her. "It's no secret. My mother is dead."

"I didn't mean—"

Jordan continued going down the line, removing items and tossing them in the basket. She grasped his arm and stopped him. "Look, I'm sorry. I . . . I shouldn't have said that. I'm angry. But it's not your fault."

Rain streaked her face, which filled with a tenderness he hadn't seen before. Perhaps she hadn't been thinking before she verbally attacked him, but what did it matter? He was leaving the minute he earned enough money for driving school.

He counted to three between a flash of lightning and the rumble of thunder that followed. She seemed more interested in standing there and probing him with questions than in taking down the clothes.

"Jordan, I really didn't know. I was forbidden to talk about—"

"Her shunning?"

He moved to the other end of the line. And then he saw his pants. He felt the air leave his lungs. He snatched them off the line and put his hand inside the pocket. Jordan closed his eyes, holding in emotions that were too big.

"What's wrong?"

Before he said something he would regret, he marched off.

"I don't understand," she said, chasing him.

He ignored her, climbed the porch steps, pressed his shoulder against the door, and opened it.

"Those were the pants with the coffee stain. I got the stain out of your shirt too. I thought you would be grateful." The sincerity in her eyes didn't alter how he felt.

He pressed his lips together, keeping the churning words in check. Unable to speak, he motioned with a stiff nod at the door.

She stepped closer. "Won't you tell me why you're upset?"

"I need a few minutes alone." He waited for her to move so he could close the door, but she stiffened like a cement pillar. Stubborn, curious woman.

He placed his hand on her lower back and guided her to the door, then shut it hard to send an unspoken warning.

Jordan took the wet, crimped photograph and attempted to smooth it. The ink was sticky and made a mess of his mother's face. He leaned against the door and closed his eyes.

Her sobbing on the other side of the door rattled his nerves. He jerked the door open. "Why are you still—" What was she doing sitting on the ground in the pouring rain? He flew off the porch and grabbed her arm. As he lifted her up, the bright blue eggs on the ground caught his eye.

"The nest fell off the windowsill," she said with hitched breath.

"I'll put them back." Jordan squatted down beside the robin eggs. At least they appeared to have survived the fall. Not wanting to handle the eggs, he looked around the ground for a few sturdy sticks and leaves.

"I wonder where the mama bird is," she said softly.

"I'm glad she isn't here. She might abandon the nest if she thinks we've messed with her eggs." He used the sticks to scoot the eggs onto the leaves and back into the nest, then balanced the nest between the two sticks and lifted it to the window ledge.

"What was in your pocket?"

Rachel stared at the rain draining off Jordan's hat and falling on his broad shoulders.

He turned without saying anything and went into the house.

Rachel tilted her face upward, allowing the warm rain to dilute her tears. "He's hurting. I see the pain in his eyes, God."

Nathaniel chanted prayers that only his Master understood. Transparent light radiated within him. In a chorus of echoes, he said, "His ears are open to your prayers, child."

Rachel splashed through the mud as she ran to the clothesline. She grabbed the basket, leaving the other items on the line, and ran into the house.

Mamm entered the sitting room, looked at Rachel's shoes, and wagged her head in disapproval.

Before she opened her mouth with her well-meaning, future-*fraa* instructions, Rachel acknowledged her shortcoming. "*Jah*, I know." She had tracked the muddy trail from the door to the sofa. "I'll mop the floor."

Mamm bent down and lifted the dress from the top of the pile. "This isn't too wet," she said, feeling several areas of the garment before spreading it over a chair in front of the wood-stove.

"I think most of them were dry before it started to rain." Rachel pulled Jordan's shirt from the basket and studied it. She'd been so concerned about getting the coffee stain out, she hadn't thought about checking his pockets.

"Lord, show me how to make it up to Jordan," Rachel mumbled.

"Why? He's the one who was irresponsible and left the stuff in his own pocket." Tangus wedged himself between her and the woodstove. "You don't even know what was in there. Probably nothing important—like Kayla's cell phone or some other worldly treasure. What else would have any meaning to Jordan?" Tangus exhaled, and ash dust from the woodstove blew out the cast iron door and fluttered to the floor.

Mamm snapped a towel, then spread it over a stool. "I thought we could make potato soup tonight. You could make a rhubarb pie. Afterward I'll read you Iva's and Fanny's letters. Have you written to them lately?"

"*Jah*. I send a letter once every few days."

Rachel took some of the drier pieces from the basket to fold. "Did you know that Jordan's *mamm* died?"

Mamm straightened the towel over the stool. "*Jah.*"

"Has he said anything to you about it?"

"I didn't want to pry." She pulled the stool closer to the woodstove. "I've wanted him to feel at home here. He can speak or not as he pleases, so long as it isn't dishonoring God."

Rachel's throat dried. She swallowed hard. Since his arrival, she certainly hadn't made him feel welcome. "I'll bring some rhubarb in after I mop the floors." This time she would add sugar. Perhaps he might view it as an apology.

"Your heavenly Father is pleased." Nathaniel's brilliance magnified.

Tangus contorted his body to avoid the light reflecting off Nathaniel's bronze form. As the heavenly host sang praises, Tangus collapsed on the floor. Spread sheet-thin, Tangus disappeared under the door crack.

Rachel hurried through the afternoon chores and took great care preparing the evening meal and the rhubarb pie. It wouldn't be long before Jordan and *Daed* would have the milking finished.

Mamm stood at the window. "It looks like the Davys are here to retrieve their horse."

Rachel stopped stirring the soup and stood on her toes next to her mother. She smiled. With the horse gone, Kayla would have no reason to pay Jordan any more visits.

Pepper balked and backed away from the trailer. His head up high, eyes wide, he pawed the ground. She wondered why anyone would want such a green, high-strung horse for their daughter.

The heavy scent of garlic drew her away from the window to check the progress of the biscuits. She jabbed a fork into the dough. A few more minutes and they'd be ready. Rachel filled the kettle with water to heat for coffee.

"The horse is loaded." *Mamm* pulled away from the window and went to the cabinet.

"Finally," Rachel said, setting out the plates and silverware.

Mamm brought out four cups and set them on the counter. "Don't forget to check your biscuits."

Rachel pulled the biscuits from the oven and slid them from the cookie sheet to a plate. Golden brown and still soft—just how she'd hoped. She breathed in the savory aroma.

The outside door opened and closed, and a single set of footsteps entered the kitchen. Rachel glanced over her shoulder at her father.

"Where's Jordan?"

Daed sat. "He's gone to help unload the Davys' horse."

Rachel's smile faded. She brushed her hands on her apron. "We can keep a plate warm for him."

"Don't look for him to *kumm* back. He asked to be released."

Chapter Twelve

Rachel scooped a can full of oats from the grain barrel and poured them into the feed bucket. Her father hadn't said anything since he started milking. His quietness, no doubt, had to do with Jordan leaving yesterday. Rachel wanted to apologize for the way she'd treated Jordan, but the more she dwelled on his leaving with Kayla, the more determined she became that they didn't need him. *She* didn't need him. And once she and *Daed* had the fields done, *Daed* would realize it too.

She poured grain into Clyde's feed bucket, adding extra to his portion because he would have a hard day pulling the stumps out of the field. She spoke to her father while she scratched Clyde on his withers. There was no way to know what was truly bothering her father unless she asked. "Something wrong, *Daed*?"

He lifted his head from resting it against the cow's side. "It's nothing the Lord can't handle."

"If you're upset about Jordan leaving, I'll do the fieldwork. We worked together before."

Daed pulled the bucket out from under the cow and stood. "*Nay*, Rachel." He brushed his hand over her cheek. "I'm *nett* concerned about the fieldwork. I can hire other help. I'm concerned about Jordan. His heart is troubled, and I sense he's running from God."

Rachel bowed her head, even more ashamed that she'd pushed Jordan to leave. She squeezed her eyes closed. *Lord, forgive* mei *poor actions. Don't let Jordan run far. He needs to know your peace and he won't know that until he surrenders to you.*

Nathaniel hummed as she prayed. He delighted in hearing her petition for forgiveness. "Child, this peace you are asking for your friend can also be yours when you surrender the guilt you harbor around your brother's death. It was not your hand that chose the hour of James's death any more than you placed the stars in the sky."

Daed beckoned her. "*Kumm*. Let's see what your *mamm* has cooked for us."

Rachel forced a smile and followed him out of the barn.

When they entered the house, a mixed aroma of coffee and sausage drifted from the kitchen. *Daed* doffed his hat and placed it on the hook. Rachel slipped out of her barn boots.

"Miriam, I hope that's your biscuits and sausage gravy I smell." *Daed* entered the kitchen patting his flat belly. He came up behind *Mamm*, placed one arm around her waist, and looked over her shoulder to peer into the pot. "*Mei fraa.*" He kissed her cheek. "You know how much I love biscuits and gravy."

"After twenty-eight years I should, ain't so?"

Rachel pretended not to notice their affection as she poured the coffee. *Daed* hadn't always been so forward with his feelings.

Rachel set the coffee cups on the table while *Mamm* piled the biscuits on a plate. Once seated, they prayed a silent grace.

When Rachel opened her eyes, she noticed the empty chair that in a short time had become Jordan's place. She missed his grin, his hearty appetite, and the different faces he made trying to disguise his reaction to her cooking.

Mamm sprinkled her gravy with pepper, then passed the shaker to Rachel. "I plan to send a package of baked goods and some extra yardage of material to Fanny and Iva. Would you like to add a letter, Rachel?"

"I have one started. Are you taking the package into town today?"

"Tomorrow. Sadie's bringing her letter and is planning to stay with us and sew clothes for the *boppli* today."

She'd forgotten about the planned sewing day. Rachel swallowed the biscuit. "Without Jordan here, *Daed* needs help in the field." She faced her father, silently pleading for approval.

"You can stay and sew today," he said.

"*Nay*. If we can get the dead stumps pulled

out of the field, we can start planting."

Daed cleared his throat. "I told you. I will hire someone to help me."

"Until then, you need help, ain't so?"

After a long pause, *Daed* finally answered. "*Jah*, I suppose so."

Rachel hurried to finish eating. She wouldn't risk loitering at the table with a second cup of coffee. The sooner she harnessed Clyde, the sooner she could prove to her father that they didn't need to hire a field hand.

Rachel took the dirty dishes to the sink and started the dishwater.

"What's the rush?" *Daed* sipped his coffee.

Rachel glanced over her shoulder. "We need an early start, *jah*?"

He waved his hand at her. "*Jah*, but we have enough time for a second cup of *kaffi*." He turned to *Mamm*. "What do you think of that? She's going to have me in the field all day."

Mamm handed him the cookie jar. "Then you'd better have a cookie *nau*."

Rachel finished clearing the table as *Daed* jammed a few of the cookies into his pocket.

"Don't forget they are in your pocket. I don't want my wash water full of cookie crumbs."

Rachel winced. She wished she'd checked Jordan's pockets.

Daed wasn't in a hurry to finish his coffee. Rachel went to the front door, and while slipping into her boots, she overheard *Mamm* say, "Have a talk with her, Micah. A girl her age should not work so much in the field."

Rachel worried *Mamm* would change *Daed's* mind about allowing her to work with him. She needed to get out to the barn before that happened. Rachel slipped out of the house and scurried into the barn.

Nathaniel stepped out from the corner of the barn as the door opened. Rachel nearly stumbled over the cat.

Smokey rubbed against Rachel's legs.

"*Nett nau*, Smokey. I need to get Clyde ready for the field." Smokey weaved between her legs. She squatted down. After a few strokes when Smokey stretched to meet her hand, Rachel scooped him into her arms. She scratched behind his ears and listened to his purr.

"I need to get to work," she told him, lowering him to the floor.

"Don't rush things, child," Nathaniel warned.

Rather than heed the prompting of her subconscious, she brushed the cat hair off the front of her dress while heading to the horse stall.

"Open your ears and you shall hear. Listen, and I shall lead you with sound judgment in all your actions."

Rachel peeked over the gate. "Hello, Clyde."

He lifted his head and perked his ears. The draft horse moved in Rachel's direction and, towering over the girl, nuzzled her head covering. "Clyde, you silly boy!" she said, gently nudging his nose with one hand and using the other to hold her prayer *kapp* in place. She gave his cheekbone a rub before leaving to fetch his harness from the tack area. Once in hand, she slipped inside Clyde's stall with the gear. Humming softly, she fastened the harness on the gentle giant, then led him outside, tying him to the hitching post.

She returned to the barn to get the chains. Jordan and *Daed* had talked about pulling the dead tree stumps out of the ground using chains, so she'd get those and bring them along. She located the rusty chains hanging on heavy-duty hooks near some other equipment. She lifted them off the hooks a strand at a time. As she draped them over her shoulders, she found they were heavier than she imagined they would be. Each chain link was not all that thick. But together they caused her to sag under the weight of them. Once outside, she draped them over Clyde to let him carry them out to the field.

She was ready, and *Daed* still hadn't come outside. She put her hand up to shade her eyes from the bright sun. She watched the house for a few moments, tapping her foot rapidly on the ground.

"Wait for him," Nathaniel whispered. "Wait."

"You don't need to wait," Tangus said, moving back and forth behind Nathaniel, trying to get his words to move around the angelic being. "You're a strong, capable girl. Go ahead. He'll be proud."

"Forget it," she said, patting the horse's muscular neck. "It's just you and me, Clyde. We can get it done. *Daed* will be proud." She untied him from the post, took one more look at the house, then moved toward the fields. Clyde marched alongside, head bobbing with each step, his heavy feet making solid *whumps* against the ground. The chains clanked against each other but stayed where she had put them. She patted his neck again. "*Daed* will be very impressed if we can get one stump pulled before he gets here. Can we do that, boy? Sure we can.

"Here's the first, Clyde. It's not so difficult looking, is it?" With a lot of noise and clumsy movements, she got the chains down from his back. Although they were heavy and difficult to manage, she wrapped them around a dry, gnarly tree root.

Nathaniel stood behind her. "Be careful, child." Tangus just smirked and waited.

"Pull!"

Clyde strained against his harness but didn't seem to be putting in much effort.

165

"Pull, Clyde!" He put a lot more force into his forward motion and his quick spurt of energy caused the chain to jerk, then slide off the wood. "No! Clyde! This is not how we do it."

She fastened the chains once again and hoped she had them more secure this time. She stepped back to check her work, dusting the dirt from her hands. She looked up when she heard *Daed* plodding across the field.

"I wasn't expecting you to start without me," he called. The look on his face was one she'd seen him give James. Her entire being warmed.

"Is this *gut*?" She pointed at the chain and steadied her eyes on her father, waiting for his approval.

He nodded, but the look of pride faded. He put his thumbs behind his suspenders and moved them up and down—a habit she knew meant he had something difficult to say. "I have to have a word with you."

She tugged the chain, pretending to check for tautness. "Maybe we should work first."

Daed laid his hand over hers. "It'd be best *nett* to put off our talk."

When he didn't lift his frown, Rachel drew a deep breath and reluctantly agreed.

"*Kumm* fall, you'll turn twenty-one."

"*Jah*," she agreed cautiously.

"Your sisters had marriage promises before they turned twenty-one. They had their hope chests filled. *Mamm* tells me you haven't made one article for yours yet."

Rachel chewed her bottom lip. Hadn't her parents figured out she was different from her sisters? She knew she wasn't a good cook—which was reinforced when people avoided the dishes she prepared. She didn't sew well. She left important things in pants pockets when she washed them. She would not make anyone a good *fraa*.

"Don't go past your time, daughter."

Did he really think having a hope chest stuffed with housewares would make her marriage material? Did he not see she was a lost cause? If she wasn't asked home from a singing, how could she find a husband? There had been promise until she beat the boys in that buggy race on Morley Bridge Road. And then James . . . Peter would have driven her home if Jordan hadn't interfered. She put her hands on her hips and studied her father stroking his suspenders. "*Mamm* was twenty-six when you married her. Was it because you took pity on her?"

"*Nay!*" He cleared his throat. "God took pity on me." His tone softer, he continued, "I couldn't ask for more. She gave me four *wundebaar* daughters and a *sohn*." He smiled. "I have the greatest blessing. A *gut fraa* and children who love the Lord."

"Then maybe approaching, and probably passing, twenty-one isn't too bad after all."

Clyde whinnied, giving her a perfect opportunity to end the conversation. She stepped toward him. "He's going to get restless just standing here." She gave the horse's rump a hard slap. "*Geh* on!"

Clyde's sudden, powerful, double lunge forward jerked the slack in the chain so hard it snapped. Spooked by the noise and sudden slack in the line, Clyde began to step ahead more quickly. The chain attached to his harness rig whipped back and forth with great force. And before *Daed* could react, it wrapped around his leg and yanked him off his feet.

"Rachel—" His bloodcurdling cry for help cut off as Clyde plowed the field with his body.

"*Daed*!" Rachel ran to catch Clyde. Her heart thudded. The pulsing beats deafened all other sound. "Clyde! Whoa! Whoa!" In a surreal sense that time had slowed, the clods of mud kicked up from Clyde's hooves seemed to float in the air.

Nathaniel instantly changed locations. Appearing in front of the beast, he spread out his wings.

By the time the horse stopped, her father lay moaning quite a ways from where he'd stood. Rachel ran to him and sank to the ground beside him.

Nathaniel chanted orders from the Master in a language only the beast understood. The horse obeyed and stilled.

Rachel covered her mouth and forced the hot liquid seeping up her throat back down. *Daed's* right leg, mangled and twisted in an unnatural direction, still had the chain wrapped around it. Without hesitation she tried to wiggle her fingers between the constricting chain and her father's traumatized leg.

He yelped and she yanked her bloodied hand out from under the chain. "I'm sorry . . . I'm so sorry." Her eyes welled.

"Rachel—"

She tried to search his face, but through her blurred vision, his anguished expression grew more distorted.

He ground out instructions through gritted teeth. "Get . . . the chain . . . off . . . the harness."

She leapt off the ground. Clyde's head jerked up and she froze for a second before easing over to the trembling horse so he wouldn't spook again. "It's okay, Clyde. Good boy. Atta boy." She spoke in the soothing tones she always used around the horses. "It's just me." She wanted to rush but knew that could be a huge mistake. She had to take it steady. Slow. She unbuckled the strap that held the trace, but when she went to unfasten the trace from the collar, her fingers fumbled. Then, as though she had unseen help, the harness dropped to the ground. There was no danger that he would be dragged again.

"I'm going for help."

Chapter Thirteen

Tears streamed faster than Rachel could wipe them away. "Lord, *mei daed* needs you. He's in such horrible pain." She raced up the steps and burst inside the house. "*Mamm!*"

Mamm and Sadie looked up from their sewing projects at the same time. *Mamm* shoved hers to the side, on her feet in a second. "What is it?"

"*Daed*, he's—"

Sadie joined them. "Take a deep breath."

Rachel took half a breath. "He's hurt. Bad." Her lips quivering, Rachel covered her mouth and willed her tears to subside. Unable to communicate with words, she beckoned them to follow.

"Where?" Sadie demanded.

Rachel pushed out the message, "In the field—it's his leg." *Mamm's* eyes brimmed with tears. "He . . . he needs . . . a doctor—right away." Rachel's shoulders shook as sobs erupted.

Mamm gripped Rachel's shoulders. "Which field?"

"East. Near the first stump. If Clyde hasn't moved, he's lying *nett* far from there."

"I'm going to him," *Mamm* said, already hurrying out of the house.

Rachel began to follow, but Sadie grabbed her

arm. "Take *mei* buggy and get Mr. Thon. Ask him to bring his truck."

Rachel preferred Ginger to her sister's horse, Dolly. Ginger was faster, but Dolly was already harnessed and would save time. She unfastened the horse from the post and snapped the reins the moment she sat on the bench.

Tangus inched closer to Rachel on the buggy bench. He enjoyed the hunt, the ensnarement, the prey's panic, but it was nothing compared to the thrill of their surrender when they became so entangled with dismay they didn't recognize they were being devoured. Tangus studied his victim. She blinked, and more tears rolled down her face. "Are you wondering how you can fix things?" he asked.

Silence.

Tangus never liked too much silence. He needed to keep their minds active. Silence could cause them to sink further into depression—which could be a very useful weapon—but sometimes they sensed their doom and called out to God for rescue. He spat.

He leaned eagerly toward her, waiting impatiently for her to spill her emotions so he would know what lies to feed her aching heart. He was the master, more equipped to manipulate the human mind than any other fallen angel in his ranking, and he celebrated his power.

Dolly trotted down the Thons' driveway until Rachel reined her in, set the brake, and jumped out of the buggy. She knocked hard, then closed her eyes. "Please let them be home."

The door opened. Mr. Thon smiled. "Hello, Rachel. What brings—"

"*Mei daed* is hurt. Will you bring your truck?"

"I'll put my boots on and grab the keys."

Rachel blew out a breath. "Thank you. He's in the far east field."

She ran back to the buggy and got Dolly moving. Although she wouldn't be able to keep up with his vehicle, she wanted to get home as quickly as possible. She made a U-turn in the drive as he climbed into his pickup. Waiting for him to pull out, she closed her eyes and whispered, "Lord, forgive me. Please watch over my father."

Tangus growled. "Do you really think God will forgive your carelessness and impatience that brought such great injury and pain on your daed? You were so busy trying to be prideful, and now you want God to help you? You reap the consequences of your own actions."

"God, I don't deserve your grace . . . *Daed* needs you." Her throat tightened. She knew if she hadn't been so full of pride and jealousy, this never would have happened. Her spirit lay deeply sad within her. Why should God want to help her?

She'd have to make it up to her father somehow.

His cries of pain reverberated in her heart, causing a fresh outflow of tears. She replayed the scene over and over, looking at what she could have done differently.

Worse, she could see her father's bloody, mangled leg, angled in an unnatural position. Would he even be able to farm again?

"Your daed needs you more than ever, Rachel." Tangus's accusing tone morphed into sweet and encouraging. "This is the time to show him you can do the work. Step in as a sohn would. You'll have to get up earlier and work longer hours, but that won't be too difficult for a strong girl like you. Just imagine how you'll win his favor."

Rachel blotted her eyes with her dress sleeve. A plan was forming within. Her stomach still sick with dread over her foolish actions that caused her father's injuries, her mind whirled with possibilities. She'd wake before dawn and work until the work was done—even if it took her into the night. Thankfully the daylight hours were increasing, which would give her more time to work. She sat up straighter and gave Dolly a little snap of the reins. "I can do this."

Tangus leaned back and smiled. As long as she continued in her own strength and didn't call on

God's power to work through her, Tangus held her captive.

An eerie sensation crept over Rachel as she drove the buggy down her parents' empty driveway. She looked toward the field, void of activity. Clyde stood in the corral.

Rachel jumped out of the buggy and rushed into the house.

"*Mamm*?"

Sadie poked her head around the kitchen wall. "Mr. Thon drove her to the hospital. They took *Daed* by ambulance."

Rachel's chest tightened. "Will he be okay? What did the medical people say?"

"I don't know. The ambulance crew asked a few questions about his medical history, then they carried him off the field on a long board." Sadie's eyes filled with compassion as she held out her arms, and Rachel walked into her sister's embrace.

"It's my fault." Resting her head on her sister's shoulder, Rachel sobbed, tears dampening Sadie's dress.

"Don't blame yourself. Accidents happen."

Rachel sobbed harder. The accident happened because of her mindless actions and selfish, proud desires.

"Pull yourself together *nau*." Sadie pushed Rachel out to arm's length. "You must stay strong."

Rachel swallowed her sobs for her sister's sake

and wiped her eyes. But she wasn't strong. Even though she pretended to be. Even though she planned to be. She really wasn't strong at all. She swallowed the lump wedged in her throat. "How long do you think *Daed* will be in the hospital?"

"That will be up to the Lord." Sadie peeked inside the oven. "I've started supper. You should tend to the animals and get the milking done before it gets too late."

"*Jah*, I will." After James died, Rachel's sisters took over the responsibilities of the entire household. It gave *Mamm* time to grieve, although she did so silently. Rachel helped in the barn and kept *Daed* company, even though he didn't say much either.

"You are strong. This is what you've wanted. Now you'll be in charge of the barn chores." Tangus hovered close to Rachel's side as she walked, head down, to the barn. With her weakness exposed, it would be easy for Tangus to push her further into guilt or build her pride and self-satisfaction with accomplishing the chores on her own. He could manipulate either emotion to his satisfaction. As long as she didn't call out to God.

Stepping inside the barn, Rachel shivered from the dampness. She fed Clyde, Ginger, and the other stock horses, then the calves. Finally, she checked on the expecting cows. She was especially concerned about Wendy. After Wendy struggled to deliver her first calf and then bore a stillborn, Rachel wanted to watch her progress daily. The cow appeared content, a good indication she wouldn't deliver tonight. She gave the cow a little rub on the end of her moist nose. Wendy just stared into space, chewing.

She stepped outside the barn into twilight. She walked toward the house feeling the weight of her foolishness.

Sadie set a chicken and broccoli casserole on the table in front of her that had some healthy scoops taken out of it. "I would stay and eat with you, but I need to get home before Timothy worries." She picked up two plates filled with food. "Timothy will tell the bishop and spread the word that help is needed."

"*Nay!*" Rachel lowered her voice. "I think we should wait for *Daed* to give those instructions." She wasn't ready for the entire settlement to know the outcome of her poor actions.

Sadie balanced the plates as she headed for the door. "I'll leave the decision making to Timothy. *Daed* doesn't need the burden."

Although Rachel pretended to agree, she silently vowed to finish the morning chores and be in the field before daylight.

After learning that her father needed surgery and that her mother would stay a few days at the hospital, Rachel spent a fitful night with her stomach tied in knots. Although mentally drained by morning, she determined to complete the chores as needed. She dressed, snatched an apple from the wicker basket on the table, and headed to the barn. She hurried through the morning chores and even had Clyde harnessed and hitched to the post all before the rooster's sunrise call.

She left Clyde long enough to get the chains. When she didn't find them hanging in their usual spot, she walked the length of the barn with a lantern and searched every wall stud. Not finding them in the barn, she hoped they were still in the field. Perhaps whoever tended to Clyde yesterday hadn't thought to bring the equipment in.

"You and I have a long day," she told Clyde as she led him out to the field.

Leaving Clyde at the stump, she paced the steps in the direction her *daed* was pulled. The pink sky lit the area enough to find the chains. Wet with dew, they slipped out of her hand. Rachel growled in frustration. "This is crazy. The chains will slip off the wood too."

"You must try," Tangus encouraged from a distance. He could see the animal sensed his presence, but this wasn't the time for Tangus to stir him. He wanted Rachel to succeed. Let her empowerment be driven by pride. Tangus snickered; pride led them all to a quick fall.

Rachel wrapped the chain around the stump, then attached it to Clyde's trace. She gripped his lead and called out, "Pull."

When Clyde pulled, the chain slid off the stump.

Rachel backed him up and reconnected the chain. The second attempt failed, and so did the third. She would need to come up with a different plan. From the corner of her eye, she caught sight of Timothy trekking over the furrows toward her.

"What are you doing? Do you want to get hurt too?" Timothy took the chain from her hand and dropped it on the ground.

"I have to do something." Her voice cracked.

"This is dangerous." He crossed his arms. "Are you going to tell me what's going on?"

She lowered her head. Staring at the black soil was easier than meeting his brotherly eyes.

"Rachel," he said, lifting her chin. His deep brown eyes bored into hers. "You're *nett* thinking wisely. This is *nett* a job for you."

"The field can't be cleared by itself. I have to do something."

"The chain's wet. The wood's wet. Another accident is going to happen, and Sadie would have *mei* hide if anything happened to you." He smiled. "I don't want to mess with a pregnant woman. Especially the one living in my *haus*."

Rachel cracked a smile.

Timothy bent down and grabbed the chain. He draped it over Clyde's back, then took hold of his lead. "Let's take him back to the barn."

Rachel, left with no option, followed along. She squinted at the rising sun. Not a cloud in the sky. Maybe the stump would dry by the afternoon. Her mind reeled with other ways to secure the chain. Perhaps if she wrapped a piece of old cheesecloth around it . . .

They reached the edge of the field when he asked, "What happened to Jordan? Sadie said he left."

"*Jah*, he did." She motioned to the barn. "I'll go open the gate." She sprinted ahead. Maybe Timothy wouldn't ask anything more about Jordan.

Timothy stopped Clyde at the fence and unharnessed him. After releasing the horse to graze in the pasture, Timothy picked up the equipment. "You need full-time help. More than what I can do since I've accepted the extra work to pay for the room addition."

"I can do it," she said.

Timothy shook his head. "*Nett* alone. I'll ask Jordan to *kumm* back. I'm sure once he finds out about Micah—"

"Let me," she said. "I'll ask him."

When forced to eat humble pie, she found it easier to feed herself.

As Jordan tossed a bale of hay off the back end of the pickup truck, then reached for the next one,

179

a buggy flashed in his peripheral vision. He recognized Ginger immediately. He finished hoisting up the forty-pound bale and tossed it off the truck with the others.

He pulled a bandanna from his back pocket and wiped his forehead. Rachel climbed out of the buggy. She stood for a moment and scanned the area before she headed for the barn. He grabbed another bale, trying not to react to her presence.

"Jordan?" She entered the barn and stopped beside the pickup.

"*Jah.*" He continued working, only at a faster rate. The moment she'd spoken, his heart skittered. He didn't dare look her in the eyes.

"I don't know how to ask you . . ."

"Spit it out, Rachel. I'm a little busy." He wrapped his gloved hands around the twine of another bale and lifted it waist high.

"I'm sorry to interrupt—" Her voice quivered and she spun around.

"Hey. Wait." He dropped the hay and jumped off the side of the truck. "Why did you come?"

She kept her back to him. "It's *nett* important. I can—"

Jordan reached for her arm. "*Jah,* it is." The mulish woman wouldn't have come if it wasn't important. He moved in front of her. The despondence in her eyes convinced him something was terribly wrong.

"Jordan?" Kayla entered the barn and stopped.

Her focus shifted from his hand on Rachel's arm to Rachel and then to him. "I wanted to know if we're still going riding."

He dropped his hand. "I'm not finished unloading the hay, Kayla."

"I need to go," Rachel said flatly and walked away.

Jordan followed. "Rachel, please tell me why you're here." He trailed her back to the buggy and held out his arm to block her from climbing inside.

She closed her eyes. After a long pause, she said, "I thought I could beg you to *kumm* back and help in the fields, but—"

"You're filled with pride." His breath caught when he looked into her teary glare. This was deeper than a pride issue. "I'm sorry," he said.

Kayla came over and shaded her eyes with her hand. "Well? Are you coming or not?"

"Give me a minute, please, Kayla. Let me finish my conversation in private."

Kayla threw Rachel a curious glance. "I'll get Pepper ready," she called as she walked inside the barn.

"Okay," Jordan said to Rachel, infusing as much kindness into his voice as he could. "Tell me why you came."

Rachel stared at her dress as she ran her hand over the creases. "*Mei daed* was injured in the field."

"How? How bad? Will he be okay?"

She squeezed her eyes closed, covered her mouth, and shrugged.

"Don't cry." He cocked his head to get a view of her face. "You can tell me later." He steadied her trembling shoulders. "Of course I'll help. I have one more truckload after this one to unload, but I won't be long."

She dropped her hand but kept her head down. "*Denki.*"

Jordan waited until she and Ginger were on the road before trekking back to the barn. If he hurried, he could be there before the evening milking.

Jordan climbed onto the bed of the truck.

"What's going on in Amish land?" Kayla leaned against the side of the truck.

"Micah Hartzler was injured," he said, moving to hoist the bales of hay more quickly.

"What does she expect you to do? She does know you have another job, doesn't she?"

Jordan continued dropping hay bales off the truck. They landed with a soft thump and a poof of hay dust. He'd still have to stack the bales before he left. He hoped by ignoring her, she would take the hint and leave so he could finish the job. But she continued to lean against the side of the truck, only now she rested her chin on her crossed arms and watched him work.

She stood there until he tossed the last bale off

and jumped from the pickup bed. Needing to stack the bales against the wall, he grasped the binder twine at the same time Kayla gripped his arm. He released the bale and moved his arm away from her. "I'm in a hurry."

Her bottom lip puckered. "You don't have to go, do you?" She moved in front of him, placed her hands on his shoulders, then stepped closer. "I was hoping you still wanted to go riding with me." She tilted her head, parting her lips inches from his face.

He pulled back. "Not today. The Hartzlers need help."

"And they'll get it." She rolled her eyes. "That's what the Amish do. They congregate when there's a crisis."

He skirted around her to the mound of hay. "Let me work so I can finish this before I leave."

"I thought you weren't Amish!"

He looked over his shoulder and caught sight of her scowl. "Maybe I have more Amish in me than I thought."

"My father wants to offer you a permanent position." She shifted her weight to her other hip. "Are you staying or not?"

Chapter Fourteen

Jordan entered the Hartzlers' barn and followed the lamplight to the new calf pen. He sneezed as he came up to the railing of a stall where a large cow shifted about.

Rachel spun around, her hand clutching her chest. "I didn't hear you *kumm* in."

"Sorry, I didn't mean to startle you. I stopped at the house, but no one answered the door."

Her shoulders relaxed. "*Daed's* still in the hospital." She ran her hand over the cow's back and spoke softly. "*Mamm* won't be home until after his surgery."

"Surgery?" He figured her father's injury was serious enough considering how desperate she was to hunt him down, but something as serious as surgery had never crossed his mind. Jordan sneezed again and looked around the immediate area. *Where is that cat?* He scanned the rafters with no success. Jordan eased into the stall. "Why are you in here? Is something wrong with the cow?"

"Wendy's pregnant."

"Yes, I know. So don't you think you should leave her alone?" The cow bellowed and Jordan backed into the gate. His eyes were trained on the cow as she moved to the other side of the pen. "They can be unpredictable."

Wendy craned her neck in his direction and mooed. He opened the gate. "Let's go. The cow's restless."

Rachel shot Jordan an aggravated look. "If she's annoyed, it's because you keep talking."

He couldn't leave Rachel in there. The gate hinges creaked as he reentered. Wendy kicked at him but missed. He lunged toward Rachel and grabbed her arm. "Come with me."

Once he had her outside the stall, Jordan cornered her against the wall. "Don't you know to leave a pregnant cow alone?"

She hunched over to duck under his arm, but he shifted and stopped her.

He tilted his head to look into her eyes. "Are we going to argue or get along?"

She just looked at him.

"You asked me to come back. Tell me if that's what you still want." He waited patiently, staring into her stubborn eyes. When she didn't reply, he dropped his arms and went to the door. "I'll ask Timothy and *Onkel* Isaac to round up some men."

"*Nay*, wait." She took a step forward and grasped his arm.

Her touch caused a spasm to travel over his muscles to the tips of his fingers. His chest swelled. For sure if she moved any closer, she would discover the effect she had over him.

"I want you to stay. But . . ."

Jordan's smiled faded. "But . . . ?"

She moved back to the birthing pen. "Wendy had problems with her last pregnancy. The calf was stillborn." She looked him hard in the eye. "I want to help. This was *mei bruder's* cow."

"And you know what to do?" He certainly didn't. Another reason to ask his *onkel* for help.

"Maybe. I felt the calf kick so I know it's alive right now."

Jordan grinned. "I almost felt the mom's kick. She missed me by a few inches."

Rachel held back a laugh.

"You think that's funny?" he teased.

Her expression sobered. "I would've felt awful."

The lamplight's glow softened her skin tone and rendered him speechless. He noticed the light flickering in her eyes. Why hadn't one of the unmarried men spoken for her?

"*Denki* for *kumming* back." She drew a deep breath. "I'm sorry I treated you so badly that you left."

He swallowed. He wasn't sure he could keep a safe distance from her with this sudden transformation. It'd be easier if he stirred up some friction between them. But with Micah injured, he couldn't possibly provoke her intentionally. He tended to do enough of that unintentionally.

"I had other reasons for leaving."

"*Ach*," she whispered. "Kayla?"

He didn't want to answer. He didn't want to talk about Kayla. Especially with Rachel. He yanked the barn door open, then placed his hand on her back between her shoulder blades to direct her outside. "What's for supper?"

"I made chili and cornbread earlier. It just needs warming."

"Oh, so you can cook more than just eggs?"

She elbowed him. "Of course I can."

"Wait." He stopped abruptly. "There's something I want to show you before it gets dark." He beckoned her to follow.

Curiosity lit her face. "What is it?"

He directed her to the corner of the *grossdaadi haus*. "Look." He pointed to the nest on the windowsill. "They hatched. I saw them when I dropped off my stuff."

Cautiously she moved forward, climbed the steps of the stoop, and leaned toward the window. Turning back to him, she smiled. "Three. They all made it."

He came up beside her. "We shouldn't bother them. The mama bird must be hunting worms close by."

"They don't look like robins. Instead of being red, they're spotted."

"I think the red coloring comes later."

He stepped off the porch and Rachel followed, still sporting a wide smile. A shudder spread along his nerves.

"I, um . . . I should . . ." He pointed to the pile of firewood when he couldn't stop stammering. "Firewood."

Her smile widened. "*Jah?*"

He grinned. How did he buckle so easily under a simple smile? The setting sun didn't help. The golden glow highlighted her freckles.

"I'll bring some wood and meet you in the house." He hoped to regain some of the strength that her smile had drained from him.

"Okay." She walked away, and glancing back, she said, "Supper will be ready in a few minutes."

Something had sparked between him and Rachel. He faced the woodpile trying to focus on something else. Kindling. There wasn't much cut that was small enough to fit inside the cookstove. Taking the ax in his clammy hands, he barely held a grip on it as he began to split the wood, chopping more than was needed. A good bit more.

After loading his arms, he headed to the house. As though an unseen presence met him as he stepped through the door, his soul filled with warmth.

"Jordan, you're experiencing a portion of God's peace. There is rest in His arms," Nathaniel reassured in a whisper.

A sulfuric vapor crept inside from under the threshold, and Tangus materialized from the floor planks. His laugh expelled a putrid vitriolic stench.

Eight sets of rhombic-cut eyes roamed the room, recording any infractions. Later, in the midnight hour, he would broadcast the accusing images over Jordan's subconscious. Creating a mind-set to cultivate self-condemnation was a powerful tool. If Jordan crumbled and Rachel continued to move toward her selfishness and pride, he would own both their souls.

Tangus attached himself like a bush brier onto Jordan. He cupped his hands around Jordan's ear. "You don't want to stay here. There are so many new things to experience, places to go. You've gone without all your life; follow me and I'll equip you to soar. Go back to Kayla—her companionship will keep you warm and happy."

Nathaniel hummed, blocking the piercing frequency and interrupting the fallen angel's hypnotic flow, but he couldn't force Tangus to retreat. Only his charge could make such demands, and only in the name of Jesus were strongholds loosened and souls set free.

Jordan set the larger pieces of wood in the firebox next to the stove in the sitting room. Noticing the filled ash tin, he walked it outside and emptied it in the garden. His mother always insisted the ashes helped lessen the acidity of her tomatoes.

He glanced at the staked-out section of Rachel's garden and recalled the long hours he spent with his mother. Most of their meals came out of the garden they planted. Some nights supper wasn't much more than fried tomatoes or cucumber sandwiches. His mother used to say that people paid a lot of money in fancy restaurants for cucumber sandwiches and fried green tomatoes. But those fancy restaurants didn't pay his mother much for the produce she sold them. At one time, his mouth watered for a juicy hamburger. Now he would give anything for another one of his mom's sandwiches.

Jordan glanced over the rows in Rachel's garden. It looked as though she'd planted plenty of cucumbers if the seed packages on the stakes were any indication.

He tapped the bottom of the ash pan before bringing it back into the house. Since most nights in May were historically cool, he made a fire to keep out the chill. Then he gathered the smaller pieces of wood and brought them into the kitchen.

Rachel stood in front of the stove, trying to stir and dodge splattering chili at the same time.

"How's it coming?"

"Oh. It's fine."

She obviously didn't know what the term *simmer* meant. Sauce had splattered on the counter, even the wall. He tossed the kindling into the metal tin box next to the stove and swept the loose oak bark off his shirtsleeves.

"Here, let me help," he said, taking a pot holder

from the counter. He lifted the pot and placed it on a wire cooling rack, then stirred the chili as it finished sputtering.

Rachel pulled a clean spoon from the drawer. "Want a taste?" She dipped it into the chili, held her other hand under the spoon to catch the drippings, and offered it to him.

Sampling the spoonful, his eyes watered. He fanned his mouth.

"Spicy?"

He shook his head while grabbing a cup from the cupboard. Turning on the tap, he filled the cup with water, then gulped it. His throat cooled.

"It's still too hot to eat. Let's give it a minute or two," he said hoarsely.

Rachel picked up the pot holder. "I warmed the cornbread too." She opened the oven and pulled out the loaf pan. Her anticipatory smile turned to disappointment.

Jordan craned to see the contents. "It looks good."

"It burned."

"That part can be cut off." He turned to the counter. *Salt. Pepper.* "Where's your sugar?"

Rachel opened the pantry door. With her brows slightly askew, she handed him the container.

"Do you mind?" He held it over the chili. "Sugar will offset the acidic tomatoes."

"I don't think you can hurt it."

He added the sugar, studied the pot, then

sprinkled another layer of sugar. As he stirred the mixture, Rachel came up beside him with a spoon.

She dipped out a sample and took a bite. "Not bad."

The tip of her tongue darted out from her mouth to clean the residue off her lips.

Without thinking, he placed his hand on her cheek and slowly traced the crease of her mouth with his thumb. "You missed . . ." Suddenly aware of their closeness, Jordan blinked, forcing himself to pull away.

"I like it." Her great big eyes looked up at him. "The sugar was a *gut* addition."

He spun to face the stove. "What do you think? Has it cooled enough? I think so. Let's eat. Do you have bowls?" Of course she had bowls. His heart clamored inside his chest.

"I'll get them," she said.

She bumped into him and he nearly tripped trying to get out of her way. "I'll just—" Jordan pulled out a chair at the table and sat.

Rachel set the dishes and silverware on the table. After placing the pot of chili on a pot holder and a few slices of white bread on a plate, she sat with him.

He lowered his head.

"Jordan." Her voice soft.

He glanced up. "Yes?"

"Will you say a prayer for *mei daed* too?"

"Of course." The depth of her blue eyes bored

into his soul and he couldn't turn away. Nor did she. And then he realized what she was asking. "Oh. Do you want us to pray together?"

She nodded and bowed her head.

He cleared his throat. "God, we give you thanks for the food, and we ask that you be with Micah in the hospital. Amen."

Nathaniel extended his wings, lifting the sweet aroma of Jordan's prayer. "Your supplication has gone before the Master's throne."

Tangus recoiled as Nathaniel's manifested glory intensified. Tangus hated retreating almost as much as he hated when people prayed together. A force not easily broken. He would wait. Other opportunities would arise—they almost always did.

Rachel smiled. "*Denki.*"

"You're welcome." He picked up his spoon, thinking that he hadn't prayed aloud for a meal since long before his mother passed away.

He took a bite and smiled. "It's good. I've never had chili with potatoes in it."

"They were getting ready to go bad."

"Once a week, my mom would clean out the refrigerator and make a meal using all the leftovers." He stopped, surprised. He'd never shared stories about his mother before, yet with Rachel it came so easy.

"I'm sure she created some interesting meals that way." She blew over her chili.

"Interesting, yes. But not always good." Snapshots of unusual meal concoctions flipped through his memory. In a strange way, they were good memories.

"*Ach*, I'm sure she was a good cook."

"Aren't all Amish women?"

Rachel's smile dropped.

He hadn't meant his statement to be insulting. He scrambled to find something to fill the uncomfortable silence he'd created. "Have you ever tried the combination of vegetable soup and tuna casserole?"

"Together? *Nay*." Her nose scrunched.

"See! Your cooking isn't bad." He waved his loaded spoon as he spoke.

She retrieved the cornbread still on the counter. "How large of a slice do you want?"

"Large." He winked.

"You're . . . *befuddled*."

"And that means . . ."

"It's how we say you're mixed up." She twirled her finger in circles. "In the head."

"I suppose when I added tuna to soup, I was for sure."

"*Ach*, so that concoction was *your* creation?"

Jordan scraped the bowl, getting the last spoonful. "My cooking improved."

"Anything would be an improvement over tuna

soup—even my chili." She stood and reached for his empty bowl. "Do you want more?"

"No, thank you. I'm full."

Rachel gathered the dirty dishes from the counter and placed them in the sink.

Jordan brought the other dishes over to her. "What should I do? Wash or dry?"

"Neither." She took the ever-present kettle from the stove and poured warm water from it into the sink. "I'll *redd-up*."

"Then what will I do while you work?" He slipped his arm around her and skimmed some suds from the water's surface. When she turned to look at him in surprise, he dabbed her nose with the bubbles.

With a whoop that could only mean she declared war, she scooped a handful and reached for him. He was too quick, stepping aside as she attempted to slather him with the frothy soapsuds.

"You missed." He laughed and darted out of her reach again. "Nice try, but you—" A sound in the hallway distracted him for the split second it took for her to take advantage of the moment and lather his face.

Timothy and Sadie appeared in the kitchen entry. Timothy looked from one to the other, amusement in his eyes. "I see Rachel convinced you to *kumm* back."

"*Jah*," Jordan said, surprising himself that he'd used the Amish term instead of *Englisch*. The word had popped out so easily, as though it had always been part of his vocabulary. He snagged a towel and wiped his face. His eyes burned and he needed to spit out the soap she'd gotten in his mouth.

Sadie put a hand underneath her swelling belly as though to give it support. "We wanted to check on you and see if you needed anything."

"We have all we need." Rachel plunged her hands into the soapy water and began to wash the dishes.

Timothy put his arm around Sadie's shoulders. "We can visit another time."

Sadie hesitated but allowed Timothy to guide her to the door. "Talk with you later," Sadie called out just before the door closed behind them.

Jordan leaned against a cabinet, closed his eyes, and squeezed the bridge of his nose between his index finger and thumb.

Rachel blew out a breath. "*Ach, doplich*, ain't so?"

Doplich? Jordan cocked his head.

"Awkward."

"I bet that's what they're saying too." Jordan stepped up to the sink. "You need help?"

She paused a moment, then dunked the soapy bowl into the rinse water. "Okay."

Between the two of them, it didn't take long to finish. Jordan didn't know what kind of conversation to have with this beauty so close to him, so he said nothing and just drank in the fresh scent of her as they moved in a sort of dance—scrape, wash, rinse, dry.

"I'm done," Rachel said as she pulled the plug, then folded the washrag and set it next to the faucet.

Jordan gave the last dish a polishing swipe and dropped the towel onto the counter. "Me too."

"Would you like to sit on the porch?" She ran her hand over her dress, pretending to straighten it. "You don't have to. I just thought—"

"Okay." Jordan grasped the lantern by its handle from the counter and gestured toward the door. Rachel preceded him and stepped outside. She smoothed her dress beneath her and sat on the top step. She tilted her head back. "There aren't any stars tonight."

"They're there, just hidden by the clouds." Jordan sat on the step below hers and leaned against the opposite rail. "It might rain."

"It would be nice if it held off until after the fields were planted."

"It would."

Several minutes of silence passed between them. Jordan had so much to say, yet so much he shouldn't say. He wanted to just reach over and touch her slender fingers that were splayed on the step.

Rachel continued to look skyward, as though searching for more than just stars. "Do you ever wonder . . ." Her voice trailed off, sounding sad and in need of something he didn't know if he could give.

"Wonder what?" he said as softly as he could, hoping that would encourage her to continue.

She left her star search and searched his face instead. "Can I ask you a question?"

"Sure."

"Do you still have Kayla's phone?"

That was by far the last question he expected. Rachel fussed with her dress folds as though the answer wouldn't matter.

"No. I only used it to look up information about truck-driving school. Why?"

"I thought if you still had it you could call the hospital and check on *mei daed*."

Even with the limited light of the lantern, he could see her eyes glazed with tears. "I know you're worried about him." His mind fumbled quickly for some sort of comfort. "You prayed for him, right?"

"*Jah*," she whispered.

"Then of course he's going to be all right." Jordan stood to go. He didn't want her to see his doubt. After all, prayers hadn't helped his mother.

Chapter Fifteen

After Jordan took care of the animals, the morning downpour kept him from working in the field. He'd hoped the weather would clear by noon, but still the rain came. He trotted across the yard to the house, holding a slicker over his head to keep some of the rain off.

As he stepped inside the kitchen, he craned his neck toward the stove but couldn't see what was inside the pot. "Something smells good. Do you want help?"

Rachel smiled. "You can pour some milk."

He opened the cabinet and removed two glasses.

Rachel took the silverware from the drawer and placed it on the table next to the plates. "Did you check on Wendy?"

Jordan stopped pouring the milk. Since when did cows need a midwife? "She's still pregnant." At least he hadn't seen a calf in the pen.

He set the drinks on the table, then pulled out a chair and sat. He couldn't tear himself away from staring at the strands of straw-colored hair that peeked out from under her *kapp*. He needed to focus on something other than her. "Did your *daed* make this table?"

"*Mei bruder*, James, did." She placed the

covered dish in the center of the table and lifted the lid. Her lips twisted into a contorted expression.

Jordan moved to see what was in the dish. Steaming, milky, chunks-of-something filled the bowl. He relaxed back into his chair.

"It looks interesting."

That wasn't a lie. Trying to guess what floated on the creamy surface and whether it was edible held his interest. A little.

Rachel sat in the chair opposite him and bowed her head.

After spending a moment silently watching her, he bowed his head and said his quiet grace. Once he opened his eyes, she handed him the serving utensil.

"Your brother was a fine craftsman." He dipped the scooper into the dish and unloaded the ladle onto his plate. Although he shoveled himself another portion, her eyes still looked sad.

"What do you call this?"

"You haven't eaten *hinkel* dumplings before?" She took the ladle from him and filled her plate.

"None that looked like this," he mumbled. Jordan reached for the fork, then thought better of it and chose a spoon instead.

He sampled the floating chunks. The tightly packed ball of flour lodged in his throat. His eyes watered and he forced a hard cough and pounded on his chest to get his breath back. He chugged half the glass of milk. "Is this the first time you've made it?" he asked, his voice hoarse. He twirled another gummy flour ball with his spoon in the cream base.

"*Jah.*"

"Thought so."

The rich blue of her eyes and her hopeful look amused him.

"You probably shouldn't bring this to a get-together. Not if you want to find . . ." The words caught in the back of his throat.

"Finish your sentence." She pinned her eyes on his.

"Don't you want to find a husband?" He looked down at what she called dumplings. "An Amish man wants a good cook and someone to sew his clothes." He held his tongue before adding what Timothy had told him about her competitiveness. He'd already said too much.

"You forgot to add, have his children."

He shoveled the food into his mouth so fast he thought he might choke.

She blew out a breath. "You should concentrate on learning how to farm."

"I don't want to be a farmer." He stood and picked up his empty dish. "And I'm not Amish," he said under his breath as he walked to the sink. He pointed to the dishes. "Do you want help?"

Her daggered eyes glared. "*Nau* you think I can't clean up? Amish women can wash dishes —before they become a *fraa*."

He hadn't meant to stir her up to that extent. But he couldn't resist one last poke. "I forgot. You can add watching the cream separate to the *fraa's* list of duties. Can you do that?"

"*Ach!*"

"I was teasing you."

She lifted her head and ignored him.

He headed outside. Spending too much time inside with her was dangerous. He shouldn't have mentioned what Amish men wanted in a wife. The moment he did, the idea of Rachel married bothered him. He'd already spent a great deal of time thinking about her, despite promising himself not to get involved. He wasn't ready to join the church, and certainly not for the wrong reason, like falling in love.

Something was missing in the Amish way of life. Their unmovable faith seemed anything but simple. He appreciated his *onkel* taking him into his home after his mother died. He obeyed the house rules, attended church meetings, and respected his *onkel's* request not to bring discord into the community. Yet he had no desire to speak with the bishop about becoming Amish.

Jordan's gut twisted from the expanding clumps, which had gummed up in his stomach like a heavy wad and felt like he had eaten horseshoes. He would need a long walk just to keep the mass of flour from cementing.

• • •

Rachel scrubbed the caked flour off the bottom of the dumpling pan. Jordan's comment kept replaying in her mind. She'd accepted not being a good cook and never had much of a reason to learn to sew, but when Jordan pointed out those facts, it hurt. She hadn't realized how much she wanted to please him when she prepared the *hinkle* dumplings.

She rinsed the pan and set it aside. "Lord, I stopped praying about finding a husband when it became clear no one would ask to court me. I thought I accepted your will. I don't want to have feelings for Jordan." Jordan's wide grin flashed in her mind. She squeezed her eyes tighter. "Have mercy on me. I can't keep him out of my thoughts."

"Rachel?" Jordan stuck his head inside the kitchen door.

She winced. Had he heard her prayer?

"Why don't I drive you to town so you can visit your father? The ground is too wet to work in the field. Come on. I have the buggy ready."

"*Denki.* That would be very kind." She looked at her clothes, then touched her prayer *kapp* and pushed the stray strands of hair back in place.

"You look nice," he said. "I'll wait for you in the buggy."

She wasn't sure what to make of his gesture of kindness. And it didn't make sense that he would point out her lack of skills to be a *gut fraa* and then tell her she looked nice. Rachel extinguished the oil lamp. *Ach*, it shouldn't matter what he thought. She was grateful for the ride to town. She snatched her shawl from her bedroom and wrapped it around her shoulders as she stepped outside.

He stood next to the buggy until she stepped inside and sat on the bench. He had put out a hand to help, but she had not accepted it. She could get into a buggy by herself.

Jordan seated himself inside the buggy without a word. He gathered the reins, then snapped them, the horse instantly obeying the command.

Rachel gave her attention to the wild bull thistle growing along the roadside. The purple thistle contrasted nicely against the green weeds in the ditch. She liked the colors of spring but actually enjoyed the different shades of green the leaves turned even more.

Jordan cleared his throat. "I'm sorry about what I said earlier."

"About what?" She assumed he meant the comment he made about her dumplings, but watching him squirm gave her a little satisfaction.

"I didn't mean for it to sound like you aren't marriage worthy. You are . . . I'm sure you'll make a good wife . . . for an Amish man."

Why she wasn't married wasn't a topic she wished to discuss with him. "You said you were looking into truck-driving school. Is that what you want to do, drive a truck?"

"As a truck driver you get paid to travel."

"Where do you want to go?"

"Everywhere. It's hard to imagine the vastness of the ocean, the mountains, or the Grand Canyon. I want to see it all. Deserts and plains. Even the massive cities. From what I've read, and the pictures I've seen, I'd really like to experience San Francisco, Seattle, Boston—"

"I've never been out of Hope Falls." She was unable to imagine ever wanting to leave where she lived.

"It doesn't take long to get a Class A license, and most companies will reimburse your schooling," he said with excitement in his voice.

"You found that out using Kayla's phone?"

He navigated a turn before answering. "She has the Internet on it."

Kayla's worldliness had certainly impressed him. "What does she think about you becoming a truck driver?" Rachel's stomach rolled. Did she really want to know what Kayla thought?

Jordan stood at the doorway of Micah's hospital room, paralyzed by memories of his mother's last days. Antiseptic penetrated the air, constricting his lungs. He leaned against the door frame, knees wobbling beneath his weight. He should've stayed outside with the horse. His reaction to seeing Micah like this was unexpected and unsettling.

"It's *gut* to see you, Jordan." Micah winced and both Miriam and Rachel moved closer to the bedside.

Miriam gestured to the IV tubing. "Push your pain button."

"I'm okay." But his deep-furrowed brow indi-cated otherwise. "*Denki* for *kumming* back to work." His neck muscles tensed as he blew out a slow breath.

"Of course."

Rachel's powdery-white complexion masked her normal radiance. Tears brimmed as she stared vacantly at her father's leg suspended above the bed by some form of mechanical traction.

"I want to speak with Jordan alone," Micah said.

Miriam reached for Rachel's hand. "We'll take a walk. Maybe go to the cafeteria for a cup of fancy *kaffi*."

Jordan wiped his sweaty hands on his pants. He waited for Rachel and Miriam to leave the room before he eased closer to the bedside.

"Is something—" Jordan swallowed, his throat dry. Of course something was wrong. Micah wanted to speak with him alone.

Micah frowned. "I'm sorry. I'm sure being in a hospital brings back painful memories of your *mamm*."

"Yes, sir."

"I wish Rachel hadn't asked you to bring her." Micah winced again.

"She didn't. I offered. Are you in pain?" Jordan took a few steps toward the door. "I can get the nurse for you."

"I'll be fine."

Jordan took the seat by his bedside. "Rachel didn't ask me to bring her. The field's too wet to work and we were both concerned about you."

Micah forced a smile he couldn't hold.

"Are you sure you don't want me to call a nurse?" The same useless feeling washed over Jordan. He couldn't do anything for his mother either.

Micah closed his eyes and finally pushed the button to deliver a dose of pain medication. "Will you do something for me?"

"Anything."

"Have patience with Rachel. She's going to balk at brotherly advice, but try to work in unity."

"We've been getting along."

"*Gut.* I worry about her. She's unlike *mei* other daughters."

Rachel was unlike any woman Jordan had ever known. In some ways, he worried about her too, more so than he should.

Within a few minutes, the pain medicine took effect and Micah closed his eyes. Jordan sat with him quietly until Rachel and Miriam returned, their faces shifting into expressions of deeper concern.

"The pain medicine knocked him out," Jordan said, standing and offering Miriam the chair. Her eyes were shadowed with exhaustion as she gratefully accepted it.

"I'll wait in the hall." Jordan stepped out of the room. He didn't want to rush Rachel if she wanted to stay longer, but the smell of disinfectant nauseated him.

A few minutes later, Rachel came out of the room sniffling.

"Are you okay?"

"I guess." She wiped her face with a wad of tissue. She didn't look okay.

They walked down the hall, the silence broken only by Rachel's sniffling. Jordan wanted to comfort her during the short elevator ride to the lobby but kept his hands at his sides in the elevator as well as to the end of the parking lot where Jordan had tied Ginger to a lamppost. As he untied the horse, Rachel climbed inside the buggy.

"Micah's going to be okay," Jordan said, climbing in beside her.

Her eyes filled with tears. "It's hard seeing him in pain."

"I know." He released the brake, clicked his tongue, and snapped the reins.

"Was your mother in the hospital a lot before she died?"

"Yes." He maneuvered Ginger onto the shoulder of the road. Thankfully, Rachel didn't ask more questions. She sat with her hands folded on her lap and looked away from him. His heart felt linked with hers. He knew the pain of seeing a parent in the hospital with nothing you could do to help. He was grateful, however, that her father would be coming home.

A few blocks later, Jordan turned the horse into the parking lot of the IGA grocery store, pulled up to the entrance, handed Rachel the reins, and jumped out. "I'll be back in a minute. I just want to grab a few items."

Rachel expected Jordan to pull a pie out of the grocery bag he'd set on the counter inside her kitchen, but he brought out an eggplant. She crinkled her nose as he unloaded the remaining items: chicken, cheese, tomato sauce, and bread-crumbs.

He turned on the tap water and rinsed the eggplant. "Want to help?"

"Sure."

"You can slice this." He handed her the wet eggplant. "I'll get the chicken ready."

Rachel took a knife from the drawer, and while she cut the eggplant, she kept him in sight. He moved around the kitchen with ease. First he washed the chicken breasts, then dipped them in eggs and coated them in crumb mix.

"Once you've cut the eggplant, layer it in the bottom of a cake pan."

"Okay." Having him instruct her in cooking tasks felt awkward. Naomi would tease her for certain. As awkward as it was, she liked it.

After frying the chicken in a greased skillet, he placed the pieces on top of the eggplant, poured the tomato sauce over the ingredients, and placed the pan in the oven.

"While this bakes, we have time to feed the animals." He headed to the door as though on a mission.

She trailed him out to the barn. "What do you call that dish?"

"Chicken and eggplant parmesan." He held the barn door open for her. "Ever have it?"

"*Nay.*"

He gathered the water buckets and headed outside while she filled the feed buckets with grain.

"What about milking?" she asked after they had fed all the animals.

"Let's eat first."

Stepping inside the house, the thick scent of oregano caused Rachel's mouth to water. She tried peeking around his shoulder as he sprinkled cheese on top of the chicken, but he blocked her view. "Go sit," he said, slipping the pan back into the oven.

She opened the cupboard and reached for the plates, but Jordan took her hand and led her to her chair. "Sit. I have everything under control." It amazed her to watch him. He moved about the kitchen with a sense of belonging and comfort. It was nice that she felt she could learn from him, and he wasn't mocking her less-than-admirable cooking ability.

A few minutes later, he placed two plates of food on the table and took his seat across from her. After prayer, he watched as she took the first bite, holding his breath until she finished chewing.

"It's delicious." She took another bite.

"I'm glad you like it."

She waved her empty fork. "Don't fill your head with *hohchmoot.*"

He tilted his head. "Hot air?"

"Pride."

He cut a bite for himself. "I'm glad you like it that much."

"I suppose you'll remind me of that too."

"For certain." He winked.

Rachel's face heated. She expected him to call her Red, but he lowered his head and focused on eating.

Their conversation moved from topic to topic as they ate the delicious meal. They mostly told funny stories of things they did when they were small children. When they had eaten all they could, Rachel stood to collect the dirty dishes.

A moment later the back door opened and Sadie and Timothy came in.

"*Ach*, Rachel, something smells *gut.*" Sadie looked at the pan. "What did you make?"

211

"It's chicken and eggplant parmesan. Jordan made it."

Sadie's brows raised and she glanced at Timothy.

"Don't get any fancy ideas," Timothy said. "Anything I cooked wouldn't be edible." He turned to Jordan. "You need a hand with milking?"

"Sure."

Once Jordan and Timothy were outside, Sadie spoke to Rachel. "You two seem to be getting along *gut*."

"*Jah*, I suppose so." Rachel picked up the kettle. "Want a cup of *kaffi*?"

"*Nay*, I have to give up caffeine." Sadie sat and propped her legs up on the chair beside her. "*Mei* legs are swollen and *mei* heart is racing."

"Is that normal?"

"I suppose. The midwife wants me to watch my weight. She says every pregnancy is different."

Rachel emptied the hot water from the kettle into the sink.

"Do you want help?" Sadie lowered her legs from the chair.

"*Nay*, I'm fine. You rest." Rachel pulled a dishrag from the drawer. "Have you started making clothes for your *boppli* yet?"

"Some. I've been given some too, mostly boys' clothes." She rubbed her belly. "But everyone tells me I need to be ready for twins."

"I'll help you sew."

Sadie looked surprised. "What's up? Something

is if you're offering to sew." She shifted in her seat, trying to get more comfortable. "Tell me about Jordan. Is he talking about joining the church?"

"He wants to be a truck driver." Rachel continued washing the dishes. She didn't want to chance Sadie recognizing disappointment in her expression.

"I'm sorry to hear that."

Rachel used the back of her hand to wipe some stray hair from her cheek. "I don't know why."

"Keep your distance. You don't want to fall in love. Unless he's committed to the church and—"

Rachel held up her sudsy hand. "I know." She wiped her hands on her apron and took the cookie jar off the counter to distract Sadie's thoughts. "Want a cookie?"

Just as Sadie reached her hand inside the jar, the back door opened and Jordan and Timothy entered. Timothy took one look at the cookie in Sadie's hand and frowned. "The midwife said you've already gained more weight than you should for your entire pregnancy."

"Since when did your *fraa's* weight bother you?" Rachel had never heard him mention anything about Sadie's appearance.

"Since her blood pressure has soared." He winked at Sadie. "You know what the midwife said."

Sadie put the cookie into Timothy's outstretched hand. "He's right. I don't want bed rest."

Rachel passed the jar to Timothy. "You'll eat an extra one for Sadie, *jah?*"

"I'd be happy to," he said as he put his hand in the jar.

Jordan reached for one next. "Timothy thinks we should burn the stumps instead of pull them out."

"It'll be safer."

Rachel filled two glasses with milk. One she handed to Timothy and the other to Jordan.

"Rachel and I can work on the stumps in the morning." Jordan dunked his peanut butter cookie into the milk.

"Bishop Lapp has gathered a crew to help with the planting tomorrow."

Rachel twisted her apron around her hands.

"Is there a problem?" Timothy asked.

"*Nay* . . . I just . . ." She looked at Sadie. "What will I make to feed them all?"

"You could always make *hinkel* dumplings. Those are easy to prepare."

Rachel glanced at Jordan's lopsided grin. No, *hinkel* wasn't an option. "Any other ideas?"

"You could make *yummasetti*. There should be a jar of canned hamburger in the cellar."

"Thank you." Rachel was not pleased with her options, but the simplest way to drop the subject was to agree with her sister.

Timothy drained his glass of milk and set it next to the cookie crumbs spilled on the table. "We should head home, my *fraa*." He stood and helped Sadie up from the chair, his eyes filled with concern and care.

I want a husband like that. It was like Rachel's heart whispered the prayer to God. She felt herself blush, as though the others had heard her thoughts.

"Don't worry about tomorrow," Sadie said. "There will be plenty of food."

Rachel forced a smile. Her sisters didn't understand. They couldn't. They were so different from her. Why had God made her that way?

She waited until Sadie and Timothy were gone before turning to Jordan, hand on her hip, pretending to be annoyed. "I saw your expression."

He didn't deny what she saw. "It doesn't matter. I ate dumplings today and I'll eat them tomorrow."

"I don't believe you."

"Try me." He stepped toward the door, reaching for the handle. "You want to take a walk?"

Rachel's heart fluttered. "Sure," she said, keeping her tone neutral.

"I want to check out the stumps that need to be burned."

Together they stepped outside and down the stairs. They ambled silently to the east field. Rachel marveled at how she almost never felt uncomfortable with the silence that often accompanied them when they were together.

At the first stump, Jordan walked around the perimeter, eyeing the gnarled deadwood. Rachel watched him, noticing everything about how he moved, squatted, inspected the problem before him. She liked how he took it all in, seeming to examine it carefully within before coming up with a solution. His decisions didn't appear to be rash or impulsive.

Jordan straightened and Rachel pretended to be interested in something off in the distance. "Let's go find the other ones. On our way I'd like to check out the river."

Rachel froze.

"I found some old newspapers in the little house and I read about the angel sighting and—" He stopped and turned. "You're not coming?"

Rachel held her aching heart. "I don't go to the river anymore." She drew in a hitched breath and pivoted so she wasn't facing him. "And there hasn't been an angel around here in two years."

Nathaniel sighed. "I've been here with you all along, child. I've been assigned to encamp around you and minister to your needs." He lifted his focus upward. "Why do they need to see before they will believe?"

"I'm sorry. I forgot about the river . . . and your brother."

She looked down at the dirt. "Who told you about James?"

"Micah told me," he said softly. "I'm so sorry. I didn't mean to stir up painful memories."

Unable to speak, she nodded.

"Open your heart. God hears your cry," Nathaniel whispered.

Jordan took her shoulder and gently turned her toward the house. "Let's go back and sit on the porch."

She walked with her head down, needing to say something she was ashamed of. "I didn't like you at all when you first *kumm* to stay."

"So you say." He gently nudged her. "You pointed out how my milk bucket wasn't full."

A funny image came to mind—Jordan flexing his stiff hands after milking. She lifted her head, smiling. Then the smile faded as the image grew fuller. "I didn't treat you well." She scuffed her feet over the damp soil. "I've wanted to help my father since James died, and then you *kumm* to stay and—"

"And you think I've tried to take James's place?"

"Haven't you?" She didn't want to sound accusing. She just wanted to know.

"I needed a job. That's all."

She didn't like the twinge that pricked her heart at his words.

217

He nudged her shoulder with his. "I still don't get all the milk out of a cow."

She cracked a smile.

They took a few steps in silence when Rachel just let the words come. "James planned to marry Katie Bender. They were going to live in the *grossdaadi haus* and he was supposed to shoe horses with *Daed*." Her words ran together. "I didn't want an outsider to replace James in *mei daed's* heart."

Chapter Sixteen

Thick smoke from the burning stump engulfed Jordan when the wind shifted. All morning the dense, soot-filled air had trailed them each step they took.

Rachel coughed but didn't attempt to move. He reached for her elbow and guided them both out of the flow.

"Go inside. I can handle this," he said.

"I want to help." She rubbed her sooty hands over her eyes, leaving a ring of black smudges around them.

"You look like a raccoon."

She wiped her eyes but made them darker.

Jordan reached for her hand and brought it away from her face, turning it palm up so she could see the soot and dirt.

She laughed. "I made it worse, didn't I?"

"Oh no. I kind of like it." He moved in front of her, pretending to study her face. "You missed a few places." He dragged his dirty thumbs over her cheekbones, then dotted her nose. "Now you're irresistible." The words slipped out before he could catch them.

Rachel heard. He could see it in her eyes. But he couldn't tell what she thought of them. He dropped his hands and moved to check the fire—the easiest way out of his mistake.

"This stump is under control."

He picked up the water buckets. "Let's go get the last one."

Rachel grabbed the shovel and a bucket. "Do you think that one is too close to the woods?"

"It might be." He studied the stump as he approached. Because it wasn't centered in the field like the others, they could plant crops around it without much difficulty. On the other hand, the surrounding trees looked fine, and their green leaves were still—the breeze had died down.

Jordan set the buckets on the ground and took the shovel from Rachel. Within a few minutes, he'd created a long trench separating the woods and the stump.

"That barricade should help keep the fire from spreading." He swept his shirtsleeve over his sweaty brow, then doused the dead maple stump with the turpentine and set it on fire.

Black smoke curled from the burning stump to the sky. Beside it, Tangus exhaled, his sulfurous breath adding to the dense cloud. He sang, enticing other demonic spirits to join him in circling the flame. As they did, they thickened the blanket of smoke. The suspended soot particles began to choke the subjects.

Jordan covered his mouth and nose with his hand. He placed his other hand on Rachel's lower back, directing her to move with him to the opposite side of the wall of smoke.

Tangus sucked in the fumes and exhaled a hideous discharge from deep within his core. His companions joined in the folly of chasing the twosome's every move with their poisonous, powdery vapors.

With the embers stirred, sparks flickered toward the wooded area. The subjects were blinded with smoke and didn't see the brush ignite.

Nathaniel whirled in revolutions no human eye could follow. Disguised within a cyclone of sand, he moved over the wooded area and smothered the fire.

"God has not permitted you to destroy the land," Nathaniel declared.

"I'm just amusing myself," Tangus called out from behind his evil colleagues. With so many sets of eyes to mask, Tangus hated being anywhere near the light Nathaniel radiated from standing in God's presence. Walled off by his companions, he used them as a shield to brazenly approach the fire. After a quick stirring of the roasting embers, sparks skittered toward the subjects.

Rachel shielded her eyes from the flames' roaring intensity, trying to find her way out.

"Rachel!"

She opened her eyes to see Jordan drop to the ground, swatting his flaming shirtsleeve.

"Help him, God," Rachel cried out loud as she snatched a water bucket and tossed the water over his arm. The flame extinguished. She dropped the bucket and collapsed to her knees next to him. "Please, God, don't let him be hurt too badly."

"Thanks," Jordan croaked. He lifted his unaffected hand to her face. "Don't cry. You prayed and God answered." He winced and dropped his hand.

She stared at his arm. He needed more water. She reached for another full bucket.

Jordan rolled to his good side and boosted himself upright. "I'm not—"

She drenched his arm with the water.

"What was that for? The fire was out." He wiped his wet face with the sleeve of his unaffected arm.

"Even a turkey keeps cooking after it's removed from the oven." She eyed another bucket.

"No more. I'm—" he rasped. "I'm—"

"You're wheezing."

He pushed off the ground and stood. "I'll be all right." But as he spoke, his neck and chest muscles retracted with each laborious breath.

Rachel doused the smoldering stump with the remaining bucket of water. Steam hissed from the charred wood.

Jordan doubled over, coughing.

"Let's get you help." Before he denied assistance, she put her arm around his waist. Although his breathing had eased by the time they reached the yard, she didn't want to take any chances. "I'll harness Ginger and take you to the clinic."

"No. You can bandage it as well as any medical person." He waved his good arm in the general direction of the *grossdaadi haus*. "Let's go inside so I'm sitting down when you slap the salve on me."

"You need a *dokta*. It might get infected."

"No. I'll be fine." He steered her around the corner of the little house.

Rachel gave the door a nudge with her hip. Once inside, she helped him sit on a wooden chair, then lit the lamp to get a better view of his arm.

"What's the diagnosis, Doc?"

"I need some supplies. I'll be right back." She hurried to the door, mentally compiling a list of things she would need. Scissors, bandages, soapy water . . . Where did *Mamm* keep the burn cream?

She scurried over to the main house and worked swiftly to fill a basket with first aid supplies. The last thing she did was empty the cookie jar into a plastic baggie and toss the cookies in the basket.

On her way back to Jordan, she glanced at the field. A trace cloud of black smoke hung over the area. "Lord, I ask that you place a hedge of protection to contain any lingering embers. And please heal Jordan's arm."

The maple tree leaves overhead rustled in a sudden gust of wind. Beyond, a cyclone of sand swept over the field, snuffing out the fire. She stood, astounded, as the cyclone dissipated as quickly as it had appeared. She would have to go check it out later. Right now Jordan needed her help.

"Doc, so good of you to make a house call," Jordan said as she entered.

She lined the medicinal items up on the table and debated the next step. Until the arm was fully exposed, she wouldn't know the extent of the burn. First she needed to get a basin of soapy water ready.

"Cookies?" He leaned toward the table and reached for the bag.

She playfully slapped at his hand. "Those are for you—if you're a *gut bu.*"

She headed into the kitchen, added water to a basin, then shaved pieces of the bar of soap to make sudsy water. After getting a towel from the drawer, she carried the basin into the other room and set it on the table. She rested her hand on her hip and frowned playfully at Jordan.

Jordan pulled the cookie away from his mouth. "What? I'm being *gut*," he said as cookie crumbs spilled from his lips.

She tried not to crack a smile. "Well. All right. Perhaps a sweet snack will soften the pain coming."

"Pain? There's going to be pain?"

She rolled her eyes at his pretend shock. "Of course there's going to be pain, silly," she teased. "The borax in the soap is bound to cause some discomfort as I clean out the wound. I'll make sure to be as rough as possible."

He looked up at her with an impish little-boy look, and for a moment, she felt something she didn't want to feel. She turned away, scanning the items in front of her, and selected the scissors.

"Don't think because I'm compromised here, you're going to cut my hair."

She snipped the air with the scissors. "Why *nett*? It's *mei* chance to work on my hair-cutting skills." She reached for his arm. "Seriously. I have to cut your shirt."

Although the shirt was damaged beyond repair, she carefully snipped the cloth on the seam. Rachel sucked in a deep breath once she exposed the wound. She stared at the raised red area. No doubt it'd blister the size of his fist.

"Don't faint on me," he said, easing his shoulder out from under the suspender strap.

Rachel turned away as he pulled his unaffected arm out from the sleeve and let the shirt fall to the floor. She dipped a rag in the sudsy water, then squeezed out the excess. Turning back to him, she said, "The area needs to be cleaned so it doesn't get infected." She gingerly dabbed the washrag over the burn.

Jordan winced.

"I'm sorry." She pulled back the washrag, paused a moment, then rinsed the rag before continuing.

Jordan clenched his teeth.

When she finished cleaning the wound, she tossed the rag into the water basin.

Jordan's body relaxed and he exhaled deeply. "Done?"

"*Nett* yet." Rachel picked up the aloe stems she'd clipped from the potted houseplant. She split open the spiny leaves and squeezed out the clear gel. "This might hurt," she said, smearing a layer over the affected area.

"Might?" His jaw twitched.

"It's supposed to be soothing." Because of the severity of the burn, the plant probably wouldn't bring much pain relief. "You need to see a *dokta*." She wrapped the entire gauze bandage around his arm, then paused to examine her work.

"That it?"

"*Jah*, but you need to keep it clean." She began packing the unused supplies into the basket.

"Okay."

"And dry."

"Do I get another cookie *nau*?" He reached around her for the baggie of treats.

She felt her face flush. "I, uh . . . sure." She stepped out of his way to pack up the supplies and to get her emotions back under control.

"Thank you, Rachel."

"*Jah*," she said without facing him.

"I suppose I better put a shirt on." He ambled toward the bedroom, still talking. "The others will be here shortly to start planting."

Her breath caught in her throat. Alone with him, shirtless, wasn't something she wanted to explain to the bishop. She left the supplies on the table and fled the house.

For a moment Rachel didn't know what to do with herself. Her heart raced, her thoughts jumbled, and her emotions screamed something at her she couldn't understand. *Be practical,* she told herself. *What needs to be done?* The practical took over, and she marched to check on the area that had been on fire. When she got there, she stared in disbelief. The fire had consumed the entire stump, yet the area around it was covered in sandy white soil.

She peered up at the sky. "God?"

"Why do you stand amazed, child? God dispatched more of His angels the moment you asked for help." Nathaniel stood amid his fellow heavenly hosts. Together, the glare reflecting off their joined radiance had driven Tangus from the surroundings. Yet Nathaniel knew Tangus wouldn't keep his distance long, unless Nathaniel convinced his charges to continue with their petitions of protection.

Behind her, Jordan cleared his throat. "Fire's out."

His voice pulled Rachel away from her wandering thoughts. She smiled. "*Jah*, were you worried it might spread?"

He inspected the area. "Where did the sand come from?"

"That's what I wondered," she said, looking out over the contrasting black dirt in the field.

Jordan blew out a breath. "God's hand of protection was upon us."

"So you say."

Chapter Seventeen

Jordan redirected his focus from the stump ashes to the buggies pulling into the yard. "Here they come. I'd better get my gloves."

"Please tell me you're *nett* going to work in the field today." Rachel kept pace at his side as he lumbered out of the field. "That's a bad burn. It might get infected."

"Look, Rachel. My arm's fine. And I'm not sitting in the house with a bunch of women." He waved at Timothy and pain tore through his arm. "Don't say anything about this to anyone," he said as he walked away.

From the corner of his eye, he could see Rachel cut across the yard toward the house. She meant well, but he couldn't risk the men thinking he needed pampering.

Jordan touched the bandage beneath his long-sleeved shirt and glanced at the sky. "God, others believe you will heal spontaneously. I know you're capable, but since you didn't do it the multitude of times I prayed before, I'm skeptical. So I'll just ask that you heal this wound. The Hartzlers need my help and I can't give it with this burn. So if it be your will . . . ," he mumbled.

"Good afternoon," Timothy called out as he

helped Sadie up the porch steps. "I'll be out in a minute."

Jordan could see Rachel meeting them at the door and taking the food container from Timothy's free hand. Before she stepped inside, she looked over her shoulder at Jordan and smiled. His heart skipped once. But then, when he saw Sadie touch Rachel's smudged cheek, something flared within his chest. Recalling the feel of her soft skin, he blushed and looked away.

Timothy held a smirk as he strolled across the drive toward Jordan. "I see you and Rachel worked on the stumps together." He leaned closer and lowered his voice. "You might want to wash your face."

"Mine?" Jordan dragged his sleeve over his face, then looked at the soiled sleeve.

Timothy nudged him. "I wouldn't worry about it. We'll all be covered in dirt after working in the field."

Jordan swept his hand toward the gathering men. "I'm surprised so many came."

"There are still more *kumming*. Andrew Lapp will bring his four-horse team."

"This is amazing."

"*Jah*," Timothy agreed. "That's our way. We help one another in times of need."

"I'll be back in a minute. I need to get my gloves." He waved at the others as he jogged to the little house. He was pleased. With so many workers, it was likely the crops would be planted by the end of the day.

Jordan grabbed his gloves off the table, then returned to the group. As he slipped them on, he couldn't help but feel somewhat of a misfit among the seasoned farmers. Micah had taught him a lot, but without much practice, Jordan wasn't feeling competent.

He glanced at the house and suddenly understood that Rachel felt the same inadequacy and turmoil about cooking.

Rachel and Naomi unloaded the food from the back of the buggy. As Naomi chatted about recent events in her family, Rachel scanned the crowd for Jordan. He stood with the group, arms crossed. She looked for a sign that he was favoring his injured arm but couldn't tell from this distance.

"You didn't hear me, did you?"

Rachel redirected her attention to Naomi. "What were you saying?"

"William and I have been sitting on the porch every weekend. We talk about many things. Often we talk about little things like what's happened in the community. Sometimes we talk about God. Or what we dream of. He is such a hard worker."

Rachel smiled. "That is *wundebaar*. And hopefully William isn't as slow as Timothy. He sat with Sadie two years before he asked her to marry him."

Naomi giggled. "I've been dropping hints about increasing the size of the garden." She nudged Rachel. "You should too."

"*Mei* garden is large enough." She didn't dare tell Naomi that she and Jordan had sat on the porch the past few evenings.

Rachel stole another glance at Jordan. This time, their eyes met. He touched the brim of his hat as he joined the others heading out to the field. A spark of hope ignited Rachel's heart. Jordan and Timothy headed into the same field with the bishop and Andrew Lapp. Perhaps while he worked with the bishop, Jordan would inquire about baptism.

"*Ach*, I see who you're staring at," Naomi said.

Rachel covered her smile behind her hand and nudged Naomi toward the steps. "I still have to prepare *mei yummasetti*."

Inside, most of the women had gathered in the sitting room to stitch their quilt blocks. A few fussed over Judith Lapp's newborn daughter. Katie Bender asked for many details, no doubt collecting information to write about in the *Budget*. She chatted on, moving her questions to probe Sadie about her pregnancy.

Rachel was glad she had tasks in the kitchen so she could avoid listening to her. She and Naomi rearranged the dishes, salads, and desserts on the long kitchen table.

Naomi filled a pot with water and set it on the

cookstove to boil while Rachel gathered egg noodles and other ingredients for the casserole.

Sadie entered the kitchen and plopped into a chair. "Can you believe Katie Bender's boldness?" Sadie rolled her eyes. "She told me I was large enough for triplets. *Nett* twins but triplets!"

"*Ach*, I didn't know you were having twins," Naomi said, getting a saucepan ready for Rachel to fry the hamburger meat.

"I don't know for certain. My midwife had to leave town unexpectedly. Something about her mother down in Florida falling and breaking her hip." Sadie fanned her face with her hand. "Is it hot in here?"

"Your face is the color of beets." Rachel reached into the cabinet and removed a glass. "I'll get you a drink." She turned on the tap water and filled the glass, then handed it to her sister. "You need to rest."

Sadie took it gratefully. "*Denki*."

The hamburger began to sizzle and Rachel stirred it so it would brown evenly.

Aenti Leah came into the kitchen, her empty cup in her hand. The oldest of all *Mamm's* sisters, she still had plenty of spunk even though she'd had her seventieth birthday last fall. Rachel braced for the critical words she knew would follow her *aenti's* appearance.

"Miriam would have brought the kettle into the sitting room if she were here," *Aenti* said.

"I'm sorry, I've been busy trying to get the *yummasetti* in the oven."

Aenti Leah ignored her apology, distracted by Sadie's ankles. "I've never seen someone with your size ankles."

Many expressions crossed her sister's face, but Rachel knew she would swallow the painful words and say nothing to her *aenti*. She didn't usually listen to responses anyway.

She peered into the pot of noodles, then glanced at Rachel. "Did you add oil so they don't stick?"

"*Jah, Aenti.*" Her *aenti* never failed to offer cooking advice at every gathering.

"Salt?"

Naomi got the kettle of hot water. "Can I refill your cup?"

Aenti smiled at Naomi. "Certainly, dear."

"I noticed you brought your needlepoint. Maybe you could show me how to do the basket weave stitch." Naomi put the kettle on the stove and guided *Aenti* Leah out of the kitchen.

Once alone with Sadie, Rachel said, "Why did *Aenti* say that about your ankles? I thought worrying about weight was vanity." She leaned closer to Sadie. "Besides, *Aenti* Leah could shed a few pounds herself, ain't so?"

Water from the noodle pot bubbled over and sizzled on the stove. Rachel grabbed a pot holder and strained the noodles. Then she assembled the *yummasetti* and slid the dish into the oven. She peered out the window toward the field. "They're making *gut* progress."

Sadie groaned.

Rachel spun toward her sister. "What's wrong?"

Sadie's face grimaced as she held the side of her belly with her palm.

"Sadie?"

Her sister puffed a few quick breaths through pursed lips.

"I'm going to help get you into bed so you can rest." Rachel weaved her arm around her sister and supported her as she stood.

"*Denki*," Sadie said once they were in the bedroom.

Rachel turned down the quilt and helped ease Sadie onto the mattress. In the few steps it took to reach the bedroom, beads of sweat had laced Sadie's forehead.

"I'll bring you more water." Rachel rushed back to the kitchen. She wished her mother were home——*Mamm* would know what to do.

Naomi slipped into the kitchen. "What's wrong with Sadie?"

"I'm not sure. Maybe it's just discomfort," Rachel said, filling a glass with tap water. "It must be very difficult and exhausting to be so much bigger than normal."

Naomi nudged her. "That might be us one day."

"*You*, you mean. Just you." Rachel nudged her back. "I'm going to be the teacher, remember?"

Naomi snorted. *"Nay.* You're going to be married too, Rachel. I know you will."

"I'm glad someone has hope, because I sure don't."

Naomi put her arm around Rachel's waist. "I do have hope. Besides, I will need your help when I am carrying my *boppli.* And I will help you with yours."

Rachel said nothing, her mind in turmoil; thoughts of wanting so much to be married being squashed by reality. It was not good for hope to be for naught. *"Hope deferred makes the heart sick,"* Proverbs said. If she did not hope in such things as were unattainable, then she would not have her heart sick, ain't so? No matter how often she spoke to God about his will, he seemed silent. Maybe he was disappointed with her as well.

Her friend dropped her arm to look out the window. "Here they *kumm.*" Naomi touched her prayer *kapp* and flitted across the room like a hummingbird drawn to nectar.

Rachel surveyed the containers of food. Everything looked in order. "I'll run this water to Sadie and be right back."

On her way out, Katie was on her way in. "Is there anything that I can help do?"

"You can set out the silverware, please," Rachel said.

"Is this your apple pie, Katie?" Naomi peeled the tinfoil off a pie pan.

"*Jah*, it was James's favorite."

Rachel froze. She knew her *bruder* loved apple pie, but she hadn't thought about it being the reason Katie always brought it to the get-togethers.

Silverware clanged as Katie unloaded the drawer. The back door opened and Jordan and Timothy entered.

"Hey, where are you going?" Jordan asked Rachel as he dusted his hands against his pants legs.

Rachel held up the glass of water. "I'll be back in a minute. I'm taking this to Sadie."

"Is something wrong?" Timothy asked.

"She's *nett* feeling well. I convinced her to rest."

"I'll take that to her." Timothy took the glass of water and moved past her in the hall.

Moments later several other men spilled inside, entering through the front and back doors. Rachel smoothed her dress with the palms of her hands and took a deep breath. She reassured herself that there would be plenty of room for all. Jordan had placed extra chairs in the sitting room, and some of the younger people would take their plates out to the porch. After all, she reminded herself, this group was nowhere near the size of the church gatherings they'd held.

She clasped her hands together as she thought about what she needed to do next. She wished *Mamm* were here. She'd hoped Sadie would help.

She'd never hosted a gathering of any kind and wasn't sure what to do.

Jordan came close behind her. "What did you make?"

She gasped. She'd forgotten her dish in the oven. "*Ach nay!*" She ran to the far end of the kitchen, grabbed two pot holders from the drawer, then opened the oven door. The heat blasting her face wasn't nearly as shocking as the stench of burnt cheesy noodles.

She pulled the dish from the oven and set it on a cooling rack. Her loud gasp and cry brought the one person to the kitchen she did not want to be there. *Aenti* Leah's frowning face halted her from checking Jordan's reaction, as she feared they mirrored one another.

Jordan took a plate and moved to the stove. "If you don't mind, I'll be first in line. Just to get the others moving, you know." He winked.

"Jordan, there is other stuff to eat," she whispered.

"This is what I want." He scooped a large portion of the *yummasetti* onto his plate. "There isn't anything wrong with this food." He took his plate to the table laden with food to add a pickle, two slices of bread, and a spoonful of coleslaw before exiting through the outside door. He stopped at the edge of the porch and leaned against the railing before taking a bite of the *yummasetti*. Rachel tried to pretend she was tidying up around the sink with a washrag, when really, she was watching him as he tasted her noodles. He didn't grimace. He didn't spit it out into the bushes. Instead, he reloaded his fork without hesitation.

Perhaps it wasn't so awful after all.

She took a dish and spooned a small sample onto her plate. When she tasted it, she did not want to reload her fork. She *did* grimace and she *did* want to spit it out. It tasted burnt. Nasty.

She looked out the window again at Jordan who was eating everything on his plate.

Either he had no sense of taste or . . . or what? Was he just being kind? Or was he trying to prove something? But what would he want to prove?

The other men, jovial and chatting about the work they'd done, passed through the line. Rachel stood in front of the *yummasetti*, blocking it from anyone who might mistakenly think it was an edible dish.

Naomi came up, holding her clean, empty plate. "How did yours turn out?"

"It burned. Don't bother."

"Well, someone took a big chunk out of it."

Rachel cast a glance at the kitchen window. Jordan was plainly visible, taking bites from his pickle, laughing as he spoke with his *onkel* Isaac.

Naomi patted Rachel's arm. "Maybe he won't find out it's yours."

"He knows it's mine and I told him *nett* to eat it."

"I'd say he likes you," she whispered. Naomi tapped her plate. "The men have all gone through the line; let's make our plates and go out to the porch."

Rachel agreed, but she refused to eat more *yummasetti*. Instead, she chose half of a peanut butter sandwich and a spoonful of potato salad.

As they stepped outside, Jordan tipped his empty plate in Rachel's direction while *Onkel* Isaac explained an idea he had for better irrigation.

Rachel followed Naomi to the far side of the porch. Katie stood on the other side, alone, staring at the *grossdaadi haus*.

Naomi pointed at Katie with her fork. "Don't you find it strange what Katie said about bringing James's favorite dish?"

Rachel thought about it. Was it strange? "They were engaged."

"But James has been gone— I'm sorry."

Two years.

Until today, Rachel hadn't given much thought to Katie's loss. Rachel lost her *bruder*, but Katie lost the love of her life. And in some ways, her future.

The screen door opened and Jordan carried another heaping plate of food—the *yummasetti*. His *onkel* had stepped away to talk to the other men, so he strolled over to her side of the porch. He pretended he didn't see her and directed his attention to William and Peter. "You should have eaten some of this. This is the best dish by far."

Peter looked at Jordan's plate. "I didn't see that."

"Me either," William said.

Jordan grinned. "Rachel made it." He loaded his fork. "It's *gut*."

Rachel caught his last word. *Gut*. He almost never used any of their words. She closed her eyes against the thought that wanted to surface. She shut it down quickly, because of course he'd use the word with his Amish friends. It was nothing more than that.

"I've had enough," William said, patting his stomach. "I'm afraid nothing more would fit."

"I think I'll try some." Peter started for the door. "I'm never too full to try something good."

"Too late. It's gone." Jordan tipped his plate.

Had he eaten the entire casserole? Surely not. So who else had? She cringed, hoping no one else felt bad about upending it in the bushes.

But why would Jordan make a public fuss about her cooking?

She took the last bite of her sandwich and noticed Katie heading alone into the woods. She drew in a deep breath; even she hadn't gone back to the river since James's death. How often had Katie gone?

Jordan leaned toward Rachel, interrupting her thoughts.

"I would like to take a walk with you after everyone leaves," he whispered. "Please. There's something I want to show you."

Chapter Eighteen

Jordan crossed his arms and leaned against the porch banister watching the groups laughing and talking around him. Some of the men rocked back on their feet as they listened. Some gesticulated to emphasize their point. A few of the younger members paired off to eat together. Children raced around in and about the adults until they were shooed away to find a better place to play.

He wanted to step off the porch and become a part of one of the conversations. But the more he attempted to mingle among the large families, the more he realized how disconnected he was from these people.

He pushed off the railing. If he had to wait until everyone left to show Rachel his surprise, he might as well muck out the barn. As he lumbered toward the toolshed to get the wheelbarrow, *Onkel* Isaac trotted toward him.

"Off to start the afternoon chores early?"

"*Jah.*" Jordan was falling more and more into using words he'd refused to use growing up as the other kids would make fun of him.

Onkel Isaac wiped his forehead with his hankie and jammed it into his front pocket. "I didn't get the chance to tell you during the meal. You did *gut* out there. Grace would be proud."

"Thank you." His mother would probably be proud that he had stayed this long with her kin. "My rows are not the straightest."

"The seed will still grow," Isaac said. "If it's God's will to send the proper amount of rain and sunshine, it won't matter if it's growing in circles."

"*Denki, Onkel.* That is more kindness than I deserve."

Onkel Isaac slapped him on the back. "God gives us all more kindness than we deserve. It's good to pass it along."

Jordan heard so many people in the world say things that sounded good but never live them out. Yet everything said here was followed up by actions that proved it.

"I don't really understand—" At that moment Jordan caught sight of Smokey hunched in a pounce position, his concentration focused on the fledglings tucked in their nest on his porch, calling for their mama to bring them food. In a flash he rushed over and scooped the cat into his arms. The cat fought to get free, his claws digging into Jordan's arm. Jordan pinned the growling cat tight against his chest until the cat stopped his battle.

The cat wasn't happy, the tip of his tail snapping back and forth. "I'll be right back," he called to his *onkel*. He sneezed all the way into the little house, his eyes watering until they dripped.

With one hand he picked up the wicker basket filled with newspaper and upended it on the floor. With determination and quick movements he shoved the cat into the basket and slammed the lid on Smokey before he could escape. Another growl came from inside the basket. "Sorry, Smokey. I know Rachel loves you, but you need to find a new home for a while."

Onkel Isaac appeared at the door. "Need any help?"

"Sure. Will you hold the lid closed while I get some twine?" He sneezed.

Onkel Isaac looked bemused. "I think I missed what happened."

"Smokey was after some baby robins—" He sneezed several times in quick succession.

"Allergic, *jah*?"

"*Jah*." Jordan rubbed his nose quickly, trying to rid it of the tickle. "Can the cat go home with you until those birds are strong enough to fly?"

"Sure."

"I'll get something to tie the basket closed." Jordan jogged to the barn, found some twine, and hurried back. He worked to secure the lid, then placed the basket in his *onkel's* buggy. "I'll come get him as soon as that nest is empty."

"Don't worry about the cat. He'll adapt to a new barn just fine," *Onkel* Isaac said as he climbed into the buggy. After a quick wave, he flicked the reins and the horse trotted down the drive.

Jordan walked to the toolshed, brushing cat hair off his sleeves as he went, sneezing every couple of steps. Once he retrieved the wheelbarrow, he rolled it to the barn. He stopped at the calving pen to check on Wendy. He didn't really know what to look for, so the extent of his checking involved looking for a new calf in the pen. He knew Rachel looked in on her frequently, so he wasn't too worried. Certainly not as concerned as she was.

Jordan filled the wheelbarrow with animal waste, then dumped the contents outside on the compost pile, his thoughts focused on the words *Onkel* Isaac had said to him.

"You shouldn't be doing that."

He looked up to see Rachel coming toward him. "If you get that burn infected—"

"It's healed."

Her cute button nose scrunched. "You're just saying that." She reached for his arm.

He moved it away. "No, really. I'm okay, Doc." He grasped the wooden handles of the wheelbarrow and gave it a push over the mound of dirt and back into the barn where he leaned it against the rafter post.

"Prove it."

He removed his gloves. "All right." He pulled the hem of his shirt from his trousers and unfastened the eye hooks. "It's what I wanted to show you." Stepping into the lamplight, he slipped his arm out of his sleeve.

Rachel lifted her hand to shield her eyes.

He stopped. "I think it's okay, Rachel. You saw me earlier without a shirt. I really don't want to make it difficult for you, so if it is, I won't show you."

Rachel lowered her hand slowly, looking uncertain.

Jordan waited.

"Okay."

He slipped his other arm out of the sleeve and peeled the bandage from the wound. "Look at this."

Her eyes widened. She took a closer look.

"It's gone."

"How can that be?" She gingerly touched his skin where the burn had been. "*Nett* even a discolored blemish."

"God healed it," he said. "It's like it never happened. Weird, huh?"

Rachel touched her prayer *kapp*. She touched the skin again, a light, feathery touch. Everything in him wanted her to continue. So he quickly slipped his arms back into the sleeves of the shirt and fastened the hooks, turning his back to her as he did so.

"*Wundebaar.*" She touched his shoulder. "Jordan, *nau* you know that God hears your prayers. He loves you."

"You aren't surprised?" His heart beat in a way that made him feel a little faint. He faced her.

She cocked her head, considering him. "Yes. And no."

"Why not?"

Her eyes looked beyond him. "The angel."

"The one I read about?"

"Yes." Her voice was as soft as her feather-like touch. Yet she still did not look at him. "He healed little Samuel."

He wanted to ask why the angel had not healed her brother. But that would be too cruel. And it didn't make sense. Why had God healed his arm as though the burn had never been there, yet her *daed* suffered greatly from his leg wound?

"I saw you tying up the basket. What was in it?"

Her abrupt change of subject took him a moment to track. Then he latched on. "Smokey."

"What? I know you don't like the cat, but that doesn't—"

He put up his hand to stop her. "He was getting ready to pounce on the baby birds."

Her flare of anger dissipated. "Did he get any of them?"

"I got to him first."

She put her hand to her chest. "*Gut.* I'm glad. *Denki.* Did you give him to your *onkel*?"

"Yes, just until those birds can fly. Okay? Then I promise I'll go get him."

"Okay." She fingered the strings of her prayer *kapp*.

"I know how important he is to you."

She looked up at him, her eyes filled with gratitude.

They stood there an awkward moment. Jordan cleared his throat. "I want to finish mucking out the barn before I . . . leave."

Her forehead crinkled. "You're leaving?"

"The fields are all planted."

"Will you be going back to work for Kayla Davy's father?"

"No. I might be an *Englischer*, but I'm not interested in her."

She looked as though she didn't believe him. She watched herself smooth the folds of her dress as though she couldn't look at him as she spoke her next words. "You don't have to be an *Englischer*. Bishop Lapp can help you."

"Rachel, I . . ."

She looked at him, her eyes speaking words he could not understand.

"Do you think I've changed my mind?" He tried to speak gently, but it seemed as though his words slapped her. "From the very beginning I told you I wouldn't be staying. That I'm not Amish and never planned to be."

Confusion filled her expression. "I don't

understand. You were so kind to eat the food I cooked even though it was terrible. I thought . . ."

Realization hit him of what he had done. "Rachel, I'm sorry if I've given you the wrong idea."

"Then why—"

"I ate your food so the unmarried men wouldn't find out it was burnt. I want them to see you in a different way. I want you to be chosen—" He couldn't say any more. The clenching in his stomach and the sickness in his heart stopped him.

She wrapped her arms around her waist. "Why do I need to be seen in a different way?"

"Well . . . Timothy said you haven't attracted a husband because—"

"Because I can't cook?"

"Partly. But that's not new information, is it?"

"*Nay.*" Tears sprang to her eyes and she blinked several times. "What else did he say?"

He considered whether or not he should tell her more.

"Please tell me."

"You're too competitive. It's hard for a man to feel he is weaker than a woman."

She put her hand over her mouth, tears beginning to slip down her cheeks.

"I'm sorry. I didn't want to hurt you." He rubbed the back of his neck.

"You said *mei* cooking wasn't that bad."

"I'm not Amish." He kicked a clod of dirt,

248

wishing he could kick himself. "And never will be."

"So you said."

"I told you, I want to go different places. See the country. Understand why my father left us."

"And you have to drive a truck to do that?" He couldn't miss the sarcasm in her voice.

"It's a good living. Nothing to tie you down."

"Fine. Go. But I think you're confused."

"Confused about what?"

Her eyes flashed. "Everything."

Rachel stepped out of the house when she heard the car driving down their road. She shielded her eyes from the setting sun, wondering who among the *Englisch* would be coming down their drive. When she recognized the car, she gave a shriek of delight. "*Daed*! *Daed's* home!"

Jordan emerged from the barn, wiping his hands on a rag.

Rachel ran down the porch steps and threw open the rear passenger door. She leaned in to give her father a hug. "I'm so glad you're home. How's your leg? Are you still in pain?" She knew she sounded as though she were ten years younger, her words spilling out in bunches.

Daed forced a smile. "The pain isn't bad. It's *gut* to be home."

Rachel moved out of the way when she felt Jordan's tap on her shoulder. "Let me help you,

Micah." Jordan leaned over to put one arm around Micah's shoulders and offer the other for Micah to use as leverage.

Mamm retrieved a bag from the trunk and set it on the ground. Rachel put her arm around her mother's waist. "I missed you, *Mamm*." She released her hug and took a second bag from the trunk. "I'll get them both, *Mamm*. You go help *Daed* get settled."

Mamm gave her daughter's cheek one stroke with the back of her finger. Rachel closed her eyes to bring the gesture into her heart.

"Your father refused the crutches the hospital wanted to send home," *Mamm* told her, looking at the two men; *Daed* limping toward the house, favoring his injured leg, and Jordan at his other side, lending support.

"If I have to depend on crutches," *Daed* said, "I'd rather make *mei* own pair. Their price is ridiculous." He gritted his teeth. "But I don't expect I'll need them."

Mamm threw up her hands. "There is no convincing this man of anything." She moved ahead of them and up the steps to open the door.

"The fields are planted," Rachel said.

Daed smiled at Jordan. "*Gut, denki.*"

"It wasn't just me." Jordan shifted underneath the weight of her father. "The entire settlement came to help."

"That's what a community is for," *Daed* said.

"But it is far easier to give than to receive."

Mamm held the door while the men moved slowly up the stairs, her father grimacing with each one. At the top, Jordan stood sideways to allow her *daed* room to come through the door. *Daed* held on to Jordan's shoulder until he reached the wooden chair in the sitting room. Once seated, he sighed and the deep lines across his forehead smoothed over. "*Denki*, Jordan."

"Of course. You're welcome."

Mamm pushed another chair closer for *Daed* to prop up his leg.

Rachel sidled up alongside her father. "Can I get you something to drink?"

"Water, please."

Rachel and *Mamm* went into the kitchen while Jordan stayed with her *daed*.

Mamm's brows crinkled as she looked at the containers of food spread out on the counter. "What is all this?"

"Leftovers from the work bee. The rest is in the ice *haus*." Rachel removed two glasses from the cabinet.

Mamm uncovered a container and peeked inside. "I see we have plenty for supper tonight."

"*Jah*. It was *gut* of the women to leave the leftovers." Rachel filled the glasses with water, then addressed her mother. "Sadie's legs are so big, *Mamm*. She can't seem to catch her breath with any activity. Is that normal?"

"Sometimes." *Mamm's* face collected in thought. "She should still be checked."

"Timothy said she's *nett* supposed to overdo things. I told Sadie I would keep up with weeding her garden."

"And we'll do the canning together. But we'll talk about that later. See to it that your *daed* gets his drink."

Rachel headed to the sitting room but stopped when she heard *Daed* and Jordan's conversation.

"Would you consider staying longer to work?"

Rachel held her breath, waiting behind the wall for Jordan's reply.

"I suppose you'll need some help while you're laid up."

"*Jah*, I will," *Daed* said.

"Sure, I'll stay. I'll keep up the chores until your leg is healed enough for you to do them yourself." Jordan's voice sounded hesitant.

Rachel let out the breath she'd been holding. "*Denki*, God. Maybe now Jordan can find his way to you." She moved to the sitting room as though she came directly from the kitchen. She handed one glass to her father and one to Jordan, then sat on the floor and looked up at her father. "*Daed*, I've missed our family devotions. I hope you feel up to reading the Scriptures tonight."

Daed smiled and glanced at Jordan. "After the milking we can all read together."

Jordan kicked off his boots at the door in the *grossdaadi haus*. He hadn't planned on staying—until Micah asked him to. He wouldn't stay any longer than he needed to. He didn't want Rachel drawing any more wrong conclusions.

He respected Micah and so remained after the meal for devotions. But joining the family in order to listen to a Bible reading did not mean he would talk with the bishop. He didn't need to. He knew what Bishop Lapp would say, "Seek the Scriptures."

He lobbed his hat over the hook.

"Wise words," Nathaniel said, wishing the advice would resonate with the young charge's soul. "Let the God of hope fill you with joy and peace in believing. Abound in His hope, for there is understanding in His Word."

Nathaniel's radiance infiltrated the ethereal realm with an iridescent glow. He had managed to keep the predator at bay. But how long would Tangus pace the perimeter and not attack the charge with his cursed lies?

Unless Jordan called upon the Father, Nathaniel's limited powers would not reach their potential. He longed to intercede. Other hosts of heaven spoke with the Master on their charges' behalf with prayers that never ceased. Songs of praise saturated the throne room of grace and nullified the accuser's petty grievances. Oh, how Nathaniel longed for activity to bring before the King.

"God delights in the praise of His people."

Nathaniel stirred the hearth's bed of embers, and sparks of fluctuating light drew Jordan to the fireplace. He infused a lulling chant of Deitsch hymns like Jordan's mother sang to him as an infant and smiled as Jordan leaned in toward the sound.

Jordan's back stiffened. Dazed with bittersweet childhood memories, he stood from the stone hearth, moved to the rocker, and buried his face in his hands. He hummed the tune playing in his heart, tears brimming his eyes. To shift his attention away from the painful remembrance, he picked up the Bible from the side table.

He set it on his lap, keeping it at the place in Isaiah where it had fallen open.

"Fear not," he read, "for I am with you; be not dismayed, for I am your God. I will strengthen you, yes, I will help you, I will uphold you with My righteous right hand."

Jordan closed his eyes, a shiver piercing his soul; it was the same passage Micah had read only an hour ago.

For the fifth evening, they gathered in the sitting room to listen to *Daed* read the Scriptures after supper. Tonight Jordan fidgeted on his seat.

Rachel counted him changing positions eight times before *Daed* finished and closed the Bible.

"Did you have a question, Jordan?" *Daed* asked.

Jordan shook his head, then stood. "*Denki* for supper," he said, directing his gratitude in *Mamm's* direction.

"There's a nice breeze tonight," Rachel said, following Jordan to the door. "I think I'll sit outside awhile." She hoped Jordan would join her, but he lowered his head, said a quick good night, and ambled across the yard.

She eased onto the wooden swing and, with the gentle lulling of crickets chirping, closed her eyes.

Sometime later she woke with a start when Jordan jostled her shoulder. She shifted to make room for him on the seat.

He sat down beside her. "I know what you're up to." He kept his voice low.

She yawned. "What are you talking about?"

"I'm not ready to talk with the bishop, so you can stop messing with my Bible."

She pulled her brows in, confused. "Jordan, I haven't touched your Bible." She hadn't even gone inside the *grossdaadi haus* to gather his dirty clothes.

"Then who keeps opening the Bible? Every night it's opened to the same passage your father read." He combed his fingers through his hair.

Something fluttered inside her. Was God doing yet another thing for Jordan? "I haven't touched your Bible. Perhaps the window was open."

"Rachel, you were right when you said I'm confused. I am. I just didn't want to admit it. But that doesn't give you permission to make this harder on me." He stood, the moonlight revealing his glare. "We both know the Bible can't open itself."

"God is *nett* a God of confusion." Rachel began to push the swing back and forth ever so slightly. "Can you explain how the burn on your arm disappeared?"

"What are you saying?"

"Maybe God's trying to get your attention."

Chapter Nineteen

The next evening Rachel avoided eye contact with Jordan during supper. After he put his plate on the counter, he made up an excuse to leave, successfully avoiding devotions. His absence made it difficult for her to pay attention to the Scriptures.

Once *Daed's* reading ended, Rachel excused herself to take a walk, hoping to clear her mind. She hadn't gone too far on the wooded path before the sound of snapping tree branches startled her. She had seen white-tailed deer plenty of times at dusk while walking through the woods. She surveyed the area, but having limited light, she couldn't make out anything. She cocked her head.

Whistling? That certainly wasn't wildlife. Then, coming around a bend in the path, was Jordan, hands in his pockets.

His whistling stopped. He looked as startled to see her as she was to see him.

He touched the brim of his hat in greeting, then nodded toward the river. "The water level is low."

"It hasn't rained much."

He removed his hat and ran his fingers through his hair. "Are we going to just talk about the weather?"

Rachel looked down at her dress and straightened the folds. "What were you doing? Looking for an angel?"

"Why would that matter to you?"

"Seek God, not angels. Angels only act upon His orders." Nathaniel peered upward. "You're merciful to those who call upon Your name. How do I reach them with Your love?"

"I guess I've only seen trouble come from seeking what one cannot find. A promise not meant for them."

He slid the brim of his hat round and round through his hands. "Where were you headed?"

"Not the river." She didn't intend for her tone to sound sharp. Rachel reached for the birch tree and peeled off a section of bark. "It's true about the angel, you know. Two years ago, Andrew Lapp's *fraa* encountered an angel at the river. Katie wrote about it in the *Budget*. She couldn't stop talking about the angel, and the more she talked, the more I wanted to find him." She turned her attention to the golden sunset.

Nathaniel created a gentle breeze with his wings.

Jordan stood completely still.

Rachel blinked a few times to chase the tears away, then wiped her face. "I rushed through chores and forgot to close the sheep pen. James noticed they were out and went to look for them." She looked at the rustling leaves above. "Apparently one sheep was stuck in the river briers. James fell in trying to free it, and the current swept him under. That's what Katie said. She was with him when it happened."

"I'm sorry." She knew his eyes searched for contact with hers, but she would not give it.

"I said some harsh things to Katie." Her voice broke. "But the accident was *mei* fault. I shouldn't have *kumm* looking for an angel. I should have known I wouldn't find him." She looked away.

He kept quiet. She was grateful for the silent permission to continue her difficult revelation.

"I was so foolish to go to the river searching for the angel. I worried about such unimportant matters."

"Did you seek the angel for answers?"

"*Jah.*" She swallowed hard. "I should not have cared if a *bu* didn't offer to drive me home from the singings. *Narrisch*, I know."

"No, it's not." He touched his palm to her cheek. "They're all crazy. And blind."

He looked into her eyes as though trying to say more but lacked the words. His palm pulled her closer until their lips were so close . . .

Rachel yanked away, her heart ready to explode. For a split second her eyes looked like a frightened animal's. And then she ran.

Jordan trudged toward the house. What was he thinking? Had he kissed her like he wanted, he would've complicated everything. He glanced behind him on the trail. Rachel not in sight, he dropped his pace. Hopefully she wouldn't linger after dark in the woods.

His heart ached listening to her talk about James. No wonder she didn't want to spend any time at the river. He shouldn't have gone there with hopes of finding an angel either.

Reaching the clearing, a pair of headlights caught his attention. He trotted toward the Hartzlers' driveway.

Kayla climbed out of her truck.

"Is something wrong?"

She looked him up and down. "Hello to you too."

He smiled. "Sorry. I didn't mean to sound rude."

"I came over to give you a message." She dug in the back pocket of her jeans.

"A message?"

"Yeah. Remember when you borrowed my phone?" She tried to straighten the crumpled paper. "Apparently you posted something on a trucker site?"

"Oh, sorry." He grimaced. "I should've told you."

"Well, you got a reply from someone named Clint Engles." She handed him the paper. "I printed it off my e-mail."

Jordan squinted, trying to read the tiny print in the dark.

She pulled his arm. "Come on. You can sit in my truck and read it."

His heart raced. He had never expected his father to contact him. Jordan climbed into the passenger seat of her pickup and removed his hat.

She flipped on the interior light.

For a moment, he tried to recall something more than his father's wavy dark hair. He couldn't. His hands trembled as he tried to read the paper.

Dear Jordan,

When I saw your post inquiring about me, I was thrilled. It's been a long time since I've seen you. You're a man by now, almost twenty-one. I miss that I wasn't a part of your youth. I hope, since you were looking for me, that you've forgiven me.

I want to see you. Please contact me again.

Clint Engles

He looked up from the paper. "He wants to see me."

Kayla rolled her eyes. "Yeah, I read it." She pushed a few buttons on her phone and handed it to him. "Write him back."

"Now?" His heart kicked up more beats. "I don't know what to say."

"Tell him . . . Well, you might want to first tell him your friend gave you the message." She giggled. "You probably don't want him thinking your e-mail name is Rodeo Girl."

"Oh, great."

She laughed harder.

Jordan glanced at the blank screen. When he looked up, he spotted Rachel in the headlight beam. She continued to the porch and looked over her shoulder before entering the house.

Jordan took a deep breath. He stared at the screen briefly, then typed a response.

Clint,

I didn't think you would contact me. I'd like to see you too. I'm staying in Hope Falls.

Jordan

He hit Send, then slapped his hand on his forehead. "I forgot to say I wasn't Rodeo Girl."

"Oh well. Guess you'll have to let him think you wear pink when you ride."

"You think that's funny." He tried holding a phony scowl but laughed anyway. "Thanks for bringing me the message."

"I'll let you know if he contacts you again." She shifted on the seat to face him. "Is everything going all right here?"

"I'm doing well. They're really good people."

"I see your hair is growing out." She tugged at a section of hair covering his ear. "Cute ringlets."

"You're embarrassing me." He slapped his hat back on his head.

Her phone dinged. She glanced at it and held the phone out toward him. "He responded."

Jordan's heart started up again. His father. Right now just a wave of technology away. He read the message.

Jordan,

My refrigerated trailer on my rig broke down, so I'm waiting for a loaner trailer to finish a few deliveries on the west coast. Then I'll head to Michigan. I'll contact you when I get to town. I won't be in Michigan long, but if you want, you can ride along with me from there. It'd give us time to catch up.

Clint

Jordan stared at the screen, not sure how to feel now that he might actually get to spend time with his father. It didn't seem real. "He's coming to Michigan and wants me to go with him on his deliveries."

Kayla smiled. "That's great. When is he arriving?"

"I'm not sure. His rig is being repaired. He said he'd contact me when he gets to town."

"I'll let you know when he does." She glanced at the house. "I think we have someone watching us."

Jordan peered at the upstairs window just as Rachel pulled away.

He gave Kayla back her phone. "I should let you get home. We have church tomorrow."

"Of course."

As he climbed out, he looked up at Rachel's bedroom window, now empty. His stomach knotted.

Rachel stared out the window in disbelief. One moment Jordan attempted to kiss her, and the next, he was sharing another girl's company—in her truck. With the light on in the vehicle, Rachel could see them with their heads together, laughing.

How dare he toy with her heart.

She moved away from the window. "God, I wanted him to kiss me. I am so foolish to have believed his words to me." She dropped to her knees beside her bed. "Lord, I ask that you forgive me. I've had a bad attitude for so long. Please forgive me. Help me to become the person you want me to be, a person pleasing to you. I love you, God. And I place *mei* trust in the plans you have for *mei* life. Even if they don't include Jordan, or marriage."

Nathaniel chanted praises to God. He celebrated his charge's repentant heart because of the glory her sacrifice of praise offered to God.

Jordan stole a glance at Rachel seated on the women's side of the barn. If today was like the other church services he'd attended, it was likely the bishop would dismiss them shortly.

During breakfast she refused to make eye contact with him. Either she was upset that he'd almost kissed her, or she was upset about him sitting with Kayla in her truck. Whatever the cause, he didn't want her angry.

The moment the service ended, he headed toward the women's side. Rachel stood with Naomi, and although Rachel glanced at him, she didn't smile.

A heavy hand clapped his shoulder. Jordan turned to find Timothy standing beside him.

"Micah's making *gut* progress."

"He only limps slightly now."

"I'm glad you've stayed to help him. As swamped as I've been, I wouldn't have had much time." Timothy glanced over his shoulder toward the women. "How are you and Rachel getting along?"

"She's a great person."

Timothy crossed his arms and grinned. "*Jah* . . . and . . ."

"She's upset with me. Is that why you're asking? Did she tell Sadie something?" Jordan furrowed his brows.

"Not that I'm aware of. Why is she upset?"

"I sat in Kayla Davy's truck to read and respond to a text message. Rachel saw us. Now she's avoiding me." He kept silent about trying to kiss Rachel.

Timothy's brows rose.

"She thinks I'm interested in Kayla. But I'm not." He reached into his pocket and pulled out the note. "My father contacted me through Kayla's e-mail." He handed it to Timothy, not sure why he was compelled to explain his actions.

Timothy read the note and handed it back. "How long has it been since you've seen him?"

"Years. The only thing I remember is he had wavy dark hair." Jordan folded the paper and slipped it into his pocket. "He's a truck driver." He glanced at Rachel. She, Naomi, and three other girls, whose names he couldn't ever get straight, stood together by the far table.

"I need to talk with her," Jordan said. He quickly realized this wasn't the place. Not with the entire church membership eyeing them.

Timothy clapped Jordan's shoulder. "Pray about what to say. Maybe leaving isn't the answer."

Chapter Twenty

Rachel crawled on her hands and knees, sloshing the sudsy water over the plank floor.

Sadie entered the house, her arms loaded with material for sewing. "*Ach*, you've got a cool breeze in here."

"I opened the windows to air the place out." Rachel pushed off the floor and slid barefoot over to her sister. "The floor's slippery, so watch your step." She wiped her hands on the front of her dress, then reached for the bundle from her sister's arms. "*Mamm* took *Daed* into town for his appointment. They shouldn't be gone too long."

"Spring cleaning?" Sadie teetered as she crossed the floor.

"*Jah*, I want to surprise *Mamm*." Rachel set the stack of material on the kitchen table. "How are you feeling?"

"Very pregnant." She lowered herself onto the chair and let out a slight groan. "It feels like an effort just to breathe."

"Isn't that what all pregnant women complain about?"

"*Jah*. So now I know."

"Would you like a cup of tea?"

"Water sounds better." Sadie propped her legs up on the opposite chair and puffed out a few quick breaths.

"Are you sure you feel up to sewing today?" Rachel filled a glass with tap water and handed it to her sister. "Your face is flushed and you look tired."

"You sound like Timothy."

Rachel smiled. "Perhaps you should listen to your husband." She filled another glass with water and sat across from Sadie.

"He would have me on bed rest." Sadie rolled her eyes. "I have too much to do before the *boppli* arrives." She winced and shifted into what looked like an uncomfortable position. Leaning to one side, Sadie held the lower section of her belly. "If the *boppli* isn't kicking *mei* bladder, it's poking at *mei* ribs." She shifted again and the tension eased from her face. "Tell me about Jordan. Have you two had much time to talk?"

"About what?" Had word already spread about Jordan sitting in the truck with Kayla?

"Staying in the settlement? Joining the church?"

"*Nett* any more than what I told you." Rachel took a drink, then set her glass on the table. "He wants to be a truck driver."

Sadie frowned. "Don't stop praying for him."

"It's hard." She played with the glass, watching the water slosh gently inside it.

Sadie reached across the table and tapped Rachel's hand. "I pray for you to find someone like *mei* Timothy. He is a *gut* man, Rachel. And a *gut* husband." She flinched. "I want you and I to raise our children together."

Leaning closer, Rachel whispered, "You need to listen to your *wundebaar* husband and rest." She bounced to her feet. "I think I heard the door. *Mamm* and *Daed* must be back." Rachel rounded the corner and stopped.

Jordan was looking down at his boots and the tracks he made across the floor. "Sorry, I didn't know you were mopping." He looked at her, embarrassed. "My footprints are going to dry and leave a film."

"I suppose you have a secret for removing it." She placed her fisted hand on her hip.

He grinned. "Don't use soap." He craned his head toward the kitchen. "Is Micah back from town?"

"*Nay*, is something wrong?"

"Maybe nothing, but I think someone should check the cow."

"What's wrong with the cow?"

"She's acting strange. Why don't you come with me?"

Rachel shoved her feet into a pair of boots near

the door. "Sadie," she called out. "I'm going to the barn. I'll be back soon."

Jordan pulled the door open and let her out first. Together they walked quickly to the barn.

"What's she doing that's strange?"

"You'll just have to see."

Rachel rushed inside the barn and over to the railing and peered at the cow. Wendy stood with her tail raised and her back arched. Anyone could see what was happening. "She's ready to deliver."

He took a deep breath. "Okay. What do we do?"

"Boil water," she said in an urgent tone.

Jordan snapped a quick nod. "I'll do it." He spun toward the entrance.

"Hey." She waited until he looked at her. "I'm joking." She smirked until he squared his shoulders and crossed his arms.

"So what do we do?"

"We wait and see if she needs help." Rachel glanced at Jordan. "How long has she been like this?"

"Most of the morning."

"In contractions? When did her water sack break? Why didn't you *kumm* get me earlier?"

"Take a deep breath." Jordan mimicked breathing in through his nose and exhaling slowly.

"Tell that to the cow."

Wendy's abdomen tightened, actively trying to force the calf out.

"Funny."

"I'll get the supplies ready." She headed for the storage room at the back of the barn, hoping when the time came she would recall all the steps her father followed when extracting a calf.

She flipped the wooden latch on the door to the storage room and fumbled around the long workbench for a pack of matches to light the lantern. Once she had the room illuminated, she worked fast to gather the supplies. Rags to wipe the calf's nasal passages, iodine to apply to the umbilical area . . . She scanned the shelf for the mineral oil but settled for a container of lard.

Jordan entered the room. "Do you need help?"

"*Jah*, grab those ropes and chains hanging from the wall stud."

Jordan did so without asking questions.

"Hopefully you won't need to use all this," she said, moving past him to return to the pen.

"Me?" He followed close on her heels.

She glanced over her shoulder and smiled. "You're the farmer. I just watch the cream separate." She set the supplies down outside of the pen and glanced in at Wendy. Still standing. That was good. She remembered working with James and *Daed* trying to get Wendy up so they could apply the mechanical traction device.

"I've never delivered a calf before," Jordan said.

Neither had she, but she'd watched a few deliveries. She squatted next to the supplies and grabbed the bar of soap. "You need to get prepared," she said, heading for the door.

He trekked behind her. "Okay. What's first?"

Once she reached the pump, she handed him the soap. Without saying anything, she pumped the handle to prime the water.

"Here, I can do that." He handed her the bar of soap and took control of the handle. "Are you still sore about the other day?"

"What about it?" She lathered her hands.

He stopped pumping. "That I almost kissed you."

She pushed up her sleeves, then lathered her forearms. "Did you try to kiss Kayla too, or did you actually do it?" She looked at the dry pump opening, then at him. "I need water to rinse."

"I've never wanted to kiss her." He pumped the handle until water spewed with the force he put into pumping. "I wanted to kiss you. You ran away."

She scrubbed her hands more aggressively than needed. "I think you're confused about Kayla."

"What if I was?" He sounded sarcastic, demanding.

"God is *nett* the author of confusion."

He shook his head and quit pumping. "How long before your *daed* returns?"

"Hopefully soon." She stuck her hands under the water and rinsed. She needed to concentrate on Wendy instead of Jordan and Kayla. Rachel had looked forward to the day she could prove her skills, but not like this, not without her father's help.

The screen door creaked and Sadie stuck her head out. "Is everything okay?"

Rachel continued rinsing her hands. "*Jah*. Wendy's going to deliver shortly is all."

"Is all," Jordan huffed under his breath.

"*Ach*, that's *wundebaar*." Sadie went back inside.

Rachel stepped away from the water. "Your turn." She tossed him the soap.

Jordan rolled up one sleeve at a time. "I thought animals didn't need help birthing their young."

"*Jah*, most don't." She wished Wendy wasn't one who did.

When he finished washing, he raised his hands and the water dripped down his forearms. "Now what?"

"We see if she's progressed." Rachel headed back to the barn.

"And if she hasn't?" His words ran together as he kept her pace.

"We wait." She paused at the entrance. "If she senses you're nervous and becomes excitable, her labor might be delayed."

"That's good, right?" He must have read her facial expression because his smile faded.

"Delaying labor might endanger the calf."

Finding Wendy straining in an awkward head-down-and-back-arched position, Rachel's breath caught. This calf wasn't waiting much longer. She unlatched the gate.

Jordan grabbed her wrist. "Where are you going?" His eyes darted between her and the cow, then steadied on her. "She . . . she looks uncomfortable. She might kick."

Wendy snorted and shifted her stance, and her abdomen muscles relaxed.

"She stopped. That's good, right?"

"Maybe."

"Maybe?" Deep creases spread across his forehead.

She had to find something to keep Jordan occupied. "Do you have the time?"

He dug his hand into his pocket and pulled out a watch. "Half past two."

"*Denki.*" She turned and studied Wendy.

It seemed forever before the cow bore down again for another contraction. When Jordan reported the time, only ten minutes had passed. The cycle repeated in ten-minute increments for the next two hours before the contractions appeared to stop completely.

She kept her eye trained on Wendy. "How long has it been?"

"Twenty minutes," he said.

Wendy kicked her hind foot up against her stomach. A few minutes passed and Rachel said, "How long *nau*?"

"Eight minutes."

"Let's get her into the birthing chute." She pointed to the narrow, standing-only-space pen. "In there." Rachel eased into the stall, took hold of the cow's halter, and tugged hard. Wendy wouldn't budge.

Jordan slipped into the stall. "Why are you trying to move her?"

"*Daed* puts the ones not progressing in there to keep them standing while he pulls the calf out." She beckoned for him. "Give her a nudge."

"I'm probably going to get kicked," he mumbled.

The cow strained as another contraction began. This time, amber fluid gushed out and soaked Jordan's shirt and pants.

"*Ach, gut.*" Rachel smiled.

"Good?" Jordan echoed. "You could have warned me."

She didn't remember the fluid being that viscous. Her smile faded. The calf might be stillborn. Rachel yanked on the halter, but Wendy dropped to her front knees, then rolled on her side.

Jordan stared wide-eyed at the cow.

Rachel reached between the fence boards and grabbed the can of lard.

"Hold out your hands." She opened the lid.

"Why?"

"I'm going to grease you up." Rachel scooped a handful of lard out from the can, then reached for his hand. His forearm muscles tensed as she lathered him with lubricant.

Jordan jerked his hand away. "Oh no!"

"Shh." She looked at Wendy, but the motionless cow didn't seem concerned with his raised voice.

Jordan leaned closer. "I don't know what to do."

"We need to know what position the calf is in." At least that was what *Daed* told James.

"Are you crazy?" His voice rose again.

She disregarded him and crouched next to Wendy. She picked up the cow's tail and gently pulled it to the side, then beckoned Jordan. "*Kumm* on." When he hesitated, she released the tail. "Jordan, I'm *nett* strong enough to reposition the calf."

He snorted but moved close enough that Wendy swatted him with her tail before Rachel had a chance to grab hold of it again.

"I don't think she wants us in here."

"It really doesn't matter what she wants right now. We will do what is best even though it may not feel like it to her."

"Why is this necessary?" He looked very uncomfortable. If this wasn't such a serious situation, it would be funny.

"Wendy needed help during the last delivery. I watched *Daed* and James do this." She stroked the cow. "You see anything?"

His face skewed as he reluctantly looked at the cow. "No."

"Then go inside."

"You're joking, right?"

275

She gave him a look that he obviously under-stood. She wasn't joking.

Jordan inhaled a deep breath and inched his hand closer to the opening but jerked it back before making contact.

"You can do it. Hold your fingers close together." She demonstrated. His jaw twitched.

He rolled his shoulders, cranked his neck side to side, then finally lifted his hand to the birth canal. His face turned a paler shade.

"Are you okay?"

"I might vomit."

His voice quivered and he looked away from her. She never considered he might have a weak stomach. He needed to focus.

She didn't see anything but Jordan's arm. "Do you feel the calf?"

He snapped his head in her direction. With teeth clenched, he said, "I don't know how to describe what I feel."

"Is it a hoof?"

"I think I'd know that." He snorted.

She leaned closer. He was only in mid-forearm. "*Daed* was in as far as his elbows."

He closed his eyes and his Adam's apple moved down his neck. "There's a foot."

"Front or back?"

His eyes shot open. "How would I know? It's not like I can see it." Jordan's face contorted as Wendy strained in a contraction. He removed his hand and bolted for the corner of the stall. Bent at the waist, he dry heaved.

Rachel scooped out a mound of lard and slathered it on her hand and forearm. She knelt beside the cow, and with one hand repositioning the tail, she slipped her other hand into the warm canal.

Jordan knelt beside her and took hold of the tail. "Sorry."

Touching something hard, she blew out a breath. "It's a front hoof."

His face contorted. "How do you know?"

"Three joints." She gripped the leg and tugged. The calf moved. Rachel smiled. "He's alive."

Wendy contracted, wedging Rachel's hand between the abdominal wall and the calf. But the cow's forceful strain didn't stimulate any additional calf movement. Rachel groaned. She waited until the contraction ended before removing her hand. "We better get the chains ready."

Jordan swallowed.

She pushed off the floor. "Something's stopping the calf." Her greasy hands slipped as she tried to unlatch the gate.

"Let me get it." Jordan wiped his hands on his thighs, then clicked the bolt and swung the gate open.

Rachel stepped out, but Wendy's laborious snorting summoned her back into the pen. The gate slammed shut behind her at the same time.

The cow's abdomen moved violently while her legs locked in a stretched-out position. Alarmed by the cow's sudden colicky action, Rachel hurried to reapply another coat of lard over her hands.

One hoof was out.

Jordan opened the gate, with the chains draped over his shoulder. Staring at the protruding leg, his face drained of color.

When the contraction ended, the foot disappeared back into the birth canal.

He gestured at the cow. "Is that normal?"

"I don't know. I've never seen it happen before." She squeezed her eyes closed. "Oh God, please let this calf live. In Jesus' name, let it live." She opened her eyes as Jordan was closing his.

"God, I agree with the request. Amen." He opened his eyes and a faint smile appeared at the corners of his mouth.

Wendy kicked her hind leg up against her abdomen. Under the pressure of the cow's forceful strain, the calf's hoof reappeared, but it quickly retracted again when the cow stopped pushing.

Rachel's throat tightened and her vision blurred with tears.

Jordan moved closer. "Don't break down now. What do we need to do with these chains?"

She shrugged, too choked up to give a reply.

"Rachel, that little guy wants to come out of there." Jordan handed her the chains, then lathered his hands with a thick layer of grease. He slipped his hand inside before Wendy contracted, then looked up at Rachel. "The other leg is turned. How do I get it unstuck?"

She quickly found the end of the chain. "Loop this above the ankle joint."

"Then what?"

"*Daed* always told James to pull with each contraction. Then hold with an even traction between each one."

After attaching the chain, Jordan withdrew his hand and steadily held the chain.

"Pull," she said when Wendy contracted.

The contraction eased.

"Hold."

After another round of pulling, the other hoof appeared, and after that, the calf's muzzle. Rachel wiped the thin membrane away from the calf's airway. "*Nau* she needs to push the shoulders out."

Jordan aided Wendy, and after several minutes of forceful contractions, the rest of the calf slid out, landing on the bed of straw.

Rachel took a piece of straw and wiggled it inside the calf's nostrils. "Rub his sides to get his lungs moving."

Jordan massaged the rib cage, then thumped hard a few times until the calf breathed. He gazed at Rachel. "You're amazing." His smile widened. "I mean it. You're amazing."

"*Nett* me. God is amazing. Don't you forget, Jordan Engles. We prayed about this, and God extended his grace."

Wendy and the calf both stood and the calf bonded with its mother.

"I'll thank him for making you amazing." He patted his chest with a slimy hand. "If I wasn't covered in gunk, I would kiss you." He moved toward her and paused as if waiting for her permission.

The rattle of the gate hinges startled them both. Rachel rose as her father limped inside the pen.

Daed gestured to Jordan's clothes. "Difficult delivery, *jah*?"

Jordan spread his arms so Micah could see it all. "*Jah.*"

Daed put his hand on Rachel's shoulder. "Go on in the *haus*. I need to talk with Jordan alone."

Chapter Twenty-One

Micah cleared his throat. "What are your intentions with *mei* daughter?"

Jordan swallowed hard. He hadn't expected such a direct question. Micah must've overheard him say he wanted to kiss Rachel.

"I'm *nett* so old that I don't see how she looks at you," Micah said.

"I'm fond of Rachel." *Fond?* He felt a lot more than fondness toward her.

"I know your father contacted you, *sohn.*" Micah stroked his beard.

"He wants to take me on his truck route."

"And driving a truck is something you want to do, *jah?*"

Jordan drew a deep breath. Only a few weeks ago he could've answered with an immediate yes. Now, choked with uncertainty, he couldn't form a reply.

"If you go . . . don't take *mei* daughter." Micah's firm tone contradicted his watery eyes.

Jordan's stomach knotted. "I understand. I'll keep my distance from her. You have my word."

The lines on Micah's forehead disappeared. "You're a *gut* man."

The words were hollow in Jordan's heart. With his feelings for Rachel growing stronger every day, it would be difficult to keep his word.

"I know you've struggled since your mother died, and living here hasn't been easy," Micah said.

Jordan remained silent. He rubbed his watering eyes, leaving a greasy film from the calf delivery on his lids. His stomach rolled.

Micah pulled a handkerchief from his pocket and handed it to Jordan.

Jordan wiped his face with the cloth. "She told me before she died . . . she'd made peace with

God. She wanted me to find the same peace. But I don't know how."

A stretch of silence passed between them before Micah spoke. "Have you considered that God might be trying to show you the way?" As though he hadn't expected Jordan to reply, he continued, "Don't be so stubborn that you refuse to listen. The sheep hear the Shepherd's voice. Your heart hasn't turned to stone . . . or you wouldn't be drawn to seek him." Micah picked up the chains. "I'll get these boiling."

"I can do that." Jordan reached for the chains, but Micah didn't release them.

"*Nay.*" He patted the pen slats. "It's *gut* to spend a few minutes with a newborn calf." Micah limped out of the barn.

Jordan leaned against the pen and stared at the newborn. "Thank you for saving the calf, God. It means a lot to Rachel." He squeezed his eyes closed. "And Rachel means a lot to me."

Tangus slithered along the barn rafter above Jordan. "Micah thinks you're trouble. He knows you'll never be righteous like them. You're not Amish."

"That is not the truth." Nathaniel hovered over Jordan to block the enemy's view. "Remember what your mother said, 'My kinfolk will welcome you. Your father will find you there.' Jordan, the Father is here. Call to Him, for He waits for you."

Tangus dropped down to the straw floor and shielded his eyes from Nathaniel. "Your father did find you. He wrote you a letter."

Jordan smiled. "My mother was right. I have found my father here."

Tangus lifted his tattered wings away from his eyes to steal a glimpse at his ethereal adversary. "You underestimate my power, Nathaniel. I've manipulated the human heart since those worldly creatures were created. They all stumble. Some fall. And some I bury in their guilty pleasures."

Jordan watched the calf, suckling on its mother, and grinned at the stubborn little gal. Rachel sure proved to be a good midwife to the cow. He stayed for a while observing the miracle before him.

As Jordan closed the barn door, Rachel was hitching Ginger to the buggy. His heartbeat skipped erratically. He needed to keep his promise to Micah and keep his distance, but the moment she looked up from fastening the strap and smiled, he veered toward her.

"How's the calf?" Her smile lingered.

"She's nursing. You want to go see her?"

"*Jah*, but I can't. Sadie's sick and I'm driving her home." She squatted to reach the strap dangling under Ginger's belly, then looped it through the ring. "I plan to stay and help her."

"When you get back will you take a walk with me?" She needed to hear the news about his father from him.

She paused and eyed him as though she could see into his soul. "I suppose, if you promise to tell me your secret for getting those old floors to shine in the *grossdaadi haus*."

Jordan smiled. "One part vinegar and one part vegetable oil."

She shifted her attention to her sister waddling toward them. Rachel leaned close to Jordan and whispered, "Sadie's rasping like her lungs are filled with fluid."

Sadie handed Rachel a jar of canned chicken broth and pulled herself into the buggy. Once she sat on the bench, Rachel handed her the jar.

Jordan followed Rachel to the driver's side. "How long will you be gone?"

"A few days." Rachel glanced at the barn. "You'll look after the calf, *jah*?"

"*Jah*. If you promise not to race that horse."

"I only like racing those I can beat." Rachel smiled as she released the brake. "I'll wait for you."

Rachel wished she could have stayed home and gone for a walk with Jordan. The intensity of his stare had warmed her core.

Beside her, Sadie squirmed on the bench like a child at the close of a three-hour church service.

Rachel glanced at her sister. "Are you feeling worse?"

"The same. I'm light-headed and hot—like *mei* insides are cooking." Sadie arched her back and placed her hand on her side. "This pressure feels different." Sadie's forced smile slipped into a frown. "I wish I knew if this is normal."

Rachel reached for her sister's hand and gave it a gentle squeeze. "You need rest." She flinched along with Sadie as the buggy wheel dipped into a pothole.

Sadie closed her eyes until Rachel stopped Ginger in front of the house. Rachel jumped out and came around to her sister's side. As Sadie eased off the bench, Timothy came out of his shop and ran over to them.

"What's wrong?" He looked with concern at his *fraa*.

"I need to rest, is all." Sadie's lips pursed. "It will pass."

"How long have you felt like this?" He wrapped his arm around her and carefully helped her down.

"It *kumm* on me sudden."

Rachel followed them inside the house. "She said she feels hot on the inside."

Timothy helped her into the bedroom. After lowering her on the bed, he placed his hand on her forehead. "You feel warm."

"She needs to be checked," Rachel said.

"*Jah*, maybe so."

"You two stop talking about me like I'm *nett* here," Sadie protested. "The midwife is still out of town."

"I'll bring you some water." Rachel left the room, filled a glass, then took it to her sister.

"She's going to take a nap," Timothy said.

Rachel set the water glass on the bedside table.

"*Denki*," Sadie mumbled.

Timothy helped her to sit long enough to sip the water, then he gently lowered her to the pillow. "Do you need another pillow?"

"*Nay*, I'm fine *nau*." Sadie closed her eyes as Timothy kissed her forehead.

Rachel had always admired his attentiveness to Sadie. His love for her was obvious both in the way he looked at her as well as in his actions. Rachel stifled a sigh. "Are you hungry?"

Sadie rolled her head against the pillow. "But you can make something for Timothy, please."

Rachel touched her sister's arm. "You must eat something after your nap. I'll warm some broth."

Her sister closed her eyes without replying.

Rachel slipped out the door behind Timothy. "She needs to eat something for the *boppli's* sake."

"*Jah.*"

"*Mamm* sent a quart of her chicken broth. I'll add some vegetables and make soup."

"*Denki.*" Timothy paused at the end of the hallway, his face full of concern. "I have some work to finish in *mei* shop." He eyed the bedroom.

"I hope it's *nett* the *gut* Lord's plan for Sadie to miscarry the *boppli*."

Rachel clasped her hands. "We will pray for God's grace."

"And mercy." Timothy then began mumbling something about buggy wheels as he headed outside.

Rachel drew a deep breath as she stepped inside the kitchen to inventory Sadie's pantry. Pushing back the pantry curtain, she found a container full of dried homemade egg noodles. She filled a pan with water, added the stiff noodles, and placed the pan on the stove. She poured the broth into a separate pot.

After the broth had simmered, Rachel ladled a bowl and let it cool on the counter. Timothy entered and wiped his feet on the braided rug. "How's Sadie?"

"I was getting ready to take her some broth."

Timothy took a spoon from the drawer, grabbed the bowl of broth from the counter, and headed for the bedroom. A few minutes later, he reappeared in the kitchen and set the bowl on the counter. "She's still sleeping."

"Here, I made us some vegetable and noodle soup." Rachel placed two steaming bowls on the table and some sliced bread on a plate. "I'm worried about her."

"Me too." Timothy pulled the chair away from the table and sat.

Rachel sat across from him, bowed her head, and said a short prayer asking God to watch over the *boppli* and to bless the food.

Timothy blinked a few times, then peered in the bowl while stirring the soup with his spoon. "Do you think she's been sick all day?"

"She said no, but I was helping Jordan deliver a calf. So I don't really know."

He forced a smile. "How did Jordan do?"

"For *nett* wanting to be a farmer, he did okay. He did what needed to be done."

"I'm *nett* sure he wants to be Amish either." Timothy buttered his bread before he took a bite.

She wasn't sure if he meant his words as a caution to guard her heart, or merely as a statement of fact. But the words jolted everything within her. She stared at the chunks of carrots in her bowl. She hadn't realized how deep her desire was for Jordan to accept their faith.

"Don't fall in love with him," Timothy said as he reached for the salt.

She focused on her soup, acknowledging his warning with a reluctant nod. She spooned some soup into her mouth. Timothy's words wouldn't have stung if she didn't already love Jordan. She swallowed and looked at Timothy. "He's confused about the faith. I've asked him to speak with the bishop, but—"

"*Ach*, Rachel. You're smitten already." He gave her a knowing look and dipped his spoon into the soup. "He doesn't plan to stay."

"I know," she said in a whisper. But every part of her wanted to believe he would. Rachel's heart grew heavy. She sipped the soup, thankful that Timothy had become quiet. When they finished eating, Rachel tidied up the kitchen, then reheated the simple broth for Sadie.

She paused at the sitting room where Timothy sat with an open Bible on his lap. The sight warmed her, reminding her how important it was to have a husband who loved God with all his heart.

She continued down the hallway to the bedroom. "Sadie?" she whispered. "I made you some soup." Rachel set the bowl on the dresser and lit the oil lamp.

Sadie didn't respond.

Rachel sat on the edge of the bed. Heat radiated off her sister's body. Her face looked as though she'd spent too much time in the sun. The redness had spread over Sadie's cheeks, and her forehead was dotted with perspiration. "*Ach*, God, protect the *boppli*. Sadie will be devastated if she loses it." Rachel rushed out to the sitting room.

"Sadie needs medical attention *nau*."

Without speaking, Timothy closed the Bible, crossed the room, and headed toward the bedroom. He took one look at his *fraa* and spun around. "Sit with her." His voice raspy, he cleared his throat. "I will get help."

Chapter Twenty-Two

Jordan stood on the porch and watched the sun setting over the Hartzlers' cornfield.

The door creaked as Micah stepped out. "A fine *nacht, jah?*" He moved to the stairs and beckoned for Jordan to follow. "Let's check the crop."

Shoving his hands into his pants pockets, Jordan walked beside Micah. The fading sunlight hadn't affected the temperature. Nearly nightfall and the heat index was probably in the 80s. Before he came to live with the Amish, Jordan never thought about giving thanks for simple things like a breeze. He smiled. He'd finally grown accustomed to wearing long sleeves in the heat and having a tight, collarless shirt hug his sweaty neck.

Micah stood at the edge of his cornfield, fingering a cornstalk.

Jordan did the same. "Knee high by fourth of July, right?"

Micah took off his hat and dabbed his head with his handkerchief. "Probably *nett* this year. With the late planting and lack of rain . . . well, that will be up to God, won't it?" He replaced his hat and tucked the cloth into his back pocket.

Jordan felt the weight of this setback on his shoulders. "I should have—"

"*Nay.* God knows the beginning from the end."

"But I shouldn't have left."

"God will provide." Micah clapped Jordan's shoulder. "This is the farmer's life. Some years are plentiful, some years we scrape by." He chuckled. "We have never gone hungry."

"That's what my mother used to say when our garden was drought stricken."

"Having a garden, you've seen the fruit of one's labor." Micah grinned. "You have a farmer's heart."

He might have been able to soften to the Plain lifestyle, but he wasn't a farmer. He panicked when the cow needed assistance and had only recently filled the milk bucket without his hands stiffening.

"You did a fine job delivering the calf."

"Rachel did that. I didn't even know the cow was in labor."

Micah crossed his arms, looking amused.

"I'm serious. Rachel told me what to do. You taught her well. She saved the calf and maybe the cow too."

"Perhaps." Micah crouched to the ground, scooped up a handful of dirt, and inspected it. "I only wish she would give as much attention to cooking and sewing as she does to being a cow's midwife."

Afraid an affirming comment would somehow betray Rachel, Jordan clamped his mouth tight. Her cooking wasn't horrible. And despite what the unmarried men believed, a little bit of competition with a woman wasn't sinful, unless the men were bitter when they lost. It only bruised their masculinity, and they wouldn't admit it.

Jordan cleared his throat. "I think I'll go back to the little house."

Micah stood, the rich earth falling through his fingers. "*Jah*, it's getting dark."

Nathaniel decamped from the field and plodded along with his charge. He entered the house behind Jordan and brought a swift breeze inside with him. Just as Nathaniel had hoped, Jordan noticed the fluttering Bible pages and picked up the Word of Truth.

"Ask, Jordan, and it will be given to you." Nathaniel's voice penetrated the earthly realm. Yet his charge denied the calling. Jordan stood motionless, void of conviction.

"Seek and you will find." Nathaniel's exhale carried another prompting. "Ask."

Rachel's hands trembled as she attempted to thread the needle. She pulled the blue thread taut while gazing at Sadie's closed bedroom door. Thankful to have a project to bide the time, she tied a knot on the long end of the thread. She'd finished sewing the first shirtsleeve while waiting for an update on her sister's condition, but neither Timothy nor his mother, Anna, had come out to tell her anything.

She joined the two sections of blue fabric and began her stitching. The way this evening was going, she might have the new shirt for Jordan completed before she heard anything.

The bedroom door opened. Rachel shoved her sewing to the side and stood.

"Her fever broke," Timothy reported. "*Mamm* made her an herbal tea that she was able to hold down."

Rachel followed him into the kitchen. "And the *boppli*? Did Sadie say she feels kicking?"

Timothy smiled. "*Jah*. I did too." He took a glass from the cabinet and turned on the tap. "Would you look for a letter in the desk? The midwife sent information of who to call if we needed someone." He sipped some water and tossed the rest in the sink. He placed his hands on either side of the sink and stared despondently out the window into the darkness.

Rachel went to the sitting room, opened the roll-top desk, and found a stack of mail. She recognized Fanny's and Iva's handwriting on most of the letters before coming across the one the midwife had sent.

Rachel tiptoed back down the hallway and peeked inside the bedroom. Anna King sat next to the bed, her head bowed and eyes closed. Rachel tiptoed closer. The floorboards creaked and Anna opened her eyes.

Rachel neared the bed. "Is she sleeping?" she whispered.

"*Jah.*" Anna's warm smile couldn't mask her fatigue. Rachel spotted the dark circles under her eyes immediately and wished Timothy would have gone after her *mamm* instead. Sadie had mentioned last week that her mother-in-law had been ill.

"Can I get you anything, perhaps a cup of *kaffi?*"

"*Nay, denki.*"

Rachel watched her sister and smiled. Sadie's moist, rosy complexion looked flattering compared to her normally pasty skin tone. She sat on the edge of the bed and couldn't resist the urge to place her hand on Sadie's belly. She frowned and changed hand positions when she didn't feel movement. Then the unborn life made its presence known. Rachel caught her breath at the wonderment. *Denki, God.* The baby kicked again, harder this time.

Anna leaned forward in her chair and touched Sadie's forehead. Unable to read the woman's expression, Rachel frowned. "Is she hot?"

"*Nay.* I think she's doing fine." She let out a long sigh and leaned back in the chair.

"I'll be back in a minute. I have a letter to give

to Timothy. I think he's outside on the porch." Rachel scooted out the door and down the hall.

Timothy entered the house. "I had to get some air." He motioned to the bedroom. "Any changes?"

"*Nay*, but your *mamm* doesn't look well. Her eyes are sunken and she's tired." She handed Timothy the letter.

"*Mamm's* still recovering from the flu." He unfolded the letter and read silently. A smile crept over his face. "She should be back in town tomorrow."

"That's *gut*." Rachel breathed easier.

He folded the letter and jammed it into his pocket. "I'm going to check on Sadie and *mei mamm*."

Rachel followed him. As Timothy crept closer to the bedside, Rachel went around to the other side.

"Let me take you home," Timothy said to his mother.

"I can stay and look after Sadie."

"*Nay*, Mamm, you're exhausted."

"I gave *mei* word to Sadie that I would help with the delivery if the midwife wasn't back in town." She looked at her son and her expression softened. "All right. Just be sure to fetch me if anything changes."

"The midwife will be back tomorrow. I think we'll be fine until then." He moved to the bedroom door. "I'll harness the buggy for you, *Mamm*."

"Denki, sohn." Once Timothy left the room, Anna turned to Rachel. "If she wakes up and can sip another cup of tea, I think it will help her upset stomach. She was complaining earlier about pains on her right side, but they eased up with the tea."

"Okay." Rachel followed Anna to the sitting room, where she grabbed her sewing. When Timothy poked his head inside and said the buggy was ready, Anna left and Rachel went to sit beside her sister.

Sadie hadn't stirred while Timothy was driving his mother home. He stepped inside the bedroom. "How is she?"

Rachel set her sewing aside. "She's still sleeping."

Timothy crept closer and sat on the bed. He gently touched Sadie's cheek. "You had me worried, *lieb*," he said under his breath to his *fraa*.

Timothy's compassion for Sadie reminded Rachel of the way *Daed* looked at *Mamm* when he thought no one was paying attention. Rachel stood, wanting to give them some privacy. "I'll be back in a few minutes."

Timothy mumbled something inaudible as Rachel left the room. After loitering in the kitchen for several minutes, she meandered back to the bedroom.

Timothy's hand was on Sadie's belly, a smile filling his face. "He's as sturdy as a horse," Timothy said, looking up at Rachel.

"You're talking about a *boppli, nett* a horse." She gave him a playful smile. "And maybe it's a *maydel*."

A grin spread over his face. "I suppose we'll know that soon."

Nathaniel positioned himself at the head of the bed and kept watch over the room. Except to continue ministering to Rachel, he hadn't received additional instructions. He wanted to offer some form of comfort to the man—even a small amount of peace in the midst of this trial. But a response to the man's requests for comfort from the Savior had not yet been given. Even Nathaniel didn't understand delays from the Almighty.

Chapter Twenty-Three

Jordan stepped aside as flames shot up from the forge. The blistering heat created pellets of sweat that scattered across his forehead.

They needed rain.

Until Micah mentioned the uncertainty of a good harvest, Jordan hadn't thought much about the weather, other than wanting it to rain so the unbearable heat would subside. He shaded his eyes, searching the cloudless blue sky for any indication of rain. Not even a shred of a cloud.

"This shoe repair won't be difficult. I already trimmed and rasped the hoof." Micah pumped the accordion-like bellows over the coal. Next he hammered the molten iron into shape, then submerged it into the water bucket.

In anticipation of which tool Micah would call for next, Jordan selected the driving hammer. He admired the handle's fine wood-grain finish, turning the beautiful tool over and over in his hand.

"That's the hammer *mei* father made," Micah said.

"He was a fine craftsman."

"And a fine man." Micah picked up the mare's leg and positioned the hoof, then held out his hand. "I'm ready for the hammer *nau*."

Jordan handed him the hammer. "The wood's almost soft."

Micah tossed it in his hand. "It gave me plenty of calluses." Micah positioned the square nail and pounded it into the hoof.

"Have I showed you how to make square nails?" He set the next nail.

"Not yet." Jordan turned when a pickup entered the driveway.

Micah looked up and frowned. "That's Kayla Davy's truck."

"*Jah*," Jordan replied.

"I don't like having too many people around a horse I'm shoeing. Would you see what she needs?"

"Sure."

Jordan sauntered over to Kayla's truck as she stepped out. "What's up?"

She smiled and pulled her cell phone from her pocket. "Your father sent you another message."

Rachel propped more pillows behind Sadie to help her sit up, then handed her a plate of scrambled eggs.

Sadie stared at the eggs, then looked up at Rachel. "I won't hold any of this down."

"At least try. You've gone too long without eating. It isn't *gut* for the *boppli*." Rachel set a glass of milk on the side table next to the bed. "You probably never thought you would take instruction from your younger sister, ain't so?"

Sadie reached over and squeezed Rachel's arm. "I'm glad you're here." She took the fork and began to poke at the eggs, pushing them around the plate. "How is Timothy doing?"

"He certainly misses your cooking." Rachel giggled. "The other *nacht*, I boiled *Mamm's* broth dry. By the time I added enough water, it no longer tasted like chicken."

Sadie cracked a smile.

"I want to show you what I've been working on." Rachel plucked her sewing off the dresser. She sat on the edge of the bed and unfolded the material. "It's a shirt."

"*Jah*, it looks great, Rachel. You will be a fine seamstress yet."

"It's for Jordan. I used one of Timothy's shirts as a pattern, only I made it a larger size." She folded the royal blue material. "You can look at it later when you're feeling better."

"I'm sure you did a—" Sadie grimaced.

"What's wrong?"

"I woke earlier with pains in *mei* side, and here they come again."

"Pains? The *boppli*?" She pushed the shirt aside.

Sadie's forehead wrinkled and sweat sprouted on her forehead. "Take this food away, please."

Rachel grabbed the plate. "I'll get you a cool rag." She hurried out of the room and wet a washcloth with cold tap water. Sadie let out a sharp cry and Rachel rushed back.

Rolling to her side, Sadie clutched her belly. "I'm going to be sick."

Rachel spotted a small tin trashcan next to the dresser and handed it to her sister. "Use this—"

Sadie tensed, hung her head into the can, and vomited. She lifted her head slowly, as though it weighed too much, her eyes droopy.

Rachel pulled the can from Sadie's arms as her sister fell back against the bed.

The stench inside the can was so strong, Rachel's stomach rolled. She peered at the greenish bile-looking stuff and fear shot through her. "I'm going to fetch Timothy." Rachel moved to the door, taking the foul can with her. Without taking time to slip into her shoes, she dropped the waste bin outside and raced barefoot across the lawn to his workshop. She yanked the door open. "Something's wrong with Sadie."

Timothy dropped his mallet and pushed past her.

Rachel followed but couldn't keep up with his long strides.

Sadie's cry carried down the hall. "The *boppli*! The *boppli*!"

As Rachel entered the bedroom, Timothy was bending over the bed, stroking his *fraa's* cheek. "Stay calm, Sadie." He kept his voice even, but when he glanced at Rachel, panic filled his eyes. "I have to get help."

"I'll hitch the buggy."

"I'm faster." He sped to the door.

Rachel followed. "I've never delivered a *boppli*."

"I haven't either. Keep her calm. Maybe the *boppli* won't *kumm*." Timothy glanced down the hall, then returned his focus to Rachel. "I'll stop at *Mamm's haus*, then go after the midwife."

"Do you have the letter in case the midwife isn't back yet? You'll need the emergency number she sent."

"Don't panic, Rachel," he said, barely holding back his own. He pulled the crumpled letter from his pocket and stuffed it back in.

Rachel opened the door for Timothy. "Take Ginger, she's faster."

Sadie screeched.

"Hurry, Timothy." Something told her this wouldn't be anything like delivering a calf. She headed back to the bedroom. Ach, *Lord, let the* boppli *live* . . . "Please, God," she whispered as she stepped into the bedroom.

Sadie was curled into a fetal position with her arms clutching her knees. "Something's *nett* right."

Rachel placed her hand on Sadie's forehead and gasped. "You're boiling." Beet-red patches had developed on Sadie's face. Rachel clutched the wet rag and spread it over her sister's forehead. "Timothy's gone for help."

"I'm frightened. Promise me you'll be here to help with the *boppli*. If anything happens—"

"Help is *kumming*. Don't panic."

Please don't panic.

Jordan read the message again. "He's here, in Hope Falls?"

"I contacted him and said I would give you his message," Kayla said.

"He's in town," Jordan mumbled to himself.

Her brows arched. "Isn't this what you wanted?" Kayla touched his shoulder and he flinched. "Jordan?"

He looked over at Micah hammering, then turned his attention toward the kitchen window. Rachel wasn't home, he had to remind himself. He'd already caught himself trying to catch a

302

glimpse of her standing in front of the window several times today.

"I shouldn't have contacted him for you. I'm sorry." She tossed the phone onto the front seat.

"Don't be." He stopped her before she climbed into her truck. "I'm surprised he responded. I never expected him to . . . care." Jordan hadn't expected his stomach to knot either. This was his dream—wasn't it?

Kayla smiled. "Well, do you want a ride into town?"

"Can you come back in an hour or two? I have some errands to run first."

She looked beyond him toward the shoeing area and smiled. "Okay, I'll see you in a couple of hours." She climbed into the cab of the pickup and cranked the engine.

"Jordan?" she called from her window opening.

"Yes?"

She held up her phone. "Do you want me to call him to say you're coming?"

The glare reflecting off the phone's rhinestone case was too distracting; he looked away. "That would be nice, thanks."

Sweat trickled from under his hat and rolled down the back of his neck. Saying good-bye wouldn't be easy, especially to Rachel.

"Everything okay?" Micah lowered the horse's hoof and stepped away from the animal. "You look dazed. Something troubling you, *sohn*?"

"My father's here. In Hope Falls." The words sounded foreign. *My father . . .* His father wanted to see him.

Micah's eyes glazed. "You being here meant so much to me, so much to us. *Denki*."

"I appreciate you giving me a job and a place to stay." Jordan tilted his face upward, as though his eyes could reabsorb the tears.

Micah unlatched the horse and handed the lead to Jordan. "Would you put the horse back in the stall? I'll be back in a minute." He lumbered toward the house.

Jordan's chest tightened. "This is the right decision," he reminded himself.

Tangus hovered in the barn shadows. "Why are you even doubting? Haven't you longed for this day since you were a child? Weren't there times you prayed for it?"

Jordan led the horse into the stall and closed the gate. Not ready to leave, he wandered over to the calf pen. The calf walked around its mother. She was so steady and sure of herself. It was hard to believe she had needed a few thumps on the chest to get her to breathe.

Micah came up beside him and leaned against the pen. "She's putting on weight, *jah*?"

"She looks strong."

Micah moved off the fence. He dug into his

pocket and pulled out a wad of cash. "*Denki* again—"

Jordan backed away. "No, I won't take it."

Micah extended his hand. "This is your money. You earned it."

Jordan gently pushed his hand away. "You said the crops might not make it. You'll need the money to get through the winter."

Micah smiled. "I also told you that God will provide. He will. He's never left us hungry." Micah reached for Jordan's hand and forced the money into it. "You've given me more than help with the farm. I hadn't realized the deep void in *mei* life after losing James." He pressed his lips together before speaking. "*Nau* I'm aware of *mei* need to surrender that to God."

Jordan swallowed hard. For Rachel's sake, he hoped that she had regained her rightful place in Micah's heart. Jordan cleared his throat. "I need to see Rachel before I leave." He watched as Micah stroked his beard. "Is that okay with you?"

After a brief hesitation, Micah cleared his throat. "And what if *mei* daughter wants to follow after you?"

Helplessness shrouded Rachel as she dabbed a cool cloth over Sadie's forehead. In the short period since Timothy had gone for help, her sister's face had become redder and her eyes bloodshot.

Sadie spoke between gasps. "I can't—breathe."

"I think you'll breathe easier if I get another pillow." Rachel hurried across the hall into the other bedroom, grabbed the two feather-stuffed pillows, and fluffed them before positioning them behind her sister's back. "Better?"

"Something's wrong, Rachel. Something's very wrong."

"The *boppli* wants to make an early arrival, is all."

Although her panting seemed to ease with the added pillows, her nostrils still flared with every breath. Rachel propped the window open a few inches. Then, gazing at Sadie sweating profusely, she decided the breeze might cause a chill. She closed the window as a buggy pulled into the driveway.

Rachel met Anna at the front door.

"How is Sadie?" Anna asked.

"She's beet-red and having a hard time breathing. Where's Timothy?"

"He went after the midwife. I sent word over to your *mamm*. She should be here shortly too."

"*Denki*." Rachel led Anna into the bedroom.

Anna sat on the edge of the bed and placed her hand over Sadie's forehead. "Sadie?" She looked up at Rachel. "How long has she been like this?"

"Hot?"

"*Nett* responding." She tapped Sadie's shoulder. "Sadie?"

306

A car drove past the window and Rachel shot out of the room. Before the midwife pulled her bag out of the car, Rachel had the door open, ready to usher her inside. "I'm glad you're here."

"I got back in town last night." The woman rushed up the porch steps. "Mr. King said his wife is in labor."

"*Jah*, she's boiling with fever too." Rachel waited for her to enter, then closed the door.

Already familiar with the house, the midwife headed to the bedroom.

Rachel stepped inside the room as Anna King moved aside for the midwife. "Let's give her some privacy," she whispered to Rachel.

Rachel swiped her sewing off the dresser. Once they were in the sitting room, she asked, "Do you think the midwife can stop the labor? Sadie's *nett* at term."

"There've been plenty of premature *bopplis* who do just fine. God willing, this one will too."

"*Jah*." *God willing.*

Rachel finished attaching the last hooks and eyes to the shirt. Then, not having anything else to keep her occupied, she paced the length of the room. "I wish there was something for me to do." She glanced at Anna. "Would you like *kaffi*? I could heat the kettle."

"*Nay*, I'm fine." Anna folded her hands and bowed her head.

Rachel prayed as she paced. *God, I try* nett *to*

ask for much, but mei *sister really wants this* boppli. *She'll be a* gut mamm. *She and Timothy will train up the child as your Word instructs* . . .

Another buggy entered the driveway. It passed by the sitting room window so quickly that Rachel didn't know if it was Timothy or *Mamm* who had arrived. Seconds later, the door flew open.

Timothy looked back and forth between the two of them. "How's Sadie? Did she have the *boppli?*"

Anna rose from the chair. "The *boppli* hasn't *kumm*, and the midwife is with her *nau*."

"I want to see her." Timothy's eyes watered. "She needs to know that I'm here."

Rachel's throat tightened. "I'll tend to Ginger." She sucked in a deep breath and shot out the door. Her heart ached seeing Timothy fight back his tears.

Ginger nickered as Rachel approached, then dropped her head and blew at the ground. Her neck foamed with sweat.

"*Gut* girl, Ginger." Rachel untied the reins from the porch banister and walked Ginger to the barn so she could remove the harness. She unfastened the top strap and moved to the other side of the horse. The gravel crunched and she looked up.

Jordan sneezed. He sneezed again as he climbed out of his buggy.

"Bless you." Just then Smokey jetted out from the wicker basket inside Jordan's buggy.

"Smokey!" She swooped him up in her arms, glad to have his comfort. She buried her face in his soft fur and he began to purr.

"I tried to catch you on the road." Jordan went over to Ginger. "You were driving crazy." Concern etched his face. "Do you want to kill yourself?"

Rachel set Smokey on the ground. He wove contentedly around her ankles. "It wasn't me. Timothy was fetching the midwife."

Jordan's hardened expression melted as he looked at the car parked in the drive. "What's going on?"

She attempted to keep her words calm, though inside she was terrified. "Sadie's probably going to have the *boppli* early." She wanted to be inside, but with Anna and Timothy there with the midwife, she would just be in the way.

"Will they be okay?"

Rachel looked at him, wishing she knew the answer. "Only God knows. And he is *gut*."

Jordan began to say something, but Rachel stopped him. "Wait here."

"Where are you going?" Jordan called.

"I won't be more than a minute," she replied, sprinting to the house. She snatched the shirt from the chair and darted back outside.

"I made this for you." She handed him the shirt.

Jordan unfolded the fabric. "Wow, you made this, really?"

"I worked on it all *nacht*." His pleased reaction warmed Rachel's heart.

"And here I thought you couldn't sew." He looked at it again. "This is nice. Thanks."

She eyed his broad shoulders and chest. "Your shirts are thin." *Tight too.*

He grinned. "*Jah*, so you say."

She mentally compared his shoulder size to Timothy's. Jordan's shoulders were broader and his chest and neck thicker.

Jordan grinned as he folded the shirt. "I'll treasure it. Especially knowing how much you don't like to sew." Rachel followed him as he placed it on the bench of his buggy.

He pulled the equipment off Ginger and carried it to the tack area of the barn.

Rachel followed, feeling jittery. She wanted desperately to be inside with Sadie. It was difficult to plant herself here, in this moment, no matter how much she cared for Jordan. "Why are you here? Why is Smokey with you?" In light of what was happening inside the house, she felt her questions were silly and mundane.

He hung the harness on the nail next to the others. "I told you I would bring the cat back."

"*Jah*, when the birds had left the nest."

"I was on my way to take Smokey to your house, but then I saw Ginger and I chased you, or who—"

"Why were you taking him back home? The

310

birds aren't ready to fly and you're allergic to cats." She tilted her head, trying to figure him out. "I don't want you to be sneezing." She stopped. Her words froze as the possible reason for Smokey's early homecoming became apparent. "Jordan—" She bit her bottom lip.

Jordan moved closer. "I need to talk to you." He reached for her hand, his eyes boring into hers. "I didn't want you hearing it from anyone else."

"Hearing what?" A lump constricted her throat.

He squeezed her hand. "I'm leaving. I'm going with my father."

Rachel blinked back tears. "I thought you'd started to like it here. I thought . . ."

"Please don't cry. I'm sorry." He dropped her hand and rubbed the back of his neck. "I didn't plan it this way."

She reached for his arm, her eyes searching his. "Then don't go."

His muscles tightened under her grip. "I told you I wanted to learn to drive a truck, remember?"

"I know," she said softly—but she hadn't really believed he would go.

"I won't forget you." His voice quivered and he paused. "You mean a lot to me."

"Then don't go. Stay. You don't have to—"

"I already said yes." He stepped closer. "This isn't easy for me either."

She stared, unable to speak.

"You'll find someone and forget about me." He

lifted her chin to look into her eyes. "You will."

Did he really believe that?

"You and I both know I won't." She blinked to clear her vision, but more tears burned her eyes.

"Then I'll come back for you."

"You'll forget about me." She tried to move her chin from his hand, but he wouldn't release his grip.

Jordan looked deeper into her eyes. "I won't ever forget you."

"I won't forget you either." She also wouldn't forget the emptiness in her heart.

"I have to go," he whispered, releasing her chin.

He opened the door and the flash of sunlight blinded her. As her eyes adjusted, she could see Kayla's truck pulling into the drive.

Mamm climbed out of the cab, a look of alarm on her face. She thanked Kayla for the ride before she hurried up the porch steps.

Kayla's window lowered. She stuck her head out the window. "Jordan, you weren't back yet and Miriam needed a ride. I thought I might find you here."

Jordan grabbed the shirt out of his buggy and turned to Rachel. "She's giving me a ride into town."

"Of course." Her voice felt distant, as if coming from someone else. Someone stronger than she was.

"Micah said he would make sure my *onkel* gets

Blaze and the buggy back." He reached into his pocket and pulled out the cash Micah had given him. "Give this to your *daed.*"

"Why?"

"Just promise me." He climbed into the passenger side of Kayla's truck. "Take care." He rolled down the window and stuck his hand out until the truck was no longer in sight.

Rachel shuffled into the barn. She cried while she tended to Ginger and lingered in the barn until her emotions were controlled. On her way back to the house, the door flew open and Timothy bolted outside. He grabbed both her arms, panic not only in his eyes but in every part of him. "Rachel, hitch the buggy for me." He sprinted back to the house.

Chapter Twenty-Four

Rachel had the buggy rehitched by the time an ambulance pulled into the yard. Ginger spooked at the scream of the siren, prancing in place, her head high, eyes wide.

"Whoa, girl." She pulled the reins and set the brake. With the horse nervous, she couldn't leave Ginger alone. She fixed her eyes on the door and waited for a signal from Timothy . . . from anyone. Rachel squeezed her eyes closed and whispered another prayer. "God, please watch over the *boppli*."

The screen door creaked and Rachel opened her eyes. Two paramedics wheeled Sadie out on a stretcher. The midwife kept stride, rattling off numbers that meant nothing to Rachel, except when the midwife reported Sadie's extremely high blood pressure.

The paramedics loaded her sister into the ambulance. Timothy placed one boot on the bumper, ready to board, but a crew member held up his hand and said something Rachel couldn't hear. Timothy backed away from the closing door.

He ran to the buggy. "Slide over." He climbed inside and snapped the reins. "God willing, the Thons are home and one of them can drive me into town."

Rachel opened her mouth to ask why an ambulance was needed but then shut it. Timothy was lost in a pensive stare, praying with his lips moving and eyes open. Something she should be doing. Rachel bowed silently and quoted the Twenty-Third Psalm.

"*Denki*, God, they're home," she said as Timothy pulled into their *Englisch* friends' driveway. He stopped Ginger, tossed the reins to Rachel, then jumped out. After a quick rap on the door, it opened.

"*Mei fraa*—my wife—was taken to the hospital. Can you please drive me there?"

Simon reached into his pocket. Keys jingled in his hand as he started to his truck. "Let's go."

Rachel called out, "I'll bring your *mamm* and mine." She doubted Timothy heard her comment as he slammed his door closed.

Mary appeared in the doorway. "Is there an emergency?"

"*Jah*!" she called. "Sadie was taken to the hospital by an ambulance."

"I'll get my keys and drive your family into town."

Directed to the second-floor waiting room by a hospital staff member, Rachel, *Mamm*, and Anna King found Timothy alone in the room.

He lifted his head when they entered. "Sadie's in the operating room."

Mamm covered her mouth, and Anna placed her arm around *Mamm*'s shoulder. The two mothers leaned toward each other, pushed together by mutual fear.

Nathaniel unfurled his wings and moved beside Rachel as she eased closer to Timothy.

"What did the *dokta* say?" Rachel practically held her breath.

"I didn't understand the fancy words. Something about her blood pressure and toxemia. I didn't even get to see her before they rushed her to surgery." He stopped, attempting to get his emotions under control. "They had me filling out paperwork."

The wait drained all of them. If they spoke at all, it seemed to be more of a mumbling to themselves rather than something important to be heard. Timothy paced, his hand to his bearded chin, eyes cast to the ground, lips still moving in near-silent prayer.

Finally, a white-coated man appeared in the waiting room doorway. "Mr. King?" The doctor stepped into the room and approached Timothy. Everyone froze.

"This is what I've been waiting for." Tangus sprang off the ceiling and landed next to the doctor.

"*Jah?*"
"You have a daughter," he pronounced with a grim smile. "Five pounds eleven ounces."

Tangus spun gleefully. He edged closer to Rachel, but Nathaniel's protective covering prevented him from sidling up next to her ear.

Mamm and Anna brightened, chattering about the baby being a girl, her weight reasonable for a preemie. "Is she okay?" *Mamm* asked. "The *boppli*. Is she okay?"

"Timothy, didn't you hear? It's a girl." Rachel touched his arm, but he stiffened. She followed his pinned stare. Her breath caught in her chest. The doctor held her sister's prayer *kapp*. Why would he have—

Timothy cleared his throat. "And Sadie?"

The doctor paused, pain and sadness in his eyes. "I'm sorry. She didn't make it."

Mamm gasped, her hand flying to her chest.

Timothy backed up until he nearly stumbled over a steel chair. He sat and dropped his head into his hands, his head wagging in disbelief.

Rachel's surroundings blurred. In a slow-motion delay, she moved from *Mamm*, smothered in Anna King's embrace, over to Timothy— whitewashed and speechless—over to the doctor, still dangling Sadie's prayer *kapp* as if he'd pulled it out of a lost-and-found box.

"What happened?" Rachel's voice cracked. "She *kumm* to have a *boppli*. A baby."

"You only prayed for the baby, remember? Not your sister. Now she's dead. If you had prayed for her, things might have been different!" Tangus strutted toward Rachel. "Now what do you think of your God?" His chest inflated and he flexed his wings with pride and self-empowerment.

"My job will be easier now," he said to Nathaniel.

Nathaniel steadied his hand on his sword and waited for word sent from God.

The doctor stepped into the center of the room. "Mrs. King suffered from a syndrome called HELLP. The toxemia caused her liver to rupture; we couldn't save her." He paused, allowing Timothy to soak in the news.

"Suffered. Did you hear him?" Tangus closed his eyes to block the glare radiating from Nathaniel's iridescent form and weaseled through an opening to get closer to Rachel. "Sadie suffered," Tangus repeated.

Rachel gasped.

The doctor extended Sadie's *kapp* to Timothy.

"Would you like to speak with a member of the clergy staff?"

"*Nay.*"

Rachel opened her eyes as she heard Timothy's choked reply. He stared at the prayer *kapp*, his eyes budding with tears.

"If you have any questions, the nurse can page me." He waited a moment. "I'm sorry about your loss, Mr. King. I did everything I could to save her."

Rachel swallowed hard. "What about the baby?"

"The pediatrician is still examining her. The neonatal intensive care unit is located on the third floor."

Rachel's numbed senses couldn't distinguish between the hum of the Coke machine and

Mamm's muffled cry. She already struggled to live without James. How could she possibly live without her sister too? Rachel's knees weakened. The room spun. Suddenly her legs went limp, and she wobbled before a firm hand caught her and supported her weight. For a brief moment she saw someone whom she conceived in her mind as Jordan.

"Rachel, you better sit down." Timothy guided her into the cold steel chair.

Mamm slid into the seat beside Rachel. They clung together for what seemed like hours, sobbing.

Jordan paused at the restaurant's entrance. Since the eatery and the truck stop shared the same building, truck drivers made up the majority of patrons. Among the array of different ball caps, dingy T-shirts, and men with the common trademark of an oil rag tied to their belt loop, finding his father might prove difficult.

He scanned the crowd. One person made eye contact with him, but Jordan ruled him out. The man's polo shirt didn't fit what he imagined a trucker would wear.

"Take a seat wherever you can find one," said the waitress pouring coffee at one of the nearby booths.

"Thank you," Jordan replied.

The nicely dressed man slid out of his seat and

approached. "Jordan?" He extended his hand.

Jordan stared. They were the same height; the man's eyes were the same shade of green as his. His hair, although strewn with gray, was wavy like he remembered.

"You look how I imagined," the man said.

Jordan pulled himself from his surreal trance. "And you . . . ," Jordan said, unable to complete his thought even in his own mind. He lifted his hand and grasped his father's with a firm grip.

"I'm Clint—your father." He motioned to the booth. "Are you hungry? I haven't ordered yet."

Jordan nodded, although he doubted he could eat.

Clint stepped aside to allow another patron to pass through the entrance. "Let's get out of the walkway and sit so we can talk. It's good to see you."

Jordan smiled. For someone who hadn't tried to make contact over the years, his father sounded genuinely pleased to meet him now. Jordan followed him to the booth and slid onto the seat opposite him. He glanced out the window at the rows of parked trucks. A mix of excitement and panic sped through his veins.

"I took you for a ride when you were about five. Do you remember?"

Jordan tried to dredge up the memory but couldn't.

"You were young." He leaned to the side and

pulled his wallet from his back pocket. He flipped open the bifold and smiled as he removed a photograph and passed it to Jordan.

"You carry a picture of me?" Jordan stared at the old photo of him as a child kneeling on the seat holding the steering wheel. He wished he could remember that day. He wished he could remember a lot of things.

His father looked delighted with the memory. "You couldn't see over the dashboard."

"Where did we go?" He handed the picture back.

"You rode with me to fuel up, then we ate lunch in a diner something like this." He seemed warmed by the memory. "It was only ten miles but we had a great time. You pretended you were the truck driver 'going far, far away.' " Before he replaced Jordan's photo in the wallet, he paused to look at another picture and Jordan caught a glimpse of his mother's photograph before his father slipped Jordan's picture over hers.

His father cleared his throat. "Now look at you. You don't need a booster seat to reach the table."

"Nope. Haven't needed one for a couple of years now." Jordan felt so off balance. He studied the stranger across the table. "What do you want me to call you?"

His father crossed his arms on the tabletop. "Clint is fine with me." He winked.

Chapter Twenty-Five

Rachel slipped her hand into the incubator glove and stroked the crying baby's cheek. Since Sadie's death, the days crept by at an incredibly slow pace.

"She's responding to your touch," the nurse said when the infant quieted.

Rachel marveled at how strong the newborn's lungs had become in her five days of life. "I wish I could hold her all the time and not just for her feedings."

The nurse patted Rachel's shoulder. "It won't be long. This little girl is a fighter. She's gaining strength every day."

"He gives power to the weak, and to those who have no might He increases strength." Rachel had quoted the verse from Isaiah multiple times in her mind. Today was the first time she'd verbalized the scripture aloud.

Nathaniel towered over the incubator. Since the infant's birth he had maintained his post. Hearing his charge quote the same words that inspired Isaiah filled Nathaniel with praise. "Indeed, God will increase the babe's strength and yours as well."

Rachel glanced at the nurse. "What did the doctor say about her being released?"

"If she maintains a normal temperature and the blood tests return within normal limits, I think the doctor will clear her for discharge in the next day or so. She's eating and has gained a few ounces." The nurse smiled. "I'll get a bottle ready and you can feed her."

"Thank you." Rachel loved feeding time. It meant that she could cuddle the baby in her arms and rock her in the chair. She wished Timothy spent more time with his daughter, but she also understood he needed to make funeral arrangements.

With the funeral set for the day after tomorrow, Fanny and Iva had time to make the trip home from Wisconsin. *Mamm* hadn't been allowed to spend time with the baby since she had developed a fever and sore throat. At least with her sisters' arrival, the sad occasion would have a glimmer of comfort for *Mamm*.

The nurse returned with a small bottle of formula that she handed to Rachel. "If you'll take a seat in the rocker, I'll bring the baby to you." She unlatched the door of the incubator and opened the hatch.

Rachel sat in the cushioned rocking chair and spread out her arms to accept the fragile bundle. She nestled her niece in the crook of her arm as best she could while wearing a paper gown.

"I'll be at the desk doing paperwork. Push the red button if you need anything."

"*Jah*," she said, softly touching the baby's fingers. She gazed at the suckling infant. "You look like your *mamm*. Her eyes were blue too." Rachel's throat constricted at the thought of the baby never knowing Sadie.

Rachel worried about Timothy. He hadn't even chosen a name, and the woman from the medical records department had inquired every day. She explained she needed the information to fill out the birth certificate, which must be completed soon.

The incubator labeled *King infant girl* sounded cold and detached.

The last few days blurred like a dream spoken in a foreign language. So many worldly things to accept. Rachel wanted to bring the clothing Sadie had sewn for the baby, but the nurses insisted that they needed access to the IV lines and the hospital clothing had snaps for that purpose. The hospital staff also rejected the idea of the baby wearing the traditional white *kapp*. However, once the nurse explained how the knitted pink hat kept the baby warm and how critical it was to maintain the baby's temperature, Rachel understood.

The door opened. A tall man entered the room. Dressed in a paper gown over his clothing, a mask covering his beard, and a blue hospital cap in place of his straw hat, Rachel barely recognized Timothy. He no longer looked Amish.

"How is she?" He moved toward her with obvious apprehension.

"*Wundebaar.*" She eased out of the chair. "Sit here and I'll hand you the *boppli.*"

Timothy sat and Rachel lowered his daughter into his arms.

"She's so small," he said, gazing at his daughter.

"*Jah.*" She handed him the bottle. "I'll give you some time alone with her." She hadn't taken more than a few steps toward the door before he called her in a panicked voice.

"*Nay,* please stay."

She turned. His eyes were wide. She came back to his side.

"I don't know what to do," he said.

"It *kumms* natural in time." She watched with wonderment how tiny the baby was in his arms and how carefully he held her. "She is pretty, ain't so?"

"Like Sadie." His eyes turned glossy. "Maybe you should . . . take her." His voice fractured as tears drained from his eyes and soaked into the paper mask he wore.

Rachel's eyes pooled with tears, hurting for him as well as herself. She dabbed her face with her gloved hand, but the latex material couldn't soak up the wetness. Timothy looked just as desperate to hide his pain. He stared at the ceiling.

Rachel understood he needed time to grieve,

but bonding with his daughter was important too, and he didn't seem comfortable with that.

"Look, she's almost finished the bottle." She took a cloth diaper and draped it over his shoulder.

Timothy flinched.

"Go ahead, you'll do fine."

He slowly lifted the infant to his shoulder and lightly tapped her back.

"That's *gut*," she reassured.

"She isn't doing anything."

"She will."

After a few more taps, the baby burped.

"Well, *Daed*, what do you think of your daughter *nay*?"

He stiffened, then motioned Rachel to take the baby. After passing off his daughter, Timothy walked out of the room, tearing off his mask and wiping his eyes.

Rachel rocked the baby. *God, this child needs her father. Please show Timothy mercy during his time of grieving. And, God, I ask that you direct me in how I can help him.*

"Rachel, give Timothy time to come around," Nathaniel whispered. "He must first accept God's will before he can be the father God has called him to be." Nathaniel brushed the tips of his wings over the infant's cheek. "You are precious in God's sight, little one."

After a few minutes, Timothy reentered the room. "I spoke with the nurses at the desk," he said, his voice quiet and soft. "They said she can go home in the morning."

Rachel smiled. "I suggest you name her so her birth record is complete."

He sobered. "I've been thinking about it. I keep coming back to how Sadie wanted her name to be Ella Sue."

"After *mei mammi, jah*?" Rachel smiled.

"I told Sadie I wasn't fond of the name . . . *Nau* . . ."

"Sadie would be pleased, Timothy."

The nurse stepped into the room. "How much did she drink?"

"The whole thing." Rachel held up the bottle.

"That's good. What about a bowel movement?"

"I haven't noticed, nor have I changed her diaper. She's probably in need of a fresh one."

Rachel hadn't adjusted to using disposable diapers. At home, the baby would wet through a cloth diaper and that would be the signal to change it.

"I'll take her," the nurse said. "I need to get her vital signs and temperature again."

Rachel released the baby. "Her name is Ella Sue."

"That's a beautiful name." The nurse looked at the sleeping infant. "For a beautiful little angel."

Ella Sue fussed the moment the nurse placed her on the counter and removed her diaper.

Timothy leaned close to Rachel. "What is she doing?"

"It is strange, isn't it? They weigh her diaper." She pointed to the clipboard next to the scale. "The nurse told me they record everything Ella takes in and puts out on that chart."

"Why?"

"It's a way they can see if her kidneys are working." She tipped her head toward the door. "Want to take a walk to the cafeteria?"

"Sure."

Once outside the nursery, Rachel removed the mask, hair bonnet, and disposable gown and tossed them in the designated trash. "Wearing this gets hot after a while, ain't so?"

"*Jah.*" Timothy tossed his used coverings into the trash can. "This place smells like death."

Rachel inwardly agreed. Her throat burned from the chemical scent. *I can do all things through Christ Jesus who strengthens me. I need your power, Lord. Show me how I can help Timothy.*

They stopped in front of the elevator and Timothy pressed the Down button. He jammed his hands in his pockets and lowered his head. "I don't want to be here," he said.

"Neither do I," she said, sadness welling up inside her. "God has a plan."

He shot her a sideways glare but said nothing.

Rachel straightened her shoulders, pushing her own pain to the back of her heart. "Concentrate on your daughter. She needs you." Her words felt empty and true at the same time. The gap Sadie left was powerful, deep, and painful. Yet the helpless *boppli* was here now, and she did, truly, need her father.

The elevator door opened and they stepped into the crowded compartment. With the button for the lobby already lit, Rachel clasped her hands and looked down at the green marble tile. Once the door opened again, she stepped into the main lobby and waited for Timothy.

"The cafeteria is this way," she said and began to walk down the newly familiar hallway. A lump grew in her throat. At least in the nursery holding the baby, she felt useful. This silence gnawed at her nerves. She swept her hands over her apron and blew out a breath as they entered the cafeteria.

Timothy headed for the coffee station. He filled two disposable cups, then turned to her. "Are you hungry?"

"*Nay*. Naomi brought me a basket of lunch." She surveyed the large metal pans of food along the serving line. "You should eat though."

"There is plenty at home. *Mei mamm* and others in the community have seen to that. They have brought too much food."

At the register, Timothy put his hand into his pocket and pulled out a few dollars. The worker gave him back coins, which he shoved in his pocket before picking up the coffee cups. He stopped at the condiment stand and removed the plastic lids from the cups. He reached for a packet of sugar, then paused. "I forgot, do you take cream or sugar?"

"*Nay*. Black is *gut*."

The corner of his mouth turned down and she knew he was remembering how Sadie liked her coffee extra sweet.

"There's a table next to the windows." Rachel pointed to the far wall that overlooked the court-yard.

"Okay." He carried the cups and followed her across the room. Timothy sat facing the window. "It feels like a nightmare." His focus drifted to her. "Does it feel that way to you?"

"*Jah*, I suppose it will feel this way for a while." She didn't like remembering the dark time after James died. And how she still hadn't seemed to finish walking through it.

She didn't deny struggling to understand God's will. In their own quiet way, everyone busied themselves with tasks to keep the grief at bay. Timothy made funeral arrangements; in spite of being ill, *Mamm* cleaned the house in preparation for Fanny and Iva's arrival; and Rachel tended the baby.

"Part of me died," he said, his voice barely audible.

Rachel dabbed a napkin against the corners of her eyes. What could she say? And there was the big question looming over them. How would Timothy rebuild his life without Sadie—and with a baby?

Water trickled down the courtyard fountain, with bright violet shades of impatiens circling the collecting pool. She should've suggested they sit on one of the outdoor benches. The sounds of nature would be more soothing than the clang of cafeteria dishes. "Do you want to move outside?" she asked.

Timothy continually stirred his coffee with the tiny plastic straw. "We wouldn't hear if they paged us."

"*Jah, gut* thought." Although with the noise level in the cafeteria, she wasn't sure they would hear their names if they were called there either.

He took a sip of coffee, then lowered the cup to the table and slowly ran his finger around the rim. "*Denki* for staying so many hours with the *boppli*."

"I'll be happy when Ella can go home. One more day."

He continued to trace his finger around the cup rim. "I heard Jordan left."

"*Jah . . .*"

"I'm sorry. I know Sadie—" He cringed.

"What is it?"

"I was trying to move the conversation away from Sadie. But then I started to say that Sadie had prayed about you getting married when she recognized a budding relationship between you and Jordan."

"*Jah*, she told me so too." Rachel dabbed her eyes with the napkin again. "But Jordan made it clear he wasn't Amish."

"*Nett* many *Englischers* become Amish."

And Jordan wouldn't be one of the few either. Rachel sipped her coffee, which was quickly becoming lukewarm. "The flowers are beautiful."

After a few minutes of silence, he drained his cup. "Are you ready to go back upstairs?"

Rachel took another drink to finish hers. "*Jah*. I don't want to leave Ella too long."

They tossed the empty cups in the trash and walked to the elevators. Rachel pressed the Up button and waited. The floor indicator lit as it made its way to the ground level.

Timothy cleared his throat. "Do you mind if I go back home? I still have to meet with Bishop Lapp."

"I'll stay with Ella. You do what needs to be done." The door opened and Rachel stepped inside. "I'll let the nurse know you'll be here tomorrow to sign the papers."

"*Denki* again."

The doors closed and Rachel shut her eyes as the elevator climbed. "God, show me how to comfort Timothy during this trial. He's hurting, but I can't see through my own pain to know what to do for him."

Chapter Twenty-Six

Rachel stood between her two sisters during Sadie's funeral, which was being held inside Sadie's house. Her family hadn't yet finished grieving the loss of James, and here they were preparing to bury another family member. The suffocating silence tore at her heart.

The Amish didn't memorialize the dead with lavish flowers or long speeches of what the deceased had meant, but Rachel knew people were reflecting silently.

She was.

Sadie had always looked out for Rachel. Sadie made sure Rachel had a ride home from the singings. Sadie never once implied that Rachel's presence on those rides had interfered with her dates with Timothy.

She glanced at Timothy. He clutched Ella in his arms and kept his head low throughout the service.

As was custom, Bishop Lapp finished reading a hymn from the *Ausbund*. After the portion of the service at the house, everyone made their way to the line of buggies.

At James's funeral, after the service in the house, the bishop read a few scriptures at the graveside and the men dug the grave. Later people came back to the house. Sadie's funeral would be the same. The talk would be simple. Then the cows would need to be milked and the animals fed.

Fanny nudged Rachel's side. "Are you going to take one last look?"

Rachel sucked in a deep breath and leaned against her sister as they shuffled toward the coffin. Timothy had moved the long kitchen table into the sitting room to support the casket. Dressed in a simple black dress, white wedding apron, and prayer *kapp*, Sadie looked at peace. Rachel pulled out the wadded hankie she'd tucked up her sleeve and dabbed her eyes. She wanted this day to end. She stepped away from the coffin before she cried outwardly.

Fanny and Iva dropped back with Rachel. *Mamm*, *Daed*, and Timothy remained at the casket. The three sisters leaned on each other for support and walked outside, weeping. A few minutes later, *Mamm* and *Daed* came out of the house and joined them in the yard.

When Timothy finally came out, he stopped next to Rachel. "Will you take Ella?"

Rachel held out her arms. She welcomed the distraction and nuzzled the *boppli's* neck.

"*Denki*," he said hoarsely. He signaled a few of the men who had been waiting outside, and together they headed back inside the house.

Rachel cradled the sleeping child and rocked her gently in her arms. She wanted to block out the vision of Timothy overseeing the sealing of the coffin.

Iva leaned closer to Rachel and pulled back the small quilt to peek at Ella. "She's a beautiful *boppli*, ain't so?"

Rachel nodded, unable to push the lump from her throat to speak. She glanced at the sun directly overhead, then covered Ella's face.

The door opened, and Timothy and the other men carried the casket over to the waiting wagon and eased it onto the bed.

Nathaniel stood at the graveside. His duty was to oversee his charge by fending off the enemy and showering Rachel with peace.

He rustled the oak branches, providing a gentle breeze. With his outstretched wings, he filtered the light that fell on Rachel as she held his newest charge. "Your sister is at rest."

He lifted his face to the sky and soaked in God's love. Empowered by his Master, Nathaniel spoke into the breeze. "To everything there is a season, a time for every purpose under heaven. A time to be born and a time to die . . ."

Rachel pressed the infant tighter against her chest and closed her eyes. *Have mercy on this child. Have mercy, I beg of you, God, have mercy on Timothy. My parents too. They've lost two children, Lord, and they are heavy with sorrow. Give them strength in your Son's name, I ask.* Aemen.

White Sweet Everlasting flowers covered the field and their balsam scent penetrated the breeze. *How ironic.*

Bishop Lapp made the final words brief. He bowed his head, a signal for the men to use their ropes to lower the plain casket into the ground.

The first shovelful of dirt landed on the coffin with a thud. Rachel shuddered.

"Are you okay?" Fanny whispered.

"I guess," Rachel said, but nothing was okay. She focused her attention on the baby sleeping in her arms. The innocent newborn held no worries about tomorrow. Precisely the way God intended his children to rest in him.

Birds chirped and the leaves overhead rustled, but that didn't distract Rachel from hearing every shovelful of dirt thump. Thankfully, there were plenty of men shoveling and they filled the grave within minutes. Outside of a few faint murmurs, there was silence.

Bishop Lapp lifted his hand for the men to stop. They eased the shovels onto the back of the wagon, but they still clanged. Another shudder crept up Rachel's spine.

As the others moved toward the buggies, Rachel kept watch on Timothy standing alone at the grave. He removed his hat. His head down, she could see his lips moving, but his eyes were open. Praying or saying good-bye to Sadie, she couldn't tell.

Her family walked together in heavy silence. Rachel fell back a few steps so she could take a moment at her brother's grave. Katie Bender stood there, alone, head bowed and shoulders shaking. Rachel's vision blurred. She kept walking.

Daed climbed into the buggy. "Timothy said *nett* to wait for him. He doesn't think he can eat anything." *Daed* released the brake and clicked his tongue.

As they drove away, Timothy returned to the grave, his hands clasped together in front of him, his head bowed.

"He will work out his sorrow," *Daed* said, as though reading everyone's thoughts. "His faith will see him through this season."

Rachel wondered if *Daed's* talk was more for *Mamm's* benefit. After he made the statement, he reached for *Mamm's* hand and held it, something Rachel had never seen him do in public.

Back at Timothy's house, the long table had been placed back in the kitchen and was loaded with food the women had prepared. Under any other circumstances the community would welcome a feast.

Rachel doubted if she would partake. Her

stomach rumbled, but the thought of eating wasn't appealing.

Naomi came up beside Rachel and wrapped her arm around Rachel's waist. "I'm sorry about Sadie."

"*Denki.*"

"The *boppli* is beautiful." Naomi's voice cracked.

Rachel tucked the blanket around her niece. "She looks like Sadie, *jah*?"

Naomi wiped her tear-streaked face. "*Jah*, she does."

Iva came over to them. "I'll hold Ella while you get yourself some food."

Rachel held her bundle tightly, reluctant to give her to anyone. "I'm *nett* hungry." She looked around the room. "Is Timothy here? You could make a plate for him."

"*Gut* idea," Iva said and walked away searching the crowd.

Naomi took her elbow and walked her to a place where they could speak more privately. "I heard Jordan left. How are you doing?"

"I'll be fine." Rachel kept her eyes trained on Ella and rocked her arms slowly.

"You don't sound convincing to me."

Tears pooled, blurring Rachel's vision. "Naomi . . ." Her voice squeaked. "I'm going to sneak off and change her diaper." She faked a smile. "I'll be okay. I know for certain, I will." She glanced at the door. "Your parents are saying their good-byes. I'll see you on Sunday. We can talk then."

"That would be good."

Rachel slipped down the hall to the bedroom to change the baby's diaper. She hoped that if she took her time, the guests would leave and the house would be empty.

She lowered the baby into the cradle long enough to light the lamp wick. As she struck a match, a shadow moved and she gasped.

"It's me." Timothy stood from the chair in the far corner and moved closer to the light.

"I'm sorry. I didn't know you were in here. Ella needs a new diaper. I won't be long. Unless you want me to take her—"

"It's okay," he whispered.

Ella fussed but stopped the moment Rachel scooped her into her arms. "She's probably hungry. It's been almost two hours since her last bottle."

"I'll have one warmed." Timothy headed out, and by the time Rachel had finished changing the diaper, he had a warm bottle ready.

Rachel held his daughter out to him. "Do you want to feed her?"

He cleared his throat. "I'll take the next feeding."

She maneuvered the baby to her shoulder and attempted to test the temperature of the formula.

"Maybe you should sit." He put his hands on the back of the chair to steady it for her.

"You think I'm clumsy?"

He smiled slightly. "I'd rather you *nett* take any chances." He helped her into the chair. "I admit, you appear more capable than me." He sat on the edge of the bed. "How hot is the formula supposed to be?"

"Warm is all." She gestured for his arm. "Let's see your wrist." She sprinkled a few drops over his outstretched arm. Meanwhile, Ella rebelled. "Warm, *jah*?"

"*Jah.*" His jaw twitched as he watched the wailing infant. "We've made her mad."

"She's just telling us what she wants. It's her only way." Rachel brought the baby into the crook of her arm and gave her searching mouth the warm milk. "And what about you," Rachel asked Timothy, "did you eat?"

"I will later, after everyone's gone."

"You need your strength."

He mumbled something under his breath and looked at the ceiling.

A few minutes of silence passed before Rachel asked, "Would you please bring me a burp cloth?"

He took a folded cloth from the stack on the dresser. "I was wondering," he said, bringing the cloth to her. He sat on the bed. "I need help with the *boppli*. *Mei mamm's* planning to stay during the *nacht*, but I'll need someone during the day."

Rachel smiled. "I'll *kumm* tomorrow."

"Denki." Timothy blew out a breath and rose from the bed. "She needs a woman's nurturing." He crossed the room and slipped out the door.

A father's care too . . .

Rachel arrived at Timothy's house shortly after sunrise. "How did Ella do last *nacht*?" she asked Anna.

"Gut, but you have that little one spoiled already." Anna closed the door after Rachel entered. "I had to coax her to take a bottle from me."

"She ate though, right?"

"Ach, jah. Once she got used to *mei* voice." She lifted her hand to cover a yawn. "Those feedings every two hours wore me out."

Rachel followed Anna into the kitchen. She couldn't wait to hold the baby. "Is Ella sleeping?"

"Jah, but she should wake soon."

"And Timothy? Is he resting too?" Rachel picked up the kettle, checked the water level, then set it on the stove.

"He said he couldn't sit idle so he went out to his shop." She sighed. "I'm worried. He wouldn't eat breakfast."

"I'll see that he gets a warm lunch." Rachel motioned to the kettle. "Would you like a cup of *kaffi*?"

"Nay, I still have to make breakfast for *mei* husband," she said. "Tell Timothy I'll be back tonight."

Rachel waited for Anna to leave before she tiptoed to the bedroom to check on Ella. The baby fussed. "Shh, it's okay." She gathered the baby in her arms and checked the diaper. Wet.

She softly hummed a High German tune as she changed Ella and the baby stopped fussing. Afterward, she cocooned the infant in the soft blanket and carried her out to the kitchen to prepare a bottle.

Within a short time, Rachel had the baby fed, burped, and back to sleep in the crib. It was too early to make lunch, so she needed something to keep her busy. The floors needed scrubbing after all the foot traffic through the house for the funeral. She found the rag mop and pail on the back porch and looked under the sink for cleaning detergents.

Before adding the soap, Jordan's formula came to mind. She put the detergent back, found the jug of vinegar and the container of vegetable oil, and measured out equal parts. The combination of Jordan leaving and losing her sister left an unmendable void.

As she moved the mop back and forth over the floor in slow rhythm, her emotions seemed to move with it. Guilt to loneliness to resentment to grief—astounding grief. And when the wood grains shined from Jordan's concoction, an anger she couldn't identify or understand burned through her veins.

She heard the door open, and Timothy had walked halfway across the sitting room before she had a chance to tell him the floor was wet. He stopped, looked behind him at the tracks from the door, and mumbled, "Sorry."

Rachel sniffled, wiping her face with her dress sleeve. "It's all right." She rested the mop handle against the wall and tiptoed over the wet floor to the kitchen. "I'm sorry. I haven't started cooking yet."

"Don't trouble yourself. I'm heading into town for material." He took a thin notebook from the kitchen drawer and did his best to follow the same muddy boot prints, apologizing as he did. He took his hat from the hook. "I shouldn't be long."

Rachel resumed mopping, going back over the floor that had the footprints. When she finished the floors, she dusted the windowsills and filled all the lamps with kerosene. She kept busy with things that didn't alleviate the sorrow that threatened to consume her.

She stepped down into the cellar's cool dampness to find something to prepare for their meal. She inventoried the covered dishes left over from the funeral supper. She looked at each one, not truly seeing them. Her chest tightened as reality poured in. Sadie was gone. The kindness of others surrounded her in the form of casseroles. Rachel collapsed to her knees, put her face in her hands, and sobbed.

When the tears began to subside, she eased herself up. Brushing off her knees, she stood, determined to move forward. Yet even the simple task of choosing between the three-bean casserole and the macaroni and cheese overwhelmed her.

Nathaniel knelt beside Rachel. "He gives power to the weak, and to those who have no might He increases strength." He hoped his prompting would bring to remembrance the scripture she had quoted in the hospital. "Your strength shall be renewed through the Lord."

Rachel rubbed her eyes. "I am weak, Lord. I ask for your strength." Even as she spoke the words, her voice fractured and she couldn't hold back the tears again. She drew in a hitched breath and concentrated. The meal needed to be prepared. Ella would wake and be hungry again soon. Rachel had plenty of chores to keep her mind and hands occupied.

"*Jah*, just keep busy," she said aloud. She chose the three-bean casserole and a jar of pickles, then climbed the wooden stairs to the kitchen. She set the containers on the counter and looked out the window. Timothy's buggy was parked by his shop.

Rachel set the table. An hour passed and Timothy still hadn't come inside to eat. With Ella asleep in her crib, Rachel decided to walk out to the shop.

When she entered, Timothy pivoted away from her, but not before Rachel caught sight of his wet face.

"Lunch is ready," she said softly.

"I'm *nett* hungry."

"There's a lot of food left over from—"

"I said I'm *nett* hungry!"

She flinched at his harsh tone and backed out. She would give him the space he obviously needed.

She considered sending someone for the bishop. He could help Timothy through this time.

Rachel kept a plate warm, but Timothy never left his shop. Throughout the afternoon and while she drove home that night, she prayed, cried, and prayed some more. By the time she reached her house and tended to Ginger, she was exhausted.

Mamm, her two sisters, and Katie Bender sat at the kitchen table, each working on separate quilt blocks. *Mamm* pushed her sewing aside and stood when Rachel entered the room. "Have you eaten?"

"*Jah.*"

"How're Timothy and the *boppli*?" Fanny asked, her eyes red and a bit puffy.

Rachel wondered how much she should say. "Ella slept most of the day and Timothy closed himself off in his workshop." *And I fell apart on the cellar floor.*

"Poor Timothy." Katie's needle went through the fabric in careful, even stitches—without the long pauses Rachel always had. "It's going to be difficult bringing up the *boppli* alone."

"Rachel is there. She's doing a good job of helping him." *Mamm* touched Rachel's cheek with tenderness. "The water in the kettle is hot if you want tea."

"*Denki, Mamm.*" Rachel opened the cupboard and removed a cup. She poured steaming water over the tea bag and took her cup to the table. Taking a seat beside Fanny, she asked, "How long can you stay?" She hoped for her mother's sake that it would be another week or two.

"Our bus leaves the day after next." Fanny put another stitch into her quilt block before she looked up. "I wish we could stay longer, but with this being our first winter in Dalton, we have so much canning to do before it turns cold." Fanny's words sounded light, but her face held a deep sadness. The sisters battled Sadie's death differently. One tried to live a normal life, the other was barely able to take one step in front of the other.

"Maybe we can afford to make a trip back in a couple of years," Iva said, her voice laced with longing.

"That would be *wundebaar.*" Rachel tried to sound positive. She dunked her tea bag a few times, then placed it on the saucer. She would rather her tea be weak than steeped too long and keep her from sleeping. "What's it like in your new settlement?" Something felt wrong about speaking of such mundane things when a beloved person was missing from the table.

Daed joined them, the *Budget* newspaper wadded in his hand. "Another buggy accident in Lancaster." He shook his head. "Those tourists are *nett* mindful of the road. They're in too big of a hurry or they're trying to take pictures while they drive. Either way they aren't paying attention."

Fanny picked up her cup and set it in the sink. "Remember how bad the traffic was after news spread that Judith Lapp saw an angel? I thought those people would never leave."

Katie paused mid-stitch. She kept her focus on the thread, but Rachel knew what she was thinking. She, too, had played a part in the community being overrun with outsiders.

Iva sipped her tea. "Katie, did you hear? Fanny plans to write for our Dalton settlement."

Katie smiled. "I'm sure you'll enjoy it."

"The bishop gave his permission. We want more Amish folks to settle. As it is, we only have twelve families."

"Once word gets out in the *Budget*, your community will grow." Even in his grief, Rachel realized, her *daed* was so encouraging. "We started out a few families and *nau* we've grown to five church districts. Next month we'll be building another *schul haus*."

Iva tapped Rachel's arm. "Wouldn't it be *wundebaar* if you got the teacher position?"

"I've been considering it."

"*Ach*, maybe she found a *bu* since we moved," Fanny said.

"*Nay*," Rachel said softly.

Daed stood. "That reminds me." He went over to the desk against the far wall and opened the drawer where *Mamm* kept the stamps. "This picture card *kumm* for you today."

Rachel stared at the postcard. "For me?" She scanned the snowcapped mountain scene on the front before turning it over. Her breath caught when she read Jordan's words.

I miss you!

Chapter Twenty-Seven

"Am I *nett* your closest friend?" Naomi had her hands on her hips.

"Of course you are." Rachel glanced around to see what church member was within earshot. Thankfully, no one. "Why do you ask?"

"You've gotten postcards from Jordan and never told me?" She stood with her arms crossed. Her fingers tapped her upper arms in agitation.

Rachel's face heated. "Who told you he sent a postcard?"

"Katie. She said you about tripped over the kitchen chair and then ran up to your room after you read it."

Rachel glanced at the women putting food on the table and lowered her voice, relieved she could tell her friend. "He only sent me one." She tried to hide her disappointment. "That was two weeks ago."

"Well?" Naomi grinned and elbowed her. "What did he say?"

"He said he missed me." Rachel smoothed her apron, hoping Naomi wouldn't see she missed him too. "We should help serve the meal." Revealing the secret to her friend was one thing. But she didn't want to admit that she'd checked the mail every day for another card or letter—but none came.

On their way to the house, Naomi asked, "Why haven't you gone to the last two sewing frolics?"

"I've been busy with Ella." She searched the crowd for the baby. Everyone wanted to love on her. "Today was the first day we've been able to bring her to church. She wasn't supposed to be around large crowds for a while." She craned her head, still searching for Ella.

"We?" Naomi's brow arched.

"Timothy and me." Rachel located Anna cradling Ella. "She is a joy to take care of."

"Surely Timothy doesn't need you to watch her every day. You're missing your youth."

"What am I missing? A few singings? I don't want to go, Naomi. My heart still aches for Sadie.

Sometimes I can barely breathe. Being with Ella helps me move forward."

"So are you just going to take care of Ella?"

"I'm thinking about asking for the teaching job when the new *schul* is built."

"*Ach*, only unmarried *maydel*s have that job."

"What do you think I am, Naomi?"

"It's only temporary."

"It isn't like someone is interested in marrying me."

Naomi gave her a wry smile. "Jordan sent you a postcard."

"One. He's probably forgotten me by *nau*. Besides, he's not Amish and never wants to be."

Ella's fussing carried over to Rachel. Anna passed the baby to *Mamm*, but Ella continued to cry.

"I should see if they need help," she said and gave her friend a hug. "I'll speak with you later, *jah*?"

"*Jah*."

"What's wrong with Ella?" she asked her mother.

"Colic." *Mamm* shuffled the baby to her other arm. "Many babies get it."

Rachel gently stroked Ella's cheek. "You're *bauch shmartzlich*, little one?"

The crying stopped.

Mamm looked amused. "She sure recognizes your voice." *Mamm* passed the baby to Rachel.

"Let's go inside. You can rock her while I heat a bottle."

Rachel found a quiet spot to rock Ella. She sat, cradling the little precious one, and hummed a hymn.

Mamm brought the bottle and handed it to Rachel. "Sadie would be happy with how much you've helped Timothy. I think you're doing a *wundebaar* job too."

"I'm *nett* sure I'm doing the right thing," she said, slipping the nipple into Ella's mouth. "Timothy hasn't bonded with his daughter. I've only seen him hold her twice."

"*Jah*, Anna is concerned about that too. She's concerned she won't be able to continue with the overnight help much longer. Her health is poor."

Rachel held the baby to her shoulder and rocked from side to side. "I'll do what I can, but he has to take an interest in her. She's his daughter."

"Chicken and dumplings is today's special," the waitress said as she pointed to the chalkboard menu.

Jordan glanced at the board. He hadn't eaten chicken and dumplings since he'd choked on Rachel's concoction.

"I know what I want," Clint said, closing his menu. "I'll take the special."

She jotted the order on her notepad and looked

over her wire reading glasses at Jordan. "And you?"

Jordan closed the menu. "Cheeseburger and fries."

"After a month aren't you sick of cheeseburgers yet?" Clint teased.

He was, but getting a good home-cooked meal in a diner wasn't likely. A decent meal would remind him of the settlement's church meals, and he'd fought those memories since leaving Michigan.

The waitress brought the food to the table. His father's chicken and dumplings lacked the floating chunks of flour like Rachel's. Jordan smiled. As bad as her cooking was, he missed it. He missed her.

"We'll reach Phoenix tonight." Clint peppered his dumplings.

"Then where?" He'd kept his eye on the map, hoping they would reach the Grand Canyon during daylight. His father followed a tight schedule, understandably so after he explained the docked pay for late deliveries.

"We have time if you want to see the Grand Canyon."

Jordan dipped his French fry in ketchup. "That would be great, but are you sure you have time?"

"As long as we're in Vegas by Saturday." He lifted his coffee cup to his mouth. "This has been a long run. After I get my refrigerated trailer back from the shop, we won't be zigzagging the states anymore."

Since leaving Michigan, they hadn't stopped other than at the required weigh stations or to eat and refuel. "It's all right. If I'm going to be a truck driver, I'll need to handle long hours on the road." The words were true, but his heart lacked his former enthusiasm.

"It won't take long to get your Class A."

"It doesn't seem like it will be too difficult." He and Clint had talked extensively about the requirements needed to get his license.

Clint jerked his thumb over his shoulder toward the rack of postcards. "I saw you studying those cards. Did you pick some out?"

"Yeah." He had looked at each one before selecting the postcard of furry white kittens peeking out from underneath a wicker basket. It was far too feminine for him, but he thought Rachel would like the kittens. A small smile came with a silly thought: at least they didn't make him sneeze.

He needed to buy stamps so he could mail this card and the others he'd bought for Rachel, but he hadn't wanted to ask his father to make a special stop at a post office.

"You got a girl back in—" He glanced up when a man stopped in front of their booth. Clint extended his hand. "How's it going, Jack?"

The burly man grasped Clint's hand and shook

it. "I wanted to thank you again for finishing my route last month."

Clint smiled. "Glad to do it. How's your daughter?"

The man shifted his weight and looked at the black-and-white checkered floor. "They thought the remission would last longer." He looked out the window. "It doesn't look promising."

Clint's smile faded. "I'm sorry. Do you need me to take another load?"

"No. Thanks though. I've stopped taking the long hauls so I'll be closer to home."

Jordan listened with sadness and disbelief. This man obviously cared about his family, so much so that he rearranged his route to be able to be near them. Why hadn't Jordan's father cared enough about his mother and him to do the same?

"I'll catch you later," the man said.

Clint gave him a thumbs-up. "Poor guy," he said as the man headed toward a table in the back. "His daughter has leukemia."

Jordan studied his father's reaction, inwardly skeptical of Clint's sincerity. Jordan wasn't proud that his veins burned with resentment. He should be proud that Clint was thoughtful of the man needing time with his daughter.

"Must be hard," Jordan said.

"I can't imagine. The road's already lonely, but he must've really felt isolated so far away." Clint added another packet of sugar to his coffee and stirred. "It's hard when you're taking the long hauls to pay hospital bills. Most truckers on those routes do it because they can handle the isolation and they don't want the same mundane route every day."

Jordan cut his eye contact and looked into his empty coffee cup. *At least some of them go home when their family needs them.*

Chapter Twenty-Eight

"*Denki.* Lunch was *gut.*" Timothy pushed away from the table.

Rachel stood and collected the dishes. "I need to leave early today."

"Why?"

Rachel set the plates in the sink. "I'm meeting with Bishop Lapp about the teacher's position."

"Why today? The *schul* isn't even built."

Rachel swept her hand over the front of her dress. "You'll be fine, Timothy."

"*Nay*, I won't be. What do I know about a *boppli*?" He rubbed the back of his neck. "You can't leave me alone with her. I won't know what to do!"

"Lower your voice or you'll wake your daughter."

"Rachel." He stepped closer and placed his

hand on her shoulder. "I'll pay you to take care of Ella. You don't need the teaching job."

Rachel frowned. She would watch her niece without pay. It wasn't about money. She merely wanted Timothy to bond with his daughter.

Timothy looked hopeful. "So you'll stay?"

Rachel cringed. "*Denki*, but I . . . I still want to talk with the bishop." Rachel touched his shoulder. "You'll do fine. I promise you will."

His shoulder tensed when Ella started to cry.

"Go get her," she said, giving him a nudge. "I'll heat a bottle." Disregarding his long sigh, she reached for a pot and filled it with water.

Ella's crying continued, but Timothy hadn't moved.

Rachel set the pot on the stove to heat. "Ella's *nett* going to stop fussing until she's fed." Without facing Timothy, she measured the powdered formula, added the water, and shook the mixture.

Timothy walked out of the room.

Before the formula cooled, Ella stopped crying. Rachel smiled. It wouldn't be long before he bonded. She tested the warmth of the milk on her wrist, then headed into the sitting room.

Timothy bounced Ella in his arms while he paced the room. When he looked at Rachel, the deep lines across his forehead relaxed. "Here," he said, extending Ella toward her.

Rachel patted the rocker. "Have a seat. I'll stay with you in case you have questions."

Ella's arms flailed as she fussed.

Timothy reluctantly sat and Rachel handed him the bottle. "Loosen up. You don't have to sit so rigid."

"That's easy to say." He shifted a little, causing Ella to cry harder. The poor child sensed his anxiousness.

"I'll be back. I'm going to get a burp cloth." She scampered to the bedroom and collected the cloth. When she returned, she paused at the sitting room entrance to watch him feed his daughter. He looked stiff and unnatural.

"She needs to hear your voice," Rachel said, entering the room. She unfolded the cloth and placed it on his shoulder. "Talk to her."

He looked baffled. "I don't know what to say."

"Sometimes I tell her how much she looks . . . like Sadie." Her throat tightened.

Timothy closed his eyes.

Rachel swallowed hard; it didn't change her throat's rawness. "How much has she eaten?"

"About an ounce." He pulled the bottle away from the baby and held it up. Ella's face crinkled. She cried and Timothy jostled her in his arms. But his jerkiness caused her to cry harder. "Maybe you should take her *nau*," he said.

"Burp her and then she can finish drinking," Rachel said.

Although clumsy, he managed to position her on

his shoulder. After several pats, she burped.

"There, you did it." Rachel walked to the door and slipped on her shoes. "She'll need to eat again in two to three hours."

"What? You're *nett kumming* back after you talk with Bishop Lapp?"

Rachel smiled. "You don't need me, Timothy. You can do it."

"What about tomorrow?"

"*Jah,* I'll be here." She slipped out the door.

Rachel choked back her tears as she harnessed Ginger. Then, as she steered the buggy onto the road, she let loose and cried. Her vision blurred as unrestrained tears streamed down her face. She pulled back on the reins, slowing Ginger to an easy trot. Perhaps she should turn around. Rachel veered the buggy off to the shoulder of the road. Cars whizzed by as she contemplated returning to Timothy's house.

"He is not alone," Nathaniel soothed.

Rachel squeezed her eyes closed. "God, this is hard," she cried.

"God holds them both in his hand."

"I should've spent more time with Sadie. I could've found time to cook and sew with her more. *Nau* I've lost that time." She pulled out a

358

tissue that she'd tucked up her sleeve and blew her nose.

"Only God holds tomorrow. He knows the beginning and the end."

Rachel bowed her head. "Lord, I don't know your thoughts. I don't understand your ways. Help me accept Sadie's death. I haven't done very good at accepting James's. God, you are Timothy's provider. Give him peace and direct him as he cares for Ella today. Give me peace too."

Rachel snapped the reins. The bishop's farm wasn't far. Maybe she would check back on Timothy after she talked with the bishop. She kept Ginger at a steady pace until the bishop's house came into view.

Naomi and William stepped out of the house with Bishop Lapp as Rachel parked her buggy. Naomi waved at Rachel, then left William and the bishop talking on the porch and met Rachel by the buggy.

"Ask me why William and I are speaking with the bishop." She smiled.

Rachel stepped down from the buggy and cocked her head. "The twinkle in your eyes says it's something about marriage, *jah*?"

"*Ach*, you know me too well." Naomi elbowed her.

Thoughts of Jordan seeped into Rachel's mind

without warning. She allowed herself a few secret moments to dream of marriage.

"Have you received more postcards?" Naomi wiggled her brows.

Rachel shook her head. She weaved her arm with Naomi's and shifted the subject back to her friend's upcoming wedding. "I'm happy for you. When is the day?"

"Two weeks from next church Sunday. It's *wundebaar*, ain't so?" She covered her mouth and retained most of her squeal.

"How are you going to keep it a secret until after it's published? You're about to burst *nau*."

"I don't know!" she whispered, excitement filling every part of her.

William strolled toward them, a bashful smile on his face.

Rachel glanced at Bishop Lapp standing on the porch. "He's waiting for me. I've *kumm* to ask about the teaching position."

"We have to visit soon," Naomi said.

"*Jah*, I suppose you'll have a sewing frolic at your *haus*. Let me know when." Rachel made her way to the porch steps. "*Gut* afternoon, Bishop Lapp."

The gray-bearded man stood aside. "Micah's Rachel, let's go inside." He opened the door and waited for her to enter, then pointed to a kitchen chair. "Have a seat."

She pressed her hand over the wrinkle in her

dress. "I'm interested in becoming a teacher for the new *schul*."

Bishop Lapp leaned back in his chair and stroked his beard. "That's a big commitment."

"*Jah*, I understand."

The bishop was a wise man, able to discern beyond what was on the surface of a person's words or facial expression. Rachel squirmed under his kind scrutiny.

"I will consider your request."

Rachel bowed her head a brief moment. "*Denki*."

"Katie Bender is also interested."

"I hadn't heard." It didn't surprise her, though.

"I don't know that she is a better fit, but she is older and has no marriage prospects," he said.

Rachel recalled Katie's despondent expression while standing at James's grave after Sadie's funeral. Katie was lonely. Still, Rachel wasn't holding her breath for marriage either.

"The *schul* won't be built until after harvest-time." He stroked his beard as he did when he pondered the Scriptures. "Perhaps your interest will change between *nau* and then."

"Perhaps, but I don't think so."

"How is Timothy? I understand you've been watching the *boppli*."

"He has *gut* and bad days." Her throat went raw.

"*Jah*, and understandably so. And you?"

"Sometimes it is hard to accept God's will."

•••

Jordan drew a deep breath at the Grand Canyon's north rim lookout point. "The air's so clean up here."

"Yep." Clint inhaled, then blew out his breath. "It's good to fill your lungs with something besides exhaust fumes."

Jordan's eyes rested on the oblong opening in the cliff. "I see why this place is named Angels Window." As he gazed at the canyon's distant shades of purples and blues, peacefulness surrounded him. Only God could create something so magnificent. He glanced at Clint. "You think up here we're closer to God?"

Clint shrugged. "Isn't he everywhere?"

"I suppose. But don't you feel a lot more peaceful here?"

Clint stared at the gorge a few moments. "Yes." He hesitated. "I think it's because we're used to the constant noise around us all the time."

Jordan knew that wasn't it. The peacefulness engulfed him. He'd never experienced such peace.

"Too much of a good thing for me," Clint said. "This change in altitude thins my blood and makes me dizzy." He motioned to the hiking trail. "I'm heading back to the lodge."

Jordan took a few steps to follow him but stopped when Clint held up his hand. "Stay. You don't get to enjoy this view every day." He pointed to the canyon's arch. "On a clear day, you can see the Colorado River through the opening."

Jordan looked over his shoulder at the massive ravine. The shadows shifting over the rock formations drew him back to the observation point.

"Draw near to God, child," Nathaniel whispered. "He's equipped your heart to seek Him." Nathaniel flapped his wings with force and sent a stiff zephyr into the dense clouds. The clouds vanished, exposing the splendid view of the Master's creation.

The postcards he'd seen in the park's visitor center didn't capture the amazing, indescribable vivid richness of the blue river against the red canyon backdrop. "God, are you here?" What Jordan thought he said under his breath echoed. An unexpected shudder rippled along his spine.

"Blessed is the man who trusts in the Lord and whose hope is the Lord." A man with a baritone voice stepped forward.

Jordan's breath caught in his throat. He hadn't heard anyone walk up.

The older man smiled and lifted his eyes to look toward the canyon. "The opening through the arch is one of my favorites."

"The Angels Window"—Jordan lifted a pamphlet— "according to the map."

The man squatted on the sandy soil. "A grand

view indeed." He looked at Jordan. "Have you looked from here?"

Jordan began to move toward the hiking trail. "I should—"

The man's eyes flickered. "Take a moment."

Jordan crouched beside the man. The view looked the same to him. Then he blinked and his perspective changed. Detailed etchings in the basin became visible. He blinked again and the image was gone. A mirage. Jordan rubbed his eyes as he stood.

"Sometimes a different perspective opens your eyes to what's been there all along," the man said.

Jordan crinkled his brows. The man wasn't making sense. He peered at the Angels Window, squinting to see if that would change his perspective.

"I don't know what—" But the man was gone. Jordan combed his fingers through his hair, then hiked toward the trail.

"Seek God with your whole heart. For those who seek, find." Nathaniel continued at Jordan's side. "God is with you. Your spiritual eyes must be opened."

Chapter Twenty-Nine

Jordan looked from one side of the boulevard to the other. He'd never seen so many blinking lights and neon signs.

"This is the city that doesn't sleep." Clint cranked the wheel, turned onto a narrow delivery access road, and stopped at the guardhouse.

"Company name, log, and driver's license," the security officer said.

"C. E. Trucking." Clint handed the man the delivery log and his license, which the security guard compared with something on his computer inside the booth. Clint glanced at Jordan. "The casinos have stiff security policies, but it shouldn't take long."

Jordan watched the man still verifying the information. "Where are we headed next?"

Clint stretched, letting out a pleased groan. "I usually take a few days to relax before picking up the next load."

Jordan liked that idea. It would give him time to find a place to buy stamps and mail the postcards to Rachel.

The security officer returned Clint's information. "Second dock on the left." He pressed the electronic gate release and waved Clint forward.

Jordan took in the large concrete building. "This doesn't look anything like the casinos we passed."

"This is the central distribution center." Clint made a wide turn. "Most trucks are unloaded here and the cargo is inspected. Later they issue the freight through vans from their distribution center." He put the rig in reverse and checked the side mirrors as he backed the fifty-three-foot trailer up to the dock. "Next week my refrigerated trailer will be out of the shop and we'll make nonstop live lobster runs out of Maine."

"Live?"

"Yep. I certainly don't understand it. I've taken frozen lobsters to the cruise ships, but out here, they want them live." He shifted to park and cut the engine. "The pay's better too." Two employees greeted him as he climbed out of the cab.

Jordan stepped out to stretch his legs.

"This is my son, Jordan. He plans to start driving soon." Clint smiled and pushed his shoulders back.

Jordan nodded his greeting because the noise from the forklifts prevented him from participating any further in their conversation.

An hour later, Clint exchanged paperwork with the foreman. He inspected the inside of his empty trailer before closing and latching the door. Inside the cab, he initialed, dated, and timed the log, setting it on the seat. "Ready for some fun?"

"Sure." His stiff body would be grateful to do something other than sit in a cab.

Clint shifted into first gear and rolled away from the dock. "Once we check into the room, I'll show you around the casino." He waved to the guard at the gate as they passed through the checkpoint. "First we'll drop the truck in temporary storage and take a cab to the casino. I'm sure you'll like the comped room at Caesars Palace."

Jordan was confused. "Comped?"

"The room's free," Clint explained.

"Because you deliver stuff?"

Clint laughed. "Because I have a fat paycheck to cash and they don't want to lose me to another casino." He eased into traffic. "I've been making these Vegas runs for years. When I first started, I picked up the next load and was out of town within a few hours. I learned that after several Maine-to-Vegas runs back-to-back, you need a few days to recoup. Besides, it was hard to pass up buffet and show vouchers. It wasn't long before they gave me free rooms."

Jordan didn't fully grasp the trucking business, but he'd grown to appreciate anytime they could sleep in a bed versus the truck's sleeper.

The "city that never sleeps" term made sense to Jordan. How could anyone sleep with the constant stimuli?

Clint pulled into the lot and veered toward the short-term parking section. Several trucks and a few RVs lined the area. He rapped on the door to the sleeper. "Throw some stuff into the duffel bags for us while I get the rig shut down and secured."

Jordan climbed into the sleeping compartment. He hadn't accumulated much clothing to pack. He did have the blue shirt Rachel made for him, but he hadn't even tried it on. Jordan jammed it and a few T-shirts into the duffel bag. He found the other bag and loaded it with Clint's clothes.

"There's a shuttle to the casinos," Clint said, leading the way to the station. "Sometimes I'll take a cab when I don't feel like waiting for the shuttle." He pointed to a barber sign. "I think after I check the rig in, I'll get a haircut. What about you?"

Jordan combed his fingers through his hair. He hadn't had a haircut since Rachel hacked it. "I'll wait in here." He plopped onto a chair in front of a large-screen TV. Unlike the other truck stops, this room had slot machines lining the walls.

On the Weather Channel—standard viewing fare for the truck driver—the weatherman reported on the heat wave sweeping over most of the nation. Michigan would be one of the hottest areas. Jordan's chest felt heavy. He rested his elbows on his knees and buried his head in his hands.

"You lose your run too?"

Jordan looked up as another trucker sat on the seat beside him.

"I've lost two Michigan runs now. They've

had massive crop failures in this heat."

The uneasy feeling in his chest grew. It was likely Micah's late-planted crops would've failed too. *"God will provide,"* Micah had said.

Jordan pressed his palms together and stared at his hands. Then words to a God he'd been ignoring for a long time came through him in a pleading prayer. *God, the Hartzlers need you. Please protect their crops and give them a fine harvest in spite of the drought.*

Jordan had never seen such opulence. As he stepped inside Caesars Palace, it was as though he were stepping onto a street in Rome. A larger-than-life statue of Caesar sat in the midst of a fountain surrounded by other Roman figures. The floor resembled a cobblestone street, and a mural of the sky on the ceiling was so realistic, it seemed that instead of nighttime, they were enjoying a gorgeous afternoon under a blue sky littered with clouds. He tried to keep his mouth closed, but he was sure it must be hanging open judging by Clint's amused laughter as he watched him. "You gawk," Clint said. "I'll be back in a moment."

Jordan felt like he couldn't take it all in. Over at the casino, lights flashed and bells blared as loudly as in the city streets. It was overwhelming

"Come on, Jordan," Clint said, coming up behind him. "We're registered. Now it's time to start the fun."

Jordan followed Clint to the casino lounge and sat on the empty stool next to Clint's at the bar.

"What will it be?" the bartender asked.

"Nothing for me, thanks," Jordan said.

"Jack and Coke."

The bartender set the drink on a napkin, and Clint pulled his billfold from his back pocket and glanced at Jordan. "You sure you don't want a drink?"

"I don't drink." Jordan looked around the casino. It looked as though everyone in the place had a drink in front of them.

"You can get a plain Coke if you like."

"No thanks. I'm good." Jordan wanted no part of this. He saw the people's faces, intent on just one more try for big money, captured by these noisy machines.

Clint took his drink and napkin to a table with a slot machine next to it. He put some money in, pulled the crank, and two 7s flashed on the machine along with a cluster of cherries.

"I think I'll go up to the room."

Clint sipped his drink, then set the glass on a napkin. "You're going up to the room now?" He nudged Jordan. "Stick around and try your luck." He pulled the slot handle and watched the rollers spin. When the machine didn't pay out, he put more money in and cranked the handle. "Addictive game," Clint said, his attention completely focused on the machine in front of him.

Jordan said nothing. The trucker's canceled Michigan run resurfaced, and Jordan thought about the Hartzlers and the other Amish families who depended on a good crop to get through the winter. It felt wrong in the face of such need to put money into the empty belly of a machine.

Clint clutched his drink and motioned for Jordan to follow. He weaved through several rows of slot machines and finally stopped at one back in the corner. "Have a seat." He patted the stool next to his at the slot and Jordan took it. "This one is the old-fashioned kind. Put coins in, get coins out."

Clint fed a bunch of quarters into the machine in front of him and did the same to the machine in front of Jordan. "Pull that lever," he said.

Jordan stared at the machine, his hands lying still in his lap. His mother's warnings about gambling saturated his mind. The noise all around overwhelmed him.

Clint reached over and pulled the lever on Jordan's machine. The spinning wheels stopped and the machine dinged with each coin payout.

"You did it," Clint shouted. "You just won two hundred bucks."

Jordan watched the trough fill with coins. He sat there staring at it, not knowing what to do. He wanted to just leave, but Clint snagged an empty bucket from the top of the machine. "Load your winnings into this," he said, handing it to Jordan, not missing a beat in continuing to play his machine.

Jordan mechanically scooped the coins into the plastic bucket.

"In a few minutes we'll go to the blackjack table and I'll show you how to double your winnings," Clint said, pulling the machine's lever.

"I can do better than double it." Tangus rubbed his hands together. "Watch my craft in action. This is my specialty." Covering Clint's hand, Tangus glowed crimson as Clint pulled the lever.

Coins dumped into the tray to the sound of the machine playing musical notes.

"Oh yeah. This is gonna be a good night." Clint scooped the coins into a plastic cup. "We're going to have a blast."

The unease inside Jordan grew until he felt like a fidgeting child. "Hey, Clint. I'm tired. I think I'll go enjoy taking a shower that isn't in a truck stop."

Clint tipped back his head and laughed. "I completely understand. But you can shower later. Relax and have fun." He glanced around the room. "Trucking would be too hard if you didn't take time to rest and enjoy yourself a little."

"Yeah, Jordan. This is a great part of the road experience." Tangus blew into his cupped hands. This was his turf. In this city, he had his choice of those to embody. Jordan included—if he couldn't entice him with a little coin jingle, then he'd bring out the fireworks. Like father, like son. "Drop a coin. One coin in any machine, and I'll make you rich."

Jordan stared at the bucket of coins, the weight beyond what he would have expected.

"Two hundred bucks. That's nothing," Tangus said, peering over Jordan's shoulder. "You wouldn't be gambling your money. Play what you won. It's free money."

"Can I bring you anything from the bar?" The blond woman leaned close to Clint.

"Sure. I'll have another one of these." He held up his Daniels and Coke.

"Rum or whiskey?"

"Jack Daniels, please."

Jordan cleared his throat. "Can I get the room key?"

Clint dug in his pocket and handed Jordan the plastic key card. "Room 708."

Jordan handed Clint the container of coins. This was certainly a side of Clint he hadn't seen while on the road. Not that he'd had much of a chance. However, now he understood Clint's lingering gaze whenever they passed a casino, usually on the outskirts of some town. He'd thought it was the curiosity of it—probably because that's how Jordan had seen them.

"Good night, son."

"Good night."

Jordan trekked to the bank of elevators. *"A gambler eventually sells his soul . . ."* His mother's words echoed as he waited for the door to open. She'd made it clear how she didn't like Jordan working for a racehorse farm. *At least the job taught your son how to harness a buggy . . .* The elevator dinged and the door slid open. Jordan entered and pressed the seventh-floor button. He looked upward but not at anything in particular. "I know how to harness an Amish buggy now too, Mom."

Jordan exited the elevator and scanned the gold-plated numbers on the doors until he found room 708. The room was impressive compared to the dumpy motels next to the interstate they stayed in on occasion. It had a refrigerator stocked with miniature liquor bottles, and the bathroom was stocked with miniature bottles of shampoo and lotions, razors, and other things. He'd use the shampoo and razors, but he'd leave the other stuff. He wouldn't be caught dead in a shower cap or smelling like Rose Dew. He flipped back the shower curtain and turned on the faucet, eager to step into the multiple jets of hot water.

He lingered in his first truly hot shower with decent water flow in weeks. Sitting endless miles on a truck seat had stiffened his joints. The hot water drained the tension from his tight muscles as steam filled the room.

He would have stayed until the water ran out, but he figured that would either be a very long time, or he would rob another hotel guest of their enjoyment of a hot shower.

Rummaging through the duffel bag for clean clothes, he found the blue, collarless shirt. He pulled it out and admired the hand-sewn stitches. He slipped it on, fastened the eye hooks, and stretched out his arms. The right sleeve measured an inch longer than the left, but to him, the shirt was a perfect fit.

Jordan plopped on the bed, took the remote, and clicked through the TV stations. He found each channel littered with gambling advertisements. He opened the drawer of the lamp table and tossed the remote inside, his mother's warnings against gambling replaying yet again.

He rested his head against the pillow and closed his eyes, thinking his mother must have known about Clint's gambling. That's why she was so insistent on reminding him of the dangers.

"Jordan, the Father is calling," Nathaniel whispered.

Jordan shot off the bed and looked around the room. He wasn't sure what to expect, but the room felt different.

"Search for God while He is near. Call out to Him and He will answer."

The hairs on Jordan's arm stood on end. He looked around the room again, sure that someone had spoken. Finding the room empty didn't calm his racing heart. Perhaps the TV would mask the eeriness. Jordan opened the drawer of the lamp table; instead of getting the TV remote as he planned, his searching fingers found a Bible. He brought it out and opened it. His hands trembled as he flipped through the pages. "Where do I begin? I've rejected your love for so long . . . Why would you care about someone like me?"

"Jordan, all have sinned. Everyone falls short of the glory of God. Read the page you've stopped on," Nathaniel encouraged.

Jordan skimmed the page. ". . . *While we were yet sinners, Christ died for us.*" He continued reading, but he stopped when an odd sensation warmed his core. He reread the scripture, this time aloud. " 'Whoever calls on the name of the Lord shall be saved.' " Jordan dropped to his knees. "I'm calling on you, Lord. I want to be saved. I want you to be Lord of my life."

Nathaniel's pearlescent wings shimmered as he stood beside his charge. "On this day, heaven rejoices. The angels sing, 'Glory to God. Praise to God, the One who is and who is to come.' "

Warm tears trickled down Jordan's face. He couldn't explain the overwhelming peacefulness.

"Dry your tears. Do you want people to think of you as weak?" Tangus materialized from the ceiling air vent. "Those ancient words won't offer comfort."

"Flee!" Nathaniel's reverberating voice struck an octave that pinned Tangus against the wall.

"I don't obey your orders. You know as well as I that some seed shall be plucked before it takes root." Tangus snarled. "I will lure him into dark places where your voice shall not prevail." Surging with boldness, Tangus propelled himself forward. "Even those ancient words tell of some who will accept but be overtaken—devoured."

Nathaniel reached for his baldric and removed the sword from the sheath. "I shall stand guard before Jordan."

Tangus raucously squawked. "Free will—I know what's been written as well as you, Nathaniel. The subject must choose to follow." He crept closer. "The power you speak of must be sought, but the mind is pliable, wicked, and can be tempted."

Nathaniel expanded his chest. "He shall be like Paul and renew his mind daily."

Tangus frowned. Paul's renewed mind inspired other unwavering followers of Jesus Christ. The kingdom of God advanced daily with Paul's teachings—he couldn't be stopped even when imprisoned.

"That's the power I speak of. The power God gives those who abide in Him." Nathaniel spoke to Jordan. "You contain the power in the name of Jesus to demand the accuser to flee. You are equipped with the armor of God—speak to this stronghold and you shall be freed."

"There are other ways to bore into his soul." Tangus vaporized into the vent system.

The room phone rang multiple times before Jordan leaned over and picked up the receiver. "Hello."

On the other end of the line, Clint yelled over background sirens. "Get down here. I hit!"

"Hit what?" Jordan scrambled to his feet.

"Payday. Don't you hear these sirens screaming? Just get down here."

Before Clint's words registered, the phone went dead.

Jordan left the Bible on the bed and hurried out of the room to catch the elevator. Once he entered the casino, he could hear Clint's voice shouting over the wailing siren.

Jordan eased into the gathered crowd. One casino worker disabled the siren on the slot

378

machine while another filled out a claim sheet and handed it to Clint.

A parade of people followed Clint to the collection booth, cheering him on. Less enthused with the commotion, Jordan hung back and waited. Soon Clint emerged from the crowd and waved at Jordan.

"Twenty-five thousand," he called out. Then he held up some tickets. "And vouchers for the buffet and show." He moved in an unsteady gait to Jordan. "You hungry?" His breath was weighted with the smell of alcohol.

Whether or not he was hungry didn't really matter. He was more concerned that eating would help soak up some of the alcohol Clint had imbibed.

"I wish you had been here to see the lights and siren," Clint said, his words slurred together.

"I was." Jordan guided him away from the casino and toward the hotel lobby. "Let's find that buffet."

"I'm not hungry. I'd rather double this money. Come on, I'll teach you how to play craps." He elbowed Jordan hard in the ribs. "It'll make a nice down payment on a second rig. We could be hauling loads cross-country together."

"Let's eat and talk about it later." This fancy place wouldn't be in the business of giving out free rooms and free meal tickets if it didn't expect to win its money back plus more. He hoped Clint sobered before he lost his shirt.

Jordan followed the signs to the buffet, the scent of sautéed garlic and onions guiding him as well. His mouth watered for something besides the greasy diner food he'd eaten for over a month. He sampled a few dishes that resembled Chinese food, then stood in line at the end of the buffet where a chef carved prime rib.

With a thick slab of meat on his plate, Jordan looked around for Clint. Ten o'clock at night and the room was full. Most patrons didn't wear the same wide smile as Clint.

Jordan weaved around the tables and sat across from Clint. He said a quick prayer, then picked up his fork. "How is it?"

"Best food I've had in months," Clint replied. "Now do you see why I drive a truck?" He cracked open the lobster tail and jabbed the meat with a tiny fork. "Wait till you see the entertainment." He winked and butter dribbled out of the corner of his mouth.

Entertainment? Jordan had seen enough billboard advertisements of feathered showgirls; he didn't need to see them perform in front of him. He took a bite of prime rib and closed his eyes. He wanted Clint to believe he was savoring the meat's flavor when truly he lacked strength to stand on his own and was silently asking for God's help.

I need wisdom. I don't want to be persuaded by

Clint. Drinking and gambling—he's not the person I hoped he was. And this isn't the life I want. Show me what to do.

Jordan opened his eyes. He cut the meat and took another bite.

Clint squinted and his head bobbed. "Why did you change into that Amish shirt? I bought you other clothes."

Jordan fingered the hand stitching on the sleeve. "A friend made it for me."

Clint pointed his fork at Jordan. "The girl you keep buying postcards for?"

Jordan paused a moment before deciding to answer. "Her name's Rachel."

Clint set the lobster pliers next to his plate and wedged his fork into the claw. "Don't make the same mistake I did."

Jordan tossed his napkin on the table and stood, rage flowing through his veins.

Clint looked confused. "Where are you going?"

"I've waited this entire trip to have a conversation with you about my mother. But I never dreamed when we did you would call her a mistake." He headed for the door.

"Jordan, wait," Clint called.

Anger drove him forward.

"I loved your mother."

Jordan stopped and pivoted to face Clint. "Why haven't you asked about her?"

Clint closed his eyes.

Jordan wasn't sure if the alcohol had caused his father to feel dizzy and close his eyes, or if he was truly searching for an explanation. "I'm going back to the room."

"Please, wait." Clint reached for Jordan. "I didn't think you wanted to talk about her. I was waiting for you to bring it up." He took a deep, shaky breath. "I know Grace died and I'm sorry."

"How did you find out?"

Clint's bloodshot eyes watered. "Usually she returned my checks with a note." He inhaled. "She always wrote the same thing. 'God provides our needs. Jordan and I are doing fine.' " He blinked back tears, then swept his hand through his hair. "Your landlord in Farmington Hills returned the damage deposit and said you'd moved out."

"Why didn't you come see for yourself if we were fine? We barely had food on the table."

"I'm not the one who returned the checks, Jordan."

"We wanted *you,* not your money." Jordan crossed his arms. "While Mom was dying, everything we had of value was repossessed . . . and you didn't care."

Clint gulped. "If I'd known—"

"You would have known if you'd come by once in a while." Pain and fury infused Jordan's voice. "You ran an extra load for that trucker to go home to his family, but you didn't go home to yours."

"We all live with regrets," Clint said under his breath. "Even your mother. She regretted leaving her family, her way of life." Clint combed his fingers through his hair. "I wanted a family. I wanted my son to know me . . . but not like this." He waved his arm over the table laden with food and drink. "I never wanted you to see me drunk or gambling."

Jordan's throat tightened.

"I'm sorry if I insinuated your mother or you were a mistake." He put his head in his hands. "I regret not being the husband and father I should've been. I regret those years I missed with you."

"You could have come back. You could have made a little effort."

"Regrets pile up until you feel it's too late to go back and fix the things you broke." He shrugged. "I guess I thought I had been too stupid too many times. I am . . . I've always been . . . ashamed." He looked Jordan straight in the eyes, a profound sadness in them. "I don't know if you can, and I wouldn't blame you if you couldn't. But . . . could you . . ." His voice trembled. "Would you consider forgiving me?"

Jordan never expected to hear those words from his father. He didn't know what to do with them. He turned them over, like they did the ground before planting, the fresh soil ready to take something and make it grow. "Yes. I forgive you."

Clint dropped his head into his open palms and cried.

Jordan waited, letting the feeling of newness flow through him. Forgiving his father released the heaviness of bitterness and resentment that he had clung to for far too long. His spirit felt lighter.

Clint took a handkerchief from his pocket and wiped his face, then blew his nose. He pulled some bills from his wallet and handed them to Jordan.

"What's this for?"

"You might need some money."

Jordan looked down at the money, fanning the bills, stunned by the amount. He tried to formulate his thoughts as he stared at the hundred-dollar bills in his hand. "I'm not going to the casino. I'm going back to the room. I don't need—" He looked up. Clint was gone, easily disappearing in the crowd.

Jordan folded the bills and stuffed them into his pocket. Thinking Clint had ducked into the men's room, Jordan entered the first one he could find. "Clint?"

No answer.

Jordan turned and nearly trampled an elderly man. "I'm sorry." He hadn't heard him come in.

"Do you know where you're headed, son?"

"I apologize. I wasn't looking where I was going."

The man's eyes flickered. The wrinkles around

the corners of his mouth deepened as his smile widened.

Caught up in the man's unique eyes, Jordan barely noticed the man had thrust a pamphlet into his hand.

"Don't lose your way home, son," he said.

Jordan glanced at the cover of the leaflet. *Roman's Road.* When he looked up to thank the man, he was gone. Jordan left the men's room and looked both ways down the hallway but didn't see the man. He passed pillars and statues of Roman gods on his way to the elevator. After pushing the seventh-floor button, he started reading. *"The wages of sin is death . . ."*

Chapter Thirty

Rachel leaned over the kitchen sink to peer out the window at Timothy's shop. If she'd known the bishop planned a visit, she would've waited to prepare supper. The two of them hadn't come out of the workshop in over an hour. She suspected Timothy was asking for guidance to deal with his grief. Bishop Lapp had spent time visiting with *Mamm* and *Daed* a few nights ago. Initially Rachel thought his visit had something to do with the teacher's position. He wouldn't offer her the position if it placed a hardship on the family.

She moved away from the window, found a fork, and opened the oven to probe the corned beef. The meat had cooked too long. The mushy cabbage resembled sludge. Rachel hauled the roasting pan out of the stove and plunked it on top of a cooling rack. She had better make some biscuits; it might be the only food they ate. At least Timothy would have the option of eating a peanut butter sandwich.

Using a memorized recipe, she quickly gathered the ingredients and prepared the dough. She floured the table and rolled out a layer of dough.

"Rachel," Timothy said.

She jumped and pressed her hand against her chest. Flour dust fell like snow.

"I'm sorry."

"I didn't hear you." She swept her dress, but her floured hands created more of a powdery mess on the forest green fabric.

"This is a bad time." Timothy turned around, his shoulders sagging and his footsteps shuffling.

"What's wrong?" she asked.

He stopped. His shoulders lifted with a deep breath, then fell. His face paled and he broke eye contact with her to clear his throat.

Rachel rubbed her hands on her apron and opened the cupboard. "Let me get you a glass of water. You don't look *gut*."

"Will you marry me?"

Her breath caught in her chest. The glass slipped

through her grasp, hit the counter, and shattered on the floor. For a frozen instant, she stared at the shards of glass.

"I know this is . . . unexpected. Probably too soon."

"I'll get the broom." She backed away from the mess, grabbed the straw broom from the corner of the kitchen, and quickly swept the glass pieces into a pile. Extending the broom under the table and dragging it over the floor, she swept the slivered pieces that had strayed. Timothy hadn't moved.

His hand clasped the broom handle.

"You're standing in the glass," she said.

He was close enough that she felt his warm breath on her cheek. He slid his hand down the broom handle, grazing hers. "I know it's abrupt to marry again so soon after—"

"Why?"

"Ella needs a mother," he said, his voice as stiff as an iron rod. Timothy dropped his hand from hers and backed up a few steps. After Rachel didn't—couldn't—answer, he scratched his bearded jaw. "I don't know of another solution."

Solution? She inhaled so sharply her lungs hurt. *He thinks marriage is a solution?*

"Ella responds to you. And—"

"Timothy," she said harshly. His mouth opened and she interrupted him by raising her hand. "It hasn't even been two months since Sadie passed on," she blurted.

"I know, Rachel. I count the days. The hours." His voice broke and he stopped to clear his throat. "I constantly relive the sight of her prayer *kapp* dangling from the surgeon's hand."

Rachel's eyes brimmed with tears. "It is hard. I think of her nearly every moment of every day too."

Timothy's eyes closed. After a moment, he opened them and said, "Rachel, I will always love Sadie. But in time . . ." He cupped his hand on her shoulder. "I know Jordan broke your heart."

She lowered her head. Shards of glass she'd missed sparkled in the afternoon sun beaming through the window.

"Here you are marrying age with *nay bu*. You don't attend the singings." He tipped her chin upward and gazed into her eyes. "Instead of being two lonely people, we can learn to love each other."

"I don't—"

"Before you say anything, look at Matthew and Leah Stolzfus. They are getting along *gut*."

"*Jah*, but after their spouses died, neither one could run a household alone with so many offspring. Combined they had sixteen children."

"They're now having one of their own. Matthew's Leah told *mei* Sadie *nett* long ago."

"*Jah*, I heard."

"Rachel, I will take care of you. You won't be alone and Ella will have a mother."

This was too much to think about.

"We've been friends these years, ain't so?"

Rachel nodded.

"And I believe you respect me."

Rachel nodded again. All those times she'd told God she wanted a husband like Timothy came back to her. All the ways he loved her sister. His kindness. His integrity.

"Bishop Lapp gave his permission. I had a *gut* talk with him."

She recalled Naomi's excitement after she and William met together with the bishop. She couldn't visualize the same excitement for herself. As much as she loved Timothy and respected him . . . But he was right. A number of couples in the community began out of practicality, not out of love.

Rachel cleared her throat. "Did the bishop mention the *schul*?"

"That job is for a *maydel*, *nett* a *fraa*."

This was so unexpected. She didn't know how to sort her thoughts. "I need to pray about such important matters . . . and talk with *Mamm* and *Daed*." She had promised Sadie she would help with the baby, never thinking it might include becoming Ella's mother.

"Okay. How long? I'd like to tell Bishop Lapp."

Why was he rushing this lifelong commitment? "This is all so sudden."

"We've known each other forever." He released

a long sigh. "Besides, Sadie had mentioned multiple times how she wished you could find a husband. I know she would've approved of you raising Ella."

"I need to sweep again before your *mamm* arrives." Rachel grabbed the broom leaning against the counter and swept under the table.

She ran it through her head again. Timothy certainly was a fine man. Someone she greatly admired. A *gut* husband to Sadie. Someone she always upheld as the kind of husband she would want. Still, the idea seemed drastic, too soon after Sadie's passing. Besides, could she marry someone she didn't love? Who didn't love her?

Timothy cleared his throat. "So you will consider the proposal?"

"You were right about Jordan. *Mei* heart is still mending. And there's bound to be talk."

"Let the *blabbermauls* say what they wish. We have the bishop's blessing."

"This is . . . unexpected." She stopped, unable to say more.

"We can make this work. Do you believe that?"

"We could." The question was, did they want to? She squatted next to the pile, dustpan in hand, and gathered the glass particles.

The door opened and Timothy's mother entered the kitchen. She glanced at her son, then at Rachel. "Everything okay?"

"*Jah*," Rachel said. "I dropped a glass, is all."

She emptied the contents into the trash can. "Ella should wake up sometime in the next hour. I made corned beef." She glanced at the pan. "It will need reheating." She took a few steps to the door before she spun to face them. "Maybe you shouldn't eat the meat. Some glass might have dropped in it." She crinkled her nose. "I'm sorry."

"I'll put something together," Anna said.

Timothy looked at her pointedly. Was he asking her permission to share the proposal news with his *mamm*? She wouldn't give that permission. There was no need to involve anyone. She had to pray first.

Rachel grasped the door handle to her house and paused to inhale deeply. On the ride home she had rehearsed what she would say to her parents about Timothy's proposal. Now, standing on the porch, she felt foolish. If she were in love, the words would spill easily. Instead a dread cloaked her. Timothy might not care what people thought, but she would. Certainly her parents would also have concerns.

She went inside, feeling jittery and uncertain. *Mamm*, *Aenti* Esther, and *Aenti* Leah chatted in the sitting room as they pinned quilt layers together.

Rachel peered over *Mamm's* shoulder. "Log cabin, *jah*?"

Mamm looked up and smiled. "*Jah*, want to help?"

Rachel glanced at her *aentis*. "In a little while." She scanned the room. "Where's *Daed*?"

Concern swept her mother's face. "Is something wrong?"

Jah, but she couldn't discuss it in front of her *aentis*.

"I need to talk to him. Do you think he's in the barn?" She bolted before they trapped her with questions she did not want to answer. If her *aentis* hadn't been visiting, she would have preferred talking with *Mamm*. Although Timothy's proposal had an odd-sounding business tone about it, and *Daed* had a *gut* business head.

Rachel jogged to the barn and yanked the door open. "*Daed*?"

"Over here at the calf pen."

With his foot propped up on the lower board and his forearms leaning on the top board of the pen, he looked deep in thought.

"Any problems?" She glanced over the rail. The calf had grown into her knobby knees.

"*Nay*, just finished mucking the pen. It's always a good thing to spend time with a calf."

"The stubborn girl is growing." Rachel sighed. "I've been too busy and haven't seen much of her lately."

He turned to face Rachel. "I heard you did a fine job delivering her."

"Jordan told you that?"

"His boastfulness of your ability was—"

"*Nett* Amish."

"I was going to say honorable." He patted her shoulder. "There aren't many men who'd risk looking incompetent to praise a woman."

"Jordan's *nett* incompetent."

Daed tipped his head back and guffawed. "*Ach*, I don't believe he is."

"Then what's so funny?" Not that she wanted to squelch his laughter. Since Sadie's death, he'd kept to himself in the barn.

"I find it interesting you're defending him. I recall a young *maydel* criticizing his milking and plowing ability."

She gazed at the calf. "*Jah*, when he first arrived, I was angry."

As *Daed's* face sobered, she braced herself for him to list the scriptures that referenced anger, but he kept silent.

"I apologized to Jordan for my actions. I was jealous he would take the place of James and me in your heart."

Daed sighed and slowly shook his head.

"You kept calling him *sohn*." She clamped her bottom lip.

Daed put his arm around her shoulder. "Jordan was a lost lamb, looking for where he belonged." He squeezed her shoulder. "I wasn't replacing James." He pulled back. "Or you."

"But you kept dismissing me from *mei* chores."

He wrapped her in his arms and rested his chin

on her head. "I liked you working with me in the barn. You're a hard worker. But I didn't want you to miss out . . . on finding a husband."

Finding a husband. She drew in a ragged breath. "I want to talk to you about that."

He pulled her back to arm's length and cocked his head. "Have you been in contact with Jordan? You're *nett* jumping the fence to run off with him, are you?"

"*Nay.*" She frowned.

He blew out a breath. "He promised *nett* to take you away."

Rachel looked down and focused on a piece of straw. "You talked with him about that?"

"*Jah.*" He lifted her chin. "I wanted him to stay, but if he didn't choose our way, I didn't want him taking you away from us. God has a plan for your life here among us. He has a husband for you."

Rachel squeezed her eyes shut. She took a deep breath. "Timothy asked me to marry him," she blurted.

Daed shifted his stance and leaned against the calf pen railing. "What did you tell him?"

"That I would pray about it and talk with you and *Mamm.*"

He stroked his beard. "Are you asking *mei* permission?"

"I don't know what I'm asking, *Daed.* I'm confused."

"Did you pray about it?" His facial expression remained stonelike, yet warmth filled his eyes.

"*Nett* yet." Unable to look at him, she focused on the calf. "Do you think it's wrong if I marry Sadie's husband?" She dragged her sleeve across her face to wipe the tears that had fallen. Without giving him time to answer, she blurted, "Timothy doesn't love me, but Ella needs a mother." Her breath hitched. "Sadie—hasn't been—gone— *Ach*, *Daed*, you want me to marry, ain't so? And Timothy is a *gut* man."

Daed wrapped his arms around her again and patted her back. "You'll know the answer after you pray about it."

"It's hard to pray when my mind is so busy."

"It is. But that is when it is most important to listen." He released her. "I approved of Timothy marrying Sadie; I would give *mei* blessing for you—if that's who God directs you to marry." He chucked her under the chin and looked into her eyes. "Don't make a decision without waiting for the Lord's reply."

Rachel knelt on the floor, resting her forehead against the bed. She closed her eyes and waited to calm her mind and shape her thoughts.

"God, I don't know where to begin. Ella needs a mother." She paused. "I know nothing surprises you, but Timothy's proposal sure took me by surprise."

Nathaniel eased down beside Rachel. "Talk to God about what troubles your heart. He's listening to your prayers."

"I cannot believe he wants to marry so soon after you took Sadie home. I guess I understand why. It would be so difficult for a man to raise a little girl alone." Rachel's heart raced and she opened her eyes, gasping for breath. "I've always admired Timothy . . . I love Ella like she is *mei own* . . . I guess this would make sense."

"Don't stop praying. Press through, child," Nathaniel prompted.
"Don't bother," Tangus said. "You're not going to get an answer."

She waited for an answer, but none came. "*Aemen.*"

Chapter Thirty-One

Rachel studied Timothy's expression as he sipped the sauerkraut soup she'd prepared. He washed it down with a quick gulp of milk.
"You don't like it?"
"I guess I'm *nett* hungry." He pushed the bowl aside.
"And your sandwich, you don't want that

either?" Rachel recalled Sadie saying that a cold meatloaf sandwich and sauerkraut soup was one of his favorite meals.

"I guess not."

"I know it isn't like Sadie's." She collected the dishes.

He slid his chair out from the table and crossed the room. "Rachel, I didn't mean to hurt your feelings."

"I understand. Sadie was a *gut* cook. *Mei* cooking won't ever be like hers." She turned away from the sink to gather more dishes and he caught her arm.

"I never liked cold meatloaf and I'm *nett* fond of sauerkraut."

"But Sadie—"

"Thought I liked it, I know." He looked sheepish. "She worked so hard to please me that I never wanted to hurt her feelings."

"Sit and I'll make you a peanut butter sandwich before I leave to help Naomi with her final preparations."

The color drained from his face. "You're leaving already?"

"You'll be fine. I made a list of things you'll need to do for Ella." She sliced a thick portion of bread.

Ella began to fuss. Rachel continued slicing the bread and ignored Timothy clearing his throat. He needed to take care of his daughter. After a moment, he trudged out of the room, unhappy with her.

"Lord, show me how to build a bridge between those two. Ella needs her *daed*," she whispered.

When Timothy came for the bottle she'd warmed, he wasn't as rigid holding Ella.

"Relax. Just talk to her." Rachel handed him the bottle. "If you don't know what to say, quote the Scriptures. She needs to know your voice."

He stared at the ceiling and blinked several times. "Sadie used to say the *boppli* could hear *mei* voice during our daily readings."

"She was right. And Ella needs to hear your voice in your daily readings again," Rachel said softly.

He closed his eyes and Rachel slipped out the door.

"Something's troubling you," Naomi said.

Rachel continued stitching the dress hem until she felt her arm tugged. Naomi took her sewing from her lap. "*Kumm* to the kitchen and help me with the *kaffi*."

Rachel hadn't wanted to dampen Naomi's get-together, and now she feared her despondence had done just that.

"I know something's wrong." Naomi planted her hands on her hips. "Why won't you tell me? I'm your best friend."

Rachel blew out a breath. "Timothy proposed to me."

Naomi gasped. "When? What did you tell him?"

"He asked the other day, and I haven't given him an answer." She reached for Naomi's hands. "I didn't want to spoil your wedding preparations. I'm sorry if I've been—"

"You've been holding out on the most important news two friends can share." Naomi laughed, then covered her mouth so the others in the next room wouldn't hear.

Rachel remembered the singing Naomi hosted when Rachel looked outside and saw Jordan isolated from the others.

"Isn't it *wundebaar*? We'll both be *fraas*."

Rachel winced at Naomi's chipper tone.

"You're happy, right?" Naomi's expression became serious.

"I'll always think of Timothy as a *bruder*-in-law." Rachel bit her bottom lip. "When I think about marrying him . . . I see . . . Sadie." She spun toward the window. "I even dream I see her."

"And?" Naomi touched Rachel's shoulder.

Rachel couldn't look at her. "She says it's okay."

"If things were opposite and your husband wanted to marry Sadie, would you be upset?"

"*Nay*," Rachel said, "*nett* at all."

Jordan stared out the bus window. After a grueling four-day journey on a crowded bus, it felt good to be in Michigan. According to the elderly man seated next to him, they still had another six hours to go before reaching Hope Falls. Jordan calculated it would be just about milking time if he caught a cab immediately from the bus station.

The man shifted in the seat. "Anxious to get home?"

Jordan smiled. "*Jah*, I am."

The elderly man pointed to his shirt. "Are you Amish or Mennonite?"

"Amish." He thought about it a moment, then repeated, "*Jah*, I'm Amish." At least he would be soon. He planned to talk with the bishop about baptism and joining the church. His mother was right; Hope Falls was where he belonged.

"I passed through Hope Falls awhile back." He smiled, a faraway look in his eye. "Nice place."

Sunlight spilled through the window and the man's eyes appeared reflective. The man reminded Jordan of someone, but he couldn't figure out who that might be. Something lingered at the edge of his memory, but he couldn't quite grasp it.

The bus slowed as it veered onto the interstate off-ramp.

"We must be stopping again." He liked the idea of stretching his legs, but he hoped this wouldn't be a long layover. He was anxious to get *home*. The bus came to a gear-screeching stop and expelled a pressurized gasp before the driver announced they were in Kalamazoo.

The man beside him stepped into the aisle and

pulled his hat out from the upper storage area. "It's been nice visiting with you."

The sun rays streamed through the window and illuminated the twinkle in the man's eyes. "You're on the right road. Stay on course, and you'll make it home." The man headed toward the exit, the flow of passengers moving him along.

Jordan tucked his duffel underneath the seat in front of him and then took his place at the end of the line of passengers. Jordan felt drawn to the man and wanted to talk to him. Through the window he could see the man disembark. He followed him with his eyes until he was distracted by the woman in front of him, who stopped to prop her foot on a seat and tie her shoe. By the time Jordan exited the bus, the man wasn't anywhere in sight. He didn't see him inside the convenience store and supposed someone had been waiting to pick him up.

Jordan returned to his seat with a can of Coke and a bag of Fritos, finding a newspaper lying there. Puzzled, he picked it up. The *Budget*. Why would the Amish paper be here? He flipped the pages to the Michigan section and read Katie Bender's column. Plans were under way for building the new school and selecting the teacher. She wrote about visiting with Fanny and Iva Troyer and wished their visit was under more cheerful circumstances. Jordan flipped to the front; the paper was over a month old. He rubbed his jaw. If their visit wasn't under cheerful circumstances, why had Rachel's sisters returned home?

Rachel glanced at Timothy seated on the bench with the other married men. Bishop Lapp was about to announce Naomi and William as man and wife. Timothy had kept his head bowed during the entire ceremony.

A heavy knot lay in her stomach. Last night after she spent a great deal of time praying, she went to sleep only to dream about Timothy. As they stood before the bishop in her dream, Timothy's hair looked as ruffled as it did today. In her dream Ella cried, and when Rachel searched for her, she spotted Sadie holding the baby. Instead of passing Ella to Rachel, Sadie placed the baby in Timothy's arms.

Rachel scanned the room and stopped when she saw Ella sleeping in Anna King's arms. Over the past few days Rachel had certainly missed caring for her niece. Although helping Naomi with her wedding preparations gave Rachel a breather from child-care responsibilities, it also gave her time to pray. Outside of the dream, she hadn't come up with a clear answer to give Timothy. And her parents hadn't brought up the subject.

The bishop introduced the married couple to the church. The service ended with a prayer, and the guests mingled to congratulate the new couple.

Rachel groaned when Katie Bender approached.

She dashed outside, but the screen door creaked behind her. Before Katie spoke, Rachel knew she'd been followed.

"Rachel, I wanted to ask you something," Katie said.

"*Jah?*" Rachel forced a smile. She hoped the news of Timothy's proposal hadn't gotten out. Katie never failed to follow up on rumors.

Katie tugged on a stray thread on her dress sleeve. "I heard you were interested in the *schul* teacher position."

"*Jah.* I talked with the bishop."

"I know that since James passed away, you and I haven't . . ." Katie's eyes watered. "I looked forward to having sisters finally after I married James." She paused. "Rachel, I loved James."

"I know you did." Rachel reached for her hand.

Katie looked at their clasped hands, tears rolling down her cheeks.

"I blamed you," Rachel said, "and I was wrong. It happened because I wanted to see the angel so badly that I left the sheep pen open."

"I was the one who suggested you find the angel." Katie dabbed her sleeve over her eyes. "I wanted to write another story about the angel. I let pride rule over me."

"I've struggled to forgive you." Rachel blinked and tears cascaded down her cheeks. "I want to move past it all. Will you forgive me, Katie?"

In response, Katie opened her arms and drew

Rachel in, giving her a warm hug. Rachel felt the forgiveness envelop her. It released something ugly that had been within her. It melted away and disappeared.

Rachel cleared her throat. "I heard you want the teacher's position."

Katie wound her fingers around each other. "I need something to do. I won't ever get married."

Rachel thought about the option that lay before her. One Katie did not have. "I'll tell the bishop I'm no longer interested." She gave Katie's hand a gentle squeeze. "Everything will work out," she said. She caught a glimpse of Timothy heading toward the buggies. "I need to see Timothy about something."

"That's okay . . . go. I'll talk with you later."

Rachel hurried to catch Timothy. "Are you leaving?"

"I am. I saw Ginger, so I supposed you wouldn't need a ride over to the Yoders' *haus*."

"*Nay*, but *denki*." The dark circles under his eyes looked more pronounced today. "Is everything okay?"

"*Jah*." He lowered his head.

"You don't sound too convincing."

He lifted his face to the sky. "I can't help but remember Sadie on our wedding day." He closed his eyes. "She was beautiful."

A knot formed in her throat. "*Jah*," she replied softly. Now would not be the right time to speak with him. At a loss for words, she glanced at the clouds. "You think it'll rain?"

"*Nay.*" He unfastened the horse from the post.

Rachel followed him with her eyes, but he climbed into the buggy without even glancing at her. "So I'll see you later?"

He nodded, then clicked his tongue to signal the horse.

"*Ach*, God, I pray that you'll direct *mei* decision." Rachel ended her prayer, hearing a baby's cry. Without turning around, she knew it was Ella's.

Just as he'd hoped, Jordan was able to hail a cab within minutes of disembarking from the bus. He leaned against the backseat of the cab and closed his eyes, eager to be back for chores.

Lord, I know in my heart Hope Falls is where I belong. Thank you for bringing me home safely.

Without much traffic on the road, the twelve miles passed quickly. Jordan leaned forward and said to the cabdriver, "It's the next house on the right." He wiped his sweaty palms on his thighs, then dug his hand into his pocket for the fare. The car was barely in park before he jumped out, hauling his duffel behind him. "Thanks," he said, handing the cash to the driver.

He lifted his hat and combed his fingers through his hair. After inhaling a deep breath and releasing it slowly, he headed up the porch steps.

Miriam answered after his first knock.

"Jordan!" she gasped. "It's *gut* to see you again."

He smiled. "It's *gut* to be back. Is Rachel home?"

"*Nay*. She's at Naomi and William's wedding." She wiped her hands on her apron. "Micah is milking cows."

"*Denki*." He turned and lumbered over to the barn.

The wooden door creaked as Jordan swung it open. Micah stood at the opposite end, releasing the cows back into the yard.

"Did I miss milking?" Jordan approached Micah.

"*Ach*, Jordan. I didn't hear you *kumm* in." Micah smiled as he met Jordan in the center of the barn. He clapped his shoulder. "How long are you in town?"

"I've *kumm* to talk with you about that." Jordan swallowed, but it didn't settle his frayed nerves.

Micah's expression sobered. "*Jah?*"

Jordan picked up the hesitation in Micah's response. He lowered his attention to the straw on the floor. *Lord, give me the words.*

"What's on your mind, Jordan?"

Jordan jammed his hands into his pockets and kept his head bowed. "I'll be looking for work again."

Micah put his hand on Jordan's shoulder. "There probably won't be a harvest. We haven't had enough rain."

"I'll work for room and board." He smiled. "I promise I won't eat much."

"Why have you returned?"

Micah's question was void of discernible emotion, and Jordan lifted his head. The way Micah stroked his beard sent a wayward shudder that spread along Jordan's spine.

"I think I've settled my stubborn ways. I want to talk with the bishop about baptism and studying the *Ordnung*." When Micah didn't immediately respond, Jordan continued, "I want to join the church."

"That's a serious commitment." Micah eyed him closely.

Jordan shifted his weight and leaned against a barn post for support. "You asked me before I left what troubled my heart."

"I remember." Micah stopped stroking his beard.

"I needed to trust God." He cleared his throat. "I've been doing a lot of praying. This is where I belong. I believe that with my whole heart.

"Before my mother died, she said my father would find me here. He did. Only I mistakenly thought she meant my biological father. Now I know she meant my heavenly Father."

Micah smiled and moved closer to Jordan. "That is *wundebaar* news." He clapped Jordan's shoulder. "I see the sincerity of your heart. I'm glad you've found peace."

"And I've found my home. Where I belong." Jordan drew a deep breath. "There's one more thing. I want to ask for your blessing to marry Rachel."

Micah's face fell and he squeezed Jordan's shoulder. "I'm afraid you're too late."

Chapter Thirty-Two

With barely a morsel of hope, and riding a borrowed horse from Micah, Jordan sped toward the Yoders' house. If Micah was correct about the timing, the youth would be splitting off to make their selections for the evening singing.

Although Micah offered his fastest horse, the Standardbreds were trotters. Despite his prodding to get the horse to break into a gallop, the gelding never broke his stride. He saved time by cutting across the fields and avoiding the road. Thankfully, the full moon wasn't masked by clouds so he had enough light to guide his way.

As Jordan entered the driveway, William and the unmarried men were loitering outside the barn. Riding up to them, he dismounted before the horse fully stopped.

"Have you started the selection?" Jordan studied the horses, but in the dark, he couldn't make out if one was Ginger.

"*Gut* to see you." William and the others circled Jordan. "When did you get back?"

"An hour ago. Is Rachel Hartzler still here?"

"*Jah*, I think." William craned his neck to look at the horses. "Isn't that third one Ginger?"

"It is," Peter replied.

Jordan exhaled. "Would you let me choose the first girl? I want to surprise Rachel."

"Sure." William waved toward the house. "They're waiting in the third room down the hall on the right."

"*Denki*," Jordan said, jogging to the house.

Once inside the house, he moved swiftly down the hall and stopped to draw a breath before knocking.

The door opened a crack. "What is your name and who are you asking for?"

He recognized Naomi's voice, but without a lamp, she hadn't recognized him at the door.

He cleared his throat. "Rachel Hartzler."

There was a muffled commotion inside the room, and the door closed.

Jordan wasn't sure if this was part of the ritual but he wasn't going to leave without talking with Rachel. He knocked again.

The door cracked opened. "Rachel isn't participating. Make another selection."

"She's *mei* only selection." This time he jammed his foot in the doorway so it couldn't be closed. "Jordan Engles is requesting—" The door swung open and his breath caught as he locked eyes with Rachel.

Her eyes widened. "Jordan, what are you doing here?"

"I asked to make the first selection." He reached for her hand. "Do you accept?"

She blinked and tears trickled down her face. She glanced at Naomi. "I have to go." She pushed past Jordan and bolted down the hall and out the door.

Jordan followed, but he collided with Peter in the doorway.

"I'm sorry, I didn't see you," Peter said.

"*Nett* a problem." He moved around Peter and sprinted toward her buggy. "Rachel!"

"This isn't the place, Jordan." She climbed in and snapped the reins.

Jordan pivoted around, looking for the horse.

"We thought you were staying so we cooled him down," William said. "He's in the stall."

"*Denki*, but I have to catch her." He rushed into the barn, bridled and saddled the horse, then led him outside. "By the way, William," he said, mounting the horse, "congratulations." Jordan reined the gelding toward the field. "Yah!"

Cutting across several acres shaved a good amount off the distance. He reentered the road a few feet behind Rachel. Because he wasn't pulling a buggy, his horse easily gained the lead. Running neck and neck with Ginger, he leaned over and grabbed the horse's reins. "Whoa," he called out, stopping her buggy.

He backed his mount up until he was at her door. "What do you think you're doing running that horse so hard?"

Instead of answering, she buried her face in her hands, sobbing.

He quickly dismounted, tied the horse to the back of the buggy, and climbed inside. "I didn't mean to frighten you by stopping Ginger like that." He reached his arm around her shoulder.

Rachel didn't resist when he ushered her into his arms. He pressed her tight against his chest and rested his cheek against hers. "I missed you," he whispered close to her ear.

Her body tensed. She pushed off his chest, but a passing car's draft shook the buggy and she sank back into his embrace.

He didn't want to let her go, but to remain parked on the shoulder of Northland Drive was dangerous. He gave her a gentle squeeze and pulled away.

"Let's get off this busy road," he said.

"Okay," she said, her voice soft. She slid to the far side of the bench. Folding her hands on her lap, she looked straight ahead.

He flicked the reins. "Just for the record, I won that race."

She huffed. "You went through the field. That wasn't a fair race." She glanced over her shoulder at the gelding tied behind the buggy. "That's *mei daed's* horse Hank, and he's *nett* faster than Ginger."

Amused, he reached for her hand, but she snatched it back. Jordan glanced sideways. If she sensed his stare, she didn't acknowledge it. She focused her attention straight ahead.

He turned off on the first dirt road.

"This isn't the road," she said.

"I know. I haven't been gone that long." He pulled back on the reins, set the brake, then swiveled on the bench to face her. "I missed you."

She looked down and pressed her hands against her dress. "I never thought you would *kumm* back for me." She lifted her eyes to him. "*Mei daed* told me how he asked you *nett* to take me away."

"I promised him I wouldn't." He slid closer to her. "Rachel—"

"Things have changed since you were here."

In the moonlight, he caught a glimpse of her watery eyes as she bowed her head. He tipped her chin and swept the warm tears from her face. He wished he'd never left. She'd needed him and he'd been on the road.

"Your *daed* told me about Sadie. I'm sorry," he whispered.

"It was all so sudden." Her voice broke. "I kept praying for the *boppli* to live. I had no idea how ill *mei* sister was." Rachel peered into Jordan's eyes. "I should've been praying for Sadie."

Unable to resist, he pulled her into his arms. He rocked her as her warm tears soaked his shirt. With his throat swelling, he struggled to form words to comfort her. Instead, he squeezed her harder against him.

"I'm sorry." She lifted her head. "It isn't proper for me to fall apart like this in front of you." She tapped his shoulder. "I got your shirt wet."

He pushed the stray strands of hair away from her face, then leaned in and kissed her cheek. His mouth moved to her lips, and deepening his kiss, he slipped his hand to her back and pressed her closer. He continued kissing her until she pulled away.

"Jordan."

His heart pumped hard, hearing her hoarse whisper. Instead of responding with words, he brought her against him in another kiss. This time he moved his mouth slowly over hers, savoring the soft texture of her lips.

She broke the kiss. "Jordan—" She scooted across the seat and cleared her throat.

"I'm not confused anymore," he said.

"Things have changed. I can't go with you *nau*."

He smiled. "I'm *nett* asking you to go away with me." He inched closer, but she scooted farther away and blew out short breaths as though panicked by his closeness.

Jordan didn't want to frighten her, so he moved back to the driver's position. "I'm going to become Amish," he said. "I realized I don't belong in the world . . . My home is here. With you . . . I believe it's God's will . . ." The longer she remained silent, the faster his pulse rose. "I plan to talk with the bishop tomorrow about baptism."

She sniffled, ran her sleeve over her face, and drew in a ragged breath. "Will you take me home *nau*?"

Jordan looked at her until she turned away. Then he released the brake and flicked the reins, signaling Ginger forward.

She sniffled a few more times but otherwise remained silent the remainder of the ride. He pulled up to the barn and jumped out.

She stepped out of the buggy and looked at him. "*Denki*," she said softly.

Jordan caught her arm before she walked away. "You can't tell me you're still going to marry him after we shared that kiss." His eyes bored into hers.

She bowed her head. "Who told you about the proposal?"

"Your *daed*." Jordan removed his hat. "A wise woman told me once that God wasn't the author of confusion."

"Why are you telling me that?" She moved some gravel pebbles with the toe of her shoe.

"You wouldn't have delayed your marriage acceptance if you weren't confused."

Her foot stilled. When she finally lifted her head, she whispered, "I want what's best for Ella." And with that, Rachel walked away.

Tangus crept along the ground, following Rachel, but Nathaniel blocked him from reaching her.

"There isn't a foothold here any longer," Nathaniel said.

Tangus ignored him. "Jordan, she doesn't love you. Go back to your father. You couldn't stay here in this settlement with her married to another man."

Jordan stared at Rachel walking to the house. "God, help me accept your will."

"See, he's made his decision. You cannot pull him from the hand of God. Flee!" Nathaniel bellowed.

"I don't run so easily." Tangus edged up to Jordan and followed him into the little house.

Jordan slumped onto the chair next to the fireplace. "God, I don't want to lose her. I thought you directed me back here. To become Amish and marry Rachel." He buried his face in his hands. "Show me why I'm here if it isn't to marry Rachel."

"You cannot persuade him to turn from God now. Not even if the girl marries another." Nathaniel drew his sword and prepared to battle Tangus.

A knock on the door startled Jordan. He jumped up from the rocking chair and went to answer the door.

"Sorry, I know it's late," Micah said.

"I wasn't sleeping." Jordan stepped aside to let him in.

"Did you talk with Rachel?"

"I'm not sure it did any good." He cleared his throat. "I think her mind is made up."

Micah frowned. "And what will you do?"

Jordan faced Micah, the truth swelling within him. "I still want to become Amish. I know it wouldn't be right for me to live here, but I would still like to work for you . . . until I can find a trade."

"Our settlement could use another blacksmith."

"I would like that."

"*Gut*. We'll start work tomorrow." Micah put his hand inside the pocket of his large work apron. "You'll need your own tools." He withdrew his hand, holding the farrier's hammer his father had made. "I wanted to give it to James." He stopped a moment and swallowed hard. "I would like to pass it along to you, *sohn*."

"What if—"

"No matter what, you are going to be Amish. I want you to have it."

Jordan held the tool, hefting it, admiring again the smooth wooden handle and the excellent craftsmanship it took to get it so balanced.

"*Denki.*" It was the best he could get out around the awe and honor he felt. "*Denki.*" Jordan's chest tightened. Anything resembling a family keepsake of his mother's was sold at auction to pay bills. Her Bible and her photograph were all he had.

Micah began to go to the door when he stopped. "I almost forgot." He pulled an oversized envelope from another pocket. "This was delivered a day ago. I forgot about it when you arrived."

Jordan looked at the envelope. Shipped overnight from Clint Engles. He glanced at Micah. "Thanks."

"I'll see you in the morning?"

"Before daybreak."

Once Micah left, Jordan tore open the envelope. The postcards he'd bought for Rachel were inside and a letter.

Dear Jordan,

When I came back to the hotel room and found your note saying you were leaving, my heart broke. I understand you want to become Amish and I wish you the best. Your mother would be proud. Enclosed is a cashier's check. This is the money I sent to your mother throughout the years. I think I told you how she returned all of my checks. I deposited each one in a savings account with hopes of one day giving it to you. Please don't return it. I know you won't put it toward a truck, but maybe you can put it toward an Amish farm.

I enjoyed our time together and I hope we can stay in touch.

Clint

Jordan glanced up from the letter and smiled. "God, you certainly provided a harvest." He laughed. "Thank you, Father."

Nathaniel stood guard until Tangus retreated completely. "Yes, your heavenly Father knows how to give good gifts."

"God is not the author of confusion."
Unable to get Jordan's voice out of her head and concentrate on praying, Rachel stood from her kneeling position next to her bed and wandered to the window. The morning sun peeked over the horizon, yet she had no desire to rush out to milk the cows. Somehow she had to settle this confusion that held her in a choke hold.

"God, why is this so hard? When I look at Ella, I see Sadie. I miss Sadie . . . Ella needs a mother to care for her. And poor Timothy, he's lost without his *fraa*. God, I think I'm the only one who understands his loss." Her voice cracked. "I didn't pray for Sadie. I knew how much she wanted the *boppli* . . ."

Nathaniel fanned his wings, creating a soft breeze. "God is the Alpha and Omega. The

418

beginning and the end. He alone holds someone's future in His hand. He alone gives the breath of life."

Rachel moved away from the window. "God, please direct my steps. Make the path so obvious that someone as simple as me can see the right way. I want your will for my life. *Aemen*." Reaching the door handle, a warm gentle breeze washed over her, filling her with peace.

Rachel entered the kitchen as *Mamm* and *Daed* were sitting down for breakfast. She glanced around the room. "Where's Jordan?"

Daed frowned and lifted up a piece of paper. "He left a note in the barn that said he had to take care of something."

Rachel's heart grew heavy. *I will follow where you lead, God.*

Mamm and *Daed* exchanged glances. *Mamm* made a slight nod at *Daed* and he cleared his throat.

"Have a seat, Rachel. I want to talk with you," he said.

Rachel pulled the chair out from under the table.

The lines across *Daed's* forehead wrinkled. "Have you *kumm* to a decision about marrying Timothy?"

Rachel's throat dried. *Have I, God?*

Mamm set a cup of coffee in front of Rachel. "We're concerned about your happiness."

"You don't want me to marry Timothy?" Rachel looked from her mother over to her father. "Ella needs a mother." She tapped her chest. "I can do that. I need to do something."

"You have," *Mamm* said. "You've been a great help with Ella."

Rachel bowed her head. "I feel guilty. When Sadie was sick, I only prayed that she wouldn't lose the *boppli*. I should've been praying for her as well."

Mamm sat next to Rachel and reached for her hand. "I prayed for Sadie. But God's decision is final, and even though we don't know his reasoning, we still trust him." She squeezed Rachel's hand. "Don't let guilt guide your decision."

Daed stroked his beard. "Have you prayed about marrying Timothy?"

"*Jah*," she replied softly.

His expression sobered. "Are you in love with Jordan?"

Rachel closed her eyes. *God, help me.*

A knock sounded at the door.

Rachel began to get up, but *Mamm* patted her hand. "Let me answer it," *Mamm* said.

From the entry, *Mamm* commented about Ella's alertness as she carried her into the kitchen. Timothy agreed, saying her eyes now followed his every move.

"*Gut mariye*," Timothy said.

"Fine day, ain't so?" *Daed* said. "Have a seat."

Timothy smiled at Rachel. "*Jah*, this is a fine day."

"I'm going to rock *mei* granddaughter in the sitting room." *Mamm* removed Ella's blankets.

Timothy pulled a bottle from his pocket and handed it to *Mamm*. "I *kumm* prepared with the essentials."

Daed glanced at Rachel. His forehead lines deepened. After *Mamm* left the room with Ella, he turned to Timothy. "I suppose you've *kumm* to talk with me."

Rachel's face heated. *Daed's* prodding was awkward.

Timothy looked at Rachel and smiled. "Actually, I've *kumm* to talk to Rachel."

Rachel froze. She never expected a bitter taste to rise from her stomach.

"Can we take a walk?" he asked quietly.

She nodded and stood. With her head bowed to avoid eye contact, she walked to the door.

Timothy followed. Once they were outside, he reached for her elbow, but he held his words until they were on the path leading to the river.

"Rachel, you've been so *gut* caring for Ella. These last few days without you have been hard." He cleared his throat. "Having to muddle through with my clumsiness, I can assure you, Ella missed you."

"I've missed her too."

He reached for her hands and squeezed them

gently. "You've put purpose back in *mei* life. *Denki.*"

His voice sounded nervous but cheery. He squeezed her hands, then released them. "I realized I can care for Ella. I'm *nett* saying it won't be hard." He shrugged. "But I think we've grown accustomed to each other."

Rachel smiled. "I'm happy for you, Timothy."

"And I'm happy for you," he said. "I hope you will still watch Ella while I'm working. I can bring her here in the morning."

"I don't understand." Rachel eyed him closely, but he continued to smile.

"I will never love you the way Jordan loves you."

Rachel's eyes watered. "How—"

"He woke Bishop Lapp early, then he stopped by *mei haus* after."

"He did?" She blotted her eyes with her sleeve.

"*Jah,*" Jordan said, walking up the trail. "I wasn't letting you go unless I knew Timothy loved you— like I love you."

"Is this really all right with you, Timothy?"

"I know what my Sadie would say . . . and she was a very wise woman." Timothy touched the brim of his hat. "I'll see you both later." He gave Jordan a nod, then split off to return to the house.

Jordan came up beside her and brought her into his arms. "I love you," he said and kissed her forehead.

"I love you too."

He pulled back, his eyes searching hers. "Will you be my date at the next singing?"

She laughed. "Are you going to sing?"

"*Jah*, I promise." He gave her a quick kiss. "I figure we have eighteen weeks to date while I take the baptism classes."

"And after your baptism?"

"Will you be *mei fraa*, Rachel Hartzler?"

Everything inside her melted and came together all at once. But she didn't want to give her answer just yet. "Well, I don't know."

"You don't know?" He looked baffled.

"There is the question of Smokey. You know I love that cat and you're allergic to him."

He laughed. "*Jah*, I am. But I will sneeze the rest of my life if it means I can be married to you."

"Well then! *Jah*, absolutely. I will marry you, Jordan Engles." She clasped her hands behind her back and swayed. "And Smokey can go live with *Onkel* Isaac."

He picked her up and whirled her around. When he put her down, he kept his arms around her waist and his face grew serious. "Did I tell you I'm *nett* a *gut* farmer? You might have to deliver every one of the calves."

She laughed. "Did I tell you I can't cook? You might have to make chicken and eggplant parmesan every night."

He kissed her cheek. "Then we're perfect for each other."

Nathaniel unfurled his wings, hovered a short time over his charges, then returned to his station in the ethereal realm where he would wait for God's call to intervene again.

Acknowledgments

"I can do all things through Christ who strengthens me."

Philippians 4:13 NKJV

As *Brush of Angel's Wings* came together, I often quoted this scripture, many times in the form of a plea. God's grace and His renewing of my strength never cease to amaze me. To Him, above all, I give thanks.

God has blessed me with a multitude of support from my incredible family and friends. My husband, Dan, your ongoing encouragement, support, and guidance have lifted me to reach higher levels.

Lexie, you are a tremendous help, especially now that you have your driver's license! Thanks for helping around the house and running errands.

Danny, you stand taller than I do, but you'll always be my miracle baby. I'm so proud of you.

Sarah, sometimes faith is difficult to measure until you're forced to walk through fire. I am so proud of the way you handled your "trial by fire" this past fall. What strength you displayed.

Betty Reid, thank you for helping to shuttle the kids to school and football practice while I worked to finish this book.

Kathy Droste, you are such a blessing. Thank you for correcting my first draft. Paul Droste (Dad), thanks for believing in me and setting up book signings.

The unconditional love and encouragement from my mother, Ella Roberts, taught me never to give up. Thanks, Mom and Bill, for your ongoing prayers and support.

To my wonderful friends, prayer warriors, and critique partners. You each know the important role that you played in bringing *Brush of Angel's Wings* to print. Susanne Dietze, Joy Elwell, Andrew Fitzmorris, Sarah Hamaker, Virginia Hamlin, Laura Hilton, Bob Kaku, Linda Maran, Anita Merchant, Donna Mumma, Ella Roberts, Gail Sattler, Mary Ann Stockwell, Linda Truesdell, Jennifer Uhlarik, and Quanda Watson.

Thank you, Mary and Simon Thon, who introduced me to the Amish while I lived with them during my college years, and to my Amish friends of Mecosta County, Michigan, who invited me into their homes.

I especially appreciate my agent, Mary Sue Seymour, and my publishing family at Thomas Nelson. Natalie Hanemann, you are truly an extension of God's grace and a powerhouse of encouragement. I'm honored to have you as my editor. Lissa Halls Johnson, you've guided me through each phase with patience and prayers. I've learned so much from your editing expertise.

Thank you! From concept to marketing, the entire fiction team at Thomas Nelson is an awe-inspiring group of prayerful people who exemplify God's love.

Reading Group Guide

1. How did Rachel's thoughts and attitudes toward Jordan encourage Tangus? Does what you say or how you act block the enemy's attack or give him more leverage to manipulate your life?

2. Rachel recognizes her jealously of Jordan and prays for forgiveness, but it isn't long before she finds fault with him again while trying to justify her wrongful thoughts. How often in your spiritual journey have you recognized the sin in your life and prayed about it only to fall back into your sinful ways? What does Jesus tell us to do?

3. Rachel's rash decision caused her father's injury. Can you think of a time when you've unintentionally hurt someone with your hasty actions? What about untamed words—can they be as hurtful?

4. What two things in James 4:7 are we instructed to do? When we resist the enemy, what must he do?

428

5. How do believers have authority to defeat the enemy? (Matthew 28:18; Luke 9:1; Colossians 2:15)

6. Describe how the adversary (Satan) seeks those whom he may devour. (1 Peter 5:8–9)

7. God has equipped believers to stand against the devil's deceit, but as believers, we must actively put on the full armor. Can you list the pieces of the armor and describe its protective abilities.

8. In John 10:10, what does the enemy come to do? What does Jesus offer? Describe what it means to live in spiritual abundance.

9. In the parable of the sower (Matthew 13:3–23; Mark 4:2–20; Luke 8:4–15), what did Jesus say the seed represented? What happened to the seed that fell amid the thorns? Compare that to the seed that fell on good ground. How fertile is your soil? Are you producing fruit?

10. Psalm 91:11 assures believers of what?

11. How much importance did Rachel's relatives place on her inability to cook, sew, and keep a tidy house? Have you ever struggled to

overcome a specific deficiency? What helped you change your circumstances?

12. Jordan and his mother lost everything after his mother became ill. How did losing his belongings affect his adult life? Was he jealous over Kayla's lifestyle? Can you think of a time you coveted something that didn't belong to you?

13. Jordan's desire to belong caused him to teeter between a worldly and Amish lifestyle. What happened that satisfied his search?